BETRAYALS

CARLA NEGGERS
BETRAYALS

Recycling programs for this product may not exist in your area.

ISBN-13: 978-0-7783-2623-6
ISBN-10:   0-7783-2623-3

BETRAYALS

First published by Berkley Books 1990 under the pseudonym Anne Harrell

www.MIRABooks.com

Printed in U.S.A.

To George Maxwell and Rebecca Martin

One

The French Riviera
1959

Annette Winston Reed hacked at an onion on the battered worktable in her airy, sun-washed kitchen. Although it wasn't her nature to fret, she noticed her hands were shaking and she was perspiring heavily. Her underarms and the small of her back were damp, and her eyes burned with lack of sleep. It's time to buck up, she silently told herself, annoyed by this betrayal of her inner turmoil. She wasn't going to let her troubles undermine her self-confidence or her sense of fun.

She refused to let Thomas Blackburn get to her. He and his four-year-old granddaughter had come down for the weekend from Paris, a typical presumptuousness on Thomas's part. Annette hadn't invited him. A Bostonian like herself, he had known her all her life. She had grown up around the corner from his house on Beacon Hill. But as much as she looked up to him, as much as she'd wanted him to admire her, she couldn't consider him a friend. He was too old, almost twenty years her senior, and perhaps knew her too well. With Thomas, pretenses were impossible.

He was at the breakfast table overlooking the rose garden, with a mug of black coffee at his elbow and the Paris *Le Monde* opened up in front of him so that Annette couldn't miss the latest blaring headline about the jewel thief who'd plagued the Côte d'Azur for the past eight weeks. He'd been dubbed *Le Chat* after the Cary Grant character in the popular American movie *To Catch a Thief.* Once again, the police promised the imminent arrest of a suspect.

This time they weren't just blowing smoke. Annette knew better.

Thomas hadn't said a word beyond a simple good-morning. He had come to the Riviera just to visit her, he'd told Annette with his wry smile, knowing she wouldn't believe him. As always, he had a loftier purpose in mind: to convince her Vietnamese caretaker, a mandarin scholar respected both abroad and in his own country, to return home. Thomas would go on and on about how Saigon needed credible centrist leaders and how Quang Tai could help save his country from disaster, and Annette would pretend a suitable neutrality, despite the prospect of losing her caretaker. She was only sparing herself one of Thomas's notorious lectures on not being shortsighted and selfish; she suspected he already knew she didn't want the bother of having to replace Quang Tai.

She sighed, frantically mincing one half of the onion. Her eyes had begun to tear, and if she didn't slow down and be careful, she'd likely chop off the end of a finger. Thomas wouldn't keep quiet for long. It wasn't a Blackburn trait.

The newspaper rustled as he turned a page, and she heard him take a small sip of coffee.

"All right, Thomas, you win," she said, whirling around with her paring knife. "What do you want to tell me that you're trying so hard *not* to tell me? You might as well spit it out, because you know you'll get around to it sooner or later."

Looking slightly miffed at her sharp-sighted observation, Thomas folded the newspaper and laid it on the table. Like all Blackburns, he was a man of impeccable moral and intellectual respectability—the kind of highbrow Bostonian that Annette usually found boring and irritating. For two centuries, the Blackburns had been outspoken patriots, historians, poets, reformers, public servants and eccentrics, if not the best moneymakers. Eliza Blackburn—the patron saint of the family—was one of Boston's favorite Revolutionary War heroines. Her portrait, painted by Gilbert Stuart, hung in the Massachusetts State House; in it she wore the cameo brooch that George Washington himself had presented to her, in gratitude for her efforts at smuggling weapons, ammunition and information from British-occupied Boston to the patriot forces in outlying areas. The Winstons, on the other hand, had snuck off to Halifax for the duration of the War of Independence. Eliza had also been virtually the only mercantile-minded Blackburn in two hundred years. She'd been the driving force behind Blackburn Shipping, which made a fortune in the post-Revolution China trade, but folded in 1812 with the British blockade and the war. That was that for a Blackburn generating any substantial income. Eliza's descendants had been stretching her fortune ever since, and it was beginning to fray.

Annette had heard rumblings that Thomas, Harvard-educated and approaching fifty, was about to launch his own business. He was an authority on the history and culture of Indochina and spent much of his time there, but how he planned to translate that expertise into a moneymaking enterprise was beyond her.

He regarded her with a calm that only accentuated her own nervousness. "Annette, I'd like to ask you a straight-forward question—do you know this thief *Le Chat?*"

"Don't be ridiculous. How would I know him?"

Her mouth went dry, her heartbeat quickened and she felt curiously light-headed. She'd never fainted in all her thirty years; now wasn't the time to start. Trying to hide her trembling hands, she set down the paring knife and leaned against the counter. She was dressed casually in baggy men's khaki trousers and an oversize white cotton shirt, her ash-brown hair pulled up in a hasty knot. If she worked at it, she could look rather stunning at first glance, but she had no illusions that she was an especially beauti-ful woman. She was too pale-skinned, too large-framed, too pear-shaped, too tall. Her near-black eyebrows were mannishly heavy and might have overwhelmed a more delicate face, but she had a strong nose, Katharine Hepburn cheeks and big eyes that were a ringing, memorable blue— her best feature by far. She'd hated her long legs as a teenager, but over the years she had discovered they had their advantages in bed. Even her husband, not the most passionate of men, would cry out in pleasure when she'd wrap them around him and pull him deeper into her.

"Annette," Thomas said.

It was the same tone he'd used on her when he'd caught her crossing Beacon Street alone at six years old. Nineteen years her senior, he was already a widower then, with a two-year-old son. Emily Blackburn, so quietly beautiful and intelligent, had died of postpartum complications, the first person Annette had ever known to die. She had only wanted to ride the swan boats in the Public Garden and had explained this to Thomas, assuring him her mother had said it was all right. He had said, "Annette," just that way—admonishing, knowing, expecting more of her than a transparent lie. Feeling as if she'd failed him, she'd blurted out the truth. Her mother hadn't said it was all right; she thought Annette was playing alone in the garden. Thomas had marched her home at once.

She was no longer six years old.

"I promised the children I'd take them out to pick flowers," she said, pulling herself up straight. "They're waiting."

She was at the kitchen door when Thomas spoke again. "Annette, this man's no Cary Grant. He's a thief who has lined his own pockets with other people's things and driven a decent woman to suicide."

Annette spun around and gave him a haughty look. "I quite agree."

Shaking his head, Thomas rose to his feet. He was a tall, lean man with sharp features and straight, fine hair that was a mixture of dark brown, henna highlights and touches of gray. The scrimpiest of the notoriously frugal Blackburns, he wore a shabby sweater that had probably seen him through his postgraduate studies at Harvard and trousers he'd let out, unabashedly leaving the old seam to show.

"I would never presume to judge you," he told her softly. "I hope you know that."

Annette held back an incredulous laugh. "Thomas, you're a Blackburn. It's your nature to judge everyone and everything."

He grimaced, but there was a gleam in his intensely blue eyes. "You're saying I'm a critical old fart."

She smiled for the first time in hours. "Not that old. Let's just say people always know where they stand with you—and you're a better man than most. Make yourself at home. I'll be back in an hour or so."

To her surprise and relief, Thomas let her go without another word.

Taking a gaggle of children flower-picking wasn't something Annette relished, even on a good day, but they quickly busied themselves plucking every blossom in sight. Surrendering to their enthusiasm, she abandoned her halfhearted effort to separate weed from wildflower and plopped down in the straw grass. It was warm in the sun under the incomparable blue of the Mediterranean sky, and the scent of wildflowers, lemons and sea permeated the air, soothing her restlessness and feeling of inundation. Down through the small field and olive grove, she could see the red-tiled roof and simple lines of her stone *mas,* the eighteenth-century farmhouse where she'd spent a part of every year since she was a girl. It was as much home to her as Boston was. In many ways, more so, for it was here on the Riviera she could be alone, with just her son and his nanny—without Benjamin, without the pressures of being a Boston Winston and a well-bred woman whose idea of fulfillment was supposed to be making everyone's life interesting but her own.

The children's zeal for flower-picking waned faster than she'd hoped, but her nephew Jared, the eldest at nine, launched a game of tag. Quentin was reluctant and terrified, his mother suspected, the girls would beat him. He was seven, a sturdy, towheaded boy with a quiet manner and a head full of dreams and ideas whose execution defeated him. A game of tag was precisely the kind of open, raw confrontation he tried to avoid. He was his father's son, Annette thought, with a lack of affection she was becoming used to. Even Quentin, however, couldn't prevail against his cousin's strong will.

The game got off to an aggressive start, and Annette nudged the flower basket closer to her. She didn't want the children in their exuberance to knock it over. The flowers wouldn't suffer; they were mostly rot. But she'd hate to have to explain why she'd tucked a .25-caliber automatic under the calico cloth lining the bottom of her flower basket.

"Bon matin, ma belle."

She hadn't heard his approach. She twisted around, but he was concealed behind the knotted trunk of an olive tree, out of the children's view. Their game was already getting out of hand. Quang Tai's six-year-old daughter, Tam, a mite of a girl, was beating the socks off the two boys and loving every minute of it, teasing them in her mixture of English, French and Vietnamese. Jared boasted he'd get her next game, but Quentin, ever the sore loser, accused her of cheating. Tam was having none of it. Jared remained neutral in the ensuing squabble, but then they both turned on him. Four-year-old Rebecca Blackburn amused herself by throwing grass on the three older children, becoming more and more daring until they finally paid attention to her.

"You can't catch me," she cried jubilantly as the two boys and Tam chased her.

Blue-eyed, chestnut-haired Blackburn though little Rebecca was, Annette had to admire the girl's spunk. In another thirty years, she'd probably be as sanctimonious as her grandfather.

Mercifully, Tam's father called from the edge of the field, and all four little monsters scrambled toward him. Annette promised she'd be along in a while and pulled her flower basket onto her lap. The gun had added weight to it.

"You can come out now, Jean-Paul," she said.

He ambled out from behind the tree and squatted down,

dropping a daisy into her basket. Annette tried to check the rush of raw desire she felt every time she saw him. It didn't work. From their first encounter weeks ago, she had been obsessed with Jean-Paul Gerard. She could never get enough of him; he could never satisfy her, sexually or emotionally. Whenever they made love she wanted more of him. Even after multiple couplings in one night, she'd awaken aching for him. He could tell her a thousand times he loved her, and she would long to hear it again—and yet never believed him. Jean-Paul was twenty-four years old and one of the most popular men in France. She was a thirty-year-old married woman with stretch marks on her breasts and abdomen.

She hated to give him up.

She noticed the sun-whitened hairs on his tanned arms. He was so handsome, so arrogantly French. Leanly built, he was a dark, sleek, wiry man, his eyes a deep brown, soft and oddly vulnerable—and keen. They had to be. He was one of France's premiere Grand Prix drivers, a risk-taking, desirable man who radiated a generous and unquenchable sexuality. He could have had virtually any woman he wanted. He had chosen Annette. She had never had any illusions that their affair would last, but she supposed she ought to derive some satisfaction at being the one to end it. He curled a loose tendril of hair behind her ear and brushed two fingers along the line of her jaw. "I missed you last night."

"Jean-Paul…" For nothing at all she'd strip herself naked and make love to him right there in the grass under the olive tree. The children and her caretaker and Thomas Blackburn and her entire future be damned. She licked her lips, parched to the point of cracking, and squinted at her lover, sitting in the shade with the bright morning sun at his back. "Have you seen the papers?"

Nodding, he sighed and sat back in the grass.

"That's why I called you." Her voice quavered; she didn't like that. She cleared her throat and forced herself not to look away. "Last night I became *Le Chat*'s latest victim. I was at the roulette wheel, wearing a Tiffany diamond-and-pearl bracelet—"

He looked pained. *"Ma belle…"*

"No, don't. Let me finish. The bracelet was a gift to me from my husband on our fifth anniversary. There's an inscription. The police…" Her throat was so dry and tight she felt she would choke. "I gave the police an exact description."

Jean-Paul accepted her words without apparent surprise or concern. "What else did you tell the police?"

Annette hesitated, then said, "Enough."

He looked away from her, his soft eyes lost in the shade.

"They've gone to your house, Jean-Paul. I would expect they're there now and have already found my bracelet—"

"You used the key I gave you?"

"Yes. Last night, while you were asleep."

He turned back to her, assessing her with the same alertness and intensity that had made him one of the finest race-car drivers in the world. This time, his craving for excitement and danger had led him astray.

"I don't blame you," Annette said, feeling stronger. "Please don't blame me. We are what we are, Jean-Paul, and I'm only doing what I have to do. I have no desire to see you in prison, and I'm aware of the acute embarrassment testifying against you in court could cause me. I have a husband and a son I need to respect me—a life that I won't allow *Le Chat* to destroy."

"I should kill you," he said calmly.

"Perhaps. But then you'd be a murderer as well as a jewel thief." She dug beneath the flowers and pulled back the calico cloth, removing the gun and a leather pouch. The automatic she held in her right hand, awkwardly; the pouch she handed to Jean-Paul. "I decided to warn you because I don't want you to be arrested and sent to jail. Here's twenty thousand dollars. A generous amount under the circumstances and enough, I should think, to get you out of the country and settled elsewhere."

He bit down on his lower lip, the only outward sign of the effect her words were having on him. "And if I choose not to go?"

"You can't win, Jean-Paul. Remember who I am. I'm giving you a way out. Consider yourself lucky and take it."

"What about the Jupiter Stones?"

She took no pleasure in how his voice cracked. In the last five minutes, she'd shattered his life. *Better yours than mine, my love.*

She said, "I don't care about the Jupiter Stones. I only care now that you get out of the country before you're arrested. Jean-Paul, I can't have what we've been together come out. Don't fight me. You'll only do yourself worse damage."

His eyes fastened on the gun, briefly, and Annette blanched at the thought he might actually force her to use it. But all at once he shot to his feet, and before she realized what was coming, he cuffed her hard on the side of the head. She sprawled backward against the tree, biting the inside of her mouth and crying out with pain as she tasted the warm saltiness of her own blood. Only by a miracle did she keep hold of the gun. If Jean-Paul reached for it, she'd kill him.

"Au revoir, ma belle."

Annette shuddered at the hatred in his voice. But he walked away, quickly disappearing in the thickets, and she brushed herself off and staggered to her feet, fighting back tears. She began to run. Through the field, her flower and herb gardens, across the terrace, and into the quaint stone farmhouse where so long ago her nanny had taught her how to dry herbs and debone a fish. Thank God Thomas wasn't around. She basked in the house's familiarity, its welcome.

She made herself and the children tall glasses of iced, fresh-squeezed lemonade and put sugar cookies onto a plate—and, in a few minutes, she began to laugh.

Baroness Gisela Majlath was buried in a simple non-religious ceremony attended by her closest friends and the tall Bostonian, Thomas Blackburn. As if his vaunted presence could change anything, Jean-Paul thought bitterly, as he hid among a stand of oaks. He stared at the plain white coffin and choked back his sobs lest anybody should hear him. He didn't want to disturb the funeral. Had the police known their missing *Le Chat* would be there, they would have sent more than a single uninterested gendarme. And the Bostonian in his frayed, pinstriped suit? What would he have done?

The stiff breeze off the Mediterranean whipped tears from Jean-Paul's eyes. Thomas Blackburn, he thought, would have done nothing.

Gisela had been a favorite on the Riviera. Her suicide forty-eight hours earlier had caught everyone by surprise and abruptly ended *Le Chat*'s welcome on her beloved Côte d'Azur. For weeks, his presence had lent a spirit of romance and adventure to an otherwise ordinary season. With visions of Cary Grant in their heads, eager young heiresses, jet-setters and bored wives of American tycoons had ignored warnings not to wear their valuable, albeit heavily insured, jewels to crowded cafés, parties and casinos. In truth, they had vied to tempt *Le Chat* to commit one of his daring robberies, each longing for the excitement and attention of being his next victim. After all, he never hurt anyone.

Even Gisela had emerged from her brush with the Riviera jewel thief physically unscathed.

If it had ever occurred. Fact and fancy were often inseparable in Gisela's quirky mind, an eccentricity that prompted more amusement than outrage among those who knew her. To be sure, her encounter with *Le Chat*—real or imagined—would never have happened if he hadn't been stalking the Côte d'Azur for victims.

Jean-Paul knew that the graveside mourners and the gossips and the snobs would blame *Le Chat* entirely for her suicide, without looking to themselves for culpability. He believed, however, that they, as much as their now-despised jewel thief, were responsible for her death.

No one had believed Gisela's blithe assertion that she was a member of the displaced Hungarian aristocracy, never mind that she had possessed the fabled Jupiter Stones until they'd been stolen by *Le Chat*.

Engaging and vivacious, she had arrived on the Riviera in 1955—from whence no one could exactly say—and immediately made a name for herself with her irrepressible charm and her unique talent for decorating country cottages and farmhouses. She never called the people she helped clients, simply "friends." Nor did she call herself an interior decorator or formalize what she did into anything as depressingly ordinary as a business. She did favors, that was all. Her "friends" always insisted on paying her, but how, she maintained, was up to them. Few ever caught her actually working. She loved to play and, especially, to take chances—with the roulette wheel, with her treks along the rocky coastline, with men. She had never made an enemy. Or, conversely, a true friend.

She had talked about the Jupiter Stones for years, but had never shown them to anyone—not that anyone had ever asked to see them. Why embarrass her? She couldn't possibly own anything so valuable. The Jupiter Stones were her good luck charm, she liked to tell people. They were the source of her boundless energy and enthusiasm for life. She rubbed them over her body every night, she told friends and strangers alike, and the stones restored her spirit.

Who could believe such talk?

The Jupiter Stones had existed. They had been a gift from Franz Josef, emperor of Austria, king of Hungary, to his beautiful, haunted wife, Empress Elisabeth. The exacting monarch, who ruled the troubled Hapsburg empire for sixty-eight years until his death at eighty-six in 1916, had had his court jewelers search the world for ten exquisite corundum gems, not just the coveted cornflower-blue sapphire or pigeon's-blood ruby, but in the other colors in which corundum was found: white, yellow, orange-yellow, green, pink, plum, pale blue and near-black. Each stone was perfectly cut, each given a name by Franz Josef himself. Four were named for the planets with a variety of corundum as their stone: the yellow sapphire was called the Star of Venus, the orange-yellow sapphire the Mercury Stone, the beautiful pigeon's-blood ruby star-stone the Red Moon of Mars and the velvety cornflower Kashmir sapphire the Star of Jupiter. Individually the ruby and the cornflower-blue sapphire—each flawless, each cut into a perfect six-sided star—were the most valuable. But as a whole, the unique collection was worth a fortune.

In tribute to his wife's unusually simple tastes, Franz Josef left the remarkable stones unmounted. He presented them to her in a ruby-red velvet bag embossed with the imperial seal. Elisabeth, it was said, took them with her everywhere. She was an incurable wanderer, and it was on one of these wanderings that she seemed to have "misplaced" the Jupiter Stones. Unlike her husband—and cousin—Franz Josef, Elisabeth, "Sisi" as she was known affectionately, wasn't an orderly person. A lover of riding and endless walks, she was generous and careless with her possessions; she could have lost the unique gems or simply given them away—as she did so often with her things— on a whim. She never said. Whatever their fate, the fabled stones weren't discovered among her countless jewels after her assassination in 1898, when, while boarding a steamer in Geneva, she was stabbed to death by an Italian anarchist who wanted to kill someone important enough that his name would get into the papers. He succeeded.

Almost sixty years later, Baroness Gisela Majlath claimed the unpredictable empress had given the stones to Gisela's mother after she, as just a girl of eight or nine, had endangered her own life to help Elisabeth after a riding accident. Gisela had inherited the extraordinary bag of gems when her mother and most of her family were killed in the two World Wars that decimated Hungary. She herself had narrowly escaped death when fleeing Budapest after the Communist takeover in 1948. All she managed to take with her were the clothes on her back and, tucked into her bra, the Jupiter Stones.

It was the sort of tale that everyone loved to hear, though no one believed it.

If Gisela had fled to the west dispossessed and penniless, why hadn't she cashed in the stones to reestablish herself? They were a family heirloom, Gisela had explained. And of course, they were enchanted; they had saved her from poverty and despair and even death. She couldn't just sell them as she might ordinary gems.

Everything changed the night she tearfully reported to the police she'd been robbed and described her ten corundum stones in detail, estimating their value into the millions of francs and admitting she had no photographs, no insurance, no proof she had ever seen the Jupiter Stones, much less owned them.

Why didn't she? The understandably skeptical police had asked what everyone but Gisela considered a reasonable question. She was insulted. Did the police doubt her word?

They did. So did all her friends and virtually everyone in France.

The gossips supplied their own answers. If the stones *were* in Gisela's possession—through whatever means— they would have been too valuable for her to afford to keep in any open, honest way. Insurance costs alone would have been phenomenal. She must have come to her senses, capitalized on *Le Chat*'s prowling about the Côte d'Azur, and hocked them, saving face by reporting them stolen. In which case, good for her.

But that scenario was far-fetched.

Far more likely she'd made up the stones altogether and had an ulterior motive for claiming she was *Le Chat*'s latest victim. A craving for attention? For notoriety? Had Gisela, too, yearned for romance and adventure?

Gisela, however, stuck to her story: the Jupiter Stones were hers, *Le Chat* had stolen them and she wanted him caught and her gems returned to her.

The gossips redoubled their efforts to come up with an explanation for what to them was decidedly *un*explainable. What if there were a germ of truth to her story and some manner of stones *had* been stolen? The idea of flighty Gisela rubbing herself with pretty rocks every night wasn't altogether implausible. She did have her idiosyncrasies. But did these stones of hers have to be the Jupiter Stones? Of course not. They could have been simple quartz or paste.

And if *Le Chat* had snatched a bag of worthless rocks… how *délicieux*.

Enjoying their own fantasies, no one noticed Gisela's growing despondency. The police didn't believe her. Her friends were enthralled with the criminal who'd robbed her of her most precious possession. The gossips were having fun at her expense. All these years, she suddenly realized, people had simply been indulging her. Not a soul had believed she had ever had the Jupiter Stones, much less been robbed of them!

Humiliated and despairing of ever seeing her corundum gems again, Gisela had flung herself off a cliff into the Mediterranean.

And everyone suddenly cursed *Le Chat* and demanded his immediate capture.

Enter Annette Winston Reed, the woman who had led the police to the true identity of *Le Chat*.

Word had spread rapidly that Jean-Paul Gerard was the culprit, and there was a collective gasp, a suspension of anger and grief, as people realized that if *Le Chat* wasn't Cary Grant, he was awfully close. The notion of the handsome, sexy Grand Prix driver amusing himself—he *couldn't* need the money—by stealing jewels went a long, long way toward renewing the romance of *Le Chat*.

But the police had their evidence, and there was precious little romance in their souls. The search was on for their missing suspect.

If they had believed Gisela…

Jean-Paul felt the tears spill down his cheeks, and he watched Thomas Blackburn lay a pink rose on the coffin. If others wondered about his presence at Gisela's funeral, Jean-Paul did not. "Thomas is a good man," she would say. "A true friend."

While the Bostonian closed his eyes in silent farewell, Jean-Paul turned away, whispering, *"Adieu, Maman."*

Tam curled up in the middle of *Tante* Annette's bed and sobbed quietly so that the other children wouldn't hear her. They would only tease her for crying. Even Papa had said she needed to be brave. France wasn't their home, he had told her. But to Tam it was. She didn't remember Saigon at all.

"Hi, Tam."

"Go away," Tam said, looking up at Rebecca Blackburn. She was only four and as big as Tam was at six. It wasn't fair. *Nothing* was fair. "I don't want you here."

Rebecca climbed onto the bed. "Why not?"

"Because I hate your grandfather!"

"You shouldn't hate my grandfather," the younger girl said. "He likes worms."

Tam sniffled and wiped her cheeks with the backs of her hands. "He's making Papa and me leave."

"Where are you going?"

"Home."

"But you live here."

"Yes, but I'm not French." She remembered her father's words: "Our home is in Saigon."

"I'll come visit you," Rebecca promised, curling up like Tam, her bare feet dirty from digging worms with her grandfather in the garden.

Tam shook her head, crying softly. "You can't—it's too far away."

"My grandfather goes to Saigon all the time. My mom sends him pictures I color, and my dad says we can go see him sometime. We'll come see you, too."

"Okay," Tam said, perking up. "Can you speak Vietnamese?"

Rebecca wasn't sure what her friend meant, so Tam demonstrated, speaking a few sentences in her native tongue. Her father said they would have to stop speaking French when they were together and speak Vietnamese instead, so she could practice.

"It sounds pretty," Rebecca said.

Tam smiled. No one had told her that before.

Her American friend jumped down off the bed and started poking around in *Tante* Annette's things. She wasn't really Tam's aunt, but she said she didn't like being called *Madame* Reed because it made her feel like an old woman. Tam adored her. She never criticized any of the children, just let them roam free in the gardens and the fields around the *mas*. Tam had heard Papa say Annette left them alone because she was bored and couldn't be bothered with anyone's needs except her own, but Tam didn't believe that. *Tante* Annette was always patient and nice.

"Oooh," Rebecca said, "look, Tam."

With her grubby hands, Rebecca dumped out a soft, red bag onto the bed, and a pile of colored stones rolled onto the white spread. White, yellow, green, blue, red, purple, black—Tam giggled. "They're so pretty!"

Rebecca carefully counted them; there were ten in all. "Do you think *Tante* Annette will let us play with them?" she asked.

Tam shook her head. "She'd be mad at us if she knew we were in her bedroom."

"Oh. Do you want to dig worms with me?"

"No, thank you."

With a shrug, Rebecca skipped out of the room, and Tam was again overwhelmed with loneliness and the fear of returning to a home she didn't know or understand. She bit down hard to stop herself from crying and fingered the colored stones. She wished she could have them to remind her of *Tante* Annette and the *mas*. If she just asked…but no, *Tante* Annette would never say yes. And even if she did, Papa wouldn't let Tam accept a gift she'd asked for.

Fresh tears warmed her eyes. *Tante* Annette had so many beautiful things. Papa said Vietnam was a poor country and they couldn't expect to have as much as the Winstons did; it wouldn't be fair to their countrymen who didn't always have enough to eat. Tam tried to understand.

But she couldn't bear to return the sparkling stones to the drawer where Rebecca had found them. Making her decision, she quickly stuffed them back into the velvet bag and ran to the caretaker's house, to her tiny room next to the herb gardens, where she hid them.

"Tam, Tam," Rebecca was calling excitedly.

Tam was certain her new friend had seen her and she'd have to give the stones back, but Rebecca ran into the caretaker's house with the longest, fattest worm Tam had ever seen.

"Isn't it cute?" Rebecca asked.

"Yes, it is," Tam said, feeling much better.

Two

Boston, Massachusetts
Thirty years later

The waiter for the unhappy vice president of Winston & Reed brought him a second perfectly mixed martini and silently whisked away the empty glass of his first. A thin, gray-haired, punctilious man, Lee Donigan had a low threshold of tolerance for two things: doing someone else's dirty work and being kept waiting. Rebecca Blackburn had managed to trigger both sources of irritation in one day.

He tried the martini. Excellent. He welcomed its soothing burn. It was his own fault he was stuck with this unpleasant task. He should have investigated the possibility that the award-winning graphic designer his public relations director had hired to revamp Winston & Reed's corporate look was one of *the* Blackburns. He had assumed a Boston Blackburn wouldn't have the gall to take on an assignment with his company. One should never assume.

Particularly, he'd learned the hard way, with a Blackburn. And especially this one.

A flash of color, a burst of energy—both compelled Lee to look up. Rebecca Blackburn caught his eye from across the busy restaurant and waved, ignoring the maître d' as she made her way to his table. Her electric personality seemed to light up the lunchtime crowd atop the forty-story Winston & Reed Building. In the few times he'd met her, Lee had observed that Rebecca was the kind of woman who never cooled off. She was always on, always moving. When her subtle, grab-from-behind beauty was added to that compulsive energy, the result was one unforgettable woman. Her high cheekbones, strong eyebrows and chin and straight nose provided the drama in her keenly attractive face, the rich, unusual chestnut color of her chin-length hair complementing the pure creaminess of her skin. Lee found himself hoping she was too professional to unleash her temper on him. That she had one he didn't doubt for a second.

She swept into the chair opposite him, a panoramic view of Boston Harbor under a clear May sky at her back. Lee's table was the best in the house. His office was just two floors down. He enjoyed working in what was commonly referred to as Boston's boldest and most luxurious building. He intended to keep his job, even if it meant doing for Quentin Reed what the president of Winston & Reed wouldn't do for himself.

"Sorry I'm late," Rebecca said.

There was nothing apologetic in her tone or her expression, and Lee's moment of guilt drowned under a fresh wave of irritation. The woman had to have known she was provoking just such a lunch as today's when she bid for the coveted design job with Winston & Reed. She should have restrained herself.

"But," she went on, "I've never been asked to lunch with a vice president who didn't mean to fire me."

Fresh words from a damn artist, Lee thought. Her eyes—a vivid, clear blue—met his just for an instant before she smiled and put her water glass to her coral-dusted lips. She looked every inch the stylish professional in a pumpkin-colored jacket over a black skirt—probably, if Lee could believe hall gossip, something she'd picked up for a song at Filene's Basement. She could afford to shop wherever she liked. Lee had to remind himself that Rebecca Blackburn was a very wealthy woman. She wasn't going to starve.

He noticed the gold dragons hanging from her ears. They demonstrated her renowned irreverence, her Blackburn independence. Even if they'd been three-dollar costume pieces—and they weren't—they would have told Lee Donigan that she wasn't one of them. She stood apart from everyone else at Winston & Reed. She didn't belong. And she knew it.

He decided not to bother mincing words with her. "You're right," he said. "We have to cancel our contract with you, Rebecca."

"Whose idea?"

"That's irrelevant."

He motioned for the waiter and nodded to Rebecca to order, not caring that he was rushing her. She was the one who'd shown up late. She ordered the broiled scrod and a salad, and he made it two. The two martinis had curbed his appetite.

"I'll have mine to go," Rebecca said as the waiter started to leave.

The poor fellow looked dumbfounded. "To go?"

She graced him with one of her most dazzling smiles. "Please."

Lee silently cursed Quentin Reed for being such a pusillanimous jerk he couldn't tell a woman he'd known since childhood to quit playing games with him and get the hell out of his company.

"I gather you don't even want to see the proofs," Rebecca said.

"I don't see what purpose that would serve."

But Lee would have loved Rebecca Blackburn to spread her portfolio on the linen-covered table and to give him a good, long look at the work she'd done for his company. As a designer, Rebecca was top-notch. Her preliminary sketches for Winston & Reed had blended the company's disparate elements, its old Boston traditionalism with its modern boldness and direction. Lee knew she wouldn't be easily replaced, if at all.

"Are you going to give me any advice?" she asked suddenly.

Her question caught Lee off guard. "I beg your pardon?"

"I've never been fired without getting unsolicited advice on how to conduct myself in the future. My favorite was from the president of the Dallas-based oil company where I worked a couple of months about two years ago. He told me I ought to get my pretty little self married and start having babies, but then he changed his mind and said he wouldn't wish a smart-mouthed nutcase like me on any red-blooded male."

Lee fervently wished for another martini. His public relations director had alerted him to Rebecca's résumé and its dizzying list of firms and cities where she'd worked since becoming one of the rags-to-riches business successes of the decade at twenty-five. She and her former roommate at Boston University had created the fun, fast-paced, irreverent trivia game Junk Mind that had become an instant and explosive bestseller. When they'd sold the rights to a Boston-based toy-and-game conglomerate, the roommate had taken a vice presidency with the company and they'd made a fortune. Rebecca, who'd designed the game board now in millions of households across the globe, had continued her drifting. New York, London, Paris, Dallas, Seattle, Honolulu, San Diego, Atlanta— she'd had jobs in them all. Not that she needed to work, but in the short time he'd known her, Lee had gained the distinct impression she didn't hold a high opinion of the idle rich—or anyone who didn't work. She'd only been back in Boston five months, making another of her periodic runs at operating her own design studio. But to make a lasting success of a studio, she would finally have to make the commitment not just to her latest project but to a place. Lee didn't know if she was running from herself, from the tragedies in her past, from her own startling success, or if she was running at all. He wondered if she was just not ready to stay put. With Rebecca, it could be just that simple.

"I'm not going to give you any advice," he said, smiling in spite of himself. "I only hope you find whatever you're looking for here in Boston. And I wish you luck, Rebecca." He extended his hand across the table. "Truly, I do."

"Would it have made a difference if I weren't a Blackburn?"

"It would have made a difference," he said, knowing he shouldn't, "if you were anyone but who you are."

Rebecca wasn't one to turn down a meal Quentin Reed was stuck paying for, but the smell of the fish turned her stomach as the elevator plunged forty stories, its doors sliding smoothly open at the cherry, marble and brass lobby. She started out.

And stopped. No. She wasn't going to let Quentin off that easily.

She marched back into the elevator, tapped thirty-nine, and nibbled on a sprig of crisp spinach on the way up. She wasn't afraid of Quentin Reed. She'd run and fetched him baking soda and water the time he and Jared Sloan had peed in the yellow jackets' nest, and she hadn't told his mother of their idiocy when she'd demanded to know why the two boys were walking so funny.

The thirty-ninth-floor reception area was, if anything, more opulent than the lobby, but Rebecca had no trouble lying her way past the receptionist into the inner sanctum of the president and chief executive officer of Winston & Reed, Boston's most prestigious real estate and construction firm. Annette Winston Reed still retained the title of chairman of the board, but the real power of the company now resided with her thirty-seven-year-old son, a circumstance that surprised Rebecca. Annette had never thought Quentin was worth a damn.

His secretary was a well-dressed, highly efficient woman who informed Rebecca she would require an appointment to see Mr. Reed.

"I'm a family friend," Rebecca said, breezing past her.

On her feet at once, Willa Johnson, willowy and fast, protested, firmly suggesting Rebecca wait while she checked with Mr. Reed—or suffer the consequences of her whisking in security.

"Mr. Reed and I," Rebecca said, "were kicked out of the wading pool on Boston Common for taking our clothes off. He was five and I was two." Supposedly, too, Jared had been the one who'd gotten them dressed and hauled them back to Beacon Hill. Mercifully, Rebecca didn't remember.

With Willa momentarily taken aback at the image of her

well-bred boss skinny-dipping on Boston Common, Rebecca slipped into his spectacular office.

Across the room, Quentin Reed slowly hung up his telephone, his pale blue eyes riveted on her. "Rebecca," he said in little more than a whisper.

It had been fourteen years.

A recovered Willa, about to strong-arm Rebecca out herself, heard the emotion in her boss's raw voice and retreated, quietly shutting the door behind her.

"Hello, Quentin."

He was as handsome as ever. Ash-haired, square-jawed, trim, even confident, although Rebecca suspected that was more in appearance than in fact. Quentin had forever been at war with his sensitive nature. He wore a conservative pinstriped suit of exquisite cut.

He cleared his throat. "What can I do for you?"

"Was it your idea or your mother's to have me fired?"

"You're not an employee. It wasn't a question of firing you."

"Semantics, Quentin. You're not going to weasel out of this one. You found out about me, told your mama and she said to give me the boot?"

He winced at her bald words, but confirmed her guess with a small nod.

"Does this mean I'm going to have the long arm of the Winston-Reed clan undermining my business in Boston?"

"Of course not." He rose, and she was surprised at how tall he was. She'd forgotten. "Rebecca, look at this situation from our point of view."

"I have. That's why I'm here. You can't stand the idea of a Blackburn earning a penny off Winston & Reed."

"You don't need the money—"

"That's not the point. Quentin…." She exhaled, wishing

now she hadn't gotten back into the elevator. "Quentin, I was hoping we could put the past behind us."

He shut his eyes a moment, sighing, and shook his head. "You should have known that's impossible."

She supposed she should have. Twenty-six years ago Quentin's father and hers—and Tam's—were killed in a Vietcong ambush for which Thomas Blackburn, Rebecca's grandfather, was directly responsible. It was a lot for anyone to put aside. But she wasn't going to give Quentin the satisfaction of telling him that.

She told him instead, "Bidding on this project was strictly a business decision on my part."

"You never were worth a damn as a liar, Rebecca. It's only your grandfather—"

"Leave him out of this."

Quentin stiffened. "You'd better leave before we both say things we'll regret."

On her way out of the luxurious office, Rebecca debated dumping her fish dinner in the trash, hoping it'd stink up the place. But she resisted, because there'd never been any satisfaction in trying to prove to anyone that the Blackburns still had their pride.

Three

—∞—

San Francisco

Jared Sloan cursed the sadist who had invented the tuxedo and had another go at his bow tie. It'd been years since he'd tied one. He'd managed all the other parts of the tux with relative ease and probably would have handled the bow tie all right, but he was running late. At least, except for cleaning, his tuxedo hadn't cost him a dime. His mother— proper Boston Winston that she was—had insisted on buying it for him years ago, and all he'd had to do was resurrect it from the back of his closet. Another failure with the tie, though, and back under his baseball cards it went. He'd wear jeans. Which would embarrass his father *and* his daughter. He'd never hear the end of what an insensitive lout he was and sparing himself that was worth another try at his tie, and maybe even the six or seven hours he was doomed to spend in his tuxedo. It was a close call.

He smiled at the sound of Mai's undignified squeal from the entry. *"Daddy!"* Then she caught herself and calmed

her voice to that of a fourteen-year-old would-be sophisti-
cate. "Dad, are you almost done? The limousine's here."

Only for you, babe. Jared successfully completed his
third try at what was, in fact, a simple knot. He quickly ap-
praised himself in the mirror. The tux's classic style helped
conceal its age; both the Boston Winstons and San Francisco Sloans would be willing to claim him tonight. He had
the strong Sloan cheekbones, dark hair, teal eyes and their
general rakish, devil-may-care look. His height—he was
six-two—and his more powerful build came from his
mother, the second of Wesley Sloan's four wives, who'd
exited from Boston society years ago and now lived on the
east coast of Canada in what she called self-imposed exile.
She'd never been so content.

"Wow," Mai said when he joined her in the entry. "Don't
you look handsome."

He laughed. "You're no dog yourself."

Mai wrinkled up her pretty face. She was a small, slim
girl, wiry and strong, with almond eyes and high cheekbones, a squarish jaw and a reddish cast to her fine, dark
hair. From the time she was a tot, Jared had tried to get her
to concentrate just on being herself. But lately he'd begun
to realize that Mai wasn't entirely sure who that was. He
tried to understand. Her mother, whom Mai had never
known, had been Vietnamese. In Vietnam, Amerasians
were known as *bui doi.* The dust of life. The expression
broke his heart, for Mai was, in a very real way, the light
of his life.

"That's not much of a compliment," she told her father.

"Wouldn't want you to get a swelled head. You're going
to be swimming in compliments by the end of the evening.
Ready?"

The glint in her eyes and the way she kneaded her hands

together told Jared his only child was champing at the bit, anxious to zip ahead of him to the elegant black limousine waiting incongruously outside their small redwood-and-stucco house on Russian Hill. But she restrained herself. A bright ninth-grader, she had lost none of the energy and exuberance of her early childhood, but was channeling it in new directions. Still, Jared found himself half expecting she'd run out and kick the limousine's tires, check under the hood, demand to try out every seat and see how every gadget worked, what every button did. A year ago she would have—in fact, her grandfather had told him, had.

Tonight, however, she walked regally out to the monstrous car, careful not to muss her gown made of clear, cool magenta fabric that exquisitely complemented the delicate tones of her skin. She quietly thanked the chauffeur by his first name, George, when he held the door for her, and tucked her knees together and her ankles to one side when she settled back into the leather seat.

Jared came around to the driver's side and climbed in beside her. He hated limousines more than he did tuxedos. At sixty-five, Wesley Sloan was an internationally renowned architect and could well afford his expensive tastes. The repeated offers he'd made to Jared to join his San Francisco–based firm were enough to make most architects salivate, but Jared, the eldest of Wesley's three children by ten years, continued to turn him down. He preferred to work solo, in the small studio behind his house, specializing in renovations, restorations and additions—"glorified carpentry," his father called it. But Jared's half sister Isabel had recently earned her graduate degree in architecture from UCLA and seemed ready to make the move up to San Francisco, something he hoped would take that last bit of heat off him. Wesley Sloan knew Jared wasn't going to change his mind, but he wasn't a man who liked to accept defeat.

If Wesley had known how much his granddaughter enjoyed riding in his limousine, he'd have tried sending it around every afternoon and never mind her father.

It was a cool, damp, foggy evening, the kind that made Jared intensely aware of his aloneness. He watched silently out the window as the car wound its way down the narrow, twisting streets of Russian Hill.

A small crowd was gathered in front of the elegant newly opened San Francisco Villa Hotel, designed by Wesley Sloan. He and his current wife were hosting their annual charity ball, a major social event on the city's spring calendar. Wesley had issued an invitation to his granddaughter every year since her twelfth birthday. This year, Jared had relented and agreed to let her attend. As he had before her, Mai would have to learn to deal with being a Winston and a Sloan on her own terms—not theirs, not his.

But as much as he believed in her and admired her spirit and self-assurance, she was just a kid. *His* kid. And he couldn't stop himself from wanting to protect her.

She tugged on his arm. "Daddy—look."

Jared was already looking. As the limousine pulled up to the curb, eight or ten huge Harley-Davidson motorcycles materialized out of the fog and formed a menacing half circle around the car.

"George?" Jared asked.

"I don't know what's going on, Mr. Sloan," the driver said. "There's no way I can pull out—we're stuck here."

"Are they going to hurt us?" Mai asked, trying to hide her nervousness.

Jared shook his head. "No, they've got too big an audience. I think they just want to intimidate us."

They revved their engines and made a lot of noise, glowering at their own reflections in the limousine windows. They were an ugly lot—overweight, tattooed, unkempt. Not one wore a helmet. Tough guys. Jared spotted two policemen emerging tentatively from the crowd. A newspaper photographer was clicking madly away.

"To hell with this," Jared muttered and turned to Mai. "Stay put."

He threw open the door as far as he could, until it touched the edge of the lead bike, and climbed out, directing his attention at the driver, a mean-eyed individual with a battered leather jacket stretched over his fat gut. Jared asked nonchalantly, "What's up?"

"We weren't invited to the party."

Jared laughed. "Consider yourself lucky."

The photographer had worked his way around the limousine behind the two policemen, who didn't appear to be in any hurry to assert their authority.

"Hate to miss a party," the biker said. He made a point of coughing up a huge clam and spitting so that it landed at Jared's toes.

Jared wasn't impressed. The guy and his pals were just getting their kicks intimidating a bunch of rich folks at a high-society gathering, only they'd picked the wrong target. Jared had dealt with scarier people than this.

"You can go in my place," he said, almost meaning it. "Got a tux strapped to that contraption?"

The biker seemed to appreciate Jared's humor and started to grin, but then Mai popped her head out behind her father and pulled his hand. "Daddy, *please* come back inside—"

"Hey—who's the gook kid?"

Jared heard Mai's sharp intake of breath and saw the

look of amusement her obvious fear and hurt elicited from the biker.

He snapped.

Putting all his weight on the door of the limousine, he lunged toward the big motorcycle. The force of the door hitting the bike's front tire caught the driver off guard and wrenched the handlebars out of his hands. He couldn't clear the bike and went down with it, catching his left leg underneath it. Jared didn't lose any time. He leaped over the fallen motorcycle and jumped on the bastard who'd insulted his daughter.

It wasn't the other bikers coming to the aid of their trapped buddy or the police jumping into the fray that stopped Jared from beating the guy senseless.

It was Mai.

"Daddy!" she cried.

He released the man's flabby throat and climbed back over the motorcycle, putting out his arms as Mai ran to him, near tears. He told her softly, "It's okay. They're just punks."

Reluctant to prolong the confrontation, the police let the bikers shove off. Jared noticed he'd gotten grease on his tuxedo and his tie had come undone. So much for sartorial splendor.

He put out his arm for Mai. "Madame?"

She giggled and laid her small hand on his crooked elbow. "I should have helped you beat that guy up."

"One hothead in the family's enough."

The photographer continued to click away, but Jared ignored him and the cheering onlookers as he escorted his daughter to her first charity ball.

Four

Almost a week after Winston & Reed had ousted her, Rebecca found herself painting her nails red and scanning a magazine article on Phoenix. She'd never lived in Phoenix. She wasn't sure it'd be smart to move there at the beginning of summer, but desert living had an exotically romantic appeal. And there wasn't much to keep her in Boston. Her fledgling one-woman studio was at a lull.

Of course, painting her nails and reading magazines weren't going to help that. She wasn't above scrambling for work. She'd worked in enough studios to appreciate the demands of the graphic design business and knew what it took to succeed. Talent alone wasn't enough—it also took sheer grit. When she'd first returned to Boston, she'd worked hard. Not wanting to hire anyone until she'd made the commitment to stay, she did everything herself. She was her own account executive, senior designer, office manager, receptionist and gofer.

Her studio occupied several airy rooms in a crummy building a few blocks in the wrong direction from the Boston Children's Museum. She'd bought the building back before real estate prices in metropolitan Boston had skyrocketed. It was on the site of the original warehouse owned by Blackburn Shipping way back in 1800. Her fellow tenants—none of whom knew she was their landlady—included a grumpy printer she'd never hire to do any of her work, an office supply wholesaler, a caterer, three or four accountants and about a dozen other strange little businesses that didn't need to rely on walk-in customers.

The telephone roused Rebecca from consideration of becoming the art director for a Scottsdale-based international resort chain. How posh. She could hit the Jacuzzi on her lunch hour and get free vacations.

She flipped on her background-noise tape and picked up the phone. "Rebecca Blackburn."

"R.J.—what's that noise in the background?"

Rebecca grinned at Sofi Mencini's voice. "My office staff busily at work. I read somewhere background noise encourages callers to take a one-woman outfit more seriously— makes them think I'm actually running a business here."

"Turn it off. I've got news."

Sofi wasn't one to fool around between nine and five; it was just now ten-thirty. The honey-haired, diminutive cocreator of Junk Mind was Rebecca's best friend and former roommate, a woman of wit, endurance and determination. Years ago Sofi had arrived at Boston University as the sheltered upper-middle-class girl from the suburbs, while Rebecca had been the outcast Boston Brahmin come home after ten years of exile in central Florida with her mother and five younger brothers. They'd both made their bids for independence—Sofi through one measured, deliberate act of will after another, Rebecca explosively. While Junk Mind was going on, Sofi had gotten her MBA and was ready when opportunity knocked to jump into corporate America. She'd never looked back.

"You've made the tabloids," Sofi said in her no-nonsense manner.

Rebecca laughed. "What, someone found out Winston & Reed axed a Blackburn?"

She grimaced at the unexpected bitterness in her tone. Until Boston, she had never taken a position without believing absolutely that this one would be the right one—that at last she'd found her niche, her home. She always worked her hardest. In terms of design, she invariably performed beyond her employer's already high expectations. While being fired or quitting did have its liberating side, it also provoked a more difficult emotion, an indescribable emptiness and sense of betrayal, a feeling of loss. But her bid for the Winston & Reed job—even, to a degree, coming back to Boston—wasn't an attempt just to get work or establish some sense of stability in her life.

What she was doing, she knew, was tempting fate.

"Yeah, I heard about that," Sofi said. "At least you won't starve without Quentin Reed's money."

"I'm thinking about moving to Arizona and taking up painting cacti. In a pinch I could sell a few off the tailgate of my truck to tourists."

"R.J., you make me crazy."

"On the other hand, I'm a designer, not a painter. I wouldn't be any good at cacti paintings."

"You don't need to paint cacti or anything else so quit this poor artist routine."

Sofi was always ready to poke fun at her friend's money habits. "So what's this about the tabloids?" Rebecca asked, steering Sofi back onto the subject.

"R.J., *The Score*'s got your picture on the front page—

and that you're currently operating a graphic design studio on the Boston waterfront. A reporter weaseled it out of one of the underlings here."

Rebecca put down the brush to her red nail polish. Sofi's news, at any rate, explained the messages she'd ignored from a reporter wanting to interview her; he'd never said what newspaper he represented. She didn't blame him. Not that it would have mattered: she'd quit talking to reporters a long time ago.

"I haven't gone near a reporter or a photographer in years," she said.

"I know."

"Sofi?"

"Think back, R.J. The fall of Saigon. Tam, Mai…"

Rebecca shut her eyes.

Jared.

"Oh, no."

Quentin Reed hesitated before pushing open the wrought-iron gate that marked the entrance to the Winston house on Mt. Vernon Street. One of the few free-standing houses on Beacon Hill, it was a quintessential Charles Bulfinch design with its pristine Federal lines, brick facade, black shutters and doors. Two huge old elms, coddled against the ravages of Dutch elm disease, shaded the brick sidewalk and front lawn, also a rarity on the Hill. Quentin had walked from Winston & Reed. Any meeting with his mother unsettled him; one called suddenly, with a request that he come at once, made him drag his heels, not so much to postpone the inevitable but to steel himself for it. He stood a moment in the shade, taking in the quiet of Beacon Hill. He could hear birds twittering in trees and shrubs; the crush of Beacon Street and the Common, of downtown Boston only blocks away, seemed distant.

Inhaling deeply, he smelled mowed grass and flowers, not just exhaust fumes, and finally he headed up the brick walk and over to the cobblestone carriageway. His wealthy mother's cavalier attitude toward security was notorious among her friends, but she refused to change. She had always loved risks and adventure, and hated the idea of living like a paranoid old woman. She considered her inside alarm system, the lock on her carriageway gate, and Nguyen Kim, her full-time bodyguard and driver, sufficient protection.

As he walked around to the rear of the big house, Quentin could feel the critical eyes of generations of Winstons on him. The ghosts, he called them. They'd always been a proud, principled, damnably lucky lot. They'd made their first fortune in the pre-revolution China trade, another in the post-revolution China trade, after they'd returned from the safety of Canada and silenced their critics by pumping money back into Boston's war-decimated economy. They were there when the Industrial Revolution had arrived and profited from a burgeoning textile industry, and like so many rich merchants and manufacturers in New England, they learned the ins and outs of conservative money management to preserve their fortune. When he married Annette Winston, Benjamin Reed was to apply those principles to her considerable assets. Instead he founded Winston & Reed.

Quentin could still see his father, a Connecticut Yankee never comfortable on Beacon Hill, standing atop Pinckney Street just after a snowstorm, with his bare head in the gusting February wind as he watched his only child careen down the steep hill on his sled. "Keep going!" Benjamin Reed had yelled. "You'll make the river yet!" He seemed oblivious to the impediments between Quentin's speeding sled and the Charles River: busy Charles Street, Storrow Drive, the median, fences, the Esplanade. Quentin would always stop at the corner of West Cedar Street, as his mother had instructed him to before he left the house, and wonder if he'd somehow failed his father for not even trying to make the river's edge. But that was the man Annette Winston had married: filled with grand ideas, but without the drive or the strategic abilities to carry them out.

In 1966, three years after his father's death, Quentin had left Beacon Hill for good. There was boarding school, then Harvard, Saigon, then a condominium on Commonwealth Avenue and a position at Winston & Reed. He'd since taken a huge apartment in the Winston & Reed–built five-star hotel on the Public Garden, but he'd surprised everyone when he'd opted for a view of Park Square over the more coveted—and expensive—view of the Garden and Beacon Hill. He and his wife, Jane, also owned a house in Marblehead on the North Shore, which Quentin adored. Jane was living there alone for the moment while they worked out problems in their marriage, but he hoped when they were back together they could abandon the city altogether, an idea he wisely kept from his mother. She expected him to return to Mt. Vernon Street. The house was his to inherit.

"Lucky me," he muttered, wishing his mother would will the damned place to someone else. But to whom? He and Jane had no children as yet. Quentin hoped a family was in their future, but right now he couldn't be certain his marriage was going to survive. There was Jared, but his cousin hadn't shown up in Boston since 1975 and wasn't particularly fond of his Aunt Annette. And Jared's daughter Mai was out. She wasn't a part of Boston, of her great-aunt's view of the Winstons. As usual, Quentin was stuck.

He found his mother in her stone garden house, transplanting pink geraniums into scrubbed terra-cotta pots. Gardening, he felt, was one of those chores Annette Winston Reed pretended to enjoy but secretly loathed. At sixty, she had chosen to play the game of representing the honor, dignity and charm of a bygone era—of being the proper Boston Brahmin dowager. She looked the part well enough with her gracefully graying hair, her reserved style of dress, her unconventional beauty. With age, she'd come into her particular kind of attractiveness; her strong features and height made her seem elegant without being frail. She sat on the boards of numerous nonprofit organizations and was generous with her time, energy and intelligence. People saw her as a well-bred, if formidable, Beacon Hill lady.

Yet there was another side to Annette Reed: the side that had made her the successful, imposing chairman of Winston & Reed, the woman who had led the company since her husband's death. It was she who had transformed it into a major player in the volatile and lucrative real estate and construction markets of the northeast United States. However, she seemed ambivalent about her power and her business triumphs. Oddly true to her own background and era, in public she credited her husband for his conception of the company and her son for running it. In private, however, she made sure Quentin knew who was in control. Yet, at the same time, she didn't hide her frustration with him for acquiescing to her will, seeing it not as respect for her abilities but as a sign of weakness in him. Not that she'd have tolerated anything else. Quentin had come to see that his mother's need to control stemmed not from strength and intelligence, as he had once believed, but from insecurity and selfishness. As for himself, he was damned if he did and damned if he didn't.

"Quentin—dear, it's so good to see you." She pulled off her gardening gloves. "Kim just put out lemonade in the garden. Shall we?"

As if he had any choice. "Of course, Mother."

"I was going to come into the office," she said, leading him out of the garden house, "but I felt this is a private matter properly discussed at home."

Quentin made no comment at her assumption that he, too, would consider the Winston house his home. She gestured to the chair at the white iron table he'd occupied since boyhood, and he sat down obediently, letting her pour two glasses of fresh-squeezed, lightly sweetened lemonade. There was the ubiquitous plate of sugar cookies as well, their sweet smell mixing with the scents of the garden, an unusually large one for Beacon Hill.

His mother withdrew a folded section of newspaper from the khaki jacket she always wore gardening. "I saw this at the pharmacy earlier this morning and decided I should call you."

She shook the paper open as she handed it across to him, her hand steady, and Quentin tried to conceal his reaction when he saw the two photographs occupying most of the front page of the popular national tabloid. He could feel himself going pale, could feel his stomach begin to burn. The picture on the left was a famous shot portraying the final American withdrawal from South Vietnam. It was seared in Quentin's mind for all time. There, again, was twenty-year-old Rebecca Blackburn carrying an infant and supporting the weight of a seriously wounded Jared Sloan as she got them all into a helicopter, only hours before communist troops entered Saigon. Rebecca's anguished expression—of shock, horror, betrayal, grief and determination—had captured the mixed feelings of so many as the nation of South Vietnam ceased to exist, and two decades of American hopes and promises ended.

The photograph on the right was a recent one of Jared Sloan in San Francisco, decking a motorcycle tough who'd insulted his fourteen-year-old Amerasian daughter, looking on from her grandfather's limousine. Quentin's gaze lingered on Mai Sloan. He absorbed every detail of her pretty face with its unusual, distinctive features. He could see Tam in her.

Tam...

After so many years, Quentin was amazed that he still felt betrayed by her, still felt such unrelenting sorrow over how they'd lost each other. She'd died that last day in Saigon. Her child—*Jared's child*—had lived.

"It's painful to look at, I know," Annette said tartly, snatching the clipping from him. "How Jared could let such a thing happen..." She broke off with an irritated sigh. "There's not much of an article. Fortunately, we weren't specifically mentioned, but they did find out Rebecca Blackburn's back in Boston. I'm afraid there could be ramifications for us, Quentin. We should be prepared."

"Mother, don't be silly. I haven't seen Jared in years—"

"That doesn't matter. He's your cousin. And if the press should learn Winston & Reed had hired Rebecca—and let her go—we could be in for some nasty publicity."

Quentin doubted his mother would ever let him forget that he'd inadvertently allowed a Blackburn to come under contract with their company. It was the sort of oversight Annette Winston Reed would never make. He said awkwardly, "You know I took care of that problem in as discreet a manner as I could."

She scowled. "There shouldn't have been a problem to take care of."

"Mother," he said gently, knowing that trying to defend himself would only make matters worse, "I'm confident I can handle the media should anyone want to pursue this story, but frankly, I doubt anyone will. What would be the point? The Blackburn-Winston thing's been exhausted twice, in 1963 and again in 1975."

Annette stiffened, annoyed. "Don't patronize me, Quentin. Your cousin should have considered us when he decided to attack that fellow."

"I doubt Jared's even thought about us in years."

"I'm sure you're right about that," she said bitterly. "Nevertheless, you'll remain alert, won't you?"

"Of course."

"And stay away from Rebecca Blackburn. She'll only cause trouble."

"Mother, she's as much a victim in all this as you or I—"

"A Blackburn a victim?" Annette fell back into her chair with a derisive laugh. "Now who's being silly?"

Regretting his unthinking comment, Quentin slipped into silence. Once he'd finished his obligatory glass of lemonade and sugar cookie, his mother allowed him to leave, with further promises that he'd do whatever he could to keep her, himself, and Winston & Reed out of the newspapers. He walked back out to Beacon Street, crossing onto the Common and stopping at the Park Street subway station. The vendor there had plenty of copies of *The Score*. Quentin bought one for himself.

His walk slowed and he felt a little faint, almost sick, as he stared again at fourteen-year-old Mai Sloan. He'd never even met her. He wished circumstances had allowed him to know his cousin's daughter. Tam's only child. But that would have meant breaching the unspoken agreement between his mother, Jared and himself. Jared's illegitimate half-Vietnamese daughter was his concern. In the unforgiving mind of Annette Winston Reed, Mai was an embarrassment to suffer, not a member of the family. To disagree with that summation would have required more courage than Quentin could muster.

And for his part, Jared seemed content with his exile from Boston, from the Winstons and the world he'd known as a child. There were times Quentin envied his cousin his freedom.

He looked again at the photograph, at Mai's beautiful almond eyes and her father's livid face, and he sadly realized there was no one he'd risk injury and the notoriety of his picture in *The Score* to defend. He wondered if Jared regretted the outburst that had landed him on the cover of a supermarket tabloid, but thought not. Jared had always been one to act on impulse, but he willingly accepted the consequences for whatever he did. Quentin had always admired his cousin's courage, his ability not to look back.

He threw the tabloid in a trash can and crossed over to Tremont Street, trying to blame the tears in his eyes on the wind. "Oh, Tam," he said, his voice choked, and flagged a cab, wanting suddenly to get back to work and immerse himself in the present. His mother was right about that: thinking about the past and rehashing it—alone, with friends, or on the pages of a gossip tabloid—would only bring them all more pain and anguish.

Best simply to forget, he told himself, yet already knowing he never would.

Annette pinched off a yellow geranium leaf and crumpled it in her hand, amazed at how stupefyingly dull her life had become. She seemed to be paying for her days of adventure and excitement with a proper late middle age. She'd always thought she'd die before she resorted to potting geraniums. And she was only sixty. Life was unmerciful.

Throwing down the leaf, she smoothed the tabloid front page on her worktable and allowed her gaze to linger on Mai Sloan. She was a pretty girl—talented, smart and mischievous, the brief article had said. She took clay and gymnastics classes, had lots of friends at the San Francisco public high school she attended. Annette's older sister, Martha, had tried to interest her in the child when she was just a baby, showing off cute pictures and telling stories, but Annette had let her know she wasn't about to forget the shame Martha's son had brought onto the family. She'd had to be quite brutal about it. Like most people who found themselves pushed up against Annette's will, Martha had chosen to retreat. Annette remembered her sister's last words on the subject: "How can you blame an innocent child?"

"I don't," Annette had replied. "I blame her father, and since he's chosen to raise the child—well, he can suffer the consequences."

Now she and Martha exchanged polite letters between Boston and Nova Scotia. There was no mention of Jared or his daughter, no pictures, no grandmother's bragging. Mai might never have been born, and that suited Annette just fine. She missed her older sister; she wasn't afraid to admit it. But their estrangement was a price she was willing to pay to preserve the honor and respect she and Quentin had earned in Boston—and their peace.

Yet Jared's child didn't look like anyone's shame. Her nephew must be a good father, Annette thought, surprised at the rush of relief she felt. Perhaps all had turned out for the best. Quentin wasn't overly bothered by this most recent flurry of publicity; that was good.

But poor Tam, Annette thought. Still, if she'd lived, would Mai be better off? Would any of them?

Annette sniffed. Why all this second-guessing? What was done was done.

She refolded the clipping and tucked it back into her pocket, then forced herself to put her gardening gloves back on and return to her planting. She wished *she* had grandchildren. If Quentin would end this ridiculous limbo with his wife and get on with starting a family, perhaps she wouldn't feel so restless, so unsettled about the future. Perhaps she ought to have Jane to tea and use her influence to encourage a reconciliation.

Annette smiled, imagining how nice it would be to have children playing in the Mt. Vernon Street garden again. She could take them to her *mas* on the Riviera, show them the olive and lemon trees, let them pick wildflowers in the fields. Yes, life could be enjoyable again, if in different ways than it had been thirty years ago.

She *had* been acting silly, she decided. There was nothing to worry about. Jean-Paul Gerard could no longer hurt her or anyone she loved. He was dead.

She'd killed him herself fourteen years ago in the hell that had become Saigon.

Five

∽⟳⟳⟳⟳∽

Jean-Paul Gerard had found the small redwood-and-stucco house on Russian Hill with no trouble, and he stayed out on the steep sidewalk, enjoying the perfect San Francisco day. It was a beautiful city. He'd flown in yesterday after discovering *The Score* discarded on a bus and had checked out the lay of the land before coming up to Jared Sloan's today. He'd slept in Golden Gate Park and had eaten cold dim sum for breakfast; he could feel it churning in his stomach now as he waited for Mai Sloan.

According to his rough estimate, she should be heading back from school in just a few minutes.

A mite of a girl came around the corner and skipped down the hill, swinging her book pack. Jean-Paul felt his mouth go dry at the sight of her shining hair, at her energy. She was so like Tam.

When she saw him, her pace slowed, and he knew she was debating crossing the street. He'd had that effect on people for many years, but couldn't get used to it. Even in the seediest areas of Honolulu, he drew nervous stares from strangers. He was fifty-four years old and could have passed for eighty with his pure white hair and his weather-beaten skin, deeply lined from years of exposure to disease, parasites, bad food, sleepless nights, alcohol and the worst—the very worst—in humankind. A livid welt of a scar ran from under his right eye down his cheek, then jutted left under his chin and finally trailed off down his neck. He didn't have a lot to live for, and people could tell, with just one glance.

"Mai?" His voice cracked, and he tried to sound less threatening, less scary than he looked. Not daring to step toward her, he went on quickly, "I knew your father in Vietnam."

Her dark eyes lit up with interest. "You did?"

"And your mother."

That drew her closer, her book pack dragging on the sidewalk behind her. "I've never met anyone besides my father who knew my mother. What's your name?"

"Is Jared home?"

"Yes—he works out back. Come on, I'll show you."

Excited now, the girl pushed open a five-foot wooden gate and led him along a stone walk, flanked with lush greenery, onto a deck. Across a postage-stamp yard was a small shed that obviously had been converted into a studio; a window box overflowed with motley petunias.

"Dad," Mai yelled over the deck rail, slinging down her pack, "we've got company!"

Jean-Paul heard a sound from the door to the house behind him and turned, spotting the U.S. Army issue Colt .45 Jared Sloan held in his right hand.

When Mai whipped around, she paled and staggered back a step. "Daddy…"

"In the house," Jared said. He stepped out onto the deck. "Now."

Mai didn't need to be told twice.

"It's been a long time," Jean-Paul said mildly.

"Get out."

"I have no desire to hurt you or your daughter."

"Crawl back into whatever hole you crawled out of and don't come near my daughter again. Understood?"

Jean-Paul nodded. "As you wish."

He backed off the deck, went slowly down the walk and through the gate, hoping he was concealing his jubilance. Jared Sloan continued to hate and fear him. *Yes!* That meant that he, Jean-Paul, had secrets yet to tell.

He had leverage.

You're crazy to go up against these people again. But what did he have to lose? His life had been shattered a long, long time ago.

He could get the Jupiter Stones. There was still a chance.

For you, Maman…

And he could have his revenge. For his mother, for himself. Maybe, at last, there could be peace in his soul. For so many years, it had been too much to hope. Now…he had to try.

Shutting the gate behind him, he found that he was crying. He couldn't stop himself. Tears streamed down his scarred face, blinding him, and the more he brushed them away, the more they came, until finally he stumbled down the street, letting them come.

There could yet be peace. And justice. Yes, he had to try.

Six

❧❧❧❧

Thomas Blackburn emphatically did not read supermarket tabloids, but anticipating her grandfather's attitude, Rebecca purchased two copies of *The Score* at a Fanueil Hall Marketplace newsstand before heading up to Beacon Hill. As was her custom, she avoided the subway and cabs and instead walked from her studio, going as much as possible by way of the renovated waterfront. She loved to stop and watch the seals outside the aquarium, or just take in the changes in the Boston skyline since she'd last lived there.

She resisted taking a good, long look at the tabloid's front page as she came to the quiet, black-lanterned streets of Beacon Hill. The famous photograph of her, Jared and Mai in Saigon was one Rebecca would never forget. She didn't own a copy. She didn't need one. Even after fourteen years, without stimulus and often without warning, she could hear the wailing of newborn Mai Sloan and feel the infant wriggling in her arms, twisting for the milk-filled breast Rebecca couldn't offer. She could feel Jared's weight against her, could see him, pale with shock and the loss of blood, his face set hard against his pain. And she could feel her own horror and disbelief, could recall every moment of their agonizing trip home.

Their Chinook helicopter had flown them to a U.S. Navy ship waiting in the South China Sea. Unwittingly, they had become a part of Option IV, the largest helicopter evacuation in history, and among the last Americans to leave Saigon. They were taken to Manila, where surgeons removed two bullets from Jared Sloan's shoulder. Rebecca had waited until his parents met him there. Then she'd boarded a plane alone to Hawaii, then on to Boston to pick up her stuff, and, finally, back home to Florida. She hadn't seen Jared or Mai Sloan since.

She had to look at the tabloid picture of a week ago, of the two people she'd gotten out of Saigon in its last tortured hours.

She stared at Jared's hard-set face. He hadn't changed. She wished he had. She wished looking at him now she saw a man she didn't remember so well, hadn't loved so much so long ago…hadn't betrayed her.

Mai, in the background, was everything Rebecca would have hoped and expected for Jared Sloan's daughter. He'd never thanked her for risking her life to get him and Mai out of Saigon, but looking at them now, suddenly Rebecca was glad they hadn't. Gratitude would only have connected them. It was better for her, and for Jared and Mai, that the cut between them—the separation—had been clean, if hardly without pain.

Rebecca cut down Pinckney Street, walking past a house where Louisa May Alcott had lived, past prestigious Louisburg Square, down to the intersection of West Cedar. It would have been shorter to have gone straight down Mt. Vernon to West Cedar, but that would have entailed walking past the Winston house, which Rebecca preferred to avoid. She had yet to bump into Annette Winston Reed. It was just as well. Rebecca was convinced that Annette had been the chief instigator behind the removal of the historic Eliza Blackburn house from the walking tour of Beacon Hill earlier that spring, something Annette couldn't have known its current owner had been trying to accomplish for years. Thomas Blackburn made no secret of his distaste at having a guide gather a group of tourists in front of his home, then relate its history and architecture, tell anecdotes about his family and, invariably, close with a sorrowful comment on the "reduced circumstances of Mr. Thomas Blackburn" that had led to the peeling paint on the shutters and trim, the scuffed door, the unpolished brass fittings, the small crack in the lavender glass in the side panel.

Over the years assorted neighbors and historical commissions and even a few politicians had written him letters or told him outright to fix up the place. He'd silenced them by threatening to paint his door vermilion. If a tour guide were particularly courageous—and there were those few—she would tell her group the gory details of the scandal that had led to Thomas Blackburn's public downfall. In his enthusiasm for "getting the facts," he had recklessly sent his son Stephen and fellow Beacon Hill resident and friend Benjamin Reed into a fatal Vietcong ambush in the Mekong Delta. Thomas had accepted full responsibility for the incident, but that didn't halt the failure of his fledgling company or keep President John F. Kennedy from passing him over as his next ambassador to Saigon. Instead the president sent another Boston Brahmin, Henry Cabot Lodge, and Thomas Blackburn had retreated from public life in ignominy.

It all made for juicy walking-tour talk. Thomas had caught one guide at it and ran out of the house, furious not that she'd brought up the touchy subject, but that she'd gotten several of her facts wrong. "People must distinguish," he'd told Rebecca, "between historical fact and one's own analysis."

Nothing annoyed Thomas Blackburn more than sloppy thinking.

Using the key he'd grudgingly given her, Rebecca entered the house through the front door. If shabby on the outside, the place was in reasonable condition on the inside, but certainly no showpiece. How like her grandfather, though, not to care about appearances. She headed straight back to the garden, one of Beacon Hill's "hidden gardens," and found him fussing over a tray of wilted seedlings at a bent-up black iron table and trying to blame her cat for their sad condition. "I saw that creature pawing them," he told Rebecca.

"Oh, you did not. Sweatshirt hasn't even been out of the house."

Thomas scowled. Not only did he dislike her cat, but he also had no use for the name Rebecca had chosen. He refused to see the connection between a gray cat and a gray sweatshirt.

"Are they dead?" she asked.

"No thanks to your cat, no. They're simply in a slight state of shock."

"From being overwatered, looks like."

Thomas made no comment, if for no other reason than he would never acknowledge that she might know more about gardening than he did. He was an intrepid gardener, but not a particularly talented or lucky one. His tiny walled garden didn't help matters. It was little more than a brick courtyard surrounded by raised beds that he and previous generations of Blackburns had planted with shrubs, perennials and annuals. A weeping birch and red maple added beauty and shade, but made the tricky prospect of sunlight trickier still.

"Don't you want to know why I came back early?" she asked.

"Boredom, I should think. You've been painting your fingernails again."

She knew she should have gotten rid of her red nails before she'd left her studio. She thrust a copy of *The Score* at him.

Thomas glanced at the two photographs and grimaced, turning away from his seedlings. He looked at his only granddaughter. "Rebecca, I'm sorry."

She was surprised. "You?"

"None of you would have gone to Saigon if it hadn't been for me."

By none, she wondered, did he mean not just her and Jared, but also Tam, Quang Tai, her own father, Benjamin Reed? Rebecca didn't ask. Over the years, she'd learned not to. She wasn't afraid of broaching the subject: she just knew it wouldn't do any good.

"Come," her grandfather said, "let's have some coffee and talk."

Talk? She wondered if he meant his version of "talk" or hers. Rebecca didn't say a word.

He heated the morning's leftover coffee in a pan, filled two cups with the rancid stuff, added milk from a jug and handed one to Rebecca, then returned to the garden and fell absently into one of the old Adirondack chairs he'd had outside for as long as she could remember. She sat across from him and tried the coffee. Worse than rotgut. But she didn't complain, watching her grandfather as he studied her. She could guess what he saw: a talented, rich woman of almost thirty-four settled neither in life nor in love. But could he guess what *she* saw? A man of seventy-nine, lanky and white-haired, not so straight-backed as he'd once been, not so proud and cocksure. Yet he still radiated the strength of character that came with the knowledge, the terrible self-understanding, that he'd made mistakes. Awful mistakes. His arrogance had left him childless, his six grandchildren fatherless and his daughter-in-law a widow at twenty-eight, and no man should have to live with that. But he had, for twenty-six years.

His thin hair lifted in a cool breeze, and he asked, "Why did you come to me?"

"I don't know."

"Don't dissemble, Rebecca. You do know."

She looked away. "When Sofi told me about the pictures," she began slowly, "my first reaction was anger and embarrassment at having the past dredged up again. I didn't even want to see a copy of *The Score*. But then..." She sighed, turning back to her grandfather. "I wondered if this wasn't the opportunity for us to talk. We never have, you know. Not about Saigon in 1975, and not about the Mekong Delta in 1963."

"Rebecca—"

"Grandfather, have you ever lied to me?"

He didn't hesitate. "No. Except about the cat..."

"Never mind the cat. About Vietnam."

"No, Rebecca. I never lied to you."

She leaned forward. "But you haven't told me everything, either, have you?"

"My mistakes and my triumphs are my own to live with, not yours. If you're asking me do I have regrets, I'll answer you. Yes. Yes, I have many regrets. And not only about your father and Benjamin. I've been to the Vietnam Memorial, and I've looked at those fifty-eight thousand names and thought about the men and women and children I knew in Indochina who are all dead. And I've asked myself what I might have done differently during my years there to prevent what came later. More arrogance on my part, perhaps. But perhaps not. The point is, I'll never know. If I've learned anything in my study of history and my seventy-nine years on this planet, it's that we have no power to change what's past."

Rebecca didn't listen easily to his words. "What about the future?"

He pulled his thin lips together. "I don't have a crystal ball. I've often wished I did. We can only do our best and carry on."

"That's it, then?"

"There's nothing I can tell you that will change anything."

"Grandfather," Rebecca said, controlling her impatience, "I'm tired of 'carrying on' without all the facts. That my picture can still make the front page of a supermarket tabloid just reminds me that 1963 and 1975 aren't going away. They're going to keep haunting us—*me*. And I have a right to know the whole truth."

"Study your history," Thomas Blackburn said stonily. "You'll discover that no one ever knows the 'whole' truth."

She swallowed hard and gritted her teeth, but suspected he could tell how angry and frustrated she was. "What do you want me to do, pretend my picture's not plastered across millions of newspapers?"

"No, Rebecca," he said, climbing to his feet. "Never pretend nothing's never happened."

Without another word, he turned back to his wilted seedlings, and Rebecca sighed to herself, wondering why she'd sought out her grandfather for advice and information, why she'd thought anything had changed. She had hoped the tabloid publicity and the simple fact that she was an adult—not the eight-year-old who'd lost her father or the twenty-year-old who'd lost her first lover—would prompt him to talk to her. There were so many gaps in her understanding of his years in Indochina, his ill-fated company, the scandal that had brought him down and changed her own life forever.

But she should have known better. Over the years, she had come to learn that if Thomas Blackburn only dealt in the truth, it was handed out precious little at a time.

Seven

⤜⥈⤛⥈⤛⥈⤚

Mai Sloan rode beside her father with her arms crossed as they drove over the Golden Gate Bridge and up into the hills of Marin County, where her grandfather lived. She hadn't spoken since they'd left the house. She had refused to pack, so Jared had thrown things haphazardly into a big canvas satchel and said if she ran out of socks or didn't have clothes that matched, tough. She'd yelled he wasn't being fair, and he'd said too bad, life wasn't fair and she might as well learn that now. Usually he made an effort to explain why he'd made a particular decision, but not this time. He'd just told her to get her things together, she was spending a few days with her grandfather. Nothing she'd said— not even when she'd called him a dictator—softened that lock-jawed look of his.

She continued to sulk as they cleared the state-of-the-art security system at Wesley Sloan's very private home in Tiberon, overlooking San Francisco Bay. Ordinarily Mai would have jumped at the chance to spend a few days there. Granddad had *everything*. But her father had pulled her from school and refused to tell her what was going on—refused to discuss the white-haired man with the scarred face he'd run off with a gun she hadn't even known he owned. Was the stranger some nut out to kidnap a Winston-Sloan? Was he connected with the motorcycle gang? *What?* Jared wouldn't say. He only instructed her not to leave her grandfather's property, even to go to school.

"Quit pouting, Mai," he said unsympathetically as they headed up Wesley Sloan's driveway. "Some things you just have to swallow."

"*I* have to swallow more than most!"

"Not true. You're one lucky kid."

"Oh, I know," she snapped back. "I could be begging in the streets of Ho Chi Minh City like hundreds of other Amerasians left behind in Vietnam. Compared to them I don't have a thing to complain about. I should always smile and take whatever anyone dishes out, *especially* my own father, since so many of us don't have fathers."

Jared sighed. "You have the right to complain about whatever you want to complain about. Your pain is yours. Just don't expect me to indulge self-pity. And you're the one who insists on measuring your life against that of the Amerasians who didn't get out of Vietnam. You can have empathy for their plight without feeling guilty because you're here and they're not."

She stared out the window, refusing to look at her father. She had been reading books and renting videotapes about the Vietnam War and the country of her birth, even trying to learn some Vietnamese. Her father told her it was normal to be confused at fourteen, urged her to concentrate just on being herself. But who was that? Sometimes she didn't know. And sometimes she hated herself for not being satisfied when so many other Amerasians suffered prejudice, cruelty and extreme poverty. They had never slept in a decent bed or felt the safety and security she took for granted. Sometimes she hated herself for not being more satisfied. She was so *lucky*. Why did she want more?

"Are you even going to tell me where you're going?" she asked.

Jared hesitated, not knowing what to say to his daughter. He hadn't since *The Score* had come out and she'd seen the picture of Rebecca, him and herself as an infant. Then the man who had shot him and left him for dead in Saigon had shown up on his doorstep, and that changed everything. Initially Jared hadn't recognized the scarred face, but then he saw the shock of white hair and the deadness of his soft brown eyes. And he'd remembered. Screams, pain, grief, his own paralyzing fear on that hot, tragic and violent night fourteen years ago in Saigon, when he'd lost Tam…and Rebecca.

He wasn't going to lose Mai.

Finally, he told her, "I'm going to Boston."

She whipped around. "Boston! But Dad—"

"Not a word, Mai. You're not coming with me. Be glad I've told you anything at all."

He could see her restraining herself from the fit she might have thrown a year ago, but she was maturing. She pulled in her lower lip and turned back to the window. She had wanted to go to Boston for years. It was the city where the Winstons had lived for generations, and where her father had grown up. And it was where he had taken her, so briefly, after their escape from Saigon. Jared tried to understand. She felt a part of her was in Boston where her father had grown up, and in Saigon, where her mother had lived and Mai herself had been born. But these were places she couldn't get to on her own. And Jared refused to take her.

"Are you going to see Rebecca Blackburn?" she asked.

Not if he could help it. Or, he was positive, if she could. The hardest he'd laughed in years was when he saw the *60 Minutes* piece on Junk Mind and found out Rebecca Blackburn was rolling in money. Served her right, reverse snob she'd always been. But he hated how much he'd hurt her, and seeing her again would only dredge up all that old pain.

He told his daughter, "I doubt it."

He had never told Mai about Rebecca's role in getting them both out of Saigon, nor about the famous photograph of them. She had cursed and screamed at him when he'd showed it to her in *The Score,* and he hadn't resented her anger. He'd have been angry, too. Rebecca, he'd explained inadequately, had been a friend.

"Then who are you going to see?" his daughter asked.

"Mai—cut me some slack, all right? We'll talk another time. I promise. But not right now."

"I just…"

"I know, kid."

He parked in front of his father's house and gathered her into his arms, wanting to hold her forever, knowing he couldn't. "You mean everything to me, Mai," he said. "I'm not doing this to hurt you."

"I trust you, Dad. You know that."

"Good. Then sit tight and let Granddad spoil you for a few days. I'll call you. And I'll be back as soon as I can."

She tried to smile. "Okay."

"Now go on."

"Aren't you coming in?"

He shook his head. If Mai couldn't wrangle an explanation out of him, Wesley Sloan just might. His daughter seemed to understand his reluctance, and she hugged him, made him promise again to call, grabbed her satchel and jumped out of the car. He watched her until she turned back at the front door and waved goodbye. He waved back, until finally she disappeared inside.

He headed out of the quiet hills of Tiberon back down to the Golden Gate Bridge and up to Russian Hill, where his house was quiet and lonely without Mai. With grim efficiency, he cleaned and loaded the gun he'd often prayed he'd never have to use. And he sat in his front room, with its fantastic view of San Francisco Bay, and watched the fog swirl in, half wishing the white-haired man would come back. If Mai hadn't been there, Jared didn't know what he'd have done, but he'd lived the last fourteen years so that 1975 didn't have to be her pain, as well.

He clenched his teeth. "It's not going to be."

But it already was, he realized, and pushed the heavy thought aside.

The next available flight to Boston left at 8:37 a.m.

He'd be on it.

Eight

◦◦◦◦

Rebecca decided not to return to her studio after her conversation with her grandfather, and retreated to her room on the third floor, overlooking pretty tree-lined West Cedar Street. She had thought she'd never see the day she became one of Thomas Blackburn's boarders. He'd started taking them in years ago, foreign students mostly. He charged them modest rents in exchange for a furnished room, a shared bath, and parlor and kitchen privileges, and he encouraged them to invite him to dinner when they were cooking something interesting and to discuss politics whenever they pleased. His current crop of boarders included a Nigerian doctoral candidate in economics, a Greek medical student, two Chinese physics students and Rebecca, who could have afforded to renovate the Beacon Hill house with its ancient plumbing and tattered drapes and upholstery and put them all up in decent apartments. But her grandfather and the boarders had their pride, and she didn't see any need to spend money renting a proper apartment in the city with among the nation's highest rents when she could stay with family, until she figured out if Boston was where she wanted to be.

The silver light of late afternoon angled through the paned window, and Rebecca pulled up an antique Windsor chair, in need of repair, and stared down at the street. Her grandfather had put her in her old bedroom, with the twin bed she'd had as a child, the marble-topped dresser with its puppy-chewed leg, the worn Persian carpet Eliza Blackburn supposedly had had shipped from Canton in 1798. Thomas had insisted upon the valuable carpet remaining in the upstairs bedroom, where it always had been; Eliza, he'd said, had been a practical woman and had intended her furnishings be used. Rebecca had quoted his words back to him when she'd spilled tempera paint on the carpet. She could still see the faded red and yellow stains. Her own furniture and things were either in storage or up at the old lighthouse she'd bought on an island off the coast of Maine. When the rest of the small, uninhabited island had gone up for sale, she'd bought it, too. She liked owning land, knowing she had places she could go pitch a tent.

She felt unsettled and raw. Looking at the quiet street, she could see herself at seven leaning out the window and nailing twelve-year-old Jared with her squirt gun for harassing her. "You'll fall, you idiot," he'd yelled, and she'd laughed and got him again.

She heard the telephone ringing downstairs. Then there was a quiet knock on the door. "Rebecca?" It was Athena, the Greek medical student; she and her landlord would blithely discuss the gruesome details of her anatomy class over the dinner table. "The telephone's for you."

Rebecca thanked her and headed down to the kitchen, where Athena was preparing a huge dish of *spanikopita* and studying pictures of carved corpses. She seemed quite happy with the outdated stove, the unstylish double-width white porcelain sink, the decades-old refrigerator, the shortage of cabinet space. The round oak table that had always been too big for the small kitchen still occupied its spot in front of the window overlooking the garden. As a little boy, Rebecca's father had carved his name in the table, in the careful, awkward letters of a preschooler. Rebecca had watched her grandfather brush his fingertips across his only child's efforts, just minutes before they were to bury Stephen Blackburn.

She grabbed the telephone.

"Rebecca," Jenny Blackburn said, somewhat breathlessly, "why didn't you warn me? I was buying groceries when I saw your picture. Are you all right?"

"I'm fine, Mother," Rebecca replied, thinking about central Florida in late May, the smells, the flowers; it would be getting hot. But her mother wouldn't notice. A handsome woman in her midfifties, with pale blue eyes and white-streaked dark hair, she had always loved the heat. Sinking into a chair, Rebecca added, "And I had no idea *The Score* was reprinting that picture or I'd have warned you. Have any reporters been bugging you?"

"A couple of local ones—young. I let them come over and look around the groves, and I answered their questions about what I've been doing for the past twenty-six years, which is raising children and citrus. I've found it's easier to bore them than to tell them to go to hell." She inhaled, then said, "Rebecca, I wish you'd just come home."

She almost told her mother she had, but thought better of it. Maybe Florida, not Boston, was her home. Jennifer O'Keefe Blackburn made no secret of her disapproval of her only daughter and oldest child's work and living habits, but she took a laissez-faire approach. "You're an adult,

Rebecca," she would say, "and capable of making your own decisions."

Ian O'Keefe—Rebecca's maternal grandfather—had no such inhibitions. He'd kept his mouth shut thirty-six years ago when his one daughter had married a Boston Yankee, but no more. He didn't approve of the way Rebecca just didn't do things the way they were supposed to be done. In February when she'd visited him and her mother, he showed her his address book and pointed out how she'd messed up his *B* section with all her moving. True to his own convictions, he'd neatly printed each of her new addresses in ink. They were all there, from her first dormitory at Boston University to West Cedar Street. His ink was born of a stubborn adherence to his own ideas about what was right, but he never gave up on her. He'd run out of space under *B* two moves ago and had had to move into the *C* section. Rebecca's five younger brothers had more or less given up trying to keep track of her; when they wanted to reach her, they just called Papa.

"I mean it," her mother went on, and Rebecca could hear the rising tension in her voice. "You know I hate to interfere in my kids' lives, but you've got no business being in Boston."

Oh, so that was it, Rebecca thought. The pictures in *The Score* were her mother's excuse for letting her daughter know how she felt about her being back on West Cedar Street. As if Rebecca couldn't have guessed. She said patiently, "My being in Boston didn't cause this thing in *The Score*. It was just a fluke—Jared being a hothead. It had nothing to do with me."

"I hate Boston," Jenny said.

"I realize that, Mom."

"It's that Blackburn pride of yours, isn't it? You just had

to go back. You can't leave well enough alone. You always have to keep pushing and pushing."

Rebecca resisted the urge to defend herself, knowing it would only fuel her mother's frustration—and her worry. Boston hadn't been an altogether lucky place for Jennifer Blackburn or her daughter.

"What do you hope to accomplish?" her mother asked wearily.

"Maybe," Rebecca said, "I just think Grandfather shouldn't have to die a lonely old man."

It was a moment before Jennifer O'Keefe Blackburn said, "He deserves to," and slammed down the phone.

Nine

~~~~~◆◆◆~~~~~

Rebecca Blackburn received the news of her father's death on a gray winter afternoon in early 1963. She was eight years old. It was Jared Sloan who came to her third-grade class at the private elementary school in Boston's Back Bay to walk her and two of her younger brothers home. A car had already come for Quentin Reed, in the fifth grade.

"There's a family emergency," was all Jared would say.

Just thirteen himself, he took hold of Nate, seven, and five-year-old Taylor and let Rebecca trot along beside him. He had volunteered to collect them and, too distraught to think clearly, his mother, his Aunt Annette and Jennifer Blackburn had let him. Jared was familiar; he wouldn't scare the Blackburns' school-aged children.

Rebecca felt her face freezing in the stiff sea breeze. "Where's Mother?"

"She had to stay with the little ones."

There were three more brothers at home: Stephen, four, and Mark and Jacob, the two-year-old twins. Once, Rebecca had heard her paternal grandfather fussing to her father about having so many children. "People will think we're running an orphanage here," Grandfather had said. Her father, who, like Rebecca, never took Thomas's grumblings seriously, had asked him since when did a Blackburn care what people thought? Thomas had strong opinions about everything, but Rebecca knew he loved her and her brothers. She remembered when he'd told them the best things came in sixes. When he was home, he liked to take her and her brothers to museums and old Boston cemeteries and let them throw rocks in the Charles River.

Not satisfied, Rebecca asked Jared, "Did something happen to Fred?" Fred was one of their cats. They had four. Grandfather complained about them, too; he said West Cedar Street wasn't a barnyard.

Jared paled. "No, R.J., Fred's fine."

"Good."

Her mother met them at the door of the Eliza Blackburn house on Beacon Hill. Away in Indochina so much, Thomas had insisted his son and daughter-in-law and grandchildren live there. Right away Rebecca knew something terrible had happened. Her mother's face was very white and tear-streaked, and she jumped off the steps and gathered her and Nate and Taylor into her arms, choking back sobs. Rebecca tried to cling to Jared. She wished he'd take her down to Charles Street for hot cocoa or ice-skating on the Common, anywhere so long as she didn't have to hear what her mother had to tell her.

But Jenny Blackburn, trying vainly to smile, thanked Jared and told him his mother was waiting for him at his aunt's house on Mt. Vernon Street.

"Will you be all right going alone?" she asked him. After all, he had lost an uncle, and, in Stephen Blackburn, a man who had been like an uncle to him.

"You don't have to worry about me, Mrs. Blackburn."

Alone with her six children, Jenny told them their father had been killed in the war in South Vietnam, where he and their grandfather had gone to help bring peace. She got out Thomas's musty globe and pointed to the country so far from Boston. Their father, she explained carefully, had gone with Benjamin Reed to a place called the Mekong Delta, and a group called Vietcong guerrillas had attacked them. Rebecca thought she meant gorillas.

"No," her mother said, "they're just people."

But why would people kill her father? Rebecca kept the image of gorillas. "What about Grandfather?" she asked, still numb with shock. "Was he killed, too?"

Jenny shook her head, and her voice cracked when she replied, "Your Grandfather Blackburn always manages to survive."

Jennifer O'Keefe and Stephen Blackburn had met in Cambridge, when she was a scholarship student at Radcliffe and he, at his father's insistence, was pouring more of Eliza Blackburn's dwindling fortune into another Harvard education for one of her descendants. Stephen was the Boston Brahmin with the impeccable pedigree. Jenny was the lively, straight-talking Southerner who planned to get her education and go home to teach college. When Stephen had shown her Eliza's headstone in the Old Granary Burying Ground off Boston Common, she'd remarked that *her* ancestors had been horse thieves and scoundrels.

She hadn't expected to fall in love with a New England Yankee, but she did, anyway.

And that was all right. Stephen was a kind, funny man— gentle, intelligent, sensual. He possessed none of his father's sometimes irritating natural incisiveness about people. In true Blackburn fashion, they were both historians, but Thomas had an uncanny knack for zeroing in on a person's weaknesses and less-than-generous motivations. It could make him difficult to be around.

"He's a sharp judge of character," Stephen would say.

Jenny believed him.

She and Stephen were married in historic Old South Church at Copley Square on a warm spring day in 1954, not long after the Vietminh routing of the French at Dien Bien Phu. Stephen had laughingly warned his bride that her new father-in-law would mark events that way. Nothing occurs in a vacuum, Thomas Blackburn was fond of saying. Jenny considered him a harmless eccentric, one of those brainy East Coast types in tweeds and holey boxer shorts. Since his wife's death in 1933, Thomas had spent as much time in Southeast Asia as he could, and more and more as his son grew up. Stephen worried about his father meddling in that dangerous part of the world. Jenny did not. She had grown up among the lakes and citrus groves of central Florida and knew a survivor when she saw one.

In late 1959, with his fourth grandchild on the way, Thomas had surprised virtually everyone who knew him when he started his own consulting firm, specializing in providing government agencies and private businesses with analysis on the political, social and economic systems of Indochina. If not amiable, Thomas Blackburn did possess intimate knowledge of the region and envisioned his company as a means of working with the people of Southeast Asia and understanding their aspirations.

Within two years, he was able to invite his son to join his firm. With Jenny's mixed blessings, Stephen accepted.

Two years later, her husband was dead.

* * *

Thomas Blackburn escorted his son's body and that of Benjamin Reed back home to Boston. Three months before, Benjamin had hired Blackburn Associates for advice and information on establishing his new construction firm in South Vietnam. He'd started Winston & Reed with his wife's money and meant to make a success of it, and he thought the Blackburns could help. Halfway between Thomas and Stephen in age, he had been friends with both men.

The inquiry into the ambush cleared Thomas of specific wrongdoing. He'd planned the excursion into the Mekong Delta and had rushed Stephen and Benjamin into executing it, but he couldn't have known the Vietcong would attack.

Or could he have?

There was rampant speculation that Thomas, in his zeal for information, had originally arranged a meeting with a group of Vietcong the day of the ambush. He canceled out—chickened out, some said—at the last minute and allowed the excursion to go on without him, apparently hoping nothing would happen if he didn't show up. Instead the Vietcong attacked, and three people were killed. Thomas had believed his position would compel the Vietcong guerrillas to leave him and his people alone.

Everyone from his daughter-in-law to a host of American military advisors and President Kennedy himself expected Thomas to defend himself against charges that he'd been arrogant or just plain naive.

He didn't.

"I accept," he told Jenny, Annette, colleagues, clients, politicians, military men and reporters, "full responsibility for what happened."

They let him.

He went back to Indochina only briefly after burying his son. His company quickly went bankrupt, and President Kennedy decided against what would have been the bold move of naming Thomas Blackburn his new ambassador to Saigon. Showing no outward sign that any of this was more than he expected or felt he deserved, Thomas continued to refuse to answer the speculative charges against him, but simply retired to his house on Beacon Hill, taking up gardening and indulging his passion for rare books.

By summer, Jenny had recovered enough from the shock of losing her husband to realize she couldn't continue to live in her father-in-law's house. She would bump into Annette Winston Reed, also made a widow that terrible day, on the streets and have nothing to say. She could see her own children becoming ostracized, confused because the Blackburn name no longer had the same resonance it once had had. And there was no money. She had six small children and a father-in-law who'd become a pariah, and Eliza's late-eighteenth-century fortune would stretch only so far.

But more than anything else, there was Thomas himself. Jenny could no longer face him every morning over coffee, listen to him scratch in his garden instead of doing something. Looking for a job. Fighting back. Starting over. Anything.

Finally, she knew she had to make a life for herself and her children away from Boston. She called her father. Of course, he told her, she could come home; he had always hoped she would.

She rented a truck and hired a couple of high school boys from South Boston to help her load it with the few things she and Stephen had accumulated during their nine years together. Her father would arrive later that morning and drive it to Florida, with Rebecca and Nate up front with him. Jenny would take the other children in the car.

Thomas watched stonily from the sidewalk. When Jenny had announced she was moving back "home," he'd refused to take her seriously. Yet there was the truck blocking the narrow street and the children pouring out to holler and run about in its empty cargo space. He was forced to admit the inevitable.

"You're running away," he told his daughter-in-law.

"So what if I am?" She had decided not to let him put her on the defensive. "At least now the children will have air."

"Air? There's plenty of air in Boston. Take them up on the roof and let them breathe all the air they want. And what's the matter with the Esplanade? The children can ride their bikes on the riverbank whenever they want. I'll take them myself. And there are parks all over the city—too many, can't afford the upkeep."

Jenny knew he was baiting her, if relatively harmlessly. "You believe children should play in the streets?"

"Why not? I did."

Pity you weren't run over, she thought. But then she'd never have had Stephen, or their children. And she hated herself for hating him; it was perhaps the best reason for leaving.

"What do you think you'll find in Florida besides alligators and poisonous snakes?"

"Alligators and poisonous snakes," she snapped back, "are better than a lot of what you'd find on Beacon Hill."

He smiled faintly. "Touché, my dear."

She sighed. "It's too late to argue, Thomas. I'm going."

"I know." He touched her arm. "I wish things could be different. I hope you know that."

"I don't, Thomas. I only know that my husband's dead

and you're willing to take responsibility for his death when no one asked you to. Now people are saying you were a communist collaborator, you're naive, you were duped, you were arrogant. If you'd considered me and the children, maybe you'd defend yourself."

"To what end?"

She jerked her arm away, scoffing. "It was difficult enough being a Blackburn before this tragedy. Can you imagine what it's going to be like now? Think of your grandchildren, Thomas. Think what it's going to be like growing up knowing their grandfather's accepted full responsibility for the deaths of three people, including their own father. Even leaving Boston isn't going to make that any easier to deal with."

Thomas pulled in his lips a moment, then sighed. "You're right, of course."

"But that doesn't change anything, does it?"

"I'm afraid it doesn't."

"The Blackburn pride," she said bitterly, and turned away so that he wouldn't see her cry.

Without a word, Thomas went back inside. He didn't come out when Ian O'Keefe arrived and helped Jenny finish packing, and finally she found him in his garden, pinching off wilted daylily blossoms.

"You'll come visit, won't you?" she asked.

He turned to her. "Not," he said, "if what you want to do is forget."

"It isn't."

"Then perhaps I'll come. Invite me."

But she never did.

Ten

❧❧

By noon the day after her picture had appeared on newsstands all over the country, Rebecca gave up all hope of getting any work done. Not that she'd tried that hard. There wasn't a whole lot to do if she wasn't going to get out there and take on new assignments. She'd thrown out her red nail polish, used up a dozen cotton balls and ten minutes getting it off her nails, and had done a few bad sketches of the replica of the Boston Tea Party ship just up the road at the Congress Street Bridge.

And answered the telephone.

It was ringing when she'd unlocked her door at eight-thirty and continued to ring most of the morning. She turned down interviews with two Boston newspapers and a regional magazine, but agreed to answer a few questions by a journalism student at Boston University who wanted to know about one of her school's famous almost-alumni. There were three calls from businesses in metropolitan Boston who offered her assignments; she took their names and numbers and said she'd get back to them. Maybe. The president of a New York advertising firm called to talk to her about becoming his art director. He said he knew her work and had thought about tracking her down for several years, but when he saw *The Score* at the train station on his way home last night, he decided he had to call. Rebecca listened to his pitch and realized why he had gone in to advertising. She was tempted, told him so, and took his name and number.

An old boyfriend from Chicago called and said he had to be in town on business next weekend, how 'bout dinner? She told him no, but thanks. After seeing Jared Sloan's picture the last thing she wanted to think about was men.

Half a dozen nonprofit organizations called with very polite, understated requests for money. Two she recognized as reputable and promised them checks, two she hadn't heard of and asked them to send her more information and two she thought sounded made up and told them to forget it.

And that was enough phone calls for one morning. She put on her message machine and headed over to Museum Wharf, where she stopped for lunch at the Milk Bottle, shaped like its name and located in the middle of the brick plaza in front of the Boston Children's Museum. She took her hummus salad to a stone bench to watch the crowd, mostly kids, tourists and young, white-collar types looking for a quick meal they could eat outside. It was a gorgeous day.

When Rebecca got up to pepper her hummus, about twenty preschoolers gathered around her bench for a carefully supervised picnic. She remembered taking her youngest brothers on picnics down by the pond at home in central Florida, teaching them about snakes and showing them how to catch frogs and lizards. In her room at night, she would describe all their activities in detailed letters to her grandfather in Boston.

She had hated Florida at first. The oppressive summer heat, the big, strange rooms of Papa O'Keefe's twenties-style house, the pond in the backyard, the endless citrus groves, the lack of neighbors, the spiders and snakes. It was all so different from Beacon Hill. But her mother had promised her she would come to love the place, and she had, in her own way. That didn't stop her from wondering what her life might have been like if they'd been able to stay in Boston. Would she have turned out to be another in a long series of impoverished, holier-than-thou Boston Blackburns? At least, she thought, their "wilderness exile," as Thomas Blackburn called it, had spared her *that*.

After she took a few more bites of her salad, Rebecca tossed the leftovers and started back toward Congress Street. She'd return to her studio and take on all the assignments she could, maybe think about the advertising job in New York. She needed to work.

A man's face came at her from the throng crossing the Congress Street Bridge, past the replica of the Boston Tea Party ship, and she stopped cold.

"My God," she heard herself whisper.

The face was even more battered now and older—so old—but there was still the slight limp, and the tough, sinewy body.

Together, they became the Frenchman from Saigon.

Or his ghost. Hanging back on Museum Wharf, Rebecca waited to see if she wasn't hallucinating from the pressures of being back in Boston and having her picture in *The Score* force her to relive the hell of April 1975.

She wasn't hallucinating.

Rebecca's heart pounded; this was no coincidence. He

had to be on Congress Street because of her. He had spotted her picture in *The Score,* looked up her studio's address in the Boston Yellow Pages and here he was.

The crowd thinned out once she'd passed Museum Wharf. Rebecca could easily make out the limping figure in worn, loose-fitting jeans and a faded, short-sleeved black shirt. With his scarred face and snowy hair, he'd never be able to melt into a crowd.

Concentrating on keeping her breathing normal so she wouldn't do something stupid like faint, Rebecca walked down Congress Street after him. Seeing him was a shock; there was no question of that. Her heart deserved to pound. But she didn't have any idea whether she should be afraid of him or not.

I suppose you'll find out if you keep following him....

There were enough people in her building and around outside that she wasn't too worried he'd try anything. And she wasn't fool enough to follow him all the way up to her isolated studio. If he went up there, he could ransack the place to his heart's content.

He wasn't going to kill her, she told herself. He'd had the chance fourteen years ago and hadn't.

Of course, by now he might have realized his mistake.

With a quick glance up to check the number, the Frenchman entered her building. Rebecca clenched both her hands into tight, nervous fists and made herself tiptoe up behind him in what passed for a lobby. He had already pressed the up button on the old service elevator.

Before she could say a word, he turned expectantly to her. "I thought that must be you following me."

His accent was only vaguely French, his voice—its timbre, its intensity—exactly as Rebecca remembered from Saigon, his eyes exactly as soft and brown and strangely

vulnerable. He took her in with a sweeping glance, and
Rebecca knew he wasn't seeing a terrified twenty-year-old
kid who expected to have her head blown off in the next
few seconds. If she hadn't put the past behind her, she had
at least gone on with her life.

She tried not to stare at his ravaged face as she searched
for a response. But what was there to say? In 1975, he and
his Vietnamese cohort, a tough, brutal man, had murdered
Tam and left Jared Sloan dying. Rebecca hadn't forgotten that
night and, she was quite certain, neither had the Frenchman.

He seemed to sense her discomfort and smiled, a surprisingly gentle, tortured smile. "I saw your picture in the
paper," he told her quietly. "I didn't know until then you'd
gotten out of Saigon safely."

"'Safely' might be exaggerating," she said, the words
not coming easily from her dry mouth and tension-choked
throat. "But we got out. I'd like to know who you are."

"I could tell you a name." He shrugged, and she saw that
he was very tanned, his muscles stringy and tough, reminding her of one of Papa O'Keefe's invincible old roosters.
"Would a name change anything?"

"If you just made one up, no. But you could tell me
where you came from, why you were there that night in
Saigon, why you're here now."

"It's better you ask no questions, Rebecca Blackburn."
Her name rolled off his tongue, as if he'd spoken it many
times. Rebecca had to stop herself from shuddering. But
he noticed, and said, "Perhaps I shouldn't have come."

"Why did you?"

The elevator creaked and groaned as it started its
descent. She would run back out into the street before she
got in there with him.

If he let her.

She shook off the thought.

"The past," he said, "sometimes must collide with the present."

The elevator dinged and the doors opened, but the Frenchman didn't go in; instead he started back toward the building's entrance. Suddenly Rebecca didn't want him to leave. She wanted him to stay and talk to her, but then she remembered the assault rifle he'd used so efficiently that night in Saigon, remembered Tam lying dead in a hot, sticky pool of her own blood. Remembered her own terror and grief and horror. And Jared. Bleeding and in shock, but not dead. Rebecca still didn't know what she'd have done if both Jared and Tam had died.

Asking the Frenchman to stick around and chat didn't make sense, no matter how much she wanted answers.

He looked back at her with those warm, strange eyes. "I'm sorry if I've frightened you," he said. "That wasn't my intention. I was your father's friend," he said, "and I believe—I know he would have been proud of you."

Then he disappeared, Rebecca too stunned by his words to follow him and demand to know what he meant. How could one of the two-man team that had murdered Tam in 1975 have known her father in 1963?

By the time she recovered enough to run back out to the street, the Frenchman had disappeared.

Her legs felt as if they were going to collapse under her, and she stumbled into the elevator, blindly pressing the button for the fourth floor. But her knees began to shake, and then her hands, and by the time she was inside her studio, fumbling into the credenza drawer, her entire body was shaking.

She found the handcrafted silver box her father had brought back from Saigon for her seventh birthday.

Inside was a deep ruby-red velvet bag. Rebecca poured out the contents onto her drawing board.

Ten beautiful colored stones ranging in color from white to near-black glittered up at her.

Rebecca shut her eyes.

Who was she kidding?

She had never really believed the colored stones she'd unwittingly smuggled out of Saigon were an ordinary souvenir. She assumed they'd been Tam's and that she'd been trying to get them out of the country, a nice nest egg with which to start her new life. Maybe Tam had been killed because of them; maybe not. Whatever the case, Tam was dead and her daughter was living a quiet life with Jared in San Francisco, and Rebecca had gotten used to pretending the stones didn't exist. It was easier that way: She didn't have to risk disturbing Jared and Mai's life with unpleasant questions, nor they hers.

But how had Tam gotten hold of these things?

Fourteen years ago Rebecca had been a scholarship student who didn't know a thing about gems. But she'd made some money since then, and she'd been around—she'd even bought a few gems of her own.

Tam's red velvet bag wasn't filled with just pretty colored stones. Rebecca suspected they were corundum: nine sapphires and one ruby.

She also suspected they were valuable.

She sighed and brushed her fingertips across their sparkling surfaces. So cool, so beautiful. Not worth dying or killing over, in her opinion.

Sliding them back into their bag, Rebecca got on the phone to Sofi. "Don't you have a friend of a friend or something who's a gemologist?"

"David Rubin."

"I need to talk to him," Rebecca said. "Your place in an hour?"

"Want me to bring the moon while I'm at it?"

"No. If I'm right, we won't need it."

Jean-Paul arrived on Mt. Vernon Street less than an hour after he'd left Rebecca Blackburn. He wished he was a better planner, but, as always, he'd acted on instinct and impulse— on feeling rather than cold analysis. He had seen *The Score* and gone to San Francisco, and then to Boston. First to Rebecca, for no other reason than to see her. Then here, to the Winston house on Beacon Hill—because he had to.

"It's like a mausoleum," Annette had told him many years ago. "I hate it. My husband does, too. He'd move in a minute."

"Then why don't you?"

She'd laughed. "Because I'm a Winston. If I'd had a brother, he'd be stuck with the place. I loathe primogeniture, but in this case it'd be a blessing."

It was, of course, a magnificent house, not a mausoleum or anything Annette Winston Reed had ever remotely considered giving up. Jean-Paul went through the unlocked carriageway gate to the back as Annette had instructed him. He had called her office at Winston & Reed and had spoken to her secretary, who'd told him her boss wasn't in the office today. Jean-Paul had urged her to get hold of Annette at once and left the number of his pay phone.

Annette had called him back right away. The only hint of the mind-numbing shock he'd just given her was a slight hoarseness in her voice.

So she actually thought I was dead.

The thought amused him.

She'd understood they would have to meet in person—

if only to convince herself the call wasn't a nightmare. Reluctantly, but ever the stiff-upper-lip Bostonian, she gave him directions to her house.

Jean-Paul entered the beautiful house in the back, then moved silently through the antiseptic kitchen and down a short hall, where dozens of expensively framed photographs hung on the wall. The people in them were all the same—smiling, rich, perfect. The men were without scars and the women without fear, and Jean-Paul had to make his arms go rigid to keep from knocking the photographs off the wall. The pain was there, the anger, the burning hate. Nearly four years in the *Légion étrangère* and five years at the mercy of the Vietcong and North Vietnamese in a prisoner-of-war camp had taught him how to control his emotions, but he could feel them exploding to the surface.

Time had resolved nothing.

He called up a self-discipline he'd forgotten he had and pulled his gaze from the private gallery, proceeding down the hall to Annette's study.

She was seated in a bone-colored leather chair at the antique French table she used as a desk. Sun streamed in through the tall windows that looked out on the elegant urban garden, making the rich woman's room seem far from the crush and dirtiness of the city.

For a moment Annette seemed unchanged, and Jean-Paul could almost hear her weeping for him as she had thirty years ago, begging him to love her. She was rich, American, older, married. She had fallen for him like a rock in a deep, still pool, drowning in her obsession. Stupidly—so stupidly—he had believed she loved him. Too late he'd learned Annette Winston Reed only loved herself.

Behind her stood a motionless, silent Vietnamese whom Jean-Paul recognized as Nguyen Kim. Kim was just over five feet tall, sleek, wiry and very tough. In Vietnam, Jean-Paul had known him as a consummate survivor. He'd been trained by the American Special Forces, and no doubt Annette showed him off as a former South Vietnamese army officer she'd generously given a job as her bodyguard. But Kim ingratiated himself with anyone who could help him—and was perfectly willing to kill anyone who wouldn't. Probably, Jean-Paul thought, Annette knew that.

He had considered she might have a gun or a bodyguard, but had risked that she wouldn't shoot him, if only not to have to explain the bloodstains on her floor.

"Well, Jean-Paul." She sat up very straight, her tone more regal than it had ever been thirty years ago on the Riviera. She had only been a rich woman then; now she was powerful, as well. "I'm beginning to think you're invincible."

He'd had the same thought about her. "I want the Jupiter Stones."

"Fine." She swept to her feet and came around to the front of the table, sitting on its edge. Her navy suit was conservatively cut and expensive, and her hair no longer fell out of its pins and made her look more innocent than she was. "Get them. The Jupiter Stones have nothing to do with me."

"You're a liar, Annette."

She laughed. "Oh, I used to love to hear you say my name. To think, I used to lie awake nights wondering if you were thinking about me. My, my, I've never been so absorbed with any man the way I was with you. But I've changed in the past thirty years. So, yes, Jean-Paul, all right—I'm a liar. But not this time."

"You'll do anything to get your way." Jean-Paul walked to the edge of the Persian carpet but stopped there, as if treading on it would suck him back into her world, back under her spell. "You only care about yourself—your own pleasure and excitement. You were that way even in bed. I should have guessed long ago what you would do to me."

"And now you hate me." She looked at him coldly, her eyes as mesmerizingly blue as he remembered, but now distant and unsympathetic. "That's your problem, Jean-Paul. I can't help you."

Looking around the study, he took in all the indications of her extraordinary wealth and thought of his own squalid room in Honolulu. Was she any happier? Any better a person?

"Do you have one of your guns handy? Or will you just wave your fingers and leave your dirty work to your body-guard?"

He thought he saw her shiver at his reminder of just how much he knew about her—how much he'd suffered at her hands—but she recovered. "I see no reason we can't resolve this problem in a civilized manner. Jean-Paul, I haven't seen the Jupiter Stones in thirty years, and that's the truth."

"So you say."

"Don't believe me, then. It's your choice."

Jean-Paul stepped onto the thick carpet, his footfall making no sound, and his gaze riveted on the powerful woman seated before him. He asked mildly, "You love your son, don't you? As much, of course, as a woman like you can love anyone."

She bristled. "Who are you to talk to me about love? Get out of my house."

Jean-Paul ignored her. "And your company," he went on. "Winston & Reed is your triumph. It would never have amounted to anything if your husband had lived. How fortunate he died, hmm? You're the Winston. You were always the one with the money and intelligence, but you insisted on being the perfect Boston woman and wife—until Benjamin's death freed you. A widow can get away with so much more, can't she? Yes. Look at Annette Reed, bravely carrying on alone."

"Get out, Jean-Paul." Her voice was low and deadly, but the Vietnamese guard remained impassive, not moving until she specifically instructed him to.

Jean-Paul persevered. "You always loved to take risks. It used to be you could satisfy your zest for risk by going to bed with the kind of man I once was." He made himself smile and move toward her, until he was so close he could have taken her into his arms. Better a viper, he thought. But he lowered his voice and exaggerated his French accent, "Aah, *ma belle,* you were a passionate woman. Have you put all that passion into your company?"

She pushed him away. "Go to hell."

Jean-Paul laughed. "We'll go together, *ma belle.*" Then he moved in close again, daring her to touch him; he saw her wince at the foulness of his breath and the ugliness of his scars. "I can destroy your son, and I can destroy your company. Quentin and Winston & Reed. Imagine them gone. What would you have left?"

For a moment she was expressionless, saying nothing. But Jean-Paul could see beneath the composed facade, could sense how angry she was—and frightened. *Could he do it? Would he?* Annette might like risks, but she wanted them to be on her own terms. She hated losing control. With Jean-Paul, she had lost control thirty years ago and had tried to drive him out of her life for good.

"Don't threaten me," she said, but her voice cracked. She licked her lips. Without lipstick, they seemed pale and thin. Still, she had never been vain about her appearance. "No one will believe anything you say about Quentin or about me. I'll have you locked up for the raving lunatic you are."

Unaffected by her outburst, Jean-Paul walked to the table and fingered a chunk of rose quartz Annette used as a paperweight. "Mai Sloan's a pretty child, isn't she?" he commented, without looking at her.

"I wouldn't know. I've never seen her, Jean-Paul. She's just fourteen—"

Annette broke off, and Jean-Paul could tell she was getting nervous. The more uneasy she became, the more relaxed he felt. She was a formidable opponent, and to get what he wanted, he had to keep her off balance. Or she would win. *Again.*

He looked at her. "Get me the Jupiter Stones."

"Jean-Paul," she said in a whisper, "let the past be."

"I can't," he replied and left her standing amidst her expensive antiques, her bodyguard's eyes following him as he disappeared.

Not until she heard the back door shut and his footfall on the cobblestone carriageway outside the open window behind her did Annette move. Then, clutching her chest as her heart throbbed painfully, she flung herself into the hall, running to the front parlor, tripping and stumbling along the way, her vision blurred by tears.

She got to the window in time to see him go through the wrought-iron gate onto the brick sidewalk.

Jean-Paul Gerard.

He wasn't even the ghost of the robust, cocky young race-car driver he'd been thirty years ago. His horrible face would give her worse nightmares than she already had about him, night after night. He seemed so shrunken and pitiful and old. Yet he was younger than she was. His yellowed, skeletal smile had stirred up her fears of dying, and she'd have given him the Jupiter Stones, just to be rid of him.

If she'd had them.

She watched him limp down the shaded brick sidewalk of Mt. Vernon toward Charles Street until he was out of sight. "Damn you to hell, Jean-Paul," she said, turning back to her silent, empty house, "why aren't you dead?"

Eleven

~~~~~~~~◈◈◈~~~~~~~~

Although Sofi Mencini's apartment in a renovated stone building on the waterfront was decorated in warm pastels and simple lines, it was as spectacular as any in Boston. Various furnishings were handcrafted, one-of-a-kind, custom-made, not because Sofi sought to be different or special, but because she knew exactly what she wanted. The effect, especially combined with the stunning harbor views, was both welcoming and awe-inspiring. A visitor knew at once that this was a successful woman with power, compassion, intelligence and humor. Rebecca wouldn't have wanted to get rich with anyone else.

"I had to cancel a meeting," Sofi said when she greeted her ex-roommate at the door. "Dare I ask what this is all about?"

"Not if you're smart."

Sofi digested that remark and could tell at once Rebecca wasn't kidding. "David's in the kitchen."

David Rubin was a curly-haired redhead in his midforties. He loved to flirt with Sofi—and, thirty seconds after meeting her, with Rebecca—but he was totally committed to his wife and their five children. Together they ran a jewelry store at Copley Place. They'd sold Sofi and her fiancé, Hank—a game-creator, ace puzzle-builder and as one-of-a-kind as everything else in her life—their wedding rings. A rumpled, cheerful man, David always seemed to have baby spit-up on his tie or the odd piece of Lego in his pockets. When it came to gems, however, he was very serious and very, very careful.

He examined Rebecca's stones for more than an hour.

Sofi and Rebecca drank iced herbal tea on Sofi's balcony while they waited. David had tried to get them to go back to the store, where he had all his equipment and reference materials, but Rebecca refused. She felt uneasy enough as it was showing the stones to him and Sofi, possibly jeopardizing their safety. Accepting defeat, David did make several cryptic calls to his wife to verify information.

"I'm not going to ask questions you're not going to answer," Sofi said.

"Good."

Rebecca sipped her tea, feeling Sofi's penetrating executive's glare. Not much over five feet, Sofi had transcended the stereotype of small women as vulnerable and weak-willed with her strength of character and high expectations of herself and those around her. Reliable, creative and direct, she thrived on the challenges of corporate life, and was good at what she did.

On the other hand, Rebecca thrived on change and taking risks with her money and her talent. She regularly drove her financial advisors in New York crazy. One had told her he'd be happy if she'd just make up her mind whether she was going to live like a rich person—she did occasionally—or a "Cinderella who can't decide if she'd rather have a coach or a pumpkin to ride around in." She had totally frustrated him by laughing. Later she'd discovered she'd been driving them all crazy and they'd decided to draw straws for who got to vent his spleen to her. He'd been the lucky winner. It wasn't business at all, he'd explained: Rebecca was on top of every penny she had and every penny she'd ever spent. It was, he admitted, just personal. Did he want out? Oh, no, working for her gave him great material for breaking the ice at parties.

"You get a copy of *The Score?*" Sofi asked.

"Uh-huh."

"Jared's still good-looking, isn't he?"

Rebecca sipped her tea. Despite Jared's failings, Sofi had always chastised Rebecca for letting Jared Sloan go. "You have unrealistic standards, R.J.," she was fond of saying.

"I think you should call him," Sofi suggested bluntly. "Sharing the front page of a supermarket tabloid gives you a good excuse."

"I don't need an excuse."

"Then how come you've waited fourteen years?"

"Sofi."

She waved her tea glass. "Yeah, yeah, I know, but I've gotten used to telling people what I think."

Mercifully, David emerged from the kitchen managing to look both excited and grim. "Where did you get these stones?" he asked.

Rebecca shook her head. "Can't say."

"Are they one of your peculiar investments?"

Leaving the question unanswered, Rebecca gave Sofi a look. She'd just met David, which meant Sofi must have told the jeweler something about her. Of course, David could have read about her in any number of gossip rags over the years, including *The Score*.

David cleared his throat and became businesslike. "You'll need more corroboration than just my say-so, but there's no question in my mind that what I've examined are the famed Jupiter Stones."

Rebecca suddenly felt light-headed. "Which are?"

"Ten corundum gems—nine sapphires and a ruby—commissioned by Emperor Franz Josef of Austria-Hungary for his wife, the Empress Elisabeth. She was unstable and quite an eccentric, and apparently she gave the stones away or lost them, probably in the mid-1890s. There's extensive documentation of each stone, so there should be no trouble verifying if these are the ones. But I should warn you that no one'll be satisfied without some explanation of how you came by them. They haven't been seen since Empress Elisabeth's day. The last time anyone even heard a rumor about them was in the late fifties when a Hungarian baroness claimed they'd been stolen from her by a jewel thief prowling the Riviera at the time. He was never apprehended—supposedly he was a French race-car driver who disappeared before the police could arrest him. The baroness committed suicide, and no one seriously believed she ever had the real Jupiter Stones."

Sofi was impressed. "How do you know all this stuff?"

David shrugged off the compliment. "Any gemologist worth his salt knows about the Jupiter Stones. The Red Moon of Mars and the Star of Jupiter—the ruby and the Kashmir sapphire—alone are famous stones, but the entire collection… Well, now I can verify that it's fantastic."

"You don't think you've made a mistake?" Rebecca asked.

"It's possible, but no, I don't think so. In addition to the stones matching the descriptions of the Jupiter Stones, the velvet bag they're in is embossed with the Hapsburg imperial seal."

"Are they valuable?"

David, ever the jeweler, smiled. "Name your price."

Twelve

His plane's descent took Jared directly over Boston proper, glittering in the clear evening air. The city of his childhood had changed. In the new skyline, he spotted the distinctive outline of the Wesley Sloan–designed Winston & Reed Building on the waterfront. He wondered if Quentin was working late, and if his aunt was there, pretending she didn't run the place when everyone knew she did.

The landing was smooth, but the inactivity of the long cross-country flight had gotten to Jared, and he couldn't wait to be out in the city and moving. All he'd done for the past seven hours was think about Mai, about Saigon and the man from Saigon and the Winstons—and about the Blackburns. Why did Rebecca have to be in Boston? He'd considered staying away because of her. But he couldn't. He had to see Thomas Blackburn; he had to get answers to the questions he'd left hanging for fourteen years.

He couldn't take any chances. The white-haired man had come to San Francisco. Obviously he had seen Mai's picture in *The Score*. Now he had seen her.

Jared took a cab to the Massachusetts State House and

walked the rest of the way to West Cedar Street. Whatever else might have changed in Boston in the past fourteen years, he supposed Beacon Hill would be pretty much the same.

And he knew Thomas Blackburn would be.

After the long flight, the exercise and the cool night air felt good. Jared took the familiar shortcuts to West Cedar Street, not even tempted to go by the house on Chestnut where he had lived with his mother after her brief marriage to his father. The place belonged to someone else and had for a long time.

The Eliza Blackburn house was in hellish shape. Jared discovered the doorbell didn't work and tried the brass knocker, in need of polishing.

Thomas Blackburn opened the door, the strong smell of curry emanating from inside the house. He squinted at Jared, then nodded with satisfaction, as if he'd been expecting him.

"Jared," he said.

"Hello, Thomas." Jared put out his hand, but that wasn't enough and they embraced briefly. Standing back, Jared added, "You haven't changed."

Thomas gave him a small laugh, shaking his head because, of course, he had changed. He was almost eighty now. He didn't stand so tall and straight, and there were more lines in his face, more weariness. Yet his eyes were still that intense blue, his gaze incisive and uncompromising as he studied Jared for a moment.

"It's good to see you, Jared."

"And you." Jared choked back his emotion. "It's been a long time, Thomas. Too long—but you don't seem surprised I'm here."

Thomas shrugged, but his expression was serious. "I suppose not. Come inside."

They went into the faded elegance of the front parlor. Neither man sat down. Jared was restless, anxious to move after his long, frustrating day. The odor of curry was even stronger inside, and he recalled that Thomas had always liked spicy food.

"You saw *The Score?*" he asked.

Thomas nodded. "Rebecca showed me."

R.J. Jared had devoured every word on her in the short tabloid article, but there'd been no mention of where she was living. One of Boston's pricey new condominiums? She was the first Blackburn in two hundred years to have money to blow, and he hoped she was enjoying every minute of it. But he couldn't think about her now.

"Jared—" Thomas broke off, sighing. "Jared, what's happened? The pictures have stirred up trouble, I assume."

"Yeah. One of the assassins from Saigon—the one who shot me—saw them and must have realized Mai made it out alive."

Leaving out nothing, Jared told Thomas about the scar-faced man from Saigon and his visit to Russian Hill, and even after fourteen years, it seemed right to unburden his soul to this aged, experienced, tortured man. The friendship they'd forged when Jared was in college and Rebecca still a kid in Florida remained intact, although in 1975, when Jared had come to Thomas shattered after his own experience in Indochina, still suffering the effects of two bullets in his shoulder, they had realized the decisions they'd arrived at that night might mean they'd never see each other again. Jared had already acknowledged, if not accepted, that he and R.J. were finished. But he'd understood then—as he did now—that whoever had shot him in Saigon had also meant to kill Mai, and could try again.

As he had fourteen years ago, Thomas listened without

interruption or any apparent reaction. Finally, when Jared had finished, he asked, "Where is Mai now?"

"My father's place, outside San Francisco."

"Good." Thomas clamped one hand on Jared's upper arm, his eyes glittering even in the dim light of the parlor. "Go back to her. Stay with her. Let me find out what I can about this man and deal with him. My guess is he's not after Mai directly."

Jared stiffened with disappointment and increasing frustration. "I'd hoped you'd talk to me, Thomas. I need advice—answers. Look, after Saigon I was so crazed and in such a state of shock, I'd have gone to Peru and opened a butcher shop if you'd told me it was the smartest thing to do. I trusted you then, and I trust you now. But Thomas... You haven't been straight with me. I can't let it lie anymore, not with this bastard showing up on my doorstep. Talk to me." Stemming his anger, Jared softened his voice and asked, "You know this guy, don't you?"

"From a long, long time ago." The old man's voice was distant, sadder than Jared would have ever thought possible. He had always seemed so impervious to anguish, but perhaps he was merely clever at hiding it from those who would take pleasure in his pain. Staring at the marble mantel where photographs of his lost wife and son were on display, he went on, "I'd assumed he never made it out of Saigon."

Jared resisted the urge to press and press hard for information. "Who is he?"

Thomas shook his head, as if cutting off his own rampant thoughts, not Jared. "You came here because you trust me, didn't you?"

Jared nodded.

Turning back to his young friend, Thomas clapped him

on the arm, his grip stronger than Jared would have expected from a man near eighty. "Then believe me," the older man said, "when I tell you the best thing you can do for yourself and for your daughter is to go home and let me see what I can root out on my own. You did what you had to do fourteen years ago. You knew then that you had to go on without answers—for Mai's sake. Well, nothing's changed."

"Mai's safe," Jared said stonily. "I'm going to find this guy. I want to know what he's up to. If it doesn't involve my daughter, then fine. If it does—"

"Jared, go home."

"I can't. I'm not running away this time."

"You didn't before," Thomas said with certainty. "You did what was right."

Jared started to argue, but stopped at the sound of footsteps in the hall.

"Grandfather, how the hell much curry did you put in that stuff? It's enough to kill a horse! My mouth's on fire and—" Rebecca went silent as she came into the parlor.

The sight of her took Jared's breath away. In her tangerine shirt and slim black skirt, she looked pulled together, gorgeous and very rich. She was older and even more beautiful, her eyes just as blue, her hair shorter, but still that unusual, very memorable shade of chestnut. And Jared realized, with a certainty that hurt, that although his life had gone on, he'd never really gotten over having loved and lost Rebecca Blackburn.

"Hello, R.J.," he managed to say.

"Jared."

Her voice was a whisper, and at that moment Jared knew that Thomas was right about one thing: nothing had changed.

Thirteen

꧁∽꧂

On a sweltering Labor Day weekend in 1973, Rebecca returned to Boston for the first time since moving off Beacon Hill ten years earlier. She came alone on an Amtrak train. Her mother didn't approve of her choice of Boston University. "Why Boston?" she'd demanded. "You've been accepted at Vanderbilt, Northwestern, Stanford. *Why* Boston University?"

Because it was in Boston, and Rebecca had dreamed about going back since she was eight. She'd restore the Blackburn name to its lofty pre–Thomas Blackburn position of respectability. And she'd do it in Boston.

But she didn't tell her mother that. She claimed she'd decided on B.U. because they had offered her the best financial aid package, which was true. Smart, fatherless and the eldest of six, Rebecca had had no trouble getting scholarships.

"You don't have to take me," she'd told her mother, and Jenny Blackburn made no pretense of her relief. She couldn't go back to Boston. And Rebecca wasn't going to make her feel she had to.

So, her stuffed duffel bag slung over one shoulder, Rebecca made her way from the train station to her dormitory, the only person on the subway not grumbling about the heat. She could have called her grandfather, she supposed, and prevailed upon him to meet her, but why bother? She hadn't heard from him since she and her mother and brothers had left Boston; he hadn't answered any of the flurry of letters she'd written to him in those first lonely months in Florida. The only reason she knew he was still alive was because her mother still got tense and nervous whenever his name was mentioned.

Her roommate was a tiny, cheerful eighteen-year-old from Westchester County named Sophia Loretta Mencini— Sofi. She owned twenty-eight belts and twelve pocketbooks. Rebecca, who had one of each, counted them. Sofi grimaced at Rebecca's meager wardrobe and the tattered, unabridged dictionary she had lugged all the way from Florida and promptly labeled her new roommate an egghead. They became instant friends.

"But why all the crayons?" Sofi asked.

"They're oil pastels. I hope to audit a few art courses, too." She'd had a flair for art since she could remember, but didn't consider it a practical choice for a career—or for erasing her grandfather's damage to the Blackburn name.

"*Major* egghead," Sofi said.

Rebecca laughed. "Just determined."

On a drizzly afternoon in October Thomas Blackburn gave up on the notion that Rebecca would come to him and instead went to her. He tracked her down at the B.U. library, roomy and nicely laid out, a better facility than he'd expected. He considered the large windows with tempting views of the Charles River an unnecessary distraction, however, and he loathed having to argue his way past the security desk. Did he look like someone who'd try to sneak books out tucked in his pants?

He found his granddaughter reshelving an enormous cart of books in the stacks and knew her at once, this little girl of his now grown-up. Thomas ached at the sight of her. At eighteen, she displayed the same unfortunate taste in fashion as her fellow students. She'd tied a red bandanna over her hair and knotted it at the nape of her neck; it was the sort of thing his wife used to wear when she cleaned the attic. Her jeans and bright gold sweater had so many holes they weren't worth mending. At least, mercifully, she was clean, the strands of hair flowing down her back from under the bandanna shining, that fetching chestnut that marked her as a Blackburn. Although she wore no cosmetics, her skin, even smudged with library dust, was radiant, and her eyes sparkled. There was an arrogant straightness to her nose—a Blackburn touch—and an altogether stubborn set to her jaw that was pure O'Keefe. Even dressed in rags, Rebecca, in her grandfather's opinion, would have looked regal, but he suspected telling her so would only have made her angry.

"A fine way to spend a Saturday afternoon," he muttered. "Does this job of yours leave enough time for you to study?"

She turned, and in the flash of her eyes, he could tell she'd recognized him immediately, but she quickly hid her surprise and, he thought, her pleasure at seeing him. "We all have twenty-four hours in a day."

"How true." Thomas lifted a discarded volume from her cart. Aristotle. He hadn't read the Greek philosophers in years. "I suppose this job of yours is a federally funded position for impoverished students?"

"Not necessarily impoverished. Work study helps students from middle-class families get by, as well. The less your family can afford, the larger your work-study grant."

"Are you at the maximum?"

She gave him a tight smile. "Not quite."

"Make work," he said.

"It feels like real work to me. I've been at it since noon. Of course, if I had a rich and generous grandfather paying my bills…"

He laughed, a faint feeling of pride rising up in him. She was a tough, outspoken young woman. If she were going to stay in Boston, she'd have to be. He found himself resisting the urge to hug her, asking instead, "When do you finish?"

"Another forty minutes."

"Good. I'll meet you downstairs at the front desk."

"For what?"

"We'll go to dinner." He winked at her, wishing it could be the same between them as it had before Stephen's death, when they'd done everything together during his home leaves and had understood each other so well. But those days were over. He'd ended them himself. "I'll take you to the Ritz."

Rebecca laughed, and Thomas had to look away so she wouldn't see his reaction. He could hear Emily in her laugh, could suddenly remember his wife as clearly as if he'd last seen her just that morning, instead of nearly forty years ago.

"You can't afford the Ritz," his granddaughter told him. "Even if you could, you wouldn't spend the money. Besides, I can't take the time to go into town."

"Marshaling your twenty-four hours?"

"You bet."

"Then we'll go to one of the disreputable student establishments on Commonwealth Avenue. You choose."

He walked off with the Aristotle tucked under one arm to read while waiting.

Rebecca chose the student union because she could use her dining card and they wouldn't have to go out in the rain. The rain wouldn't have bothered Thomas, but he understood about the meal card. His own dinner proved relatively inexpensive, and they found an unoccupied table in a corner. He was surprised by how comfortable he felt among the scores of young students and would have enjoyed striking up a dialogue at the crowded table behind them on the Vietnam conflict.

"How did you find out I was in Boston?" Rebecca asked.

"Your mother. Don't look so surprised. As much as she despises me, she believes it her duty to write me intensely formal letters once or twice a year with pictures of you all and one or two lines on your current activities."

"Do you ever write back?"

"It would only annoy her if I did."

Rebecca pulled in her lips, but he knew what she was thinking. He said, "I still have every letter you wrote to me. And I answered them all. I just never mailed them."

"Because of Mother?"

"Because of you. You were a child, Rebecca. You needed to make the adjustment to your new life, and I didn't believe you could do it with me indulging your homesickness for Boston. Then when you stopped writing, I felt I didn't want to intrude."

She gave him a long, clear-eyed look. "Sounds like a rationalization to me."

He shrugged. "Maybe it is. Tell me about school. How are your classes?"

She told him briefly, but he wasn't satisfied with superficial answers. He wanted to know if her professors were idiots, if her courses were rigorous enough, what texts were on her reading lists, whether she was required to write term papers and if there would be final exams. He had heard somewhere that young people were ignorant of geography and interrogated her on the whereabouts of Borneo, Calcutta, Rumania and Des Moines, Iowa.

"I hope," he said ominously, "that none of your professors has given you the choice between doing a paper or a collage."

Rebecca assured him none had. "You're just worried because I'm not at Harvard."

"Nonsense."

She didn't believe him. "Well, *I* think the quality of one's education depends to a great degree on the individual. A dope going to Harvard will still come out a dope."

Thomas sniffed. "That sounds like something someone who didn't go to Harvard would say."

"You're such a snob, Grandfather."

She tilted her paper cup of soda up to her mouth and got out the last of the ice, her eyes focusing on the man across from her. His tweed jacket was frayed and rumpled and his whitening hair needed a trim. Even if he'd had a million dollars in the bank, he'd probably have looked much the same. Thomas Blackburn had always hated to spend money. But there was something in his expression—just the hint of a shit-eating grin—that made her wonder if he wasn't pulling her leg just a bit and not quite the snob he was making himself out to be.

"Why did you come to see me?"

"You're my granddaughter," he said. "Just because we haven't seen or spoken to each other in ten years doesn't mean I haven't thought of you. I have, you know. Every day."

She choked up. "Grandfather..."

"Come to supper on Sunday at the house. We'll have sandwiches—bring your roommate if you wish. I'm correct in assuming you have no current gentleman friend of importance?"

Smiling through the tears in her eyes, she said, "You're correct."

"No room for romance in your twenty-four hours?"

"Not," she shot back, "if I intend to maintain my four-oh average."

By winter, Rebecca felt more comfortable in Boston and had gotten used to the idea that her grandfather had said all he was going to say on the subject of 1963—the deaths of Benjamin Reed, her father and Quang Tai, and his own retreat from public life. And what he'd said was nothing. She didn't blame him for the tragedy; she just wanted to hear his side of what had happened. What did he mean when he'd accepted full responsibility for the incident? Was there any truth to the rumors he had associated with the Vietcong? She'd started to ask him a hundred times, but stopped herself every time. He'd only call her impertinent or presumptuous for asking. He knew it was on her mind and would tell her if he wanted to.

Even after a decade, her mother's bitterness toward him was still palpable, and Rebecca wisely chose not to bring him up during her visit home during winter break. She didn't mention she'd invited him to join her in Florida.

"Stephen and Mark and Jacob don't remember you at all," she'd told him, "and Taylor and Nate just barely. They'd love to see you. And the warm air would do you good. We could all go to Disney World."

Thomas was adamant. "Your mother would slam the door in my face."

Likely enough, she would have. Or done worse. Jenny Blackburn was still holding out hope that her daughter would transfer to another school. If nothing else, she figured the cold weather would lure Rebecca back to the south. Papa O'Keefe, a plump, red-faced, incredibly hardworking man, wasn't so sanguine. "Not with that Yankee blood" was all he would say.

Winter didn't drive Rebecca south. Continuing to maintain her high average and work at the library, she used snowstorms and subfreezing temperatures as an excuse to indulge her passion for art. It wasn't painting and sculpture that seized her spirit, but graphic design. With design, she had a greater chance of having her work seen by and communicated to a large number of people. She found the process of design both challenging and enjoyable, as she took fine art's conceptual way of thinking and applied it in practical uses. The blending of artistic elements, technical expertise, inspiration and business demands appealed to her.

It was her interest in graphic design that took her to the waterfront on a brisk April afternoon. Or so she insisted. A new building was going up and one of the top design studios in the country had been commissioned to do its graphic identity—enough reason for Rebecca to justify showing up at the press conference on site.

But the architect was Wesley Sloan and the builder was Winston & Reed, and when she cut her microeconomics class and headed out to the waterfront, Rebecca had a feeling she was walking into trouble.

She just didn't know how much.

Fourteen

❧⟡❧

Jared Sloan was twenty-four that spring as he hunched his shoulders against the stiff wind gusting off Boston Harbor. He'd forgotten how cold Boston could be, even in April. Just a year in San Francisco had eliminated his tolerance for extremes in temperature. His father, however, seemed oblivious to the biting wind. Jared joined him over at the Bobcats waiting to demolish the condemned building occupying the site of Wesley Sloan and Annette Winston Reed's latest project.

"Lovely place to hold a press conference," Jared said.

Wesley, a solid man of fifty and utterly consumed by his work, laughed as his iron-gray hair stood straight up in the churning wind. "Your Aunt Annette does have a flair for the dramatic, but this one could backfire on her if a reporter gets blown into the harbor and has to have his stomach pumped. She insists the wind'll die down by three o'clock."

"Or pay the price of her wrath?"

"I wouldn't be surprised. It's good of you to come, you know."

As if he'd had a choice. Jared was an apprentice architect with his father's San Francisco firm and had contributed to the design of Winston & Reed's new headquarters in only the most minor of ways. Wesley Sloan wasn't a man who easily delegated authority, even to his son. But Jared had no illusions about why he was in Boston: his Aunt Annette was portraying her new project as a family affair, and he was family. She'd gone so far as to summon Quentin from Saigon, where he'd gone in October to work with the branch that had launched Winston & Reed at the beginning of American military involvement in Vietnam more than a decade ago. Naturally Quentin had come. He wasn't one to defy his mother's wishes and going to Saigon in the first place had about exhausted his courage. With the Paris Peace Accords, Winston & Reed was scaling back its Southeast Asian operation, and Annette had only just barely tolerated having her twenty-two-year-old son volunteer to help. Jared thought he understood. She'd lost her husband in Vietnam; she didn't intend to lose her only child.

Jared wouldn't have thought twice about defying his aunt, but he had his own reasons for wanting to accompany his father to Boston. His parents were seldom in the same city—his mother still lived on Beacon Hill—and he planned to take advantage. They'd agreed to have dinner with him while they were all in town. And then he'd hit them with his own plans to head off to the Far East. Starting June first, he would spend a year working as an architect in Saigon, under a foundation grant. He wasn't ready to be tied down to a firm, nor did he consider his architectural education complete. Southeast Asia would provide him opportunities for learning that he couldn't get in San Francisco or Boston. Wesley Sloan would see his only son's departure from his firm as a betrayal. Maybe in a way it was. But it was something Jared had to do. His student deferments had kept him out of the war, and now he felt he needed to see the country where the lives of so many of his friends had been changed—and lost. Whenever he thought of the young men his own age, of his sensitive Uncle Benjamin, who always seemed to be in the wrong place at the wrong time, and of Stephen Blackburn, good-humored and keenly intelligent, Jared knew he had to go.

"What the devil's going on over there?" Wesley Sloan grumbled. "Who's that lunatic?"

Jared followed his father's gaze down the chain-link fence securing the demolition area, where the wind had kicked up dust and debris. A woman in a bright red sweatshirt and Red Sox cap on backward was perched rooster-like atop a fence post. She had a camera strapped around her neck and was snapping pictures.

"I'll go see," Jared volunteered.

Coming closer, he saw the messy chestnut braid trailing halfway down her back and her holey jeans and sneakers. Had to be one of Boston's countless students. The woman jumped down from the fence post, landing lightly just inside the demolition area. She had a nice shape under her ratty clothes.

"I wouldn't stand in there without a hard hat on if I were you," he said.

She looked around at him, her eyes a lively shade of blue, her face angular and attractive and oddly familiar. "Of all people," she said under her breath, then climbed as fast as a monkey back up the fence, paused on the post and hopped down beside him. Her Red Sox cap came off, and loose hairs blew in her face. "What're you doing here?"

"I'm with the press conference," he said formally, bothered by her face. *Did* he recognize her? "My name's Jared Sloan. Look, this area's posted and—"

"I know who you are."

"Your face is familiar—"

She swept her cap up off the ground and grinned at him. "I would hope so."

And suddenly Jared recognized her. He'd probably known, on a gut level, when he'd first spotted her. The face, the eyes, the brazenness—he had never forgotten them. But if there was anyone he didn't expect to find in Boston, it was Rebecca Blackburn.

"R.J.," he said.

She was already heading back out across Atlantic Avenue and failed to hear him.

The Winstons had arrived, and the press conference was about to begin. Jared was supposed to line up for the obligatory family photo; he could see his father looking around for him. Quentin, suntanned and wearing a conservative suit that made him look forty, caught his cousin's eye and waved. Jared pretended not to see him. His Aunt Annette glanced at her watch. She was forty-five and, Jared suspected, relished being chairman of a thriving corporation, but she'd be the last to say so. Jared remembered her as more of a free spirit, not the unapproachable, gray-suited *grande dame* she was playing these days. He wondered if power did that to people. Or just widowhood and its responsibilities. For certain, she wouldn't appreciate his cutting out on her.

He didn't care. They could go on without him.

He ran after Rebecca.

She'd cut down a side street and was at a corner when he caught up with her, impatiently waiting to cross a narrow street clogged with traffic. "I remember," Jared said, sidling up next to her, "when you couldn't wait to be old enough to cross a street by yourself."

She fastened her bright eyes on him. "Hello, Jared."

He grinned. "Hello, R.J."

"What jogged your memory?" she asked. "You haven't seen me since I was eight."

She was all of nineteen now. "You haven't changed. Can I buy you a cup of coffee?"

She didn't even hesitate. "Sure. And I'll buy an order of French fries. We'll share."

They found a Brigham's and sat opposite each other in a booth with their coffee and fries, and the decade since Jared had held back his tears and watched the Blackburn moving truck trundle down West Cedar Street melted away. They talked about San Francisco and Florida and her five brothers and his two half-sisters. Jared said something that amused Rebecca, and in her laugh he heard the echo of the little kid he'd played with, bugged, tolerated and rescued so long ago, not in terms of years, but in how much their lives had changed since. Especially hers.

"How's your Blackburn grandfather these days?" he asked.

She didn't avert her eyes, but he could see she was tempted. "Fine."

"It took courage for him to stay on Beacon Hill. What your mother did took a different kind of courage. Everyone thought Thomas would sell the house and retire to Maine or someplace. It can't have been easy for him living around the corner from my aunt."

Rebecca was squinting her so-blue eyes at him. "Thomas?"

Jared grinned. "He insisted on my calling him by his first name."

"When?"

"A few years ago. I went to college here, and he had me

over every now and then for dinner with him and his boarders. Usually served some dish of the flaming-esophagus variety."

"Sunday nights?"

"Generally, yeah. R.J., what's wrong?"

She shrugged. "I guess I'm just jealous. I missed so many years with him—by his choice and my mother's, maybe even a little of mine. You had him when I didn't."

"He's only in his midsixties. He'll probably outlive us all." Jared winced at his insensitivity, considering her father's untimely death. "I'm sorry…."

"No, don't be. Wounds heal, Jared. I'm not angry with my grandfather for what happened to my father and your uncle. I wish I understood more about it, but—"

"But Thomas won't tell you."

"That's right. And I can't force him. It must be horrible, having to live with that guilt. No matter what happened, I don't think Dad would've wanted that. Look, you're missing your press conference."

"No problem," Jared said quickly, not wanting to leave. "By the way, what were you doing there? I won't flatter myself you came because you knew I'd be around."

She laughed. "No, I was taking pictures for a noncredit photography class I'm taking, but I really came because of the design studio your father hired. I was hoping to scarf up a press kit."

"That can be arranged. You're an art major?"

"Political science and history."

"A true Blackburn."

She shook her head. "I'm on the 'wrong' side of the Charles River."

"I just thought of something," he said suddenly, half-lying. In truth, he'd been toying with this idea since he'd realized R.J. wasn't going to tell him to go to hell and be

done with him. "There's a party of sorts tonight to cele-
brate today's groundbreaking on the new building. I didn't
think to invite anyone. Would you care to go?"

Sitting back, Rebecca eyed him with that vaunted
Blackburn incisiveness. "As your date, you mean?"

Jared coughed. "Well, yes."

"If you'd told me you'd be asking me on a date when I
was eight years old, I'd have…I don't know, kicked you in
the shins or something." She peeled a snarled rubber band
off the end of her braid and shook loose her hair, and Jared
shifted on his bench, properly dazzled. She added, "I'd love
to go. Is this thing a hotsy-totsy party?"

He laughed. "As hotsy-totsy as they come."

"Then I'd better start tracking down a dress."

She started out of the booth, but Jared put a hand on her
wrist. "R.J.—I'm glad you don't hate me."

The smile she gave him was surprisingly gentle and
filled with memories. "How could I?"

Rebecca didn't own a party dress. A short denim skirt,
yes. Jeans, sweatshirts, turtlenecks, sneakers and knee
socks, yes. But no party dress. Sofi, however, had a
solution, and it arrived an hour before Jared was to pick
her up in the form of Alex, a theater arts major who, Sofi
announced, would dress her. Before Rebecca could make
a decent protest, Alex was at her closet.

He didn't stay there long. "Your farm-girl look's a no-
go. It's a wonder there's not a pitchfork in there."

"You didn't dig back far enough," Rebecca told him.

"Funny, funny."

He tried Sofi's closet. Rebecca warned him that nothing
would fit her wildly different frame, but Alex was unde-

terred. He hauled out hangers dripping with skirts, blouses and dresses—and rejected everything.

Sofi was insulted. "What's wrong with my clothes? I bought half that stuff at Bloomingdale's!"

"Too New York. We want Boston. Something elegant and understated. Something that says old money."

Rebecca laughed. If it was one thing Blackburn money was, it was old. It was also scarce. She said, "Then all I need to do is head up to Beacon Hill and borrow some dumpy old dress stuffed up in my grandfather's attic—"

Alex suddenly clapped his hands together. "Of course!"

"I will *not*—I was only kidding. Look, thanks, but I'll figure something out."

"Rebecca, hush, will you please? I don't care about the frumpy clothes in your grandfather's attic. I have our answer."

Rebecca was dubious. "What?"

"Not what—who. Lenny."

"Lenny?"

Alex would say no more. He grabbed Sofi and disappeared. When they weren't back in twenty minutes, Rebecca was contemplating her denim skirt and her roommate's silver sequined top, but then they burst in, with Lenny, a senior theater major. Lenny wasn't short for Eleanor or Leonora, as Rebecca had anticipated, but for Leonard. He was five-ten, had a wiry runner's body and wore a short ponytail. He, Sofi and Alex all carried an assortment of evening clothes.

"Lenny finds playing women's roles both fun and instructive," Sofi said, obviously quoting him. "He thinks his openness toward new experiences ultimately will help him become a better actor and director."

Lenny made a clinical examination of Rebecca, in her ratty chenille robe and bare feet, and immediately dismissed three of the dresses he'd brought along. Rebecca made a none-too-subtle remark about the time. Sighing, Lenny posted Alex outside the door. When Jared arrived, Alex would knock three times.

Finally, Lenny said, "The white."

He withdrew his choice from the masses of dry cleaner bags, unwrapped it and held a white linen dress up to Rebecca. It had tiny white lace edging and a high collar. He said, "Perfect."

"I'll look like a virgin!"

"Of course you will."

"But…"

"You *are* a virgin," Sofi pointed out, quite unnecessarily, in Rebecca's opinion.

Lenny was all business. "You don't have shoes, I suppose?"

"Sneakers and L.L. Bean boots."

"My God. Sofi?"

"I wear a size six. Rebecca wouldn't fit in my shoes."

"I'm a size ten," Lenny said.

Rebecca couldn't believe they were having this discussion, but surrendered. "Size eight."

"Must be somebody around here who wears an eight," Sofi said. "I think Edie might."

"They must be white," Lenny instructed, "and as delicate as possible."

"Virginal," Sofi added, with a wicked grin at her roommate, and shot out the door.

The decision made, Lenny called Alex in, and together they played valet for Rebecca as though she were the star in one of their student theater productions. By now she was getting too big a kick out of the whole thing to protest. They helped her off with her bathrobe, assuring her their interest in her slip-clad body was purely professional, although Alex did make a point of telling her that Lenny might be gay, but he wasn't.

"Don't worry," Lenny reassured her, amused, "if the cretin tries anything, I'll punch him out."

"I have five brothers. If he tries anything, *I'll* punch him out."

They had her raise her arms and slipped the dress on. Lenny was bigger in the bust when he played a woman than Rebecca was, but otherwise the dress was a remarkably good fit. The lace hem came to midcalf. Ignoring Lenny's pained expression, Rebecca added her only pair of pantyhose.

"You don't have makeup, I presume?" he asked.

"I use a little Vaseline on my lips…"

"Horrors. Luckily I brought along my own palette. Sit."

She sat. He draped a towel over her shoulders and, with Alex assisting, began on her face, explaining he used only natural cosmetics and would go for a light, unpainted look. He remarked on her creamy skin, but suggested genetics and youth were responsible since he assumed she didn't bother with a proper skin-care regime.

"You know," Rebecca said, "I don't care about makeup. My ride will be here any minute—"

"We're practically home free now. And your ride will be delighted to wait. I'm assuming it's a man? Another woman might not let you out the door."

Rebecca suddenly felt self-conscious. "I could just forget all this and go in my denim skirt."

Lenny shook his head. "Relax, sweetheart. Although a little nervousness adds color to your cheeks and spark to your eyes. What do you think, Alex?"

"I think I'm going to toss her date down the elevator

shaft and take her to dinner myself." He grinned. "You like dorm food, Rebecca?"

She couldn't stop herself from laughing. "You guys are impossible, but thanks. I look okay?"

"You look smashing," Lenny said. "*Where* are your shoes?" He whisked off the towel and took Rebecca by the hand, guiding her to the mirror. "Your hair's still a near-disaster, but rather innocent-looking—and the color's magnificent."

She had to admit that in a few quick minutes, Lenny had transformed her from looking like an impoverished student to a woman who could hold her own at any party the Sloans and Winstons decided to throw. On her own, though, she still wouldn't have picked white lace.

Sofi slipped into the room, breathless, and handed Rebecca a pair of low white sandals with very skinny straps. "This was the best I could do. It's reasonably warm tonight—"

Lenny grabbed them. "But these are *perfection!*"

He insisted on slipping them onto Rebecca's feet himself. Sofi was highly entertained. "My, my, Cinderella in the flesh."

"Sofi…"

"Hey, just kidding. You look great. I mean it. If this were an Aztec party you were going to, they'd sacrifice you on the altar."

"You're a big help."

There was a knock at the door. Lenny picked up Rebecca's hand and gave it a gentle squeeze. "Have a wonderful time."

"Thanks." Rebecca gave him a hug. "I'm not used to fussing over my appearance. I appreciate what you've done, and I'll try not to ruin the dress."

"I hope your man tears it off you."

"Lenny," Alex said, "you're making her blush."

"Of course I am. I want her to have fresh color in her cheeks when she walks out the door."

Thanking them again, Rebecca shot out into the hall before one or another of the three could make one last remark. She quickly shut her door behind her so Jared wouldn't see her entourage and room filled with cast-off clothes and think she'd put any effort into the evening.

He was breathtaking in a black evening suit. "Sorry I'm late. I forgot your room number."

"You've been here awhile?"

"A few minutes." He tried to hold back a smile, but failed.

"Um… You met my roommate Sofi?"

"Was she the one running up and down the hall looking for virgin shoes in size eight?"

So much, Rebecca thought, for illusions of sophistication, but by the time she and Jared reached the elevator they were both laughing.

"I won't have her here."

Jared stiffened in anger at his aunt's words and looked to Quentin for support, but his cousin remained silent. Annette seemed hardly aware of her son's presence in the small sitting room off the elegant drawing room where dozens of guests had gathered. Jared could see Rebecca smiling as she took a glass of champagne. She was so damned beautiful. His aunt, elegant in diamonds and black silk, had pulled him aside moments after they'd arrived at her Mt. Vernon Street house.

It was her party, she was his aunt, and Jared, despite his irritation, tried to be patient. "Aunt Annette, I don't see why you're carrying a grudge against her."

"I'm not. She's a Blackburn, Jared, and while that may

be no fault of hers, it's certainly none of mine." Annette sighed, her expression softening as she touched her nephew's hand. "I know this must be frustrating and embarrassing for you, but please try and understand. There are reporters here tonight. If they find out that's Rebecca Blackburn over there, they'll be all over me—*and* her. And I'd rather not have the past dredged up right now. I'm sure she wouldn't, either. If not for my sake, then for hers, take her home."

"Mother's right," Quentin, who'd been standing mutely beside her, added.

Jared shot his cousin an annoyed look. "You don't believe that rationalization, do you? I doubt a single reporter here would care if Thomas Blackburn himself had come tonight. They just want free drinks and a chance to rub elbows with the Winstons and Sloans, although I don't think I'll really ever understand why."

With a pained look on his handsome face, Quentin started to backtrack, but Annette put up a hand and he broke off. Jared sighed, not surprised. In Quentin's place, he'd move as far from Boston as he could. Saigon was far, but Quentin was still working for his mother there—and he hadn't said a word about not coming home. Annette had given him a year, and Jared was sure that'd be all Quentin took. Before her husband's death, Annette's parenting had been nonchalant, allowing her son a generous amount of freedom. All that was sharply curtailed when Benjamin Reed didn't make it home from Vietnam. Jared didn't think Annette loved her son any more than she had when Benjamin was alive. She was just more determined to control him, although, perversely, whenever she succeeded she was disappointed in him, more convinced he was a weakling. Jared had quit trying to figure the two of them out years ago, but he did feel sorry for his cousin. No matter what he did, Quentin would never please his mother.

Annette maintained her regal calm. "Be angry if you want," she told her nephew. "Just get that girl out of my house."

Which was what he did.

To her credit, Rebecca knew exactly what was going on. "I'm being booted, huh?"

She was trying to sound as if she didn't give a damn, but Jared could see the flash of anger—and humiliation—in her eyes and red-stained cheeks. "I'm sorry," he said tightly.

She polished off the last of her champagne. "Don't be."

But he was. He'd been a fool to think his aunt would have tolerated a Blackburn in her house, and if Rebecca was going to be polite and not tell him so, her grandfather had no such compunction. They took their frustrations down to West Cedar Street, but after Thomas Blackburn politely told Jared it was good to see him, he waved off their complaints without sympathy.

"What on earth did you expect?" he asked them.

Rebecca kicked off her thin-strapped shoes and paced on the worn carpet in her stocking feet. "Am I going to be damned forever for something I didn't even do?"

It was a rhetorical question not meant to be answered, but Thomas said, "Probably," and disappeared into the kitchen.

Jared stood awkwardly in the middle of the dimly lit parlor, a fire going to take the chill off the raw spring night. He didn't know if he ought to leave or stick around. He was half-Winston and had to be an annoying physical reminder of the Blackburns' loss of prestige. For centuries, their moral and intellectual rectitude had kept them within the circles of power, even to the point of having presidents consult them on any number of topics. They had been the conscience of Beacon Hill, a shining example of "doing the right thing." They hadn't needed money to maintain their particular kind of authority. Jared could remember when Thomas Blackburn's name had evoked respect and his opinions had made people think, listen, change their minds.

An ambush in the rice paddies of the Mekong Delta had changed all that, and even if it was something the Blackburns could get used to, it wasn't anything Annette Winston Reed was likely to let them—or anyone else—forget. She wasn't a forgiving woman on the best of days, and her husband was dead because of Thomas Blackburn. If she hadn't stolen their moral authority from them, she was content not to let them earn it back.

But Jared hoped Rebecca would take his friendship with her grandfather as a cue that he didn't share his aunt's relentless hatred, nor her vindictiveness. Because Jared didn't want to leave the shabby West Cedar Street house.

He wanted, he admitted to himself, to get to know Rebecca again. When they were kids, she was the big sister to a passel of brothers and had sought Jared out just because he was five years older. She had never idolized him; that wasn't R. J. Blackburn's style. Sometimes she'd fight and kick and yell and act like a little sister asserting her independence, and then sometimes she'd find a common ground with him that was more mature than the bond she'd share with her younger brothers—something Jared could see now. At the time, more often than not, he'd viewed her as bossy as hell and a royal pest.

"I'm choking in this dress," she said, unclasping the hook-and-eye at the nape of her neck. She fastened her gaze on Jared. "You can go on back to the party, you know. I'll be fine here."

"That'd be the height of rudeness, wouldn't it? Going

back to a party my date's been kicked out of. What do you take me for, R.J.?"

"Those are your people—"

"I won't damn my aunt for being what she is," he said carefully, "but I won't defend her, either. I don't agree with what she just did to you. If I did, I'd never have taken you there tonight in the first place."

Turning her back to him, Rebecca fingered a small brass Buddha atop the marble mantel of the cold fireplace. "I believe you."

Jared said nothing. It hadn't occurred to him that she wouldn't believe him.

"Did Quentin want me out, as well?"

"I don't think so—"

"I know, it's hard to tell." She faced him again, hinted a smile. "I hadn't seen him since we left for Florida. I didn't have a chance to say hello to him tonight, but that's probably just as well." Her almost-smile broadened into a real one that was filled with energy and irreverence. "He's a handsome devil, isn't he?"

Jared laughed. "Yeah, you want his phone number? Maybe he could take you out and give his mother heart failure."

"That'd do it, wouldn't it?" Rebecca laughed, as well.

Thomas returned with a big bowl of crisp tortilla chips and a batch of his homemade salsa, hot enough to make Jared's and Rebecca's eyes tear. The old man seemed unaffected. He told them he didn't want to hear another word about the goings-on at the Winston house on Mt. Vernon and suggested they play "that game of yours, Rebecca."

She grinned, totally recovered from her humiliation at the hands of Annette Winston Reed. "That's because he always wins. My grandfather," she told Jared, "has the most incredible junk mind."

So, as it turned out, did Jared.

A handful of Thomas's foreign students joined them, and they played until midnight, when he finally threw them out. Jared drove Rebecca back to campus in his rented car and dropped her off at her dormitory, offering to walk her to the door.

"I'll be fine. It's pretty late. Sofi, Alex, Lenny and half the floor're probably waiting up for me."

"Tell them," Jared said, leaning toward her and kissing her lightly, "your virgin shoes worked."

Fifteen

〜⚬⚭⚬〜

By finals in mid-May Rebecca had turned nineteen and was head over heels in love with Jared Sloan. He made her laugh and wasn't afraid to tease her about being so compulsive about school and work. And he was self-confident enough that he wasn't threatened by her ambitions. She could be herself with him. Not just a Blackburn, not just a scholarship student, not just an egghead, not just a young, attractive, blue-eyed woman. It was liberating.

He stayed in Boston for several days after the groundbreaking for the new Winston & Sloan Building. They went everywhere together. They traipsed through Boston Common and the Public Garden, went window-shopping on Newbury Street, wandered through the Museum of Fine Arts, checked out their old haunts on Charles Street. Rebecca managed to find time for them to be together without sacrificing her work, classes or studying. Jared showed up at the library one afternoon and patiently read while she reshelved books.

When he headed back to California, he sent her postcards of the Golden Gate Bridge and jotted on the back that San Francisco was a lovers' paradise.

"Whoa," Sofi kept saying, "that man's smitten."

So was Rebecca.

Even if she knew whatever they'd started was going to come to an abrupt halt on June first when Jared headed for Saigon.

"Don't you think it's nuts for him to want to spend a year in Vietnam?" she would ask her grandfather.

"Yes," Thomas Blackburn would say, "especially now. I fear South Vietnam's a dying country."

He would then proceed to expound on the most recent trials to besiege the country where he'd spent so many years, and had lost so much. He lectured Rebecca on the devastating effects of the 1973 American military withdrawal and the Arab oil embargo on the country's economy, the suicidal intransigence and shortsightedness of the Thieu regime, the rampant corruption, the lack of interest in Vietnam of an American people preoccupied with the Watergate scandal and the future of their own president. Rebecca knew better than to interrupt when he was on one of his tirades. She had learned that, despite her grandfather's public silence, in private he spared no one his opinions. At least not her.

"But," he would eventually conclude, "I can understand Jared's compulsion to go there. I felt it myself more than fifty years ago." And he would penetrate her with his icy clear eyes. "Do you, Rebecca?"

"Not right now," she would always say. "I have to think about school and work. I don't have the time or the money to go gallivanting all over the world."

Of course, Jared Sloan did.

He came back to Boston on a warm, sunny May afternoon and found her studying for her microeconomics final on a grassy embankment overlooking Storrow Drive and the Charles River, dotted with hundreds of small white sails.

"Hey, there," he said, startling her.

She squinted up at him in the sun, and her heartbeat steadied at the sight of him, with his crooked grin and dark, sun-washed hair. Smiling, she laid down her textbook and threw herself on him, and together they fell back onto the grass.

Jared laughed. "Not a bad public display of affection for a repressed Yankee."

"Don't forget I'm half-Southerner. Where'd you come from?"

"San Francisco."

"To visit your mother?"

"To visit you."

His mouth found hers, and they rolled over on the ground, Jared ending up on top, bits of grass sticking in his hair. She relished the feel of his weight on her. His tongue flicked hot and wet against hers, and he murmured, "I could make love to you right here."

"We'd be arrested."

"All for a good cause."

She laughed, seeing the piratical gleam in his eyes. "I've missed you."

To her surprise, he rolled off her and sat up, exhaling in relief.

"Did you have any doubts?" she asked, shocked.

"Yeah," he admitted, "I did. You Blackburns are a self-sufficient lot, you know. And you, R.J.—Ms. Four-oh Average, Ms. Future Diplomat, Ms. Full Scholarship—you're about as intense as they come. They didn't break the mold when your grandfather was born."

Rebecca wasn't sure that was a compliment, however accurate he might be. She abandoned microeconomics for a walk along the river holding hands with Jared. Afterward they grabbed a couple of hot dogs from a vendor on Commonwealth Avenue and headed back to her dorm, talking all the way. When they reached her room, Jared's gaze rested on Sofi's stripped bed, closet, desk and bureau.

"Oh," Rebecca said, "she finished her last final yesterday and headed home to Westchester."

"Did she, now?"

He gave her a wildly exaggerated lecherous look and pounced, hooking one arm around her waist and tossing her playfully down on her skinny bed. Rebecca laughed—until she saw his eyes. Then she knew he wasn't just horsing around.

Her breath caught. "Jared…"

His body was strong and hard on top of hers. Rebecca could feel him breathing, feel him wanting her. A sharp stab of longing went through her—and a little fear. "Do not go Blackburn on him and tell the man you're a virgin," Sofi had warned her before leaving. "You'll scare him." Rebecca had countered that she wasn't even sure she'd see Jared Sloan again. Sofi had groaned and said her roommate was *so* naive.

He smiled tenderly and brushed the hair back from her forehead. "I thought I'd never do this in a dorm bunk again."

"Bully for you," Rebecca blurted. "I've never done it at all!" Too late, she caught herself. "I mean—"

"R.J., it'll be all right." Lowering his mouth to hers, he kissed her softly, slowly. "I promise."

She nodded that she believed him, but her practical nature asserted itself. "You're prepared?"

He laughed. "You're the one who calls me a pirate—"

"I don't mean *ready,* I mean prepared."

"I was just teasing. I know what you mean. Yes, Ms. Four-oh Blackburn, I'm prepared."

He plucked a package of condoms from his jeans pocket and set it on the edge of the bed. Rebecca didn't know whether to be pleased or appalled. "You planned this?"

"Let's just say I'm ever-hopeful. R.J." He had the grace to be embarrassed. "Has anyone ever told you that you're direct?"

She gave him a mock look of innocence. "A Blackburn direct? Imagine."

As outspoken as she was, she didn't find undressing in front of Jared easy. She felt shy and inexperienced, but the prospect of leaving the job to him unnerved her, at least for the first time. It would just be too awkward.

And in spite of her five brothers and their notorious absence of modesty, she wasn't sure about having Jared undress in front of her, either. He was tanned and muscled, but she didn't know if she should stare, look away, make a comment, or, just for a change, keep her mouth shut.

Finally he came to her on the ridiculous bed and smoothed his palms over her bare shoulders, just looking at her. "If you want me to stop...if I hurt you..."

She shook her head. "You won't."

But she wished she felt as confident as she sounded and resisted the impulse to crack a joke to relieve the strange tension that was making her mouth tingle and her skin feel almost alive. A breeze from the opened window made her shiver. Then Jared stroked her upper arms and she was hot again. She lay back on the bed, bringing him with her, reveling in the erotic sensation of her bare skin against his. They would have to take their time, she thought. She wanted to take note of everything.

But Jared had other ideas, and he communicated his urgency—made her feel it, as well—when they kissed. He explored her mouth with his tongue, matched its probing rhythm with his hips, and all her self-consciousness and nervousness vanished. *Yes,* she thought, *I want this....*

He touched her everywhere, whispered how beautiful she was, how soft and perfect her breasts were, how strong her thighs were, and she quickly stopped taking her mental notes, surprised and consumed by the shuddering abandon of her own arousal. She was bursting with a longing that made her want to laugh and cry and just hold him forever. She kept her eyes open every minute, and when he eased into her gently, carefully, she realized there was little more than a pinching tightness. Then she pulled him deeper into her, urging him on. It was the only cue he needed. His thrusts grew harder, deeper, faster, and she responded to each one with a lust that only hours ago would have amazed her, until at last she was no longer thinking, only feeling.

He came first, she seconds later, exploding as he kept pace with her, whispering for her to enjoy, enjoy, enjoy. And she did, crying out with the joy of it, with the rawness and beauty of their pleasure.

Much later, when they were back in their jeans and sitting cross-legged on the narrow bed, Jared fastened his mesmerizing gaze on her. "Come with me to Saigon, R.J."

"Saigon?" Assuming he was just kidding, she laughed. "Oh, sure, I'll just call up TWA and have them mail me a ticket."

But he was serious. "It's just a year. I'd pay your way—consider it a loan. When you got back you could pick up where you left off. R.J., you're so smart, you'll be drowning in money by the time you're thirty. We'd have a whole year together, the two of us."

"If the N.V.A. didn't overrun us first. You should hear my grandfather on the subject. Anyway, what would I do while you were off being an architect? Keep house? Make you dinner? I'm not going to take a year off from college just to hang around in Southeast Asia."

Jared eyed her a moment. "You could get a job. I don't need you to wait on me. Look, I have connections—"

"That's just my point. Jared, please try to understand. I can't let you pay my way or find me a job."

"You don't have to agree to anything that makes you uncomfortable," he said quietly. "But R.J., after all that's happened to your family, don't you want to see Vietnam?"

She swallowed, stifling a rush of tears, amazed that after eleven years she still missed her father as much as she did. Nineteen years old and the emptiness just didn't go away. She could feel him hugging her fiercely before he left for Southeast Asia for the last time. But she couldn't see his face. She didn't know why. Since she was eight she'd tried to remember what he'd looked like that hot afternoon at the airport, and she just couldn't.

"Yes, I want to see Vietnam," she said. Then she looked at Jared and added, "But on my own nickel."

To his credit, he didn't walk out on her, but leaned forward until she could see the flecks of white in his blue eyes. "Rebecca Blackburn, you are a giant pain in the ass sometimes. I'll have you know I've been saving all year for this trip." The break in tension was short-lived, and his expression grew serious again as he reached over and brushed his fingertips across the top of her hand, resting on her knee. "You might not get another chance, you know. You're letting your pride get in the way of what could be the experience of a lifetime."

"Maybe I am. But I haven't badgered you to stay in Boston and watch me suffer through my second year of college."

"I know. R.J.—" He broke off and looked away, tears glistening in his eyes. "I didn't want this to happen. I'm going to miss you."

She wanted to cry, but refused to. "Then what you're saying is we're finished."

He pulled her to him, stroking her thick hair. "No, R.J., we're just beginning."

He drove back to Florida with her. They took the long way, stopping everywhere—and sharing everything. Driving, expenses, food, themselves. Rebecca discovered that Jared wanted to make his own way in the world, too. He didn't feel sorry for himself or whine about having money, something Rebecca appreciated. He'd learned, he'd said, just to make his own decisions and not sweat the family's reactions.

Rebecca saw him off at the Orlando airport. He'd say goodbye to his father in San Francisco, then start the long journey to Southeast Asia. For days after he left, she moped, walking in the citrus groves and trying to imagine that the sweat pouring down her back in the early summer heat was from long hours of lovemaking.

Jared called when he arrived in Saigon. She took no pleasure at the loneliness she heard in his voice. His apartment was small and hot, he told her, but he was selfish enough—loved her so much—that he wished she were with him. But they understood each other. He'd done what he had to do, and so had she.

They exchanged letters through the summer while she worked at Disney World and helped in the groves and went picnicking, fishing and frog-catching with her brothers, and through the fall when she resumed classes, her job at the library, and Sunday-night supper with Sofi and her grandfather on Beacon Hill. Thomas Blackburn continued to win at her and Sofi's trivia game, and he refused to comment on the relationship between his granddaughter and Jared Sloan. Not, Rebecca was confident, that he didn't have an opinion.

"You think we're doomed, don't you?" she asked him one night in February, almost a year since she'd met Jared.

He sniffed. "That's hardly any of my business."

"Since when's that ever stopped you from stating your opinion? You told Sofi you thought her last boyfriend looked like a mushroom."

"Well, he did—and she thought so, too."

"So what about Jared?"

"I consider Jared Sloan a friend."

"And?"

"And there's a great deal of history between you and him."

"That doesn't tell me a thing."

Sighing, he patted her hand. "Your life is for you to live."

"Do you think I should have gone to Saigon with him?"

That one was easy; he didn't even hesitate. "No."

"Grandfather..."

"Vietnam," he went on, cutting off her attempt to get at the deeper issues of his own years there, "isn't a place for Blackburns."

Maybe it was that comment, that night, more even than missing Jared that made her decision for her. It didn't matter. Two weeks later she'd changed her mind.

She would go to Saigon.

Sixteen

~~~~~oↄҩↄ~~~~~

Jared was closing in on forty and as good-looking as he'd been at twenty-five when Rebecca had been in love with him. In the dim parlor light, she could make out the fine lines at the corners of his eyes and the first touches of gray in his dark hair. He'd kept in shape: his abdomen was tight, and the muscles in his shoulders and arms suggested he still liked to sail and jog. He wore good-quality jeans and a plain navy pullover.

He recovered quickly from the initial shock of seeing her again after so many years. "R.J., what're you doing here?"

"I live here."

"She's renting her old room upstairs," her grandfather amended.

Jared gave a small laugh. "I should have known a tight-wad Blackburn like you would camp out with family. Sorry for the intrusion. I'll leave—"

Thomas snorted. "Oh, please, let's not start all that non-sense. Where would you stay?"

"The Ritz."

"I have enough on my conscience," Thomas said in his

dry, understated way, "without adding the cost of an un-necessary night at the Ritz to it." He turned to his grand-daughter, still rooted to her spot in the doorway. "Rebecca, Jared is a guest in my house. I'd be most appreciative if you'd retire to your room and permit us to carry on our con-versation in private."

A polite, stuffy way of telling her to get lost. Rebecca stood her ground. "I'm not going anywhere until I find out what Jared's doing in Boston."

"If he wants you to know his affairs," Thomas replied, "he will tell you them."

"Then you'd better give up, R.J.," Jared told her, not nastily, but she got the point.

Rebecca made a face at him that would have done a twelve-year-old proud. She was still steamed from her earlier go-round with her grandfather over the French-man's appearance that afternoon. Thomas had refused to discuss how one of the two-man team that had murdered Tam fourteen years ago could have known her father or even if Thomas himself recognized the detailed description she gave him. Nor would he speculate on what the French-man might be doing in Boston, what he might want—anything. His remedy for Rebecca's heightened state of anxiety was to make her a pot of hot tea and encourage her to take a vacation. A long one. Preferably somewhere far from Boston, like Budapest.

She, in turn, hadn't mentioned the Jupiter Stones and her afternoon with Sofi and David Rubin. There were too many uncertainties, and not a single guarantee that confiding in her grandfather would mean he'd return the favor. Likely enough, he'd clam up even more. And what David had told her was too fresh, too raw. It was one thing to believe Tam had gotten hold of a few sapphires and was smuggling them into the states as a nest egg—not that she'd have needed one with Jared. But maybe she'd wanted to make a life for herself and Mai without him. After all, what did Rebecca really know about their relationship and the terms they'd come to before Tam's death? Jared certainly hadn't told her.

Still, it was quite another thing for Tam to have gotten hold of Empress Elisabeth's Jupiter Stones. Until she knew more, Rebecca would keep her mouth shut.

Not a gracious loser, she left the parlor and tried eavesdropping from the stairs. She couldn't hear much. She was about to give up when her grandfather appeared in the parlor door and glared up at her. "I'm dismayed," he said, "to see that the Blackburns' sense of honor and decency has deteriorated to the point a granddaughter of mine would stoop to listening in on a private conversation."

Rebecca jumped up and peered over the mahogany side-rail down at him. "Jared saw our man, didn't he? He must have gone to San Francisco before coming here to Boston—"

"Rebecca, if you persist, Jared will leave and neither you or I will learn anything. So I suggest for once in your life you don't cut off your nose to spite your face and please retire to your room. I'm perfectly capable of dealing with Jared on my own."

Her grandfather always went into his haughty Bostonian act when he was on the verge of losing his temper. Rebecca didn't respond and headed upstairs and stayed there.

She passed a near-sleepless night. There were haunting memories of Jared's smile, echoes of the things he used to whisper to her when they'd made love, memories of the way he'd made her feel. She doubted he was ever tormented by similar memories of her. She hadn't been his first lover.

And there were questions that kept her awake. What-ifs and fears. About the Frenchman and how his reappearance would affect their lives. About what had so unnerved Jared Sloan that he'd ventured back to Boston after so many years, back to the Eliza Blackburn house where he'd be accosted by enough uncomfortable memories of his own. About her grandfather and what he'd known for twenty-six years and had never told anyone, at least not her.

About the Jupiter Stones.

And about Mai, the hours-old infant she'd rescued from the chaos that was Saigon in April 1975. Sometime toward dawn, Rebecca flicked on her bed-stand lamp and examined the pretty, intelligent face of Jared Sloan's daughter on the front page of *The Score*. If only Mai could have known Tam.

"My baby means everything to me," Tam had told Rebecca not long before she had died.

Would the Frenchman hurt Mai?

When she still couldn't sleep, Rebecca tried to accept her grandfather for being the taciturn, unsparing man he was. He was hardest on those he cared about most—and particularly on himself.

By five-thirty, she gave up, took a shower and got dressed, not bothering with anything remotely corporate, just a shirt, jeans and sneakers. She let her damp hair dry haphazardly. Downstairs she peeked in the front parlor: Jared was sacked out on the couch with an ancient afghan pulled up over him and his clothes lying in a heap on the floor. He wasn't tossing and turning. It was all Rebecca could do not to march in there and wake him up.

Athena was already studying anatomy at the kitchen

table. Rebecca helped herself to a cup of coffee and joined her, averting her eyes from the grim photographs. A sturdy, brilliant woman, Athena was of the unshakable conviction that into each woman's life must come at least one bona fide rake of a man. Rebecca couldn't resist telling her that *her* rake was conked out in the front parlor.

"Him?" Athena was thrilled. "Yes, he's *perfect!* So handsome, no? He's broken many hearts, I'm sure. What did he do to you?"

Rebecca poured milk from a carton into her coffee. She usually had her coffee black, but one needed some protection from Athena's notoriously strong brew. "He had a baby by another woman while professing to be in love with me."

That ignited Athena, and Rebecca was pleased to see she wasn't the only hard case when it came to two-timing men. Athena ranted and commiserated and loudly suggested that Jared Sloan would make a fine specimen for her anatomy class, but she restricted herself to snorting at his sleeping figure when she headed off to med school.

A few minutes later Jared staggered into the kitchen in his undershirt and jeans, and Rebecca had to catch her breath at the memories of sleepy mornings on their trip to Florida after her freshman year at B.U. She'd dumped men and had been dumped since, but she'd never loved anyone with such abandon and trust—such naiveté—as Jared Sloan. Maybe it was because he was her first lover, maybe it was because he'd been her friend. What difference did it make? Whatever they'd had together was over.

He poured himself a cup of coffee. "Did I hear you and that firebrand med student planning to carve me up?"

Rebecca grinned. "Just a little."

"Pleasant conversation to wake up to. Bad enough I had

to fight off that damn cat all night. I thought your grandfather hated cats."

"He's not fond of them, but he tolerates Sweatshirt."

"Sweatshirt?"

"He's mine."

"I should have known." He sat across from her at the table, and he did look tired and restless. "Still hate me, R.J.?"

His expression was serious all at once, but Rebecca smiled over the rim of her steaming mug. "Only when I think about you."

"Ouch—the infamous Blackburn honesty. It serves me right for asking." Suddenly he set down his mug and ran one finger along the inside of the handle, watching what he was doing as if it were the most important thing he had on his mind. Finally he said, "R.J., I'm sorry about that business with *The Score*. If I'd known—"

"You'd still have punched that guy."

He laughed unexpectedly. "Maybe."

"No maybe about it, Sloan. You haven't changed since you were ten years old and nailed that snotty little rich kid who picked on my brothers for wearing hand-me-downs. I don't remember his name—he used to have birthday parties in the park in Louisburg Square with the maids in uniforms, silver platters, clowns."

"Which you crashed," he pointed out, his eyes dancing.

She shrugged, unrepentant. "Have squirt gun will travel."

"He's an attorney now, I hear—very upstanding. Throws parties for his kids in the park, I'm sure."

"What do you suppose he thought of our pictures in *The Score?*"

Jared looked at her. "Do you care?"

"No."

He smiled at her total absence of hesitation. "Have you had any fallout from all this?"

Twisting her mouth to one side in thought, Rebecca leaned back and gave him a long look. "Just what's sitting in front of me."

Jared picked up his coffee and gave her a teasing look. "No men calling up for dates with the rich, beautiful, famous R. J. Blackburn?"

"A few," Rebecca said, and she had to smile. He was so much the old Jared who'd never been intimidated by anything about her—her looks, her intelligence, her heritage, her high standards.

His eyes darkened for a moment. "*The Score* said you're not married."

"I'm not. Never have been—and not because of you, either. The prospect of not being married at thirty-five doesn't keep me awake nights, you know. What about you?"

He gave her a deliberate smile. "The prospect of not being married at forty doesn't keep me awake nights." Then he changed the subject. "Your grandfather's not up, I take it?"

"Not yet. He's usually an early riser. He's probably upstairs plotting ways to get me out of here so you two can pretend I don't exist."

"Still not one to sit on your emotions, are you?"

For that, she didn't warn him before he tried Athena's coffee, which was strong enough to peel paint. All he did was make a slight grimace. That proper Winston-Sloan blood of his had kicked in, she supposed.

He went on, "It wasn't my idea to throw you out last night."

"I didn't notice you asking me to stick around."

"God forbid I should come between you and your grandfather."

Rebecca gave him a skeptical look. "Yeah, right."

"Okay, I admit I was hoping you were thumbing your nose at my cousin and aunt and anyone else who thought the Blackburns would never amount to anything again and were living in the fanciest, most expensive condo you could find. I admit I didn't want to have this conversation. But you're making a mistake if you think Thomas has told me anything he hasn't told you. If it makes you feel any better, he wants me to head back to San Francisco."

"Sounds good to me." Rebecca knew she was being petty and immature but couldn't stop herself. The old hurt had gotten the better of her. "When're you leaving?"

"I'm not."

"Why not?"

Jared leaned over the table, and Rebecca saw that his teal eyes were as clear and luminous as she remembered in all her dreams of the first time she and Jared had made love. "You've seen our guy from Saigon, haven't you? He's in Boston."

"Did Grandfather tell you that?"

"No. He's no more going to blab your 'affairs' to me than he is mine to you. But it's a fair guess from his reaction to me—and yours."

Rebecca sipped her coffee, the mug poised in front of her in both hands. Her fingers weren't trembling; she hadn't gulped the coffee. As far as Jared Sloan could see, she was just fine. But she wasn't. A time and a man she'd thought she'd put behind her had reared up again, and she didn't know what she was supposed to do.

"R.J., don't hold back on me," Jared said, not as a plea or a demand, but a simple, honest request. His gaze remained intense, difficult to ignore. "My daughter's life could be at stake."

Rebecca took a sharp breath. "She's been threatened?"

"No, but this guy tried to kill her when she was just a baby. For all I know, he might try again. He was at my house in San Francisco the day before yesterday and didn't touch her, but that doesn't mean he won't. She's with my father, so she's safe for now." Jared set down his coffee mug, his expression hard and serious and very determined. "Nothing happens to Mai. I don't care what I have to do."

Rebecca was taken aback by his vehemence—by how very much he loved his daughter. And suddenly she knew, as she'd only thought she'd known before, that fourteen years ago Jared Sloan had done exactly the right thing in taking unconditional responsibility for the tiny newborn girl. Mai was his daughter. And Tam's. He had never offered any excuses or explanations. He had simply done what he'd had to do. It had meant losing Rebecca, but as painful as that had been at the time, it was now completely irrelevant.

"You're right," she told him. "I did see our man."

Jared listened grimly, without interruption as she related yesterday's encounter, leaving out the Frenchman's comment about having known her father—and David Rubin's report on Tam's bag of colored stones. Rebecca still needed time to process both developments before she could determine if they were any of Jared Sloan's business or if it were even her place to tell him. The stones might not have had anything to do with his relationship with Tam, and her violent death and Mai's illegitimacy were already enough for Jared and Mai to deal with without Rebecca throwing a fortune in smuggled gems into their faces. But that had been her judgment in 1975, as it was now.

"I don't know what he's after," she said finally. "What about you? Did he say anything—"

"No. I didn't exactly give him a chance. Mai was there. I just got rid of him and came out here."

"To see my grandfather."

Jared didn't comment.

"Why Grandfather?" Rebecca persisted. "He wasn't in Saigon in 1975. He hasn't been there since my father was killed. Look, Jared—"

"R.J., I'm not going to start a war between you and your grandfather."

"A polite way of saying you're not going to tell me a thing. Well, fine—don't." She set her mug down hard and swept to her feet. "I've got enough to do without beating my head against a wall trying to make you play fair. If you'll excuse me, I have a business to run."

As she came around the table he caught her by the arm—not hard, not long. But she drew back as if he'd given her an electric shock. His touch called up images of hot nights of lovemaking, reminded her of how much losing him had hurt, of how damned much she'd loved him. And warned her he was as sexy as ever. She could want him again. It wouldn't take much.

If she were going to be stupid.

"Stay out of this, R.J.," he said quietly, his voice even deeper, raspier than she remembered. She saw that touching her had an impact on him, as well. There'd never been any doubt in her mind he'd had a grand time for himself making love to her, no matter what had happened between him and Tam.

Rebecca narrowed her eyes at him. "I'm not a kid, Jared. I won't let you order me around anymore."

Jared looked surprised. "I never did order you around."

"Ha! You've been telling me what to do since I was two years old."

"Not a chance. R.J., you were the bossiest kid on Beacon Hill. I never managed to get you to do one thing you didn't want to do. And, in case you've forgotten, we didn't see each other during the ten years after you moved from Boston to Florida, or the fourteen since you left me to rot in that hospital in Manila. You've been free of me about two-thirds of your life." He held back a smile, his eyes giving off that pirate's gleam that used to make her groan just with wanting him. "Hey, we're practically strangers."

"A stranger isn't someone who knows—not just guesses, but *knows*—you were the one who lit the fire on Boston Common that time."

Jared grinned at their shared childhood memory. "It wasn't much of a fire, just a few twigs and leaves."

"You and Quentin and Nate were playing Salem witch trial, and I was the witch. You were going to burn me at the stake. What was I, five?"

"We weren't really going to burn you—"

"Yes, but the mounted policeman didn't know that when he smelled smoke and you took off, leaving me tied to that tree."

"R.J., you know you could have gotten free anytime, and anyway, the fire wasn't that close to you."

"The cop didn't think so. He wanted to find you and stick your toes in it, but I kept my mouth shut."

"Not out of any sense of virtue," Jared countered, "but only because you're a Blackburn and keeping your mouth shut comes naturally."

"The point is, you're no stranger and you never will be, no matter how little we see of each other." She smiled wistfully, wondering if she and Jared, if never strangers, could ever be friends again. If they hadn't fallen in love, then it might have been possible. Now—she didn't know. "Good luck with Grandfather. And if I don't see you before you leave town—well, give my best to your daughter."

Jared looked at her. "I will, R.J. Thanks."

Maddeningly, her eyes filled with tears, and she fled, running out the front door and into the cool spring air. It was damp and drizzly, a typical New England morning, and still early.

"I have no wish to discuss with you the matter of a Frenchman who might have known your father," her grandfather had told her yesterday afternoon.

She'd see what she could find out on her own.

First she'd have a big, fattening breakfast on Charles Street, and then she'd head over to the Boston Public Library, which supposedly had an impressive amount of information on the man John F. Kennedy didn't choose as his ambassador to Saigon, one Thomas Ezekiel Blackburn.

It also, Rebecca felt certain, would have something on Empress Elisabeth and her Jupiter Stones, and maybe even information on a rash of robberies on the Côte d'Azur in the late fifties.

Jared made a fresh pot of more tolerable coffee and went out into the garden, toweling off a chair. The air was cool and damp, but it wasn't raining at the moment. His coffee was piping hot, just what he needed. He inhaled the steam and tried to settle down. It wasn't easy to be around Rebecca again.

In a few minutes, Thomas came outside, wearing an ancient sweater over his polo shirt and chinos. He looked a hundred as he pulled out a chair and sat down, not bothering to towel it off. "You're not on your way back to San Francisco, I see."

"No. I called Mai last night—she's fine. Irritated with me for going to Boston without her, but she'll survive."

Thomas sighed. "I'm too old to force you to take sound advice when offered. Where's Rebecca?"

"Gone out. She says she has a business to run, but—"

"But she's got the bit in her teeth," Thomas finished for him.

"She told you our man from Saigon was at her studio yesterday, didn't she?"

Thomas fastened his incisive eyes on Jared. "She mentioned it, yes."

"You could have told me."

"I have no intention of repeating private conversations between myself and my granddaughter to anyone, including you, Jared."

Jared accepted the mild lecture with equanimity, and said, in just as mild a tone, "That's fine—until your idea of honor and discretion endangers my daughter. Thomas, R.J. knows something, and she's holding back."

"What do you want me to say?" Thomas asked calmly.

"I don't know. Did she give you any indication—"

"No. I agree with you. She's holding back."

Jared inhaled, controlling his frustration. "R.J. should get out of Boston. If this guy's here, she could be in danger."

Leaning forward, Thomas looked at Jared, his expression surprisingly gentle. "Don't be protective, Jared. Don't hover." He paused and picked bits of wet twigs and yellow pollen off his table. "Rebecca hates that."

"I don't give a damn what she hates."

Thomas smiled. "Don't you?"

Uncomfortable, Jared jumped up and abandoned his

coffee. The Blackburns were getting to him. "I'm going out for a while. I need some air—a chance to think." He glanced down at the elderly man seated at the battered garden table, wishing the last quarter-century of Thomas Blackburn's life hadn't been so isolated and hard. Thomas would say he didn't mind; he deserved the ostracism he'd endured since 1963. But Jared wondered. He added, "Maybe coming back here was a mistake."

Thomas was unruffled. "There are two seats available on a nine-o'clock flight to San Francisco. I called myself. I don't believe Rebecca's ever been."

A vision flashed in Jared's mind of taking R.J. across the Golden Gate Bridge for the first time, taking her to dinner at his and Mai's favorite Chinese restaurant.

He had to get out from under the Blackburn spell.

"I'll talk to you later," he told Thomas, his voice hoarse. He didn't wait for a reply.

Seventeen

Mai knew she would need cash for her plan. As much as she could lay her hands on. Her grandfather didn't leave large sums of money lying around for someone to slip unnoticed into a pocket. All she'd managed to grab since her plan had come into her head after dinner last night was a measly five dollars she'd found on top of the refrigerator. She'd pay him back every penny she "borrowed."

She had set her alarm for 4:00 a.m. and shoved it under her pillow so no one else would hear it go off, but it almost gave her a heart attack when it did. At least she was wide-awake. She slipped noiselessly out of bed. The house was cool and filled with strange shadows. Wesley and Maureen Sloan had no pets, so there were no barking dogs to worry about, no cats to streak out of the darkness.

Her first stop was the living room, with its dramatic view of the bay and San Francisco, glittering through the predawn mist. She checked everywhere.

Nothing.

The dining room proved equally barren. She didn't find so much as a dime at the bottom of a wineglass. It wasn't like at home, where her father always left the odd twenty-dollar bill and loose change around. She had never swiped a cent from him. It had never even occurred to her to steal from her own father; she'd always relied just on her allowance and own earnings.

He had called her from Boston. "Hey, there," he'd said, "is Granddad feeding you chocolates and letting you play with all his gadgets?"

Mai had replied that he was, but she would rather be with him in Boston. "Where are you?" she'd asked.

He wouldn't tell her where he was staying. He just wanted to make sure she was okay, that was all. "Sulk all you want," he'd added. "It won't kill you."

If she had a mother, would her father be as big a pain as he was?

Shivering, Mai went into her grandfather's study, built on a more intimate scale than the rest of the house, but still large, especially compared to her and her father's place in San Francisco. Here the view was of the garden, a magnificent, exotic place that would burst with color in the sunlight, but now, before dawn, was dark and spooky. Mai suddenly wished her grandfather believed in drapes. She got to work, going through drawers, pencil holders, filing cabinets, credenzas, anything that could possibly hold cash.

She struck pay dirt in a smooth wooden pear, about eight inches high, that opened in the middle. Inside were five one-hundred-dollar bills.

Mai had hoped for just fifty or a hundred dollars.

Stifling a squeal of victory, she scooped up the bills with one hand.

But how would she ever pay back five hundred dollars? She was saving money for college, and she could earn a fair amount babysitting and doing yard work—but five hundred dollars? She had trust funds set aside for her future, but she'd bet her dad and her grandfather would want the money paid back long before then.

She pushed the two ends of the pear together and retreated to her room, glad to be under her warm blankets, flush with money.

Eighteen

Quentin Reed finished his run with a cool-down walk across the lawn of the Winston house on Marblehead Neck, north of Boston. He had spent the night there, alone. Built in the twenties, it was a gargantuan ocean-gray clapboard house that his mother had always hated, considering it impractical and ostentatious—like her grandfather, the spendthrift Winston who'd built it. Sixty years ago the Winstons were no longer the moneymakers they had been for two centuries, but had adopted the attitude then prevalent among wealthy Bostonians that preserving fortunes was responsible and prudent, but creating them was somewhat unseemly, unless done prior to the turn of the century. This policy of conservative money management had in part led to the stagnation of Boston's economy during the first half of the twentieth century, until by the late 1950s its credit rating was in the cellar. That was when Benjamin Reed had risked Winston money to launch Winston & Reed.

By his death in 1963, even Annette had come around to the notion that making money wasn't so awful. She took her husband's fledgling company beyond even what he'd envisioned. She had the house on Marblehead Neck re-done in the early seventies, but continued to prefer the intimacy of Beacon Hill or her *mas* on the Riviera. Quentin held no strong opinion one way or the other about the house itself: Marblehead Neck jutted out into the ocean and that was all that mattered. Jane was staying at their own oceanside house, until they worked out their marital problems.

They'd had dinner together last night.

"You have to stand up to your mother," she had told him. "Quentin, don't you see? She'll respect you more if you quit caving in all the time and start arguing with her once in a while. Damn it, I love you because you're a decent, sensitive man, but those are qualities of strength, not weakness. It's time you made her realize that."

He'd had no counterargument. Maybe he was decent, maybe sensitive. People said he was, but so what? He was also weak, like his father. His mother was the strong one. At the edge of the lawn, Quentin walked out onto a flat boulder hung over a rocky cliff. Twenty yards below the tide was coming in, swirling and foaming among the rocks. The wind off the still-frigid waters of the Atlantic struck his overheated skin and rain-dampened hair, but he hardly noticed the cold. The water's edge seemed so far away, so unreachable. If he jumped, he couldn't even be sure he'd hit one of the small tide pools where the periwinkles liked to hide, never mind the ocean. Wherever he landed, he wouldn't live long. Eventually, the tide would take him.

He shook off the morbid thought. What was the matter with him?

Last night he'd dreamed of Tam. He hadn't in years. She had seemed so real to him. Every detail about her was etched clearly in his mind: her long, fine, black hair whipping over the front of her shoulders as she turned to him with her dazzling smile. Her delicate and incredibly beautiful face. Her shining dark eyes and small, sensitive mouth. She had seldom worn makeup, and even as an adult she'd resembled a pretty child, a fact that had never failed to incense her. She would call him a racist, sexist American pig, and he would agree and apologize, remarking on her intelligence and self-reliance. They would end up in bed, where she proved herself an artful, skillful lover, very much an adult.

"I can't live without you," he had told her so many times.

He had awakened sweating and wretched, with those same words on his lips. For a long time afterward he was positive he could smell the light, expensive perfume she favored. She would never tell him its name; it was her secret, she would say. She had always loved mysteries and secrets.

The run had only been marginally cathartic. He had already notified his secretary he would be in late, but maybe he'd skip going into town altogether. He could just stay here and walk on the rocks. They'd be slippery in the persistent drizzle; he'd have to be careful.

Or not.

He smiled bitterly in the cool wind. It would be a tragic accident, wouldn't it? Would his mother miss him or revel in the attention her grief would elicit? First the young widow, now the childless mother.

"Jesus," Quentin breathed, trying to shake off his depression.

He started back toward the house, his wet sneakers squishing with every step and bits of grass sticking to his legs. He remembered how he'd once fantasized about living here with Tam, filling the giant house's cavernous rooms with their children. As he progressed across the drizzle-soaked lawn, he could almost see them running to him, crying "Daddy" as he scooped them up.

Why couldn't Tam have continued to love him? Why couldn't she have forgiven him?

Then he realized a figure *was* coming across the lawn, not a child, but a man. Quentin blinked, thinking his imagination had run wild. Yet as he drew closer, the figure remained, becoming clearer, and he saw the shock of white hair, the limping gait.

The Frenchman. Jean-Paul Gerard.

Quentin slowed, but didn't bolt, as perhaps would have been smart. He could easily outrun the older man. Still, no matter what Quentin did, the Frenchman had always been able to find him in Saigon. He would find him in Boston, as well, if that was what he meant to do.

When they were face-to-face, Quentin cleared his throat and said, "You've come to kill me."

Gerard laughed the terrible laugh of Quentin's nightmares. "Don't tell me—you also thought I was dead. Or did you only hope I was?"

"I haven't thought about you in years."

More laughter. But there was no corresponding twinkle in the Frenchman's dead eyes. The laughter faded, and he said, "Liar."

True enough. "What do you want?"

"Not to kill you," Gerard replied, matter-of-factly. "No, my friend. Nothing will ever be that easy for either of us. I have no wish to harm you. Our arrangement from Saigon is finished, for both of us."

Their "arrangement" had been nothing short of blackmail. Quentin had arrived in Saigon in October of 1973—nearly eight months after the Paris Peace Accords—

despising those of his Americans who'd exploited the country they were supposed to help and protect, who'd supported an underlife of prostitution, drugs and desperation. Then, so easily, so *stupidly,* he had become one himself. Preying on the fears of a beautiful Vietnamese woman, he had gotten her to fall in love with him—or at least pretend she had. When he'd gone home to Boston and didn't return fast enough to suit her, she'd assumed the worst. She never even gave him a chance. Instead, she had fallen into Jared Sloan's arms, and Quentin had come to wonder who had used whom.

But Gerard hadn't blackmailed him over his love affair with Tam. Through his own naiveté, Quentin had gotten involved with a network of American civilians running drugs into the United States. Jean-Paul Gerard had found out and threatened to bring his "evidence" of Quentin's involvement to the head of Winston & Reed—unless Quentin paid. So Quentin complied. Thousands of dollars he paid, until his only escape was to admit everything to his mother and beg for her help. Her solution was to make him stay home. So he did, in August 1974, accepting his first management position at Winston & Reed, but expecting—hoping—Tam would understand that he really did love her and would return for her.

But he had never gone back to Vietnam. What would have been the point? He would have had to defy his mother and risk another encounter with Gerard. And Tam had found another man.

Quentin envied how relaxed the Frenchman looked, as if he didn't even feel the chilly air and drizzle. "Your mother has something I want," Gerard said calmly.

"That's absurd." Quentin couldn't hide his shock. What could Annette Reed and this troll have in common?

"My mother wouldn't have anything a lowlife like you would want."

Gerard grinned, his stained and missing teeth revealing decades of abuse. "You don't think so? She's a very rich woman, my friend."

"If it's money you want—"

"It's not. None of this need concern you, but it can, if she refuses to cooperate."

Quentin summoned what courage he could. "Stay away from her. If you—"

Gerard waved him silent. "Please, I don't have time for this 'protective son' nonsense. Your mother needs no one's protection, least of all yours. She has a valuable collection of sapphires. I want them. If I were you, I'd make sure she gets them to me."

"You're mad."

"If not by now, then no doubt soon. But that changes nothing, my friend. The sapphires." Gerard's eyes were piercing, suddenly very much alive. "You tell her, all right?"

Stunned, Quentin watched the frightening man limp back across the lawn, moving with confidence and a strange dignity. He continued down the driveway and disappeared beyond the evergreens that gave the grounds privacy and an air of seclusion. If he'd wanted to, Quentin could have chased him. Demanded answers. Throttled his thin, ravaged figure. But despite his scars and limp and advancing years, Jean-Paul Gerard had proven himself a surprisingly resilient man.

Did he have proof of what Quentin had done in Saigon? Would he have to go to his mother again and beg her help to keep the one stupid mistake he'd made fifteen years ago from continuing to hang over his head?

Quentin shuddered. As usual, he simply didn't know what to do.

* * *

Jean-Paul climbed into the nondescript sedan he'd stolen out of the Boston Common garage. He had no money for rentals. Satisfied that he'd put the fear of God into Quentin Reed, he drove out to Route 1 and headed back down to Boston, keeping within the speed limit. Annette would know he wasn't going to give up. He'd keep turning the screws harder and harder, until she surrendered the Jupiter Stones.

"Yes, *Maman*," he whispered, "we will succeed."

He stopped along the way for coffee and candy bars, his staples the past few days. He'd dozed no more than an hour or so at a time since he'd seen *The Score* in Honolulu. There would be time for sleep later. He needed to stay awake. Last night he'd seen Annette's bedroom light on well past midnight and imagined her plotting ways to kill him, and he'd seen Jared Sloan come to the Blackburn house on West Cedar Street.

They were a problem, Jared Sloan and Rebecca Blackburn.

He would deal with them next.

In Boston, he left the stolen car on Cambridge Street at the west end of Beacon Hill and felt no remorse. He'd picked a car with a near-empty tank of gas and was leaving it half-full.

Quentin showered, shaved and dressed, and feeling more in control of himself if no calmer, he dialed his mother's Mt. Vernon Street number from the bedroom telephone.

He hung up before she could answer.

She would be coming into the office later today. He would see her there and talk to her in person. He would have to be careful. Even under pressure, his mother had extraordinary self-control, but Quentin hoped he would be able to see through any smoke screen regarding the Frenchman and these sapphires he was after.

Had his mother once done something stupid for which Jean-Paul Gerard was trying to blackmail *her?*

Impossible.

More likely, Gerard was using what he had on Quentin to force him to get his mother to relinquish something valuable—sapphires—that she had acquired through legitimate means. Quentin would once again be the loser: his mother would relinquish the gems to protect him and keep what he'd done fifteen years ago from coming out and embarrassing them both. She would hold his mistake over his head forever.

He couldn't let that happen. She wasn't a woman to understand and never one to forgive. If he intended ever to gain her admiration and respect, he couldn't let Saigon resurface.

What if *he* could get the sapphires and give them to Gerard?

Mulling over that possibility, Quentin went out to his car and finally decided that whatever he chose to do, he couldn't afford to make a mistake. If he did, the Frenchman would be waiting. And so would his mother.

"I often wonder what this company would have become if your father had lived," she had once told her only son. "Don't be like him, Quentin."

Too late, Mother, he thought. *I already am.*

Nineteen

For the first time in twenty-six years, Thomas Blackburn walked to the end of West Cedar Street and turned up Mt. Vernon. Staying away from the Winston house was the one concession he'd made during his self-imposed exile; he and Annette Reed simply didn't need to bump into one another. If anyone was going to move off Beacon Hill, it would have to be her. Occasionally he'd spot her on Charles Street, and would do his best to avoid her without ducking behind lampposts or otherwise going out of his way. He assumed she did the same.

Billowing gray clouds had again gathered over the sun, and although it was morning, the temperature was dropping. Thomas could feel the dampness in his chest as he headed up Mt. Vernon Street. All he needed now was to have a heart attack and drop dead in front of Annette's doorstep. She'd be mortified, and his grandchildren would never forgive him.

He grunted with morbid amusement. What would Rebecca do with the Eliza Blackburn House? He'd left it to her in his will. She was the eldest of the grandchildren, and with her substantial fortune she could afford the taxes and upkeep. Sometimes he'd wished his own stubborn pride had permitted him to take her money and fix up the place, but that wasn't his way—and it would have spoiled the perverse pleasure he'd taken in thumbing his nose at the Annette Winston Reeds of the city by continuing to take in student boarders and refusing to paint the shutters. Yet Thomas hoped all that would be finished by his death. He hoped his granddaughter could enjoy spending her money to restore the famous house, and that his descendants could understand what he'd done and why, and take pride again in being Blackburns.

That was what he wanted, he thought: a future in which, even if no Blackburn chose to live there, Eliza's beautiful home was returned to its original gracefulness and charm and put back on the Beacon Hill walking tour. It would be a fitting symbol of the restoration of the Blackburn name.

He suspected it was what Rebecca wanted, as well. Although she hadn't admitted as much to him, he was convinced it was the chief reason she had come back to Boston. Time, her success, her money, her extraordinary spirit and talent—they were all to erase the stain Thomas Blackburn had put on the family. Two centuries of excellence, high standards and achievement had crumbled with his one terrible mistake.

But Rebecca was being naive, and perhaps so was he. It would take more than his death and her accomplishment to make things right again on Beacon Hill. No matter what the Blackburns did, there would be Annette Winston Reed to remind everyone that her poor husband was dead, along with Thomas's own son and his Vietnamese friend, and that Thomas Blackburn had killed them.

His heart was thumping along rather erratically when

he came to her house on Mt. Vernon, but he was only perspiring lightly and his chest pain had abated. From here on
he'd be fine. Damned if he'd give her the satisfaction of
dropping dead at her feet.

The front gate was open. Her flowers were in better shape
than his. When he was just a little boy, Thomas remembered
his mother walking him over to the Winston house. She had
pointed to it as an example of high-style Adam architecture
and remarked on the elliptical fanlight, the Palladian window
in the second story above the elaborate front entrance, the two
end chimneys, the roof balustrade, the cornice-line modillions
and dentils. An art historian, she had taken up the cause of
architectural preservation immediately after the signing of the
Armistice; if still alive, she would have gladly signed letters
protesting her son's neglect of the Eliza Blackburn House.

His mother had lived to see her only grandson married
and her first great-grandchild born. She had adored Jenny
O'Keefe almost as much as Stephen had, even understood
her ambivalence about raising a family in the city and leaving her own father alone in Florida, coping with the lofty
expectations people had of anyone—including herself—
bearing the Blackburn name. "Being married to a Blackburn can be a devilish experience," she'd said.

Thomas shook off his daydreams and rang the doorbell
in Annette's gleaming, perfect entrance.

Nguyen Kim opened the door. Thomas had heard
about him from the neighbors and one of his student
boarders from the early 1980s, a Vietnamese refugee
studying at M.I.T. who had seen Kim on Mt. Vernon, and
he made her nervous. Probably, she said, Kim had saved
his own skin in 1975 without even considering the fate
of his countrymen.

Thomas inclined his head politely at the straight-backed Kim. "I'd like to speak with Annette."

"It's all right," the lady of the house said from within the large foyer. Kim quietly withdrew, and Annette came into the doorway. "Well, Thomas, it's been a long time. I was wondering if you'd show up. You might as well come in before the neighbors see you."

"They wouldn't give a damn. People don't care about what you do as much as you'd like to believe they do."

She feigned amusement. "Already lecturing me?"

"Just stating the facts."

"Go to hell," she said mildly.

Leaving the door open, she went into the formal parlor. Thomas assumed he was expected to follow and did. For the first time in more than a quarter-century, he really looked at Annette. Time had had its effect, but she was still a striking woman, more regal perhaps, more withdrawn. She'd been so high-spirited and deliberately unconventional as a girl, so adventurous and irrepressible as a young woman. If only she'd been more comfortable with who she was, if she could have applied her energies to building a company sooner. What if she hadn't been born to money, influence and rigid expectations? She could have founded a company like Winston & Reed, anyway. But perhaps not. Being born a Winston was just an excuse for the mistakes she'd made. As much fun as she'd been in her youth, Annette was selfish and self-absorbed, and one needn't be rich to have those faults.

Playing the polite hostess, she offered him sherry, but he shook his head. "You've turned into the kind of *grande dame* you always despised."

She shrugged. "People change. I've grown up, Thomas."

Opting not to go into the office today, she had put on

her gardening clothes and supposed she looked like any other frumpy Beacon Hill housewife. What did she care? Thomas knew her accomplishments; she didn't need to "dress for success" to prove herself to him. *I don't even need to prove myself to him—who the hell's he?* After a sleepless night, she had hoped a morning in the garden would allow her to think. Those damned pictures in *The Score* and Jean-Paul's ultimatum had shattered the fragile status quo that had existed in her life—in all their lives—for the past fourteen years. That Thomas Blackburn had chosen now of all times to invade her life wasn't unexpected; his timing was notorious.

Annette felt his incisive gaze on her as she sat on the edge of a Queen Anne sofa. Knowing her guard was standing in the hall, she said in a normal voice, "Kim—would you bring coffee, please?"

Thomas remained standing, looking rumpled and old. "Why did you let me in?"

She gave him a cool smile. "Would you believe pity?"

"No."

"Anyone else would. You're a broken old man, Thomas. You're right—I shouldn't worry if anyone saw you outside. People around here don't talk about you anymore. Most don't even realize you're still alive." She leaned back, wishing she could look as relaxed and unconcerned as he did. Yesterday had been a harrowing day. "No, Thomas, the only reason I let you into my house without a fight was to spare myself the torture of having to listen to whatever threat or promise you cooked up to get me to agree to have this conversation. So go ahead. What's this all about?"

"Jean-Paul's in town."

"Yes, I know."

Her answer was too abrupt, her voice too cold. Annette

didn't like that because it indicated Gerard's reappearance had disturbed her. She preferred to show Thomas Blackburn she was absolutely in control and unafraid, that *she* had the upper hand. Kim entered the room with an elaborate tray of coffee and warm scones, a pot of wild strawberry jam and whipped butter. He set it down on the antique table in front of her and poured two china cups, offering one to her guest first. Thomas accepted. With Annette served, Kim withdrew. As always, she appreciated his absolute discretion and efficiency.

With deliberate nonchalance, she sipped her coffee, set it down and pulled a needlepoint pillow onto her lap. She'd made it herself, painstakingly needlepointing a trailing arbutus—the Massachusetts state flower—in the center, another of those tiresome proper ladies' hobbies she'd taken up to fill the lonely hours of her semiretirement, when she wasn't undoing Quentin's mistakes at Winston & Reed.

Thomas went on, "He wants the Jupiter Stones, doesn't he?"

"Presumably. That, however, isn't my problem. I don't have them. I don't care whether or not you believe me, Thomas," she went on, "but I assure you if I had the damned things I'd have given them back to him years ago. They were a stupid bit of revenge for what he did to me. I had no idea he'd hold the grudge for thirty years."

"You ruined his life," Thomas pointed out.

"He ruined his own life."

"I suppose it depends on one's point of view. It must have come as an enormous shock to you to discover your twenty-four-year-old French lover was a jewel thief. How did you feel about turning him in?"

She ignored his half-sarcastic, half-critical tone. "I did what I had to do."

"Don't you always," Thomas said. "What went through that keen mind of yours when the police didn't catch him?"

"What do you think? I was afraid—"

"Afraid he'd come back for the Jupiter Stones? Afraid he'd come back for revenge?" Thomas seemed amused. He took just one sip of his coffee before setting it down. "No, Annette, you didn't consider the possible consequences of your actions—you were simply relieved. With Jean-Paul a fugitive, you wouldn't have to testify against him and risk having your affair made public. It's even possible," he went on, calm and arrogant, "that you helped him elude the police and get out of the country."

Annette laughed derisively, stretching one arm across the back of the sofa. "You think you're the only one, Thomas, honorable enough to risk the exposure of unpleasant personal facts. When I discovered Jean-Paul was *Le Chat,* I did the right thing. Why can't you give me any credit for that?"

"When one does something because it's right," he said, "one doesn't expect 'credit.'"

"You goddamned bastard—"

He smiled. "I thought you didn't care what I thought?"

Letting her stew, he turned to the beautiful marble fireplace and restored his own composure. Dealing with Annette Reed had never offered him much tranquility; she'd set him on edge since she was a little girl. He'd always prayed she would overcome her selfishness and insecurity—her exaggerated fear of making a mistake—and allow her carefree, daring and fun nature to emerge.

A photograph of Benjamin and Quentin on the mantel caught his eye. They'd been such a pair, that particular father and son. Both sensitive, both daring in their dreams, both tentative in life—not like Annette. She thrived on adventure and risk as a mask to her basic insecurity. In her youth, she'd had her affairs. In middle age, her company and her solitary life. What would she have become if Benjamin had lived?

And Quentin. Would his father have recognized his son's sensitivity and helped him come to terms with the positive aspects of his dreamy nature?

Thomas abruptly turned away from the photograph. What-ifs were among the worst forms of torture an old man suffered, he'd decided. Benjamin Reed had died when his son was ten and had left his young, self-absorbed widow to raise him alone.

It was done. So be it.

"I believe you," he told Annette, "when you say you don't have the Jupiter Stones, if for no other reason than if you did, you'd have stuffed them down Jean-Paul's throat and let him choke on them."

Annette leaned forward and spread a scone with jam. "You don't like me because I'm a powerful woman now and no longer give a damn what you think. You don't like strong women, do you?"

"My dear, if you'd been a man you'd be a powerful, selfish man instead of a powerful, selfish woman. Don't flatter yourself. There's no double standard at work here."

"Isn't there? How often are men accused of being selfish? Almost never. They're single-minded, devoted to their work, determined. It's women who are considered selfish."

"I don't deny what you say, Annette, but I've seen selfish men—and none of this excuses your behavior."

"What behavior? That I wasn't a gung-ho wife and mother?"

Thomas sighed. "You're making excuses, Annette, where there are none to make. No, you haven't been a good mother to Quentin—but you were a rotten parent long before you became chairman of Winston & Reed. Working or not working has nothing to do with your basic selfishness. You're a good businesswoman, but that doesn't make you immune from being responsible for your other failings. It wouldn't if you were a man."

"Get out of my house, Thomas." She threw down the scone, but was pleased to see her hands weren't shaking. "I don't have to listen to your insults and senile drivel."

"I don't want your feud with Jean-Paul harming anyone else. Do you understand that, Annette?" Thomas's heart was beating erratically again. *God help me from giving her the satisfaction of seeing how upset she still can make me.* He went on carefully, "As powerful and strong as you think you are, my dear, you don't respond well to personal pressure."

"And you do?" She sat back, hating him, but unable to pull her eyes from his aging figure. "Damn you to hell, Thomas, for thinking I want anyone hurt over this business with Jean-Paul. Yes, I'm sure he wants the Jupiter Stones. He must believe that silly woman Gisela's claim they were real, in which case they must be enormously valuable—a pity I misplaced them. But he knows I'd pay him to stay away from me. So it has to be more than a simple profit motive at work here, don't you think?"

"It makes no difference—"

"Not to you, I'm sure. I'm the one who turned him in and, as you say, ruined his life. Has it ever occurred to you that his conviction that I have those stones has kept him from coming after *me?* He doesn't just want the stones." She swallowed hard, looking for some way to make herself seem more composed, then gave up. "He wants revenge, Thomas. Don't you see that? As soon as he get the stones, he'll come after me."

I hope he does, Thomas thought, and he walked over to her, moving slowly and stiffly after his long day. Yet he could see from Annette's expression that she wasn't looking upon him as a man approaching eighty whose body was beginning to fail him. She was remembering their days together in Saigon, when Annette had wanted nothing more than for him to love her.

He leaned in close, so that she could see the yellow in his eyes, the wrinkles and the liver spots on his hands and face, the sagging skin, so that she could know that time, too, would catch up with her. He didn't give a damn about being old. He had seen too much death, was too close to it himself, to let it worry him. But aging, dying—they wouldn't sit well with Annette.

"Understand me, Mrs. Reed," he said coldly. "I don't care if Jean-Paul Gerard exposes you for what you are or even if he kills you. I only care that his obsession with the Jupiter Stones and your belief that you're worth saving at any cost don't spill over and ruin the lives of any more people I care about." He straightened up and simply refused to breathe hard. "I'll do what I can to keep him away from you—but not for your sake."

She suddenly looked like a petulant adolescent who wanted to stick her tongue out at him. "You're wrong about me, Thomas. *I've* suffered, as well—"

"You don't know what suffering is."

"I lost a husband because of your arrogance!"

"You see, Annette, you phrase everything in terms of yourself—you've suffered, you've lost. Suffering isn't just when you yourself are hurt. It's when someone you love is hurt. What's unfortunate, but obvious and probably unchangeable, is that you only love yourself."

She stuck her chin up at him. "Go to hell."

"Simply do as I ask." He gave her a nasty smile. "Think, my dear. What if after all these years I decided to talk?"

"Kim!"

The Vietnamese appeared immediately, but Thomas waved him off and walked himself out.

Annette splashed more coffee into her cup and gulped it down, her hands shaking violently. She should have shot Thomas. She had guns in the house. She'd learned how to use them—*would* use them. She should have filled him with lead and watched him bleed. Who was *he* to judge *her?*

No one would have blamed her for shooting him.

Poor Mrs. Reed, they would say, having to endure being accosted by that vile old loser who'd killed her husband.

Anyone else in her position would have shot him.

She'd loved Benjamin! And she loved her son. Quentin was her baby—

Ignoring Kim, she ran to her study and removed the Browning automatic from her desk drawer.

Thomas had left the front door open. She rushed out to the steps with her gun.

He was already gone.

"I hate you, Thomas Blackburn...*I hate you!*"

If only she believed it.

Twenty

A little before noon, Jared entered the unprepossessing building on Congress Street where Rebecca's studio was located. There was no building directory. He asked a scrawny, ink-covered man in a printing office for directions. "Fourth floor" was all he said, and that ungraciously. Not bothering to thank him, Jared took the creaking elevator and entertained himself by considering ways the building could be renovated, if the owner had the funds and the imagination for such a task. Even a few gallons of paint would do wonders.

The studio's entrance looked like something out of a Humphrey Bogart movie with its windowed door, black Gothic lettering and never-used brass mail slot. Jared peered through the milky, patterned glass, but he couldn't see much. There didn't seem to be any lights on inside. He knocked.

No answer. He wasn't surprised. Walking alone through the Public Garden and the streets of Back Bay had started him rehashing his conversations with Thomas and Rebecca Blackburn, trying to put pieces together. He had already known Thomas hadn't told him everything, but he hadn't expected the same from Rebecca. Not because she was any more forthcoming than her grandfather: being a Blackburn, she was naturally tight-lipped and outspoken, each when it suited her. The problem was, Jared hadn't anticipated her knowing anything *he* didn't already know. A stupid mistake on his part.

He fished out the set of keys he'd swiped from Rebecca's spartan room on West Cedar Street. He had guessed that she might be off on a mission of her own, but he was determined to check out her studio for anything that could lead him to the honest, *complete* answers neither she nor her grandfather would give him. Maybe he'd find something, maybe not. At least he was taking some kind of action and not just sitting around twiddling his thumbs or drinking Athena's overpowering coffee.

The third key he tried worked.

The studio was pure Rebecca Blackburn. Everything about the large, airy rooms suggested the woman who worked here was intense, exacting, high-energy and, more often than she should be, irreverent.

Nothing suggested she was anywhere near as rich as she was.

Jared flipped on the overhead lights. On a less gloomy day, there would be adequate sunlight from the huge paned industrial windows that looked out onto the street. It wasn't much of a view. Rebecca could have afforded the best views of the Boston skyline, the Rockies, the Alps, Central Park…San Francisco Bay. Whatever she wanted. But therein lay the contradictions that made Rebecca Blackburn not only a captivating, exciting woman, but also so hard to figure. Part of her wanted to have money and surround herself with the good things money could buy, to take pride in what her creative talents, business acumen and entrepreneurial drive had earned her. Jared could see that side of her in her choice of original prints for her walls, in her state-of-the-art equipment, in her quality pens and pencils and markers and all the other tools of her trade. In one corner, she had on display her many design awards and mementos of the game that had made her rich: the game board she'd made at eighteen for Sunday nights with Sofi and her grandfather, the original handcrafted game pieces, framed copies of the first Junk Mind poster.

He started with a cursory search of her flat files and reference library, not sure what he expected to find. He was momentarily distracted when he came across photographs of her five brothers, some with wives and children, and it bothered him that he couldn't tell who was who. He remembered the Blackburn boys as toddlers and little kids, but he didn't know them as men. Next to their pictures was a photo of Jenny and Stephen Blackburn on their wedding day. Jared, just four, had been the ring-bearer.

The elevator creaked down the hall. Jared wasn't worried about getting caught; he'd shut the door on his way in. But then he heard footsteps, saw R.J.'s silhouette in the translucent glass and knew there wasn't much way around it—he was going to scare the shit out of her.

Of course, he should have remembered with whom he was dealing.

Rebecca kicked open the door and said, "I should have you arrested, Sloan."

So much for scaring her. He eased down onto the stool at her light table and took note of the color in her cheeks, the load of papers in her arms, the way his heart started thumping when he saw her.

"How'd you know it was me?" he asked.

"Art."

"The printer?"

"He said some good-looking guy was asking for R. J. Blackburn. The good-looking I wouldn't know about, but you and Sofi're the only ones who still call me R.J. You pick my lock?"

He waved her keys at her. She snatched them out of his fingers. He said, "Your bedroom looks like an eight-year-old lives there—except for the Victoria's Secret underwear."

Spots of color appeared on her cheeks. "Nice of you to notice."

"How could I not?"

"You could have stayed out of my things," she snapped back, dropping her load of stuff onto her drawing table. "What were you looking for?"

He shrugged. R.J. had never been one for hypocrisy, and for that reason alone he'd never considered that she'd deliberately omit critical details—skirt the truth, in other words, if not out-and-out lie. Her last words to him at the hospital in Manila—and he'd always believed them—had been "Go on your way, Jared. I have nothing else to say to you."

Like hell, sweetheart.

He said, "I was looking for what you know about our guy from Saigon that you haven't told me."

She turned cool, a sure sign he had her. "Like what?"

"There, you see? That's not a direct lie, but it's not the truth, either. You know what. You talked to him."

"I told you that already. He was here yesterday—"

"And you said—and I quote—'I recognized him straight off as the Frenchman who shot you in Saigon.'"

She clamped her mouth shut.

Jared was losing patience. "You want to tell me how you knew he was French?"

"From his accent," she said, neatening up her stack of photocopied papers. "He said something that night after he shot you."

"What did he say?"

"I don't remember exactly."

"There you go again. You don't remember *exactly*. But I'll bet you remember generally what he said. Rebecca, I have a right to know!"

She inhaled deeply, controlling herself. "You're a fine one," she said, "to be talking about someone's rights."

He sprang to his feet and raked both hands through his hair in frustration and guilt, but couldn't think of a thing to say. Rebecca was on firm ground there, and she knew it.

"You've stayed out of Boston for fourteen years," she said, "but as soon as you spotted the Frenchman outside your house, you flew here and went straight to my grandfather. Why?"

"You'll have to talk to him about that, not me." Jared studied her a moment, and he had to admit that she was as maddeningly captivating as she'd been at nineteen. His curse to notice, he supposed. "Believe it or not, R.J., I didn't punch that guy on the motorcycle just so I could mess up your life. Thank your grandfather for me." He sighed; obviously he wasn't going to get anywhere with either Blackburn. And what right did he have to involve them in his problems? "I won't be staying on West Cedar Street tonight."

He felt her eyes on him as he headed for the door, and he wondered what words he'd put in her mouth if he could. *Stay…I'll tell you everything, Jared…I've thought about you a lot over the years….*

Definitely time to back out of her life.

"Have you seen Grandfather yet today?" she asked.

Jared pulled open the door. "He came down a few minutes after you left and said we ought to head to San Francisco."

Rebecca's smile surprised him. "He didn't recommend Budapest to you?"

In spite of himself, Jared grinned. "No—I think he must have decided San Francisco's more romantic."

And he left before he started saying things he had no business saying and forgetting how mad he was at Thomas Blackburn and his rich, beautiful and totally unfathomable granddaughter.

Rebecca resisted the temptation to follow Jared only because she had work to do. Not design work; she'd already given up any illusions of drumming up clients today. A couple of hours at the Boston Public Library had netted her a biography of Empress Elisabeth that mentioned the Jupiter Stones, a couple of articles on the Côte d'Azur robberies in 1959 that Rebecca photocopied and stuck in a file folder and stacks of information on her grandfather and his downfall. She checked out what she could and copied what she couldn't and carted it all back to her studio to go through in privacy.

A 1963 article from *Time* was on top of her pile. There were pictures of Thomas Blackburn as a Harvard professor in 1938; in Saigon in 1961 with his Vietnamese friend, the popular mandarin scholar Quang Tai; in Boston in 1963 at the funeral of his only child. This last picture also showed Stephen Blackburn's penniless young widow surrounded by their six children at his graveside. They all looked exhausted and still in the grip of grief and shock. It was a photograph Rebecca had never seen until that morning. As far as she knew, her mother had never bothered with any of the news pieces probing the tragedy. She'd certainly never mentioned them.

Steeling herself, Rebecca began to read.

The Winston & Reed Building on the Boston waterfront was one of the best of Wesley Sloan's timeless designs. Jared was impressed. He had never seen the finished building, but found that models and photographs didn't do it justice. His father was a hell of an architect, but that didn't make Jared itch to join his firm and design skyscrapers himself. He was content working out of his one-man studio behind his house on Russian Hill.

Still smarting from his encounter with Rebecca, he entered the luxurious lobby and took the elevator to the thirty-ninth floor. He had no idea what he'd say to his cousin Quentin. *The child that could have been yours is a great kid and I'm not going to let anything happen to her.*

At least it was a start.

Being a Sloan, he got past the receptionist with no trouble and almost got past Willa Johnson, Quentin's secretary. But her boss had just gotten in, he wasn't having the best of days, and Jared couldn't just walk in, cousin or not, without her checking first.

She checked. Quentin, it seemed, had no desire to see his cousin Jared.

"I'm sorry," Willa said, as if that ended the matter.

It didn't. Jared commented that he was sorry, too, and marched past her to Quentin's office. He could hear her calling security, but that didn't trouble him. Without hesitating, he pushed open the heavy walnut door.

"Call off the dogs, cousin."

Quentin looked so pathetic Jared almost took pity on him. Then Mai's face came to him. He could see her stubborn pout when he'd said goodbye to her in Tiberon, and he could hear her saying "Oh, Daddy" in that way she had, as if he was the biggest idiot who'd ever lived.

And Tam's face came to him. So trusting and innocent even as it crumpled in pain and horror when the first of the assassin's bullets struck her. And Rebecca's face, pale with shock, defeat, betrayal.

Jared had no pity for Quentin Reed.

"Jared—" Quentin's voice cracked under the strain of seeing his cousin for the first time since Tam's death. In his business suit and huge, elegant office with its stunning harbor view, he looked out of place, like a little boy dressing up in his father's clothes and playing boss. He cleared his throat and pushed back his executive's leather chair. He didn't get up. "Jared, it's good to see you, but I can't visit right now. I wish you hadn't barged in here like this."

Jared moved in closer, noting how awful his cousin looked. "What's got you so scared? It can't just be seeing me again. Has a certain white-haired man with a scar running from one end of his face to the other been to see you, as well? Come on, Quentin. Call off security and let's talk."

"None of this concerns you."

"He was at my house and that concerns me."

Quentin jumped to his feet, but didn't seem to know what to do with himself once he was standing. He shoved his hands in his pants pockets, then pulled them out. He looked out his bank of windows, then swung back around to face Jared, as if he thought his cousin might decide to shoot him in the back.

"Talk to me, Quentin," Jared said, holding back his anger and frustration.

Quentin drew himself up straight. "I have nothing to say to you. You were the one who walked out on your family.

If you think you can just strut back in here and call the shots—well, you're wrong."

Jared shook his head in disbelief. "You know, for years I felt a little sorry for you. You lost a father who had faith in you and were stuck with a mother who didn't—"

"My mother has faith in me."

"Think what you want to think. I'm just telling you what *I* thought. I quit feeling sorry for you when we were in Saigon together and you used Tam."

"I loved her!"

"Right—sure, you loved her. Then why didn't you marry her?"

"Because of you, Jared," Quentin said, as if that should have been obvious. He sounded pained and so sorrowful, Jared briefly wondered if he might be wrong, but he'd learned a long time ago that Quentin believed what he wanted to believe. He went on in that same pathetic tone, "You were the father of her baby. I would have come back for her, but Tam didn't want me. She wanted you. How could I have married her when she didn't love me?"

The arrival of two beefy security guards spared Jared having to answer. They called him sir and were very polite about it, but they didn't take his word for it that he was leaving. With a nod from their chickenshit boss, they took him to the elevator, stuffed him inside and joined him for the ride down to the lobby. Then they escorted him outside and mentioned they'd be keeping an eye out should he decide to bother Mr. Reed again.

Jared glanced back as he crossed the plaza in front of Winston & Reed, where tulips were closed up in the gloom and pedestrians weren't lingering today, and he saw the two beefs posted at the door.

He gave them a mock salute.

And then got out of there, fast.

* * *

Quentin fled into his private bathroom, splashed cold water on his face and shook unscented cornstarch powder into his armpits and down his back, hoping it would absorb the sweat pouring off him. First Jean-Paul Girard, now Jared. Jesus, next thing Tam's ghost would walk into his office and point her finger at him and demand to know why he'd killed her.

You can't think like that!

"Oh, Tam," he sobbed, sinking his face into his hotel-weight hand towel. "Tam, Tam…whatever happened to us?"

Forcing himself at least to feign calm, he dried his face and returned to his office, informing Willa he didn't want to be disturbed. If she didn't feel capable of monitoring his calls and visitors, she should commence finding a replacement at once. Ever the professional, Willa didn't bore him with excuses.

Then he dialed his mother's Mt. Vernon Street number and held his breath until she answered. Even her hello sounded strong and ever-capable. Quentin felt tears spring to his eyes. Why did he always have to be the one to fall apart?

"Mother, it's me," he said, and he could hear how small and inconsequential he sounded. "I wanted to tell you…I thought you should know Jared's back in town."

Annette didn't miss a beat. "How wonderful," she said with heavy sarcasm. "So's your blackmailer from Saigon."

Quentin's heart pounded; he was sure he'd faint. He couldn't speak.

"Charming individual, isn't he?" his mother went on. "Has he been to see you?"

"Mother—"

"Quentin, please, don't try my patience. We both know

what you did in Saigon. You were a fool and we've had to suffer for your mistakes. But that's in the past. What I care about is *now*. We must be sensible and think about how we can resolve this situation to our advantage."

Ever since he'd been a little boy, Annette had always been able to see through him. No wonder she despised him.

"He's been to see you?" she repeated.

"Yes." Why lie?

"I assumed he would, sooner or later. And Jared?"

Quentin licked his lips, but his tongue was dry. He wished he hadn't called, wished he had the fortitude to tell his mother to go to hell and hang up. Instead he said, "He's afraid for Mai, I think."

"What a fool. Well, he's not our problem."

"Gerard—he said he wants a collection of sapphires you have."

Annette sighed. "Yes, I know."

"What are they?"

"It doesn't matter. I don't have them—"

"He insists you do."

"He can insist whatever he likes, but he's wrong. And at this point, Quentin, I'm afraid even if I did have them they wouldn't be enough."

She suddenly sounded very tired, and Quentin hated himself for taking pleasure in even this limited sign of weakness. He didn't mind strong women. *Jane* was strong. Tam had been, as well, in a different way. Why did his mother's strength bother him so much?

Finally, Annette said, "The sapphires aren't really what Jean-Paul Gerard's after."

"Then what is?"

She answered, almost to herself, "I am."

Twenty-One

Thomas Blackburn stared through the tall, paned windows of the Congregational Library reading room, gazing down at the Old Granary Burying Ground. Benjamin Franklin's parents were buried there, and the victims of the Boston Massacre and Eliza Blackburn. Back in 1892, the Congregational Association had deliberately chosen the 14 Beacon Street site behind the old graveyard for their new building to assure those who used the private library would enjoy peace and tranquility long into the future. Their foresightedness had proven worthwhile.

A squirrel scurried along the second-floor fire escape and hopped into one of the huge trees that shaded Old Granary, a perennial tourist favorite. Thomas could remember going to Eliza's grave with his father, and taking Stephen for his first visit when he was five or six, and then Rebecca and Nate during one of his rare home leaves in 1960. Jenny had called him a ghoul and had confiscated the children's charcoal rubbing of their famous ancestor's headstone. Rubbings had since been outlawed, due to the damage they caused the stones.

Thomas considered the reading room, with its original Tiffany ceiling, Persian rugs, fireplace and eighteenth-century portraits of famous churchmen, one of Boston's great hidden treasures. The library itself was primarily a theological library, but it was also well-known for its substantial historical holdings, obtained by virtue of the Congregationalists having run the Commonwealth of Massachusetts until disestablishment in 1831. Thomas came to the library often, if, at times, only to think.

As today.

It seemed he was never without his memories, and the older he got the more vivid they became. Gisela, Benjamin, Quang Tai...his wife, Emily; his son, Stephen. In the night when sleep eluded him, he would often wander in the garden among the shadows, talking to the friends and family he'd lost. He would explain, apologize, cry. They never answered, but left him alone in his anguish. He didn't blame them. What was there to say?

If only he hadn't been such a fool.

He could torture himself with hypothetical situations. Sometimes he did. He would see their faces with such stark vividness, and remember how they'd trusted and believed in him. Emily when, clinging to him, she would tell him her fears of childbirth, and he would reassure her that everything would be all right. It hadn't been. Gisela, his friend, who'd wept on his shoulder in her despondency over the loss of her Jupiter Stones. He had made cavalier assurances to her, as well.

Stephen, Benjamin, Quang Tai. All dead because Thomas Blackburn had insisted nothing would happen to them in that part of the Mekong Delta.

It was true, he thought. He held himself responsible for

his own son's death, a solitary burden no parent should have to bear.

He never let on to anyone the measure of his despair, of course. The sleepless nights, the agonizing walks, the countless times he would find himself drained and exhausted, perspiring and trembling like one of those stereotypical bony old men. He wanted no one's pity. Even in those terrible moments of despair, the prospect of not carrying on never occurred to him. He would never give in, if for no other reason than to be there should anyone else have to suffer for his mistakes.

"Grandfather?"

The squirrel had scrambled back onto the fire escape and was teasing another thinner squirrel. Thomas watched for a few seconds, composing himself before he turned to this granddaughter. He had left a note at the house telling where he was. Another mistake?

Looking pale and unusually serious, Rebecca held up a paper bag. "I brought sandwiches. You haven't had lunch yet?"

"No. Rebecca, something's wrong—"

"Can we eat in back?"

They went back to the stacks, where they unwrapped their sandwiches at an oak table library volunteers could use. Thomas often worked in the climate-controlled rare books room. He poured a couple of cups of coffee and sat across from Rebecca.

"You're looking grim," he told her.

"I've spent the better part of the last two hours reading old articles on the ambush." She didn't need to specify which ambush; they both knew. "I discovered several coincidences that are too much for me to swallow."

He gave her a mild look, but it felt as if something hot

and sharp had just been stabbed into his lower abdomen. "Did you?"

Her eyes seemed huge in the dim light; she didn't smile. "The driver of the Jeep that day was a Frenchman, a former member of the Foreign Legion. He was the only survivor, but he was believed captured by the Vietcong. I couldn't find his name or anything about what happened to him." She paused, then added bitterly, "I gather, though, that he's still alive."

Thomas pushed aside his sandwich, roast beef with lots of red onion; he wouldn't have blamed Rebecca if she'd sprinkled arsenic over the works. "Are you asking me what I know about him?"

"I'm not finished. I did some more digging, Grandfather, and I discovered an old 1959 photograph from the *Boston Globe*. It was taken during the trip you and I took to France. I was just four, so I don't remember much of what we did. But one of the things you did was show up at the funeral of Baroness Gisela Majlath."

She paused to assess Thomas's reaction to her dramatic announcement, but he'd had many, many years to perfect his ability to maintain his composure under the most trying of circumstances. The only reason the *Globe* had bothered running that photograph was because he was in it.

"For someone who never completed her college education," he said, "your research abilities are impressive. Of course, most research simply requires tenacity, and you certainly have that, Rebecca."

"Gisela committed suicide."

"Yes, I know." He breathed out, his memory of that dreadful day still fresh. "She was a friend of mine."

Rebecca was obviously restraining herself. "You never mentioned her."

"I had a great many friends I've never mentioned to you. I am a good deal older than you are, my dear. My friendship with Gisela was a quiet one."

Her eyes flashed. "What's that supposed to mean?"

"You're being impertinent."

"*Impertinent* is one of those words that went out with Calvin Coolidge."

"I knew Calvin in his later years—"

"Grandfather, Gisela Majlath claimed to have been a victim of a jewel thief called *Le Chat.*"

Thomas picked a bit of onion from his sandwich and nibbled on it. "Why is it," he said rhetorically, "that when the young stumble upon something new to them they assume no one else could possibly have known about it before they did? Yes, Gisela told the police this *Le Chat* stole some gems that had come into her family—"

"The Jupiter Stones."

The woman was annoyingly thorough. "Correct."

"And no one believed her, so she threw herself into the Mediterranean."

"Baldly put, but apparently, also correct."

"Apparently?"

"I wasn't there."

She digested that for a moment, then asked, "Do you want to tell me about *Le Chat?*"

"Why should I?" he replied testily. "Obviously we both already know."

Rebecca was so rigid, Thomas thought she would crack and crumble any second. "The police were going to arrest a popular Grand Prix driver named Jean-Paul Gerard as *Le Chat,* but he disappeared."

"And you're assuming he turned up in Vietnam in 1963 and again in 1975."

"I know he did." Rebecca swallowed, still working at controlling herself. "I found an old photograph of Gerard in his racing days. Turn his hair white and add some scars and we've got our Frenchman."

Thomas stared up at the milky glass flooring of the stacks. He hated this kind of deception. And for years he'd dreaded precisely this confrontation with his granddaughter. "Rebecca, you've done enough digging," he said. "Now stop. Drop this before you end up getting yourself or someone else hurt. Yes, Jean-Paul Gerard drove the Jeep when your father, Benjamin and Tai were killed in 1963. He was captured and spent five years in a jungle prisoner-of-war camp before escaping during the Tet Offensive in 1968. He's the Frenchman who participated in Tam's killing in 1975."

"And he blames you for what happened to him?"

"Undoubtedly."

Rebecca inhaled, an obvious act of self-control. "Has he been to see you?"

"Not yet. I haven't seen Jean-Paul in twenty-six years."

Her gaze was ice. "Lucky you."

Thomas shrugged. What could he say? He and Rebecca had never really talked about 1963. If he had his way, they never would. An uncomfortable silence descended between them. The two sandwiches and coffee remained untouched.

Finally, Rebecca asked, "You knew who I was talking about when I described this Jean-Paul Gerard yesterday, but you didn't mention him."

"Correct."

"Why not?"

"What would have been the point?"

She didn't answer. "What have you told Jared that you haven't told me?"

"Nothing. Rebecca, Jean-Paul Gerard was a bitter and dangerous man *before* his captivity. I can only imagine what he's like now. You should do everything you can to avoid him. That's all you need to know."

"Are you protecting me," she said angrily, "or yourself?"

Thomas rose, neither hurt nor insulted, simply determined to have his way—and that didn't include defending himself to his furious granddaughter. "I'm doing what I feel I must. If that's insufficient for you, you'll have to decide for yourself what to do about it. I've given you my advice. Now if you'll excuse me, I'm not terribly hungry."

Neither was Rebecca. She threw down her sandwich and watched her grandfather return to the reading room. The Frenchman—this Jean-Paul Gerard—had been a jewel thief and race-car driver on the Riviera in 1959. He had driven the Jeep the day of the 1963 ambush that had left Quang Tai, Benjamin Reed and Stephen Blackburn dead.

Twelve years later, Gerard had shot Jared Sloan in Saigon.

Now, fourteen years later, he had turned up in San Francisco and Boston.

Why?

Was there a connection among 1959, 1963 and 1975?

Yes: him. One Jean-Paul Gerard.

And the Blackburn family. Thomas Blackburn had attended the funeral of one of Gerard's robbery victims. He had arranged the trip into the Mekong Delta. His son—another Blackburn—had been killed. And, in 1975, Rebecca Blackburn had saved Mai Sloan and gotten her, Jared and herself out of Saigon.

Along with the Jupiter Stones. She mustn't forget those. Were they another connection?

"I was your father's friend, and I believe—I know he would have been proud of you."

But how could a man like Jean-Paul Gerard and Stephen Blackburn have been friends?

Giving up on her sandwich, Rebecca wrapped up the leftovers, stuck both sandwiches in a small refrigerator and went after her grandfather.

The woman at the front desk said he'd just left. "You can probably catch him."

"He didn't say where he was headed?"

"No. A friend of his had just come in, and they went off together."

Sloan. "Tall, dark hair, good-looking?"

"Oh, no. This one had very white hair and quite a scar—"

Rebecca ran.

The sun, breaking through the clouds, glistened on the rain-soaked lawn in front of the Massachusetts State House. Thomas held his umbrella in his left hand, using it as a sort of cane as he studied Jean-Paul Gerard. War and time—and his own stubbornness—had left him ravaged and old and mean, a shadow of the carefree, daredevil young race-car driver he'd been thirty years ago. Thomas didn't find it easy to look at a man who'd suffered as much, and as needlessly, as had this relentless Frenchman. Yet he still could see Gisela in the soft brown of the younger man's eyes, in the shape and sensitivity of his mouth, and he wondered if he was being too harsh or if, at least, there was hope.

"I want him to be happy, Thomas," Gisela had said. "That's all I've ever wanted."

She had been so proud of her only child. Nevertheless—and Thomas had never understood why—she had persisted in her refusal to acknowledge him as her son. She maintained that Jean-Paul preferred to shroud himself in

mystery, pretending that he'd come from nowhere and letting people—women, especially—fantasize about his
origins. It was a part of his mystique. That he was the illegitimate son of a popular woman who claimed she was
a displaced Hungarian aristocrat certainly would have had
its romantic side. Only after they were both gone, Gisela
to her grave and Jean-Paul to Sidi Bel Abbès and the *Légion
étrangère* as a fugitive, did Thomas consider that it was
perhaps Jean-Paul who was protecting his mother, not the
other way around. For the popular young Frenchman had
to have known that telling the world he was Gisela's son
would have stimulated a scrutiny to which her life couldn't
have stood up.

"You're an old man now, Thomas," Jean-Paul said with
unmistakable satisfaction. "Are you starting to smell the
dirt in your grave?"

"I don't believe I'm as old as you yourself are, Jean-
Paul. You've had a hard life. I'm sorry." He added softly,
"Gisela never wanted that."

"Don't give me your pity, old man."

"Consider it commentary, not pity." Thomas felt himself
tiring already and put more weight on his old, sturdy
umbrella. "She won't give you the stones, will she?"

Jean-Paul's eyes—so suspicious now when once they'd
been eager, trusting, filled with an unshakable zest for
life—narrowed as he considered Thomas's words. "I
haven't even seen her."

"I don't believe you, Jean-Paul," Thomas said quietly,
giving him a small, sympathetic smile. "You've never been
an adept liar. Perhaps if you'd recognized this many years
ago you'd have saved yourself—and others—a good deal
of anguish."

"And you? Think of all the anguish you'd have saved if

you'd thrown yourself into the Mediterranean thirty years ago instead of Gisela."

Thomas looked at him. "I have."

Jean-Paul clenched his fists at his side. "I want the Jupiter Stones, old man. Nothing more. They belonged to Gisela, and I intend to get them back. Don't try and stop me."

"You can't beat her. You of all people should know that."

"I'm not trying to beat her."

"You're playing with fire," Thomas said, his tone deceptively mild. Seldom had he been so serious. "You played with fire thirty years ago and got burned, and now you're doing it again. It's time to forget those stones and move on."

The Frenchman inhaled slowly, his eyes never leaving the older man, then he tried a new tactic. "Annette says she doesn't have them."

Thomas shrugged. "Perhaps she's telling the truth."

"She's not," Jean-Paul said softly. "She doesn't know what the truth is. But I didn't come for your approval of my actions. I know Jared Sloan is in Boston, and so is your granddaughter. Tell them to stay out of my way. And you, too. Let me do what I have to do."

"Jean-Paul—" Thomas sighed, breaking off. He put out a hand to the younger man, but Gerard stepped backward, as if afraid of any perceptibly amiable gesture. "I've made terrible mistakes. I've been arrogant and unthinking, but like you, I never thought my decisions would have negative consequences. Jean-Paul, be better than I was."

"Go back to your books, old man. I've said all I intend to say."

"I'll stop you if I must," Thomas said in a low voice.

The Frenchman laughed, a sandpapery sound in which his years of suffering resonated more plainly than any threat. "You go ahead and try."

Leaving Thomas on the sidewalk in front of the State House, Jean-Paul trotted back across Beacon Street and onto Boston Common, disappearing in the shadows as the clouds once again closed over the sun. Drops of rain landed on Thomas's nose and cheeks. He started to put up his umbrella, but discovered his knees were trembling and he needed its support for walking. With the rain increasing, he debated a moment, then headed inside the State House and down a quiet hall to the portrait of Eliza Blackburn. She looked rather like Rebecca. Thomas felt his eyes burning with fatigue and raw emotion as first he studied Eliza's face, then the cameo brooch George Washington had given the plucky Revolutionary War heroine; the brooch itself was now on display at a museum in Concord.

"Well, Eliza," he whispered hoarsely, "I've made a fine mess of the Blackburn name, haven't I?"

He thought he could see her smile, hear her whisper back to him, "All for a good cause, my son." But of course he knew that was impossible. They were only the words he wished he could hear, from someone, but never would.

Jean-Paul was out of breath by the time he reached the Park Street subway station on the Tremont Street side of the Common. He slowed down, wheezing and totally disgusted with himself. In his two years with the *Légion étrangère,* he'd been able to run ten miles without getting winded, carry a seventy-pound load on his back for days, drink all day and screw all night, and the next morning spot a spider on a roof a half-mile off. His acute vision had been the envy of his fellow soldiers and had contributed to his skill as a marksman. Even after his five years as a prisoner of war, when he'd suffered malnutrition, isolation and severe brutality, he could see better than most, if not as well as he once could.

"Hello. It's Jean-Paul Gerard, isn't it?"

He whirled around and saw Rebecca Blackburn standing too close behind him, her face drained of color.

"I followed you," she said. "I saw you and my grandfather talking."

Jean-Paul found himself wanting to touch her, not in any romantic, sexual way, but as the child she'd been in picture after picture Stephen Blackburn had shown him on hot, lonely nights in Saigon. He couldn't bring himself to speak.

"What were you and my grandfather talking about?"

"About how foolish you would be to stay after me," Jean-Paul said quietly.

Rebecca gave him a cool look, her cheeks regaining their color. "You were in the Mekong Delta with my father when he died."

So she knew. Jean-Paul all at once felt very tired and not nearly as confident in his purpose as he had. Perhaps he should have left *The Score* in the newsstand and remained in Honolulu.

Rebecca eyed him with impatience. "And you're a jewel thief."

But her voice quavered, and she hesitated, suddenly looking frightened when he took another step toward her. He could see how very blue her eyes were, how dark the lashes, how creamy her skin. Just knowing she was in Boston should have been enough to keep him away. Wherever he went, he brought agony and death. Perhaps Thomas Blackburn was right; he would never win.

"Stay away from me," he told Stephen Blackburn's beautiful daughter. She paid no attention to the rain pelting on her chestnut hair and soaking her blouse. He could see the clear outline of her breasts under the wet fabric. He put out a hand, as Thomas had to him, and didn't blame her when she drew back. And he said, "I'll only hurt you."

She raised her squarish chin. "I'm not afraid of you."

"Perhaps you should be."

As she considered his remark and her own response, Jean-Paul suddenly understood that this wasn't a woman who discouraged easily. She would keep coming and coming and coming until she'd found answers. She had spotted him talking with her grandfather and followed him onto the Common, a reckless act considering how little she really knew about him. He would have to be more alert.

"I'm not going to be put off," she told him.

"Then you're a fool."

He drew back one hand and before she could react, he cuffed her hard on the side of the head. He kept his expression grim and menacing, forcing himself not to grimace as her eyes widened in shock and pain and she staggered backward.

Around them, people backed off.

Blood spurted from Rebecca's mouth and it might have been Jean-Paul's own for the pain he felt.

She didn't scream. She put one hand up in front of her face in belated self-defense, but Jean-Paul couldn't bring himself to strike her again. Instead he moved very fast to make certain that few onlookers witnessed what he'd done. Another blow and someone would call the police.

"Stay away from me," he said through gritted teeth, and fled into the Tremont Street traffic. Horns blared, brakes screeched. He wouldn't have cared if a car hit him. Picking up his pace, ignoring the ripping pain in his chest, Jean-Paul darted down a side street.

* * *

On the Common, Rebecca broke away from the crowd that had gathered around her and ran hard through the rain, trying to catch up with Gerard. She wanted to ask him about the Jupiter Stones—to give them to him if they were what he wanted. Then he could take the stones and go off and leave them all alone.

But she'd lost him.

She brushed one hand at the blood that had dribbled from her cut lip down her chin. She ended up smearing it, probably making her injury look worse than it was. How dramatic. Her head throbbed and she felt stupid. She finally gave up on finding the Frenchman among the lunchtime crowds and headed back up to Beacon Hill. She thought of her grandfather and his refusal to talk to her, Jared Sloan and his, of Jean-Paul Gerard and his. And for the first time in her life, Rebecca though she understood why intelligence-gathering organizations had invented truth serums.

Twenty-Two

~∽⊙∽~

Jean-Paul.

Jared.

Quentin.

Former lover, nephew, son. And Thomas. What was he? Annette remembered when she'd thought he was everything to her.

She hoped if she could put them out of her mind she could assemble the scattered fragments of her thoughts into a coherent plan. But it was one of those things that was easier said than done, and she thought perhaps digging in the dirt—physical labor—would help. Sitting around waiting for things to happen was against her nature. She wasn't a passive woman.

At the first break in the rain she went back out to the garden and was on her hands and knees pulling weeds in the soft, damp soil at a raised bed when she heard footsteps on the terrace behind her. Anticipating an unpleasant encounter with Jean-Paul or Quentin, she braced herself.

"Hello, Aunt Annette."

She rolled back onto her hands and forced a smile. "Why, Jared, what a surprise."

He was one of those rare men with the capacity to see through her subterfuges and false civilities. It was just as well he'd gone to live in San Francisco. He said skeptically, "Quentin didn't warn you I was in town?"

"He mentioned it," she said, rising. "I wouldn't call it a warning."

Jared said nothing.

Peeling off her lambskin gardening gloves, Annette wished she'd gone into her office today, after all. She'd have avoided that unpleasant confrontation with Thomas, and she'd have been around when Jared had barged into Quentin's office. She didn't care about protecting her son against his cousin. She simply preferred that her first encounter with her handsome nephew in more than a dozen years didn't occur here in her garden, where she always felt so damned frumpy.

"I'm going to have to look into tighter security," she said. "It seems my excitement these days stems from wondering who might wander onto my property. It's been a long time, Jared. I was under the impression that you'd never come back to Boston."

His teal eyes—his father's eyes—bored through her. "Because you ordered me not to?"

She checked her irritation. Even as a little boy Jared had had an annoying capacity to cut through the nonsense. She feigned amusement. "As if you've ever listened to my or anyone else's 'orders.'" She climbed to her feet, noting that Jared didn't offer her a hand. "I recall I simply expressed my concern and disappointment that you'd had an affair with a Vietnamese woman and fathered an illegitimate child with her."

"Let's not rehash the past," Jared said tightly. "And let's not pretend we're happy to see each other."

"As you wish."

Annette walked across the terrace to her garden table and whisked off the plastic cover and left it to drip over one of the chairs. "So, Jared," she said, gesturing to one of the chairs. "Sit down and let's get caught up with one another. The sun seems to have come out for a bit, and I'm due a break."

She sat down herself, brushing loose dirt from the knees of her khaki pants. She was dressed casually, but expensively, in a yellow cotton shirt with the sleeves rolled up to the elbows, tan poplin pants and dusty tennis shoes without socks. She wasn't wearing makeup, and with her hair coming out of its pins, Jared saw echoes of the free-spirited woman Annette Winston Reed had been in her youth. But tragedy, the pressures and responsibilities of business and her own unyielding view of her place in the world had brought a weariness, even a hardness, to her mouth and eyes.

Jared relented and sat across from her. "I'm in town because the pictures in *The Score*—I assume you've seen them—brought the man who shot me in Saigon out of the woodwork."

"Really? How unfortunate." Annette gave him a sympathetic look. "But whatever would that have to do with Boston?"

So innocent. *Too* innocent. "You've known all along about Quentin's involvement with the drug smugglers in Saigon—"

"Oh, Jared, honestly. I can't believe you're that naive. Quentin was a rich, vulnerable young man who allowed himself to be framed for something he didn't do. The easiest course of action was for him to come home, which is what he did. If you think that has anything to do with this man who shot you, you're dead wrong."

Her directness, her confidence, her absolute certainty that she was right weren't easy to ignore. Her tone alone was enough to make Jared wonder if he were being an idiot. *Had* Gerard framed Quentin?

He was about to pursue the subject when Rebecca landed on the terrace from the carriageway.

Jared went rigid at the sight of her.

Her hair, wet and tangled, hung in her face, and blood was smeared on her swollen cheek. She was pale and shaking, but her matchless eyes were blazing, fired with determination.

And Jared knew then—even as he slid to his feet to ask her what the hell had happened—that it'd be another fourteen years before he'd have the slightest hope of forgetting her.

She pulled out a chair, hard, but didn't sit down. "Hi, there, Mrs. Reed."

"Rebecca," Annette said regally. "What on earth—"

"I'm fine."

Jared didn't take his eyes off her. She was breathing hard and obviously in pain, but he held back.

"Don't look so grim," she told the chairman of Winston & Reed. "If you hadn't had Quentin fire me, I'd be so busy working on your company's new graphic identity I wouldn't have time to poke around in the library, get beat up, come around and pester you—stuff like that."

Annette inhaled. "That's unfair."

"Maybe. Maybe not. You can answer some questions." She didn't look at Jared. "Let's begin with 1963. A man— a mercenary who'd been with the Foreign Legion—was driving the Jeep the day of the ambush. Know anything about him?"

"Why should I? Rebecca—"

"He's French. Vietnam was a French colony for a hundred years. You have a house in France."

"Let's get some ice for that bruise," Annette said. "I recall hearing something about the French driver, but as for knowing him…no, I don't think so. Yes, I have a house on the Riviera and spent some time in Vietnam myself, but I hardly know *every* Frenchman who was there. Jared— the refrigerator's in the same place as always. Would you mind?"

He didn't move. Something had happened, and he had to get Rebecca out of there—but carefully. She looked ready to explode. "Sure," he said, going easy.

"I don't need ice," Rebecca said.

"R.J.—"

"I'm not sure what people around here aren't telling me or why, or whether it'd make any difference if I knew what it was. But something's not right here, and never has been, and I'm going to keep digging and pissing people off until I find out what really happened to my father and then to Tam. And if there's anything that needs to be fixed in the record, I'm going to fix it."

Bravo for you, sweetheart, Jared thought, surprising himself, when Rebecca, white-faced and hoarse, finished.

Annette regarded the younger woman with placid amusement. Jared had always believed his aunt blamed not just Thomas Blackburn for the ambush that killed her husband, but Stephen Blackburn, as well, for having been Benjamin's friend, for having invited him along that day— just for being a Blackburn.

"Rebecca," she said, "I have no idea what's happened

to you or what you're hinting at, but there's no conspiracy of silence. Nevertheless—do what you have to do. The Blackburns always do, you know." Her gaze turned cold. "And it's the innocents like myself who suffer."

"If it's one thing you aren't," Rebecca said, rising, "it's innocent."

"Cheeky words from Thomas Blackburn's granddaughter. Frankly, I don't know how you can stand to be around him knowing he as much as killed your own father." Annette drank some lemonade, adding coolly, "Of course, that's none of my affair."

"That's enough," Jared said in a low voice.

His aunt's fierce gaze landed on him. "I'll not be told what to do in my own house. I suggest you take Rebecca home and see to her."

Without a word, Rebecca about-faced, going out the way she'd come.

Jared caught up with her jumping down from the carriageway's picturesque wrought-iron gate, the quickest way off his aunt's property. They used to have races climbing over it when they were kids. She landed neatly on her feet.

"R.J., wait for me—I'll be right over."

She pretended not to hear him. She hit the sidewalk and picked up her pace.

Jared hoisted himself up and over the fence, not with the abandon and speed he had at ten. He was so busy trying to keep Rebecca in sight that he landed awkwardly and subjected quiet Mt. Vernon Street to a string of blunt curses.

Rebecca had reached the intersection of West Cedar Street when he grabbed her by the upper arm and pulled her around to face him. "Whoa, there," he said. "Come on, R.J., what's going on?"

"Nothing."

Her eyes were shining and the swelling on her cheek and lip looked sore, if not as bad as he'd originally thought. He touched a spot of dried blood with one finger. "R.J.—" He tried to stop himself but couldn't—didn't want to. He dropped his hand from her arm to her fingers, catching them in his, squeezing them lightly. "I'm not your enemy, R.J. Who hit you?"

She shut her eyes. She didn't trust herself. Jared seemed so solid and strong that suddenly all she wanted was for him to hold her. She was sick of being alone, sick of wandering, sick of a lifetime of half truths and secrets.

"R.J.," Jared repeated, "who hit you?"

She looked at him. "The man from Saigon. The Frenchman."

He could feel his expression hardening. "I should have shot him when I had the chance."

"No, it's more complicated than that. His name's Jean-Paul Gerard. God knows what all he's done, but he didn't just shoot you in Saigon in 1975. I thought you saw everything. All these years I thought you knew."

Jared froze. "Knew what?"

"He saved my life. And Mai's."

Twenty-Three

⁓⟡⟡⟡⁓

From the first moment Jared saw Mai bundled up in her exhausted mother's arms, he knew this tiny, wriggling infant had the capacity to change his life. Already he had postponed getting out of collapsing South Vietnam because of her. She should have been born two weeks ago, when there was still at least some hope that Hanoi could be persuaded to halt its southward march.

But no baby came, and village after village fell to the communists, until, at last, shortly after six o'clock in the steamy Saigon dusk of April 28, 1975, a slippery, dark-haired girl was born to the sounds of her mother's cries of pain and joy and the shelling of the giant Tan Son Nhut Air Base just four miles from the heart of the city.

The war had finally come to Saigon.

The French nun who'd served as Tam's midwife took Jared aside several hours after the rough labor had ended. Tam and the baby were asleep in his bedroom, and the shelling had died down. But the nun—Sister Joan—looked concerned. "The baby's healthy, but Tam is very weak," she explained in English. "Her pregnancy was long and difficult, and I'm afraid so was the labor. She'll be all right, I think, but you must wait as long as possible before you take her to America."

Jared was surprised. "How do you know—"

"You must get her out," Sister Joan said, with unusual intensity for one who'd seen as much fear, sickness and death as she had in the past month. Refugees were streaming into the city by the tens of thousands. Now there was nowhere left to run, except out of the land of their ancestors. The young nun gripped Jared's arm. "The baby will get her out of Saigon. She's what the Vietnamese call *bui doi*. It means the dust of life."

It was the first time Jared had heard the expression, and he understood it at once. In a communist Vietnam, the children of American fathers, be they white, black or brown, wouldn't fare well.

Releasing him, Sister Joan continued. "There are rumors those in charge of the evacuation are letting Vietnamese women with Amerasian children pass through the system with very little question. She wouldn't even need a *laissez-passer*."

Jared had heard those same rumors. Thinking the baby would be born any second, he had let the prospect that a half-American baby would ease Tam's way out of Saigon delay their exit, despite the directive that nonessential American personnel get the hell out of the country. He couldn't think of anyone more nonessential than an American architect and a college sophomore. Nevertheless, neither he nor R.J.—as beautiful and combative as ever—would leave without Tam. And the baby was Tam's ticket out.

Still, if Tam had been able to travel safely, he and R.J. might have gotten her out sooner—somehow. Tam had no special status to get her evacuated from the country, but they'd have tried to find a way.

The problem was, the Republic of Vietnam was falling fast. The American ambassador, Graham Martin, didn't have the time or the resources to evacuate all the Vietnamese who'd likely face reprisals under a communist government. And the Americans still in the country were his first priority. It was a tightrope act: if the general population got the idea the Americans were cutting and running— which they were—there could be panic…. Vietnamese fighting Americans and each other for scarce space on planes and helicopters out…tramplings, drownings, shootings, crushed babies…Vietnamese soldiers killing and maiming the people they were sworn to protect to save their own skins. In a word, panic.

It had all happened just a month ago in Danang.

Jared promised the nun he would do everything he could to help Tam. They signed papers for the baby, and she went out into the humid, sweet-smelling night, unafraid of the curfew or the prospect of more shelling.

The apartment suddenly seemed too quiet and isolated, and Jared wished R.J. would hurry up. She was canvassing the building for food and whatever else of use she could find. Most of the other residents were American, and except for a writer-diplomat couple on the top floor, had already left the country, giving ever-resourceful Rebecca Blackburn permission to raid their cupboards. She'd produced snowy-white towels for Tam's labor, and even a tattered Raggedy Ann for the baby.

Jared tiptoed into the bedroom, but Tam was awake. Her eyelids were swollen and heavy, her skin pallid, but her haunting beauty was still there, beneath the ravages of recent childbirth, fear, exhaustion. In her gaunt face, her magnificent eyes seemed huge and so sad, even as they filled with love and tenderness at the sight of her sleeping child.

"R.J.'s out scrounging," Jared said. "How do you feel?"

She managed to smile. "Tired and sore."

He didn't doubt that. Witnessing his first childbirth had given him a new perspective on the strength and endurance of women. R.J.'s only comment was she couldn't believe her mother had gone through this torture six times. But of course, Mai made all the difference. Jared couldn't keep his eyes off her.

"Can I get you anything?" he asked Tam.

"Just water."

He had a pitcher ready and filled two glasses. Tam winced as she sat up, but didn't complain. She sipped the water gratefully.

"What's the situation?" she asked.

He knew what she meant. "Bad. 'Big' Minh was sworn in as the new president while you were in labor. A few diehards think he can still negotiate a settlement with Hanoi, but I doubt it. In cowboys' parlance, they've got us surrounded. About all Minh can do is hand over the keys to the city and forestall a bloodbath." At Tam's increased paleness, Jared regretted his blunt words. "Maybe 'liberation' won't be that bad. Most of the dying so far's been the result of panic, not communist atrocities."

Of course, the memory of communist atrocities during the Tet Offensive in 1968—the killing of three thousand civilians in Hue—had helped spark the hysteria that swept Danang. But Jared didn't need to tell Tam that; this was her country. Like so many others, her family had been decimated: killed, tortured, exiled and scattered by the decades of strife. Since her popular father's death in the 1963 scandal that brought down Thomas Blackburn, a familiar

figure to many South Vietnamese, Tam had tried to live a
quiet life. She had a small income from the life insurance
policy Thomas had insisted Quang Tai take out on himself
before returning home in 1959, and after school, used her
language skills to land a string of jobs with various French,
Australian and American firms. She hadn't done anything
to ensure her the special friendship or enmity of either the
Americans or the North Vietnamese.

Tam looked away from Jared, touching her tiny daughter on her smooth, red cheek. "I'd have written a different
ending for my country," she whispered.

"I'm sorry." Jared didn't know what else to say. "Tam,
we'll get you and the baby out—"

She turned to him and smiled. "I'm not worried, Jared.
Quentin will take care of me."

"Giap and his gang will be hanging posters of Ho Chi
Minh all over Saigon before you finally realize Quentin's
not coming back and he's not getting you out of this country. I'm sorry to be hard on you at a time like this, but
you've got to face reality." He broke off, sweating and exhausted himself. "Quentin would have to go up against his
mother to have a Vietnamese woman in his life, and he's
not going to do that."

"Everything will work out," Tam said with maddening
confidence, but she sank back down on the mattress, and
Jared could see she was too tired to argue. It'd all be moot
soon enough. With the baby born, they'd get out of the
country as fast as possible.

And from what he could gather of the situation, it
wouldn't be a moment too soon.

Right now he took Sister Joan's advice and let Tam rest.
She'd need her strength for the long trip to the U.S. After
almost eleven months in Vietnam, he was anxious to get

home himself. He'd rent an apartment in Boston, get a job there, talk R.J. into moving off-campus and living with him. She drove him nuts half the time and there was still a lot of the world he wanted to see, but there'd be time for that—when R.J. was out of school and signed up with the state department or whoever. Maybe they'd send her some-place interesting. He didn't care. The future would take care of itself. First things first: she had two years of Boston University and umpteen of graduate school left.

No, he amended silently, the first thing was for them all to get safely out of Saigon. Now.

He was glad when Rebecca burst into the hot, close apartment, still reeking with the disinfectant Sister Joan had used to clean up after delivery. Rebecca's hair was pulled back in a braid and perspiration shone on her face, but six weeks in Vietnam still had left her with more energy than most. Just two days in Saigon had made her under-stand why the people there dressed as they did. She herself had opted for linen shorts, a camp shirt, long bare legs and canvas shoes.

She dumped her paper bag of goodies on the table in Jared's combination living room-kitchen. "I've got a couple of dried-up croissants, some orange juice, some of that *chao tom* stuff and look—a jar of instant coffee."

Jared laughed. "You were born for this life, R.J."

"Blackburns have always been good at making do. It's making money that trips them up. How's Tam?"

"Fine," Tam said, wobbling in the doorway.

Jared turned to her, concerned. "Should you be up?"

"If we're to leave in the morning, I'd better get steady on my feet," she said. "I don't want to be more of a burden than I already am."

Rebecca looked shocked and sorrowful. "Tam, you're

not a burden—don't think like that." Then she grinned, obviously trying to maintain her own courage. "Come on, our midnight snack is served."

Rebecca had arrived in Saigon in mid-March as Ban Me Thuot, in what the Americans called the Central Highlands, was falling to the first North Vietnamese offensive since 1972, effectively splitting South Vietnam in half. Vietnam had been exorcised from world headlines since the American military withdrawal two years earlier, and the fall of a grubby village didn't draw much attention. Popular opinion held that Nguyen Van Thieu, the incompetent, intransigent president of the Republic of Vietnam, would launch his own counteroffensive and recapture the village. He'd broken the terms of the cease-fire often enough himself.

He didn't get much of a chance to go after Ban Me Thuot. Pleiku and Kontum fell next, and then the march was on to Hue and Danang.

For the first time in decades Jenny O'Keefe Blackburn and her father-in-law agreed on something: Rebecca had no business even being in Saigon in the first place. She had borrowed money from Sofi's father for her trip. Sofi had told him her brilliant, non-dope-smoking, impoverished roommate had to have her wisdom teeth out, but her health insurance wouldn't cover having them done in the hospital. He'd come up with the money. Rebecca had already set up an account to pay him back from money she earned typing papers and doing freelance graphic design, on top of her job and classes.

By the time she reached Jared's tiny apartment on Tu Do Street, she was run ragged. She had meant to stay two weeks at the most, but she got caught up in the death throes of the country, of being a part of history in the making. She couldn't just run back to the safety of Boston. She'd felt compelled to help and had plunged in, volunteering to work with orphans and refugees, to do whatever she could.

And she wouldn't leave Jared or Tam. Absolutely, categorically refused to go home without them.

Rebecca didn't miss a beat when she discovered a beautiful, pregnant Vietnamese woman camped out in her lover's apartment. So what? She trusted Jared. She barely remembered Tam from her visit to the Riviera in 1959, but Tam remembered Rebecca. And they shared the loss of a father on the same tragic day in 1963. The tragedy gave them a bond that transcended the years they'd spent apart and the wildly different worlds from which they came.

While they resumed their friendship, the communists continued their "liberation" of their brethren to the south.

When panic struck Danang, Thomas Blackburn did something he hadn't done since 1963: he called in a favor. An old friend, a die-hard state department type, looked up Rebecca and warned her and Jared to get out—now.

"If Thomas Blackburn's worried," he said, "it's time to worry."

Rebecca made several calls to her mother to reassure her, promising that as soon as Tam had her baby, they'd all leave.

"Leave now," her mother had said. "I lost a husband to Vietnam. I won't lose you, too. You're not supposed to be there. You don't belong there."

Rebecca felt guilty for worrying her mother, but she couldn't have lived with herself if she abandoned her pregnant Vietnamese friend.

At four o'clock in the morning Jared, Tam and Rebecca were jolted awake by the sounds of mortar, rockets and artillery fire out at Tan Son Nhut Air Base. Tam came unsteadily out of the bedroom to join Rebecca and Jared, who'd been dozing on the couch. Jared helped her to a chair, and Rebecca made coffee.

"I'll go in with the baby," she said.

Tam smiled weakly and thanked her. "You've both been so good to me."

"You'd do the same for us if our positions were reversed."

"I'll repay you. I promise—"

"There's nothing to repay."

Tiny Mai was all wrapped up in a cotton receiving blanket and snoozing in the middle of Jared's bed. Rebecca lay down beside her and just watched her sleep. Tam had told her little about her life before Jared had taken her in late last summer, but Rebecca wouldn't have been surprised if circumstances had forced her into a "sugar daddy" arrangement with a rich American or European or even limited prostitution. It was like Jared, Rebecca thought, to help out a lonely woman in need—a *friend.* Whatever he knew about Tam's situation he'd kept to himself, something Rebecca, despite her curiosity, could respect.

The baby squirmed. Rebecca loosened the blanket and peeked at her tiny red feet. "What a cutie you are," she murmured, touching the baby's mass of straight black hair, still matted down from childbirth.

The shelling seemed loud enough to shake the entire building, and Rebecca wondered if the North Vietnamese bombed Tan Son Nhut, what did that do to a fixed-wing evacuation? Airplanes needed runways to get off.

"You're so tired, aren't you, sweetie?" Her mouth was dry with fear, and she brushed the back of a knuckle gently across Mai's smooth cheek. "Getting born's such hard work, but don't you worry. We'll get you out of here."

* * *

Tam was fading fast. She had insisted on walking around the living room and kitchen area, and had collapsed on the couch. She looked drained.

"We're out of here first thing in the morning," Jared told her, handing her a cup of coffee.

She nodded. There were tears in her eyes, and he could see she was terrified. The shelling wasn't doing much for his nerves, either, but it wasn't his country going down the tubes.

He sat beside her. "Look," he said. "Quentin's got a lot of good qualities, and I can see why you feel for him. But Tam—" He sighed. His cousin had abandoned Tam: he'd cut and run. The Quentin Reed style since childhood. "He's no knight in shining armor. R.J. and I'll help you get settled in the U.S. It'll be okay."

"I loved him so much," she whispered, crying. "I thought he loved me."

Jared didn't know what to say. He neither wanted to defend his cousin nor damn him. When Quentin had come to Saigon in October 1973, he had looked up his childhood playmate from the Riviera, the daughter of another man killed during the ambush that had claimed Benjamin Reed's life. He and Tam quickly fell in love. Quentin rented her own penthouse apartment and bought her lavish gifts and made her even more lavish promises. Jared stumbled onto his secret when he arrived in town the following June, but by then Quentin was already coping with the consequences of another secret: his involvement with a drug-smuggling network that had used Winston & Reed planes for transporting heroin. He was in over his head. Jared tried to help, but Quentin only wanted to make sure he promised not to tell his mother.

"I can handle it," he told Jared.

It wasn't long before Jared discovered his cousin was being blackmailed. The situation deteriorated, and by August, Quentin had returned to Boston. Jared was appalled that Quentin could drop Tam with hardly a word, but when he confronted him, his cousin insisted he loved her and would be back.

Like hell.

Quentin had developed consummate skill at making himself believe what he wanted to believe.

Tam lost her apartment and seemed confused about why Quentin wasn't in Saigon. When was he coming back? Jared avoided bad-mouthing his cousin and invited Tam to share his apartment until she could get back on her feet. There were no breathtaking views of the river, no elegant French furnishings, no near-priceless Asian curios.

Within weeks, Tam discovered she was pregnant.

Jared volunteered to fly to Boston and kick Quentin Reed all the way back to Saigon for her, but she wouldn't let him. If she and Quentin were meant to be, he would return. She didn't want the prospect of being a father to influence his decision. She would wait.

Her pregnancy wasn't an easy one, and she was often depressed about not hearing from Quentin, waiting for him to come back to her as the months dragged on.

In early April, however, her feet so swollen she could hardly walk, her country on the brink of extinction—Tam's mood improved.

She was convinced Quentin would get her out of the country and they would live happily ever after together in Boston.

Now, Jared hated to disillusion her. He took her hand, just comforting her in silence as they listened to the shelling.

Footsteps echoed in the hall outside the apartment. It

was almost dawn and there was a curfew in effect, and the building was virtually unoccupied. Could it be another R.J.-type scavenger at work?

There was a single knock at the door. A man spoke something in Vietnamese.

Tam's eyes lit up and she jumped to her feet with a sudden burst of excited energy.

"What did he say?" Jared asked.

With a dazzling smile, she looked over her shoulder at him. "Help has come from Boston. I told you, Jared. I told you!"

Jared didn't believe it, but Tam happily pulled open the door.

She screamed and shrank back into the small apartment, and Jared, on his feet, felt his stomach lurch at the sight of the AK-47 assault rifle pointed at Tam.

Before Jared could even think of what to do, the stout Vietnamese man fired.

Tam's body jerked backward and blood spread over her front. She crumpled, falling so silently, and Jared yelled and lunged toward her, knowing he was too late.

He knelt beside Tam. There was blood everywhere, and he didn't have to touch her to know she was dead. Tears mixed with perspiration and spilled down his cheeks. She'd been killed instantly—expertly. Help from Boston… Quentin…

The Vietnamese assassin turned his rifle on Jared.

Of course, he thought, with a sudden, awful calm. Tam was one of Quentin's secrets, but Jared knew what both his cousin's secrets were.

But not R.J., not the baby. Stay in the bedroom—don't make a sound.

He willed them to be all right.

The assassin hesitated as he was joined by a white-haired, wiry Caucasian. He, too, carried an AK-47.

I don't have a chance, Jared thought.

With Tam's body lying only feet away, the white-haired man grinned at his cohort and said something in Vietnamese. The two made eye contact.

Jared took advantage of their momentary distraction to scramble and dive toward the kitchen. The two murderers were blocking the door, but if he could get to the balcony—

The gun cracked, and he felt himself flying through the air, his body out of control. He didn't know what he'd done, if he'd been hit…and he landed on the floor, hard, burning his cheek against the thin rug. For a few seconds he thought that was all that was wrong, just the rug burn, not understanding the cold, numbing sensation in his shoulder.

Then the pain started.

At the first sound of gunfire Rebecca had grabbed for the .38 Smith & Wesson her grandfather's state department friend had insisted she take, just in case—of what, she didn't ask. She'd thought he was being melodramatic. But she'd thanked the man and stashed the .38 in her knapsack.

There was another shot before Rebecca managed to get her hands on the gun. At least she knew how to shoot. It was one of the skills Papa O'Keefe had taught her that her mother would have rather he hadn't. Rebecca could do an impressive job on a coffee can.

She had to force herself not to kick open the door and swoop in with gun blazing like John Wayne.

Cracking the door, she saw Jared sprawled on his stomach, blood seeping into the carpet around him. Only her survival instincts kept her from screaming and running to him. She began to shake uncontrollably. *Jared...oh, God, no!* But she could see he was breathing. He was still alive. Now where was Tam?

Out of her view a man said something in Vietnamese.

Rebecca's mouth felt parched and her stomach had cramped up so badly she was afraid she'd double over. She stepped back and held the revolver the way Papa O'Keefe had shown her and decided her best strategy was to watch the door and wait. When—if—the bedroom door opened, she'd fire.

Everything's going to be all right. Whoever's out there is just going to go away.... Jared's going to be okay.... Tam...

Her heart was pounding and she thought she'd throw up, but she didn't have to wait long.

The door banged open, and a short, tough-looking Vietnamese man jumped into the bedroom. He didn't see Rebecca at first. She knew her revolver was no match for his assault rifle. She wanted just to melt into the woodwork, to disappear.

The assassin leveled his rifle at Tam's sleeping newborn. Horrified, Rebecca screamed, *"No!"*

She fired, braced for the kick of the gun. Her shot grazed the Vietnamese's upper arm, and he grunted, turning his attention from the baby to her. She hadn't even brought him down. Her hands were shaking badly, and sweat was pouring into her eyes, blurring her vision. She knew she had to make her next shot a good one, fast, before he could recover his balance enough to let loose with his rifle.

Another man burst into the bedroom. Rebecca thought it must be Jared, but saw the white hair, the assault rifle. *I'm dead...we're all dead.*

The intrusion distracted the Vietnamese. Rebecca used the opportunity to fire again.

Her second shot struck the Vietnamese man in the leg, and he went down, gritting his teeth, but flipped around immediately, his rifle still in hand.

The white-haired man was standing in front of the door. There was nowhere for Rebecca to run. And the Vietnamese was between her and the baby. *What kind of heartless bastard would shoot a baby?*

She couldn't leave Mai to die.

And she knew something neither the Vietnamese nor the white-haired man knew: she was out of bullets.

"There are only two bullets in the thing," her grandfather's diplomat-friend had advised her.

All this Rebecca digested in the split-second it took for the Vietnamese man to adjust his aim to take her out.

She started to dive under the bed.

But it was the white-haired man who fired. Not at Rebecca: at the Vietnamese. Stunned, she put out a hand to steady herself against Jared's crummy bureau and turned her head at the sight of the blood spreading across the man's chest. She heard him fall back onto the floor with a finality and quiet that sickened her.

On the bed, the baby began to cry.

Rebecca had no idea what the white-haired man would do next and tried to make herself speak—to beg—but no words came out.

He lowered his rifle and held it in one arm as he walked slowly toward her. "You must get the baby and your friend out of Saigon," he told her in a soft, French-accented voice. He took her clammy hand…she was shaking. "It's up to you. Do you understand?"

She tried to focus on his face. "Tam?"

"I couldn't save her." His voice choked and his eyes filled with tears. "I'm sorry."

"What…" Rebecca, too, began to sob, trying to force back the waves of approaching hysteria. "But why?"

The Frenchman touched her mouth gently with two fingers. "You will be all right," he said with confidence. "Take the baby, take your friend. At first light, leave Saigon. Go home."

"I don't know if I can…."

"You can."

Her eyes reached his. "Who are you?"

But he was already moving toward the door, and he left quickly, not making a sound.

Mai was screaming now. Rebecca looked around, feeling strangely helpless. What was she supposed to do? Sobbing, she picked up the baby, a tiny, warm bundle, and held her close, and she hushed. *Tam's dead…oh, baby, your mama's dead….*

Forcing back another wave of panic, Rebecca carried the baby with her into the living room.

She saw Tam's body sprawled unnaturally on the floor near the door and could see at once she was dead.

"Tam…oh, God…"

Jared had managed to roll onto his back and was in the process of trying to sit up, his face racked with pain. Rebecca held the baby against her shoulder and knelt beside him. His face was drained of color. But his eyes focused on her.

"Jesus, R.J.," he said.

"Don't talk. Save your strength."

"You're okay?"

She nodded, tears streaming down her face. "We'll get out of here. I love you, Jared."

He sank against the wall, unable to answer.

* * *

At 10:48 a.m. Saigon time on April 29, 1975, Ambassador Graham Martin notified Secretary of State Henry Kissinger that they were going to Option IV. It was the final and least desirable option for a full-scale American evacuation of Saigon: they were going out by helicopter. Helicopters couldn't hold as many people as planes could. That meant not all the Vietnamese who deserved to get out were going to make it.

Rebecca's state department friend showed up to make sure she and her friends got out, but was surprised to find her making her way from the apartment building with a newborn baby and a seriously wounded Jared Sloan. She had patched him up as best she could with bandages she'd scrounged from a vacant apartment. There wasn't much more she could do. He had at least two bullets in him and needed proper medical attention as soon as possible. He was in a great deal of pain, feverish, near-delirious—but determined.

"Listen, kid," her friend said when she explained what had happened. "You've got to put it behind you. Never mind the bodies. If Hanoi wants to call you in Boston with a few questions after they get into town, you can talk. Right now we've got to get you home."

He helped them get to a bus pickup point, but he had to get back to the embassy. White-faced and numb, Rebecca thanked him. He said to give Thomas Blackburn his best.

"Tell him if more people'd known what he knew back in '63, maybe—well, the hell with it. Maybe nothing. Take care of yourself, Rebecca. Call me when you finish your degree."

She promised him she would.

Then, with a diaper bag slung over her shoulder, Mai in one arm and supporting Jared with the other, she got them onto the bus, which joined a caravan edging cautiously through the city to one of the landing zones where U.S. Marine and Navy helicopters could set down.

By midafternoon, with a photographer clicking away, they climbed aboard a packed Chinook helicopter and lifted high above Saigon, on their way to a U.S. Navy ship in the South China Sea. It was hot and close in the helicopter, and Mai was screaming. Calling upon her experience as the eldest of six, Rebecca tried to comfort the baby, loosening her blanket, cooing. Tam had planned to breastfeed, but Sister Joan had left several ready-made bottles of formula for emergencies. Rebecca had stuffed them into the diaper bag, but she hoped Mai could hang on until they reached the ship. Nothing like a starving, screaming baby to forestall awkward questions from the brass. With Jared wounded and Mai barely a day old, Rebecca knew she'd end up doing all the explaining about who they were and what they were still doing in Saigon.

Mai continued to scream.

Knowing it was an old wives' tale and unless they had a rash most babies didn't give a damn whether they were wet or dry, Rebecca gave in to frustration and checked Mai's diaper.

She pulled out a deep ruby-red velvet bag wrapped in plastic.

Peeking inside, Rebecca saw the ten glittering colored stones.

Tam's ticket to freedom?

Rebecca shoved them into her pocket, wrapped the baby back up and held her close, until she exhausted herself crying and went back to sleep.

Jared grimaced and coughed a little. Someone had given him a shot of morphine during their wait for the helicopter. He still looked terrible, and despite his assurances he'd be okay, Rebecca could see he was in a state of shock not just from his wounds, but from having witnessed Tam's murder. She was grateful for having him and Mai to tend: it kept her mind occupied.

"Mai has papers," he told her. "In the diaper bag."

"Relax, no one's going to bug us about papers right now. We'll take care of the red tape later."

"No. I promised Tam, R.J. I'm not taking any chances."

Rebecca dug in the diaper bag and got out the papers and had a look. "It says her name's Mai Sloan and you're her father."

"I know."

"Is that a mistake?"

His eyes cleared as they held hers, and he said, "No."

Twenty-Four

～〜◇〜◇〜〜～

Seeing Annette Reed and Jean-Paul Gerard again after so many years combined with his poorly paced walk back to West Cedar Street had left Thomas panting and perspiring. He put on a kettle and waited impatiently for the water to boil. Nerves and exhaustion. How unbecoming, he thought. He would hate to come to the day he'd have to take a taxi to get around the city and hire someone to tend his garden for him. The expense would be aggravating enough, but the indignity—the feeling of utter uselessness—he wouldn't tolerate. He'd just stay at home and watch his garden rot if it came to that.

"You're not in a terribly fine mood, my fellow," he muttered to himself, filling his ironstone teapot with an extra spoon of loose-leaf tea and adding boiling water. The simple chore helped settle him. He brought the teapot and a cup and saucer out into the garden and set them on the dripping-wet table.

The wind and rain had done a job on his impatiens.

"Can't even keep a few flowers alive," Thomas grumbled. If he set them out, they'd have a better chance on their own. Ignoring his fatigue, he fetched his claw and hand shovel from the cellar landing and got to work.

He heard Rebecca and Jared come into the kitchen, fussing at each other. Doors slammed, feet stomped. She called him a two-timing son of a bitch who didn't deserve to be told a damned thing, and he called her a sanctimonious tight-lipped Blackburn who bowed out when the going got tough. Thomas assumed they'd finally started talking to each other. For years he'd hoped they'd accidentally meet at the Grand Canyon or somewhere and have it out. Either one would toss the other over the side, or they'd realize how very much they were meant for each other.

Well, at least *that* wasn't his problem.

Rebecca flounced into the garden and dropped into a chair, water and all. Glancing up from his gardening, Thomas could see why. She was a dripping mess herself. He climbed stiffly to his feet with his claw in one hand, dirt clinging to its sharp steel points.

With one finger on Rebecca's chin, he turned her head so he could examine her cut and bruise. "I told you he could be dangerous."

She made a face at him. "Who?"

"Our *Monsieur* Gerard. He clobbered you good, didn't he?"

"Don't jump to conclusions, Grandfather," she said, in no cheerful mood herself. She opened the lid on his teapot and peered at the steeping tea. He'd quite forgotten about it and in a few minutes it'd be strong enough he could take it out and repave West Cedar. Rebecca dropped the lid back on. "I slipped on the library stairs."

Thomas set his claw down on the able. "Lying doesn't become a Blackburn."

She fastened her sparkling eyes on him, and there was

something about her—a certain reluctant grace, an inner strength—that reminded him of Emily. If only she'd lived. Thomas had often wondered how he'd gone on without that lovely, spirited, intelligent woman he'd fallen in love with well over a half century ago. In a way he supposed he hadn't gone on, at least not very well.

"Lying doesn't become anyone," Rebecca said, "but it's no worse a transgression than withholding the truth. To me it's a case of splitting hairs."

"Rebecca…" He broke off, too tired and confused himself to attempt a halfhearted explanation—a rationalization—of the silences he'd kept. And in too ill a temper himself. "Tell me, Rebecca, do you think it your prerogative to know everything I know? To be privy to everything I've ever done in my life?"

She didn't even hesitate. "Only to what concerns me."

"And where do I draw the line? One could make the case that everything that goes on in the world concerns each one of us. There's an interconnectedness to—"

"Spare me the lecture, Grandfather."

"Yes, I believe I will," he said airily, miffed. "Help yourself to tea."

He brushed the wet dirt off his hands and knees and started back into the kitchen. Rebecca swung around in her chair. "Where are you going?"

"Up to my room." He glanced back at her. "Do I require your permission?"

She sighed. "Of course not."

"Good."

"Grandfather—"

"There's ice in the freezer," he said, and left her fuming alone in the garden.

Jared was in the kitchen already slamming chunks of ice

into a plastic bag, sure to annoy Rebecca. He started to say something, but Thomas put up a hand. Jared took the hint and let him go on without interruption.

Twenty-Five

M ai had spent the day in a state of nervous anticipation and by early evening was ready to execute her plan. She wandered out to the pool where Maureen, back early from the gallery she ran, was arranging a monstrous vase of flowers and humming to herself. She was a handsome, amiable woman, maybe twenty years younger than Wesley Sloan, though it was hard to tell. She had a college-aged son from a previous marriage and said she considered Mai more of a friend than a stepgranddaughter.

"I don't feel very well," Mai announced.

"What's wrong? Do you have a fever—"

"Just a stomachache. I'd like to stay in my room, if it's okay. You won't mind if I skip dinner? I really don't think I could eat anything."

"Of course I don't mind, sweetie. Do you want some aspirin?"

"I'll be okay, thanks. I think I just need to rest."

"Well, you let me know if you need anything."

Promising her she would, Mai had to force herself not to skip back inside. Her dad and grandfather might blame

Maureen for not seeing through her ruse, but most likely, Mai knew, they'd be too busy killing her to bother.

But as her dad said, sometimes you gotta do what you gotta do and take the consequences.

Going to Boston was something she had to do. It was more important right now than being a nice, obedient teenager. She was afraid for her father, angry at being left out of what he was doing…and sure—so sure—that the white-haired man, her dad's reaction to him and his sudden trip to Boston all had something to do with her. She was going to find her father and make him tell her what was going on. Make him be *fair*. She had rights, too. And she wasn't a chicken. She'd explain to him that it was worse not knowing, worse wondering and being scared, worse thinking maybe she'd caused her mother's death in Saigon and his breakup with Rebecca Blackburn in 1975.

She could take whatever it was he hadn't told her.

Instead of going up to her room, Mai slipped out the front door.

George was being dispatched in the limousine to pick up a Parisian couple at the airport who were spending the week as the Sloans' houseguests in Tiberon. He was out at the pool, getting instructions from Maureen.

Mai slipped into the back of the cavernous limousine and curled up on the floor, hiding underneath a tartan wool throw. It was hot and stuffy, but she'd survive. George wasn't expecting a passenger. He'd never notice her.

She was right.

He climbed into the car, and in another minute Mai felt the limousine cruising out of the hills of Marin County, over the Golden Gate Bridge and through San Francisco to the airport.

Twenty-Six

〜⤬〜

Rebecca had given up on Jared's bag of ice and was trying to cure her raging headache by planting the rest of her grandfather's impatiens. They were in sorry shape, but just might make it if he left them alone. It was suppertime, and he still hadn't come downstairs. She hoped he was all right. Maybe she'd been pushing him too hard. Even if he hated being coddled, they both had to remember he was almost eighty, no longer a young man.

Several boarders had wandered back from assorted universities and up to their rooms to unwind or study. Athena had examined Rebecca's face and pronounced that she hadn't been hit that hard.

"Not hard enough" was Jared's unsympathetic remark.

That remark made Athena laugh and forget she'd considered carving him up just that morning. They went inside together to rustle up some supper, Jared obviously having sensed Rebecca needed a chance to pull herself together.

She had told Jared Sloan everything she knew about the Frenchman and what had happened that grim morning of April 29, 1975—except about the bag of colored stones she'd found in Mai's diaper and what she'd learned about *Le Chat* and the Jupiter Stones from David Rubin and her library reading.

He wasn't just the Frenchman anymore, she reminded herself. He was Jean-Paul Gerard. She knew his name now and had to keep repeating it, not because she'd forget it, but because she wanted it to roll off her tongue the way her name did his. For fourteen years she'd hoped he hadn't been a malevolent part of that night in Saigon. It was the Vietnamese who'd been after the jewels, she'd told herself, and who had killed Tam and would have killed her and Mai if not for the Frenchman.

If not for Jean-Paul Gerard.

She had fantasized that maybe he'd been an Interpol agent and had shot Jared Sloan for his own good, to keep the Vietnamese from killing him outright.

How curiously naive.

Jean-Paul Gerard was a crook in pursuit of ten valuable corundum gems known as the Jupiter Stones. Never mind the complications: Thomas Blackburn's presence at Baroness Gisela Majlath's funeral; the Frenchman's friendship with Stephen Blackburn; his participation in the 1963 ambush; his rescue of Rebecca and Mai, and then his departure from the Tu Do Street apartment without Empress Elisabeth's nine sapphires and ruby.

Never mind all that. The bottom line was simple enough: Gerard hadn't been an innocent bystander that night.

Rebecca shuddered and stuck another impatiens in the wet dirt. Should she have turned the stones over to the authorities fourteen years ago? Should she now?

How would Jared and Mai feel when they learned that Tam had been about to smuggle a collection of famous, extraordinary gems out of Vietnam?

How had Tam gotten hold of them?

A worm crawled over her hand, and Rebecca tossed it unceremoniously out of her way and pushed the dirt up around the roots of the plant. Worms had never bothered her. Tam—

"Oh, no."

Rebecca froze and stared at the worm slinking back into the soft, moist soil.

Shutting her eyes tightly, she could see herself at four digging worms with her grandfather…could see the tears in his eyes and remember wondering why he was so upset. Didn't he like worms anymore?

She could remember showing Jared her captured worms and could hear him telling her he was going to cook them up for her supper.

And Tam.

She'd told Tam about her worms.

Tam had been crying, too, and Rebecca had tried to cheer her up and—

And she'd found the pretty red bag in Aunt Annette's bedroom.

"But they were marbles," she whispered, her knees aching on the brick terrace, the worm burrowed into the dirt. "They were marbles!"

Not marbles: the Jupiter Stones.

"Rebecca?"

Jared's voice startled her, but he caught her under the arms before she could fall backward and helped her to her feet. She knew she looked awful. She tried to smile and casually brushed her hair back, discovering dirt caked to her hands. That was right; she'd been planting flowers.

"You okay?" Jared asked.

Her eyes focused on the present, on him. His dark hair, his clear, teal eyes. She used to wake up at night and watch him sleep, wishing she could know what he was dreaming. She had loved to hear him laugh and see him smile and had trusted him the way only a nineteen-year-old really in love for the first time could.

He'd taken advantage of that trust, too, but—it was a long time ago.

The things she'd told him tonight had already rocked his balance. The man he'd hated and feared for fourteen years had saved his daughter's life. Not an easy fact to digest. Not something that slipped neatly into his own version of that night and the recent events surrounding Jean-Paul Gerard's return.

"I'm okay," she told him, and found that his presence steadied her. What, she wondered, did hers do to him?

"What's this about marbles?" he asked.

"Nothing. Just talking out loud."

He looked skeptical, but didn't press. He'd brought a tray loaded with an eclectic array of leftovers from Thomas's refrigerator: cold stuffed grape leaves, steamed Chinese dumplings, fresh asparagus and a stack of soft pita bread. Pulling dinner together had allowed him a chance to sort out what Rebecca had told him about the Frenchman's role that night in Saigon. She hadn't deliberately held back on him all these years; she simply hadn't realized his injury had prevented him from seeing what had happened.

"Who did you think killed that Vietnamese thug?" she'd asked.

"You."

That had brought her up short. "Me?"

"With the revolver that state department guy gave you."

"I thought you didn't know about that."

"A .38 Smith & Wesson stuck in a college student's knapsack is hard to miss, sweets."

"And I guess you also thought I chased Gerard off?"

He had.

She'd grinned. "With another couple of bullets, I probably would have."

Rebecca went inside and rinsed off her hands, returning with forks and plates. She stabbed a dumpling and sat down. "Jared, I'm sorry we didn't talk after Saigon. I suppose it would have been the right thing to do—to clear the air and all—but you'd been shot and I was grief-stricken…and hurt and angry. Frankly, I wasn't in the mood to do the 'right thing.' If someone had pitched you overboard, I'd probably have blown you a kiss good-riddance."

"I understand," he said.

She looked at him, wondering if he did. In simple, raw terms, he had betrayed her. Thinking Rebecca determined to stay in Boston while he spent his year in Southeast Asia, he had chosen a fling with Tam rather than months of celibacy. Yes, he'd been thrilled to see her in March. Tam knew the score, and it didn't include Jared telling his Boston lover to take a hike so he could carry on with her. What had she thought those nights Rebecca and Jared had spent together on his apartment couch while she endured the last stages of her difficult pregnancy alone in his bedroom?

Only when push had come to shove—when Tam was dead and there was no one else to claim and raise their newborn daughter—had Jared come clean and accepted responsibility for his actions.

If Tam hadn't died, would he ever have acknowledged Mai as his daughter?

But Tam *had* died, and he did take responsibility for their daughter. And he obviously adored Mai. Even if Rebecca could still get mad thinking about herself at twenty and him at twenty-five, they'd both grown up. People made mistakes. Sometimes terrible mistakes.

"I should have told you what happened with Mai and me and the Frenchman sooner," she said, "but I honestly thought you saw everything."

"R.J., I had a hole the size of Rhode Island in my shoulder—"

"And you'd seen your lover murdered. Yes, I understand that now."

Jared winced at her words. She didn't understand a thing. But where could he begin about him and Tam and Quentin? And did he have that right, after all these years?

But Rebecca, her hair blowing in the gusting wind, reached for a stuffed grape leaf, dropping it onto her plate, and finally looked at him. "Jared, I still haven't told you everything."

He picked at the thin layers of a section of pita bread, studying her. Waiting.

With a sigh, she whisked up her handbag, pulled out a red velvet sack, and dumped out the contents on the table.

The ten stones sparkled in the suddenly strong early evening sun.

Jared's eyes darkened, going from the stunning gems to Rebecca. He dropped the pita onto his plate. "R.J., what's this?"

She licked her lips. "I found them in Mai's diaper during the evacuation from Saigon."

Thomas Blackburn walked into the garden. With a pained expression, he went up to the table and ran his fingertips over the nine sapphires and ruby.

"Grandfather, I can explain."

"You don't have to. These," he said, "are the Jupiter Stones."

Thomas had shooed Rebecca and Jared out of the garden and poured himself a glass of the blueberry wine he'd picked up from the Bartlett Maine Estate Winery during an outing down east last summer, when he'd been feeling particularly alone and miserable. Four months later Rebecca had turned up on his doorstep, to start her own studio in Boston, she'd said. But it was more than that. She'd needed, finally, to sort out her feelings about the city, him, herself, and what it meant to be a Blackburn, rich, in her thirties and unattached.

The wine was dry and of fine quality, not at all the rotgut he normally associated with fruit wines. Perhaps he would return to Maine this summer and buy another bottle. He settled into his chair, pulling his sweater around his thin frame. The wind had picked up and there was, again, the smell of rain in the air. Thomas wouldn't have cared if a blizzard were in progress. His living room had filled up with students enjoying a Friday evening of popcorn, Junk Mind and television, and Jared and Rebecca had gone out for a walk to digest what he'd told them—and possibly what he hadn't.

Thomas wanted to be alone.

Seeing Jean-Paul again, Annette, the Jupiter Stones—it all had unsettled and confused him. Now he wondered if he'd told Rebecca and Jared too much: about Gisela's suicide over the loss of the Jupiter Stones, about Annette Reed's fingering of the popular Grand Prix driver as the thief *Le Chat,* about his reappearance in Saigon four years later.

"He'd been there for some time," Thomas had explained. "When he'd left France, he signed up with the Foreign Legion—no questions asked—which was headquartered in Sidi Bel Abbès until Algerian independence in 1962. That's when he quit and came to Indochina as a mercenary. He knew I'd be there. I'm not sure he realized Annette would be."

"He and Father became friends?" Rebecca had asked.

Thomas had to say yes. And to admit he hadn't warned his son about his new friend's background. He had assumed—hoped—the young Frenchman had owned up to his mistakes and put the past behind him.

But how wrong he was.

After listening quietly throughout, Jared asked, "Gerard knew it was Annette who turned him in?"

Reluctantly, Thomas had nodded.

"Then," Rebecca had said, "he has a bone to pick with her for that and one with you for the ambush. How long was he a POW?"

"Five years. He escaped in 1968."

"And somehow between then and 1975 he figured out that Tam had gotten hold of the Jupiter Stones and came after them. That's all well and good, but it doesn't explain a number of things." Sitting forward, Rebecca had counted out each item on her fingers. "First, why didn't Gerard turn Jared's apartment upside down after Tam and his Vietnamese cohort were dead? The communists were shelling Tan Son Nhut, but he had time. Did he not know the Jupiter Stones were right under his nose? Second, why wait until now to come after the Jupiter Stones? Third, who does he think has them? Fourth, something about the pictures in *The Score* must have got his attention and made him think he had a chance to get the stones—what?"

Thomas had told her they were all good questions, and then had refused to speculate on any answers. That annoyed Rebecca. Before she could get too steamed up, Thomas had hinted he was near eighty and might die on them any moment if they didn't leave him alone and let him rest. Rebecca was unimpressed. Jared, however, recognized a brick wall when he saw one and spirited her away.

Now, sipping his wine in the cool evening air, Thomas reminded himself that as much as he wanted to unburden his soul and talk about the past, he couldn't take that risk. He could not bear to lose anyone else he loved.

He'd made that decision thirty years ago.

Best, he thought, to stick to it.

Twenty-Seven

Gisela's funeral had depressed Thomas, and he welcomed his four-year-old granddaughter's company back at the Winston *mas*. Rebecca showed him her collection of worms and committed him to taking her for a walk. He avoided Annette. He continued to have misgivings about their talk that morning. There was something more between her and Jean-Paul Gerard than an exciting, handsome jewel thief and one of his coincidental victims. That it all might be none of his business occurred to him only fleetingly, for he had known Annette since the day she was born, and Jean-Paul was Gisela's son, a secret she had shared only with her old friend Thomas. He was distressed that he and Rebecca would be returning to Paris in the morning and this was how their visit to the Riviera was ending, with Gisela flinging herself off a cliff, Annette retreating into uncharacteristic silence and Jean-Paul on the run as a fugitive.

At least Quang Tai had agreed to return to Vietnam. A soft-spoken, well-educated man, Tai thought the Diem government was paranoid and wrongheaded, and he did not

approve of the communists' plans for forced collectiviza-
tion of the Vietnamese peasantry or their puritanical conviction that only their way was right. Tai understood,
however, that his people possessed a deep, abiding resentment of foreign domination; they would no more tolerate
the Americans calling the shots for them than they had the
French, the Japanese or the Chinese. Thomas didn't need
convincing, but there were those in the U.S. government
who couldn't see beyond the global communist threat to
the legitimate nationalistic aspirations of the Vietnamese
people. He hoped Tai, although just one person, could get
the right people on all sides to listen to him.

Thomas suddenly was anxious to get back to Saigon
himself. He would return to Boston with Rebecca and see
his other grandchildren, and perhaps try to convince his
daughter-in-law he was perfectly sincere when he'd told
her she was at liberty to do as she pleased with the house
on West Cedar Street, including put a swing-set up in the
garden and Porky Pig curtains in the children's bedrooms.
Why on earth should he or anyone else care? And so what
if they did?

"Grandfather, I want to go to Saigon to visit Tam,"
Rebecca announced.

Thomas had hold of her grubby, sturdy hand as they negotiated a steep incline, to the spot under a lemon tree
where the view of the Mediterranean was heart-stopping.

"I hope you can one day," he told his granddaughter.

"Tam's sad about going."

"I understand. She's lived in France most of her life, but
Saigon's her home."

"Maybe she can come visit me in Boston, Massachusetts, and we can ride our bikes."

Thomas smiled at the way his irrepressible granddaughter always said "Boston, Massachusetts" as if she were the only one who knew where it was. Jenny's doing. "Not everyone knows or gives a damn where Boston is, you know," she always told Thomas.

"Tam was crying," Rebecca said, chattering as they picked a spot from which they could sit and watch the sailboats. "She wouldn't come worm-digging. She just wanted to stay up in Aunt Annette's room and cry."

Quite an offense to a nonsulker like Rebecca. She went on, "But she felt better after I showed her Aunt Annette's pretty marbles."

Thomas stared at the little girl. "And what were they?"

"Her pretty marbles," Rebecca repeated impatiently. "I found them."

"How big?"

She made a highly unreliable boulder-size circle with her thumb and forefinger. "That big. Some were bigger."

"They were different colors?"

"Uh-huh." Pleased with her grandfather's interest, she wrinkled up her face and began reciting: "Blue, red, purple, white, yellow, green—ummm, black…umm, I can't remember."

"And what did you do with them?"

"Oh," she said solemnly, "we put them back." She jumped up suddenly, squealing and pointing. "Look, Grandfather, a *big* boat!"

Thomas nodded, distracted. His granddaughter had just described Gisela's Jupiter Stones. Real or fake, that they were in Annette's possession proved what he had begun to suspect in the past twenty-four hours: she and the dashing Jean-Paul Gerard had had an affair. Jean-Paul must have swiped the stones from his own mother to give to his lover. No wonder poor Gisela had had enough. Her son was a thief willing to steal his mother's most cherished posses-sions so he could give them to a wealthy, self-indulgent woman like Annette Winston Reed.

For her part, upon discovering her young French lover was the notorious *Le Chat,* Annette had turned him in—without mentioning their relationship to the authorities. Thomas supposed he couldn't blame her for that.

He did, however, blame her for not getting Gisela's stones back to her. What did Annette intend to do with them now that Gisela had committed suicide and Jean-Paul was dead?

Thomas watched boats with Rebecca for nearly an hour before they made their way back to the *mas.*

The next morning, they left for Paris. Two days later they were back in Boston, and within the week, Thomas was on his way back to his quiet apartment in Saigon.

It was another two years before he saw Annette again.

And another three years before he fell into bed with her.

It happened because he was tired of being alone; because his young company was doing moderately well helping American businesses understand the South Viet-namese system enough to start making money, and poorly in helping them, or anyone else in Washington or Saigon, understand the seriousness of the mistakes they were making. His hopes and dreams for this haunting, troubled country to find its place in the world as a free and inde-pendent nation were fading with the increasing corruption and isolation of the Diem government, with the quiet arrival of thousands more American military advisors, war materials, helicopters, planes and promises too easily made. Even as he dashed off persuasive letters to the Kennedy administration, the rumors had begun to circulate that President Kennedy was going to shut up Thomas Blackburn by naming him his new ambassador to Saigon.

Meanwhile, strategic hamlets went up, President Diem continued to resist needed political and economic reforms and antagonized the people he was supposed to serve, and the pot, as Thomas liked to say, began to stink. Then on January 2, 1963, there was the debacle at Ap Bac, where a small group of Vietcong routed a far superior—on paper, at least—American-advised ARVN division. Not only was the government suspect and corrupt, but so was much of the South Vietnamese military. Thomas could see the whole thing falling apart, and through it all, the Vietcong went about their business under the cover of the steamy Vietnam night.

Into this depressing mess came, in mid-January, Annette Winston Reed to see for herself, she said with a broad smile, what her husband was doing with Winston & Reed, the company he'd founded on her money. Thomas had long since stopped expecting Annette and Benjamin to talk in terms of what was theirs, together. It wasn't her first trip to Indochina. She'd visited in the fall for two weeks, but Thomas had been too busy to see her.

This time, he made a point of seeing her.

They had dinner together one night on the colonial-style terrace of the Continental Palace Hotel. Annette was impressed with the beauty of Saigon, especially its tree-lined streets and washed pastel provincial buildings that reminded her of her beloved southern France. Thomas encouraged her to see Hue, the old imperial city on the Song Huong—the Perfume River—that was the religious and intellectual seat of the country. And he wanted her to see the rice paddies of the Mekong Delta, the extraordinary beauty of the beaches of the South China Sea. He had come to love this picturesque, dangerous, divided country since his own first visit not long after losing Emily.

Annette, however, was content with Saigon. "I'm not about to go wandering around," she said, "and get shot by a Vietcong sniper."

Thomas asked her why she'd made this trip to Saigon alone.

She lit a cigarette, a recent habit she'd acquired. "Benjamin had meetings in Boston. He says he'll join me as soon as he can, but I'm not going to hold my breath."

She sounded petulant, and Thomas automatically sought to reassure her—patronizing on his part, he supposed, but he couldn't resist. And it was what she seemed to want. He said, "I'm sure Benjamin doesn't want to leave you here alone."

"I'm almost thirty-four—hardly a baby." She smiled suddenly and reached across the linen-covered table, brushing a long, manicured finger over the top of Thomas's hand. "Besides, you'll take care of me, won't you, Thomas? You always have."

She had deliberately misconstrued his comment. He had only meant that Benjamin, being her husband and caring about her, wouldn't want to be apart from his wife any longer than necessary—not that Annette required protection from him or anyone else. Still, Thomas was amused and flattered that a woman nineteen years his junior— who'd called him a "proper prig" often enough—was bored enough to flirt with him. He'd been too busy and too angered and far too depressed by the developments in Southeast Asia to indulge in flirtations. And this one was harmless enough. Situated between Stephen and Thomas Blackburn in age, Benjamin had become friends to both men. In any event, Thomas could remember Annette when he was first married and she barely toilet-trained.

After dinner they went for a long walk, up to the basilica of Our Lady of Peace at the top of Tu Do Street and over to the French Embassy, then back to his apartment. The evening was quiet and warm, relentlessly romantic. Thomas felt a familiar loneliness stinging at him.

Annette's hotel was just across the street, but he relented when she wanted to come up for a nightcap. It wasn't much of an apartment, he explained, not apologizing, just a couple of rooms, a balcony, simple furnishings and hundreds of books. She loved it.

"I get so sick of Boston," she said, running her fingers along the spines of a row of books. "All the meaningless cocktail parties, the agonizingly boring luncheons, Friday afternoons at the symphony—sometimes I could just scream. I want to do something with my life, Thomas, not just drop dead in a plate of crabmeat salad."

"So—do something."

"Like what?"

He laughed and poured two glasses of brandy. "Annette, that's up to you."

She grinned at him. "Maybe I'll become a nun."

"What would Benjamin say?"

"Oh, he wouldn't care." She spun away from the books and took the offered brandy. "He doesn't want me anymore."

Thomas felt awkward. "Annette—"

"We haven't had sex in over six months." Sipping her brandy, she looked at him dead-on over the rim of her glass, not even blushing as she enjoyed his obvious discomfort. "Does my language offend you?"

"No," he said quietly. "I just never know what to make of you, Annette—what you'll say or do next. Even when you were a little girl, you were unfathomable. Totally unpredictable."

She shrugged. "I'm selfish and like to have my own way."

"I suppose that's true."

"And I want to be loved, Thomas," she said, her voice cracking.

He cleared his throat. "A human predicament, I'm afraid."

She sniffed and suddenly said, "What would you do if I stripped myself naked right now?"

Thomas was too shocked to speak.

She laughed, delighted with his reaction. And she put down her brandy and began to unbutton her blouse, slowly.

"Annette, don't."

"When I was about fourteen or fifteen," she said, "I used to walk past your house and think about what it would be like to have you touch my breasts. Then as I got older, I wanted to feel your tongue on my nipples. Does that horrify you, Thomas?" She had her blouse completely unbuttoned and pulled it out of her skirt, so that it fell open. She had on a full slip and a lacy bra, but he could see the dark peaks of her nipples straining under the double layers of thin fabric. She smiled, her impossibly blue eyes shining with tears. "I'm awful, I know."

"No, you're not, Annette. You're in a strange country, you're confused—"

"I'm not confused. I know exactly what I want."

"Annette…"

She peeled the straps of her slip off her smooth shoulders and down to her elbows, then wriggled free so that the bodice of the slip fell to her waist. A light film of perspiration shone on her bare midriff and arms. Her bra was lacy and expensive, and she unclasped it before Thomas had a decent chance to work up another protest.

Her breasts were full and well-shaped, her nipples very dark and erect. She dropped the bra onto the floor.

"Benjamin's asking me for a divorce."

Tears were streaming down her cheeks. It was so quiet in the warm, humid apartment Thomas could hear himself breathing.

"Make love to me, Thomas," Annette whispered. "Please don't turn me away."

Distressed by his own evident arousal, Thomas nonetheless put down his brandy, swept up her bra and handed it back to her. "I'll take you back to your hotel."

"No!"

With a suddenness and fierceness that surprised him, she grabbed his hand and jerked him toward her, placing his palm on the soft swell of one breast.

"Love me," she begged. "Please…Thomas, please!"

He tore his hand away. "Not like this, Annette. I'd hate myself for taking advantage of you. And you'd hate yourself." His eyes bored through her. "We'll forget this happened."

She calmly put on her bra. "I won't forget."

She didn't. The next night she was back in his apartment, and the next. Not stripping herself or begging, but telling him how her marriage had crumbled in the last year, how lonely she was, how determined to be a good mother to Quentin despite the impending divorce.

"I'll get custody, of course," she said. "And we'll try to keep the publicity to a minimum. Benjamin and I just aren't temperamentally suited to each other. There's no point in preserving a bankrupt relationship."

"I'm sorry, Annette. I like both you and Benjamin very much."

"Don't be sorry. It's for the best—really." She gave him

a brave smile that faltered after a few seconds. "I'm just afraid men won't be attracted to me anymore. I know I'm not a ravishing beauty—"

"Don't. You're a lovely woman."

She raised her eyes to him. "Then why did you reject me?"

He smiled. "Not because I wasn't tempted, I assure you."

It was all she needed to hear.

The next night, she brought Frank Sinatra and Duke Ellington records, and they played them on his old record player and danced in his living room until midnight…and made love until dawn.

They were together every night for the rest of her ten-day visit to Saigon, and as much as Thomas was infatuated with her youth and optimism and smart-alecky ways, he couldn't shake the feeling that what they were doing was wrong. Annette was still a married woman. There'd been no formal separation, much less a divorce. He felt she should extricate herself from one relationship before launching another, but remembering Jean-Paul Gerard, realized the idea of adultery wasn't one that troubled her.

It was with both relief and sorrow that Thomas saw her off.

She promised she'd be back. "I adore you, Thomas," she said, kissing him at the airport, opening her mouth even as he struggled to pull away.

But it wasn't Annette who returned two weeks later; it was Benjamin Reed. He announced that his wife was now vice president of their company, and Winston & Reed had just landed a lucrative contract with the American government.

"Annette says we'll make a fortune if there's war in Indochina," Benjamin remarked blithely.

Stephen warned his father not to take Benjamin's hawkish talk too seriously. "Annette came back from her trip filled with all kinds of ideas of how Winston & Reed can make money over here, and they're all predicated on an escalation of direct American involvement. She's probably writing her congressman now. Benjamin's total mush around her. A few days back among the Blackburns, and we'll have him talking sense again."

But stricken by her betrayal, Thomas was no longer one to trust Annette Reed. "From something she said while she was over here, I got the impression Benjamin wanted a divorce—"

"Benjamin?" Stephen laughed. "You've got to be kidding. He *worships* Annette. Myself, I wouldn't trust her to watch my kids while I poured coffee in the next room."

Thomas nodded. What a stupid jackass he'd been.

He set out to forget Annette, and the deteriorating conditions in South Vietnam were enough to preoccupy his mind.

Then, on a warm, pleasant evening, his son brought Jean-Paul Gerard to dinner.

They'd never actually met, the Brahmin intellectual and the French race-car driver. Gisela was all they had in common, and she had spoken fondly of each to the other. Thomas was her high-minded friend whose seriousness she both admired and found amusing. They had met in Paris in 1931, when he was so hopelessly in love with Emily, and Gisela and several of her lovers—sometimes individually, often all together—showed them around their city. This was, of course, before Gisela decided to become a displaced Hungarian baroness. Then she was just Gisela Gerard, an impishly pretty young woman who loved to dance and laugh and be in love. When Emily died, Gisela didn't send flowers or a morbidly proper card, but a note telling Thomas she'd sent money to a convent orphanage in Provence in his wife's memory, and the nuns there had promised to name their next orphan girl Emily. Thomas had no idea if any of this was true, for Gisela was much better at coming up with ideas and making plans than she was at executing them. But he appreciated the gesture.

Jean-Paul was her beautiful son—her "whim," she called him, conceived in a sudden longing to have a baby. She made no demands on the father, and she herself was unconcerned about societal conventions like marriage and monogamy. World War II sobered her up some, but she retained her zest for life and was delighted when Jean-Paul set off on his own at age sixteen and became a popular and successful Grand Prix driver. It didn't bother her at all that he never acknowledged her as his mother. She'd set herself up on the Riviera as Baroness Gisela Majlath and was enjoying this new phase in her life.

Thomas had often wondered if she'd discovered Jean-Paul had amused himself by becoming *Le Chat*. Had that disappointment precipitated her suicide, or was her grief over the Jupiter Stones?

It wasn't the sort of question one put to a guest, however, and Thomas graciously pretended not to recognize his son's friend as the fugitive French jewel thief. Obviously, he'd either had to leave France without his collection of stolen jewels or had squandered their "earnings" long before now. His years in the Foreign Legion had hardened him. He was just twenty-eight, but there were lines at the corners of his eyes and a leatheriness to his skin that belied his years. His muscles were stringy and tough—he had a tested soldier's body. Thomas wondered if scores of adoring women would gather around him now, or if they'd recognize Jean-Paul Gerard as a man who'd seen too much, done too much and had very little left to lose. He had discharged from the legion, he said, to come to Vietnam, where his skills with French and soldiering could be put to use.

Thomas wondered if the young Frenchman's reasons for choosing Indochina didn't also include himself and Winston & Reed.

"You want to kill people?" Thomas asked.

Gisela's soft eyes looked back at him from the man's weathered face. "I just want to survive."

Stephen was embarrassed by his father's harsh question, but Thomas behaved himself the rest of the evening. He could see the two young men liked each other. Well, what of it? Nearly four years in the *Légion étrangère* were enough punishment for any man's crimes.

But in another week, Annette returned to Saigon, and Thomas worried about what would happen if she and Gerard bumped into each other. It was bad enough Thomas had to confront her himself.

"You lied to me," he told her baldly. "Benjamin never asked you for a divorce."

She lit a cigarette and blew the smoke Bette Davis style. "Not that he doesn't want one, I assure you. He's such a coward. Oh, Thomas, don't be mad. When will you get another chance to be seduced by a woman twenty years younger than yourself?" She grinned, totally without guilt. "You should be thanking me."

What could Thomas say? He'd known Annette her entire life and should have realized she put alleviating her boredom and having her way above any notion of honor or integrity. He'd known what he was getting into when he fell into bed with her, and if he didn't, he'd been an even bigger jackass than he thought.

"I hope," he told her, "you don't confess our foolishness to Benjamin. It would only hurt him."

She waved her cigarette. "Don't worry—he'll never know. But Thomas," she chided, "what we did wasn't foolishness. It's called—"

"I know what it's called," he said, cutting off one of her deliberately crude remarks. "You're behaving like a naughty ten-year-old. Why are you back in Saigon?"

"The same reason I was here before—to keep an eye on what Benjamin's doing with my money. Don't look so hunted, Thomas. I've had my fill of you."

"Go back to Boston."

She stubbed out her cigarette. "When I damn well feel like it."

Jean-Paul came to Thomas's apartment at dawn that night. In his bathrobe, Thomas offered him a drink, but the young Frenchman wasn't interested. He opened a manila envelope and spread six black-and-white photographs on Thomas's kitchen table.

"I didn't just arrive in Saigon," Jean-Paul said.

"So I see."

The photographs were of Annette and Thomas during their brief, all-too-torrid affair. Having dinner together, holding hands on Nguyen Hue Boulevard, kissing at the airport, and one particularly embarrassing one of Annette peeling off her blouse as Thomas opened the door to his apartment.

"Never saw me, did you?" Jean-Paul asked, pleased with himself.

"No, I didn't. Were you in disguise?"

"Just a beard. I've learned to blend into the environment during the last few years."

"I suppose you have," Thomas said steadily. "And the point of this exercise?"

Jean-Paul's expression grew serious. "I want the Jupiter Stones."

"You don't think I have them?"

"No." He glanced at the bare-breasted photograph of Annette. "But she does."

That wasn't something Thomas could argue; it was also nothing he and Annette had ever discussed. Every time he'd tried to broach the subject of *Le Chat,* Gisela and the Jupiter Stones, she'd turn him off. He'd been too stupidly considerate to press.

"And if she doesn't give them to you," he said, "you'll show these photographs to Benjamin."

"That's right. But he's just a start. I can think of a number of people who might be interested in just how indiscreet Thomas Blackburn can be—certain members of the Kennedy administration, embassy officials, perhaps even the president himself."

"You want me to pressure Annette."

"I don't care how I get the stones, *Monsieur* Blackburn," Jean-Paul said coolly. "I just want them."

Thomas pushed the photographs away. "If you'd come to me as Gisela's son, I might have helped you. But not like this."

Gerard laughed derisively. "Aren't you the courageous bastard. Look, of all people, I know what you got yourself into with Annette. All I want are the stones that belonged to my mother."

"Then deal with Annette."

He sat back in the dim light of the hot night. "I've tried."

Of course he had: Thomas wasn't surprised. And Annette hadn't come to him for help. "What did she say?"

"She told me I could rot in hell."

* * *

Two days later Annette returned to Boston without a word about the Jupiter Stones. Barely a week later she got her wish: Jean-Paul Gerard, the only survivor of a Vietcong ambush that killed Stephen Blackburn, Benjamin Reed and Quang Tai, was taken prisoner by the communist guerrillas.

Thomas had arranged for the information-gathering excursion into the Mekong Delta, into an area considered secure, although he knew there were risks. In a country at war, there always were. He hired Jean-Paul to drive the Jeep. He was good, he was tough, and it seemed Annette had called his bluff about the photographs. He had become friends with both Stephen and Benjamin, and regardless of how much he despised Annette for having betrayed him in 1959, he didn't want to jeopardize those friendships. Thomas hoped Jean-Paul, however slowly and painfully, was putting his past mistakes behind him.

Originally the trip was planned for just Thomas, Jean-Paul and Tai. At the last minute, however, Benjamin decided he wanted to go along and see for himself what was happening in the countryside, and Ambassador Nolting asked to meet with Thomas.

Stephen went into the Mekong Delta in his father's place.

From the analysis of the grim scene afterward, Tai was killed instantly, and Stephen was wounded in the leg, managing to take out at least one of his attackers with the army-issue Colt before he was killed with a bullet to the head. Two other guerrillas were killed with Gerard's assault rifle, which was never recovered.

Wounded in the abdomen, Benjamin Reed was left to die a slow, horrible death.

It was a fact the authorities kept from his widow. At first, Thomas had heartily agreed.

Within days, however, he'd decided Annette shouldn't have been spared a single heart-wrenching detail of the massacre.

"You went to bed with a viper, my friend," Tai had told him one night not long after Annette's second departure.

"You knew?"

"Yes, but I knew, too, your common sense would prevail and you would extricate yourself from her spell."

Thomas smiled. Tai had worked for Annette Reed for five years and had a right to dislike her. "Next time my love life fires up, I'll run the lady past you."

But Tai was deadly serious. "Thomas, she has contacts all over the city. With the crime bosses, with the police, with the Vietcong. She can find out anything she wants to find out and hurt anyone she wants to hurt. She used her time in Saigon well. She has the means to do whatever she wants."

"For heaven's sake, she was so green she could barely find her way to her hotel—"

"She worked fast, my friend. Trust me. I think she will use her contacts to keep tabs on her husband and make money for Winston & Reed. But don't trust her, Thomas." Tai smiled halfheartedly. "And don't get on her bad side."

But it was too late for that.

Thomas had nothing to go on but his gut feeling, Tai's words and his own knowledge of Annette, but he believed—he *knew*—she had found out about his plans and had passed the word to the guerrillas.

As he combed the city for information, he discovered enough to convince himself that Tai was right. She had the contacts, the money, the will. In one fell swoop, she would have gotten rid of two of her ex-lovers. Jean-Paul, the jewel thief and blackmailer. Thomas, the middle-aged fool.

He couldn't root out proof that Annette was anything more than the wealthy, bored woman from Boston who had spent lots of money in Saigon and talked lots of crazy talk no one hadn't heard before. He turned Saigon inside out and upside down. There was nothing that would stand up in a court of law.

And then the rumors began to circulate. "You're hurting, Thomas," his last friend in the state department had told him. "People around here think you were skipping out on a tête-à-tête with the VC that day."

Annette's doing. Her stink was everywhere, but she was safely in Boston, mourning her lost husband and clamoring for additional military aid to the South Vietnamese government.

Finally, Thomas accepted full responsibility for the tragedy that had claimed the lives of three people he loved and possibly a fourth he had only just met. If he was right and Annette had tipped off the Vietcong, then pointing his finger at her—especially when he had no tangible proof—was madness. There was the rest of his family to consider—Jenny, the children. Would Annette threaten them if he attempted to expose her?

Thomas wondered if he was being paranoid and simply looking for some way to avoid his own culpability. Common sense should have told him to stay out of her bed. Common sense should have told him to be more careful when it came to arranging excursions into the Mekong Delta.

He looked into taking Tai's ten-year-old daughter Tam back to Boston with him, but friends had taken her in and assured him she would be well cared for. Thomas wept for her and wondered if she still dreamed of the stone *mas* on the Riviera, the beautiful roses her father had cultivated, the smell of lemons and flowers and the Mediterranean Sea.

Should he have left Tai to return to his life in southern France?

"I would have come back," Tai had told him. "Remember that, my friend. You're a hard man, Thomas, but harder on yourself than on anyone else. No matter what happens to me or to my country, I don't want you to blame yourself."

Dear God, how could he not?

A month after her husband's death, Annette became chairman and president of Winston & Reed.

With the ambush, Thomas Blackburn lost all credibility. His company went bankrupt, and his chance at the ambassadorship to Saigon evaporated. If nothing else, he had put Vietnam on the front pages, and few in the American government wanted that. There were still those who preferred to do their work there quietly, effectively and fast.

Thomas returned to West Cedar Street, to his house not a half mile from Annette Reed's, and he prayed to God that with himself and Jean-Paul Gerard out of the way, she was finished.

Twenty-Eight

Annette poured herself a glass of brandy and wandered from room to room in her big, empty house, skipping only Kim's quarters in the apartment she'd made for him in the basement. She moved briskly, angrily, through the house, talking to herself, wondering if this was the sort of thing crazy old women did. But she'd been doing it for years, ever since Jean-Paul Gerard had come back to haunt her first in 1963, then again in 1974, and again in 1975, and again now.

She didn't have his Jupiter Stones.

But she wasn't going to let him ruin her life over them or anything she'd done out of self-defense.

The past was past.

She was a different person than what she'd been thirty years ago. Couldn't he see that? Couldn't *Thomas?* People grow up, she thought. They go on with their lives. They forget the mistakes they've made and the wrongs that have been committed against them. They don't hold grudges *forever.*

She had lived an exemplary life. She didn't deserve to keep suffering like this.

And damn you, Thomas, I have suffered.

Whenever she thought about sweet, gentle, boring Benjamin…well, she simply couldn't. She hadn't taken a lover since his death. Twenty-six years of celibacy: her way of honoring her husband's memory, of punishing herself for the miscalculation that had led to his death…but that really was Thomas's fault. He had known Benjamin hadn't belonged on that excursion into the Mekong Delta. He should have stopped him from going.

Thomas's fault. Not hers.

Benjamin's last words to her were etched forever in her mind. "You're a tough-minded woman, Annette. We'll be a good balance for each other."

And they would have been, too. She saw that now.

Would she have continued to have affairs? She felt no guilt about her brief liaisons with Jean-Paul and Thomas. If they'd been moral mistakes, they weren't in the sexual sense. Both men had been incredible lovers. Benjamin hadn't been hurt by her actions, as he'd had no idea she'd ever been "unfaithful" to him.

Night after night for the past twenty-six years, she'd awakened aroused and sobbing, dreaming not of Benjamin and their nights together, but of Jean-Paul and Thomas.

She refilled her brandy glass and kicked off her shoes, feeling freer and more relaxed in her bare feet.

After her disastrous affair with Thomas and the death of her husband, she—the proud, sad widow—had plunged herself into her work at Winston & Reed. Her parents and friends had excused her unseemly ambition when she'd explained to them, tearfully, that she was working hard and determined to make one business triumph after another in order to honor her husband's memory.

As American military involvement in Indochina escalated, Winston & Reed made enormous profits, and

Annette diversified and expanded its investments in the U.S. She never went back to Saigon on business after 1963. She had a trusted, astute American staff there and her own quiet network of Vietnamese contacts.

With the Paris Peace Accords, she engineered the downscaling of Winston & Reed's commitment to what she believed was a doomed South Vietnam. It just wasn't good business to continue to invest in a country she knew wasn't going to last. She had no desire to lose assets to the communists.

She fought Quentin's decision to leave for Saigon in October 1973. She could have forbidden him to go, but with the American military withdrawal and no word from Jean-Paul Gerard in ten years, she decided—moronically—she had nothing to fear. She assumed Jean-Paul must have died as a prisoner of war.

She hadn't even guessed Quang Tai's lovely daughter, Tam, would become a problem.

By the spring of 1974, Quentin had taken up with her, and Annette began to worry. When he came home for the groundbreaking ceremonies for the new Winston & Reed building, she warned her son about committing himself to a long-term relationship with a Vietnamese woman.

"But this is Tam," he told her.

Yes, indeed: Tam. His childhood playmate on the Riviera whose father had died on the same day, in the same ambush as Benjamin Reed. Bad enough Annette had to tolerate Rebecca Blackburn's return to Boston as a student and her nephew Jared's obvious interest in her. She couldn't control them. But Quentin was her son, and she *wouldn't* tolerate his continuing a relationship with Tai's daughter.

By early summer, Tam and Quentin were still going

strong, and Annette was running down the list of possible ultimatums she could give him to drop her.

Enter Jean-Paul Gerard.

He'd discovered Quentin's idiotic involvement with a ring of drug smugglers, and finally had sent him to his mother for a way of getting the Frenchman to keep his mouth shut.

Licking his lips, nervous and abject, Quentin explained the situation. "He asked me to tell you that you should know what he wants."

She did: the Jupiter Stones.

Her only satisfaction throughout the ordeal was listening to Quentin's description of Jean-Paul's haggard, malnourished, parasite-ridden body. His hair had gone completely white, and he was no longer the dashing young Frenchman who'd swept her off her feet on the Riviera fifteen years earlier. He had escaped, she learned, from his jungle POW camp in 1968 after five years of imprisonment. Obviously he'd stayed in Vietnam and was unable or uninterested in getting proper medical attention for the captivity-related conditions he suffered.

Maybe he'll just wither away and die, Annette had thought.

She'd never, however, been one to wait for providence to act. Indirectly and quietly, she let her more unsavory contacts know a confirmed report of Jean-Paul Gerard's death would please her mightily. Kim himself had twice tried to kill him and failed.

Meanwhile, Annette found her way to get her son out of Saigon and away from Tam and Gerard.

"I'll help you," she told him, "under one condition."

He didn't ask her what condition that was; he already knew.

But she told him, anyway, just to be sure. "You're not to go back to Saigon."

As Annette walked out into her damp, cool garden, she drank her expensive brandy, still able to see the stricken look on Quentin's handsome face during that dreadful luncheon in which she'd destroyed his boyish fantasies about coming home to live with Tam.

"But what about Tam?" he'd asked.

"She's survived the past eleven years as an orphan in a war-torn country. She'll be all right. Trust me, Quentin. You'll still be thinking about her long, long after she's forgotten you and moved on to another good-looking, rich, vulnerable man."

With Quentin out of the country, Jean-Paul lost his leverage. Annette half expected him to send her pictures or some other incontrovertible proof of her son's culpability in the drug-smuggling operation, but she didn't hear another word from him.

Quentin moped for weeks, until she was able to call him into her office at Winston & Reed and announce not only was she promoting him to a management position, she was also going to allay his doubts about what he'd done to Tam.

"I've never told you this," she said, "but I've had people in Saigon looking out for Tam, because I considered her father my friend and care very deeply about her, even if I strongly object to her using my son to further her own ends. My people tell me she's taken up with another man."

Her son's shock was palpable. "Are you sure?"

"Quite. What's more, she's pregnant."

"Mother—"

"And I believe you know the father. They're even living together."

Quentin didn't say a word.

Annette looked properly sympathetic. "It just goes to

show you, Quentin, that you have to be very, very careful about whom you trust."

"Tam…"

"Oh, not just Tam. The man she's taken up with is your own cousin Jared."

Annette had no idea if all she'd told him was true or not. She did know Tam was pregnant, and she did know the young woman had gone to live with Jared after losing her penthouse apartment. The rest—well, for all Annette knew, the baby could have been Quentin's or anyone else's in Saigon.

"Remember," she had told Quentin over and over during those touchy weeks, "the one person you can trust is your mother. I always have your best interests at heart."

Annette felt hot tears streaming down her wind-cooled cheeks. *Yes, Quentin, you can trust me…. I'm your mother… I love you.*

And Thomas's voice came to her. *You love only yourself, Annette.*

She threw her glass onto the stone terrace. It wasn't true!

"Bravo, my dear."

This time Thomas's voice wasn't in her imagination. Whipping around, she saw him coming out of the shadows onto the terrace. He looked like a ghost—old, pale, thin. Her heart throbbed painfully, and she debated fleeing into the house and pulling all the drapes, turning out the lights, just sitting there alone, as if trapped in a huge, cavernous coffin, all alone against the big, bad, ugly world.

He went on smugly. "It's best not to repress your emotions, but I'm too tired for arguing and swearing at each other. Annette, I have a proposition to make to you."

She eyed him suspiciously, but said nothing.

Thomas took that as a cue to go on. "I want you to tell Jean-Paul I have the Jupiter Stones."

"Do you?"

"Tell him Tam took them from you before she left France for Saigon. She didn't know what they were—she only wanted them as a memento." Thomas came into the shaft of light from the house, but it only made him look older, paler, thinner. "Tell Jean-Paul Tam sent them to me for safekeeping before her death."

Annette couldn't move. Her heart was racing, her eyes wouldn't focus, and she had to will herself not to give Thomas the satisfaction of collapsing at his feet. She said, "I don't understand...."

"I don't want you to have control over this situation, Annette. If you'll send Jean-Paul to me, I promise I'll do everything I can to get him to forget about vengeance or justice and leave you alone."

"Why should I trust you?"

He looked at her a moment. "Have I ever gone back on my word to you?"

She didn't answer, refusing to acknowledge his honesty, but knowing he was faultlessly devoted to "his word."

"Annette..."

Was he going to plead with her? She smiled at the prospect. But he trailed off and started back into the shadows toward the carriageway. "All right," she said. "I'll at least think about your idea. I'll let you know."

"As you wish," he said.

"Don't pull that sanctimonious tone on me. I never wanted any of this to happen—"

"Why not, Annette?" Thomas asked sarcastically, glancing back at her. "It's such an adventure."

"Goddamn you to hell, you arrogant bastard!"

He gave her a small, secret smile, satisfied, at least, that he'd gotten to her. Back out on the street, the night air was brisk and windy, the big houses aglow, and Thomas fancied them filled with laughter and people who cared about each other. It was a nice fancy. He had decided against polishing off his bottle of blueberry wine and instead had found himself on Mt. Vernon Street for the second time in twenty-six years—and in twelve hours. It hadn't changed since morning, or, really, all that much since 1963.

Mindful of heart attacks and headlines, he nonetheless got back to West Cedar as quickly as he dared.

Twenty-Nine

By three o'clock in the morning Jared was ready to decapitate the cuckoo in Thomas Blackburn's parlor clock and maybe strangle R.J.'s cat, Sweatshirt, who insisted on pawing his afghan and climbing over his face. Jared had counted off midnight, one o'clock, two o'clock, and every half hour in between, and now, pushing the cat off him one more time, he waited for three to sound.

There it was: "Cuckoo…cuckoo…cuckoo."

He threw off his afghan and sat up on the couch. His mind was spinning with images and questions, with R.J.'s still-beautiful smile. They had walked past sundown, trying to sort things out, but often talking about nothing—the little old lady who used to run the chocolate shop on Charles Street, whether that was really Mrs. Caldwell's silver in the antique shop window and had she gone broke, this year's citrus crop in Florida, the backless dress in the Newbury Street boutique window. Rebecca had shoved the Jupiter Stones into her handbag, which she slung cavalierly over her shoulder.

"Aren't you worried about getting mugged?" he'd asked.

"That'd solve all our problems, wouldn't it? We could send Gerard after some poor mugger."

Thomas was still in the garden when they'd gotten back, and Jared hadn't liked how he'd looked: ashen-faced and a million years old, knowing things he wouldn't tell.

Knowing things both he and Jared knew and hadn't told anyone, including Rebecca.

Seeing her again hadn't made the lie he'd let her believe any easier to bear. But he had felt he had no choice.

In 1975, still weakened from his weeks in the hospital in Manila and then Hawaii, Jared had come to Thomas for advice. He hadn't known who else to go to, who else would understand Quentin and Rebecca and Tam and a man's responsibility to an innocent child in the way Thomas would.

"Do what you feel you must," Thomas had counseled him. "It's all anyone can ask of you."

So he had. And in so doing, he'd lost R.J. Already burned by two men in her life—a father who'd promised to come home and hadn't and a grandfather who'd ruined her family's good name—she hadn't been easy on a lover who'd admitted he'd fathered a child by another woman.

He raked his hands through his hair. The hell with this. He pulled on his jeans and tiptoed upstairs to Rebecca's room on the third floor, half expecting Athena to streak out of her room with a carving knife.

Light angled through her cracked door. Jared knocked, softly.

"It's open," she said.

Rebecca stood in her window, looking down at the street, and Jared's stomach clenched at the sight of her, draped in a silk satin nightgown that probably had set her back as much as she'd used to make summers working in the O'Keefe citrus groves. It was cream-colored with tiny yellow flowers embroidered along the neckline, softening the stark expression on her angular face. She was tough, this woman he'd once loved. Tough on others, tougher on herself. "Cut yourself some slack," he used to tell her during their too-short time together. "It's okay to be human." *And let me be human, too,* he'd wanted to say. *Let me make mistakes.*

In her book, he had.

Seeing her in the expensive, feminine nightgown highlighted how she'd changed. Fourteen years ago, every time she'd spent a nickel on herself she'd thought about her college expenses, her five younger brothers, the starving, the homeless, the poor. Jared wondered if she'd agonized over buying the nightgown or had accepted it was okay to spend a few bucks on herself.

"I thought you might be Grandfather," she said.

"Not old enough. Mind if I come in?"

"Of course not—have a seat." As she moved away from the window and climbed onto her childhood bed, she caught his look and laughed. "I know it's ridiculous, my living her like an eight-year-old, but it's been good."

Jared pulled up a chair and sat down. He noticed the light scent of the powder she'd used after her shower and could see a dusty streak on her throat. With her hair hanging down and her cheeks flushed and that damned nightgown, she looked like a beautiful virgin princess, but he thought better of telling her so.

"Your bruise doesn't look so bad now," he said.

"It's fine. You couldn't sleep?"

"No."

She leaned back against the headboard. "I've been up here pacing and thinking and—I don't know. Sometimes I think I was too hard on you, Jared. It was easy just to blame you for what happened between us instead of looking at myself, as well. It was so long ago. We were in such different places in our lives." She caught herself and smiled suddenly. "Never mind. You don't want to hear this."

"No, go on. Please."

She talked for a long time, exposing herself to him in a way she never had before. Coming to Saigon and witnessing the collapse of South Vietnam had had an impact on her that he'd been too blind or stupid or just too convinced of her indomitability to have noticed at the time.

"I looked around that devastated country and realized my father had died there trying to do some good and it all amounted to nothing. Zero, Jared. People were still fighting and suffering and what could I do about it? I was overwhelmed. I'd set some fairly tough goals for myself. I had years of school ahead of me. I was going to set the world on fire and clear the Blackburn name—and when I was in Saigon, all that seemed so selfish and useless. There were people running scared for their lives, people without homes or food—little kids with no one to take care of them. I looked around and realized that I could work the rest of my life and maybe—*maybe*—make a small difference. So why bother at all?"

Her eyes were huge and glistening in the soft light, and she explained that even without Tam and Mai, she didn't know what she'd have done when she finally came home from Saigon. Finally, she quit school, got a flunky job as a designer while taking art classes, and worked on Junk Mind.

"It took me a while," she said, "but now I'm really glad I made my fortune coming up with a game that brings people together for a few laughs the way Junk Mind does. I've shot a man, Jared, and I've seen people suffer and die violent deaths. It doesn't bother me a bit to know something I created entertains millions of people. And the design work I do doesn't make any great artistic statements, but that's okay." She grinned at him. "Me, I appreciate a nicely designed restaurant menu."

"Are you sorry you didn't finish your degree?" he asked.

"I don't know. Sometimes I think when I settle down I'll get back to it. In case you haven't realized, I've moved around a lot. And here I always thought you'd be the wanderer. That was another thing that worried me, you know. Not only are you half Winston and the Winstons and Blackburns haven't exactly gotten along the past quarter-century, but you're half-Sloan—and an architect on top of it. You father hasn't set any records for lasting relationships, and you know what they say about architects—don't get attached too soon. You were just twenty-five, Jared. Never mind the rest of it. We just weren't ready for each other."

She winced at her choice of words, as if after fourteen years things might have changed. But that was the hard part of the past few days, of seeing his picture and having him turn up in Boston. She was discovering how much she still cared about Jared Sloan.

"You've settled down though, I see," she said lamely.

Jared smiled. "It's not easy to pick up and go with a kid."

"I suppose not. Do you like San Francisco?"

"Sure."

"Ever miss Boston?"

"Occasionally. It's where I grew up—I have memories here." His gaze rested on her. "Some are tougher to forget than others."

Rebecca shifted, suddenly feeling awkward and exposed, and she asked quickly, "Do you think you'll ever bring Mai here?"

"She'd give her eyeteeth to come, but it's not going to happen."

He got up and went to Rebecca, sitting on the bed next to her, knowing he had to tell her. Maybe that was why he'd come up to her room. Not because he couldn't sleep or because he wanted her to explain why she hadn't given him a chance after Saigon, but simply, because he needed to talk.

At last.

He brushed her hair behind her ear and grazed her bruised cheek with one finger. "Rebecca," he said, passing over her nickname, "I want you to promise you'll hear me out."

Her brows furrowed, and the Blackburn incisiveness was there in her gorgeous eyes. But she said, "All right."

"I never slept with Tam."

"So Quentin Reed is Mai's—what? Her biological father?"

The shutters banged in a gust of wind. On the end of Rebecca's bed, Jared shut his eyes and nodded. It was the first time he had ever heard those words spoken aloud: *Quentin is Mai's father.*

"And Mai doesn't know?"

He listened for it, but there was no hint of accusation in her voice. Did Rebecca sympathize with the hard choice he'd made? He had told her everything: Quentin's secret affair with Tam, his stupid involvement with the drug-smuggling scheme, his return home. Jared could still remember the disgust he'd felt toward his cousin, who'd suddenly treated Tam as if she had never existed. Jared couldn't understand why she continued to believe in him, but she did. And he'd kept his promise to her not to tell anyone—not even Rebecca—about the affair she'd had with his cousin. Hothead that Rebecca was, she never would have kept her mouth shut, killing Jared's hope for Tam to begin a new life after her baby was born.

"No, Mai doesn't know," he said, and he looked at Rebecca. "Do you think I want her knocking on Quentin's door so she can see what her real dad looks like? At the very least he abandoned Tam and made it clear he didn't want to have anything to do with their baby. At worst, he had Tam killed and tried to have Mai killed."

As she listened in rigid silence, Jared explained how, the night Tam had died, he'd come to realize she'd contacted Quentin and had cajoled, begged, bribed or threatened him to get her out of Saigon and back into his life. Maybe she'd presented him with an untenable ultimatum, or maybe he was just a coward who couldn't face up to what he'd done. Either way, two assassins had shown up at Jared's Tu Do Street apartment to murder Tam and try to murder Mai… and had almost killed Jared and Rebecca, just because they were there and in the way.

"Now I don't know," he went on heavily. "I don't know if Tam's translation of what the Vietnamese told her through the door was accurate—or if she was hearing what she wanted to hear. She was exhausted and scared. She just couldn't believe Quentin would abandon her and their baby. But that doesn't explain the gems in Mai's diaper, Jean-Paul Gerard, *Le Chat,* Baroness Majlath—" He broke off with a tired huff. "I don't know anymore. There must be a link here we're missing."

Rebecca hugged her knees against her chest and nodded at him, white-faced. But she didn't speak. She was thinking about Quentin leaving a young woman pregnant and alone, and only because she knew Annette Reed could she understand, if never condone, what he'd done.

Mostly she was thinking about the colored "marbles" she had found in Annette's bedroom thirty years ago, and how much they'd cheered up Tam.

Was that their link?

She shook off the thought. It was something to save for later, when she didn't have Jared's warm blue-green eyes searching her face for secrets and answers and maybe a little understanding.

"You told my grandfather everything about Quentin?"

Jared nodded. "R.J., I was scared to death. I didn't know if Quentin had gone completely off the deep end and would try again to kill Mai—or even me. He knew I'd found out about the smuggling. He knew I knew about him and Tam. Maybe he'd decide he couldn't live with the prospect of me blabbing and would have me killed. The point is, I didn't know what he'd do."

"And Grandfather advised you to take Mai and go?"

"No. That was my decision. He supported it. I'd just signed my name as Mai's father so it'd be easier to get her and Tam out of Saigon. That kind of stuff went on all the time those last few weeks. But I had the papers—they were legal." He couldn't go on; his throat was tight, his stomach aching with tension, and he could see Mai at two years old climbing into his lap, saying *Daddy*. "She's my daughter in every way."

Rebecca stretched out her legs, her toes grazing his thigh, and he sensed her confused, raw emotions. "You did what you had to do under the circumstances."

"I ran," he said.

"You saved a child from a father who didn't want her and may have tried to have her killed. I don't think that's running."

"That's what I've been telling myself for years. For

months after we got to San Francisco, I'd hear a noise and wonder if it was another of Quentin's assassination teams come to claim us." He sighed, trying to release some of the pent-up tension. "But what if I was wrong? R.J., what if Gerard and that Vietnamese were after a fortune in gems that had nothing to do with Quentin? When I saw him this morning, he acted as if I'd stolen Tam from him and he believed I did father Mai."

"A rationalization?" Rebecca suggested.

"Maybe. He's always been good at believing what he wants to believe." Jared laughed suddenly, sadly, at the complexity and sheer incredibleness of it all. "Murderers, orphans, thieves, secrets, a fortune in gems—all we need now is a monkey to collect nickels to see the show. But we'll sort this mess out, R.J."

"Together," she said. It wasn't a question; it was a demand.

Jared gave her a long look, and he wasn't surprised to discover that despite fourteen years apart, he still knew R. J. Blackburn. "Okay. What's eating you?"

She pulled her knees back up under her chin. "Nothing."

"Like hell. You've been trying to be nice and understanding, but that's not your way, R.J. Tell me the truth. You think I should have come to you after I got out of the hospital instead of to your grandfather."

"Not necessarily," she said.

"You'd already left Boston," he pointed out.

She flashed him a look that told him his guess was right on. "So? I was in Florida. You could have flown there from Hawaii just as easily as to Boston. You didn't trust me to have enough sense to *help* you work things out."

"You were twenty years old."

"We all have to grow up sometime."

"I was afraid Quentin would have you killed, too."

She faltered, a little of the color going out of her face. "You were protecting me," she said, flattening her legs again, practically kicking him off the bed. "We could have figured something out. Talked to the police. Hired body-guards. Something."

"There was no proof. No trail, Rebecca. Nothing—"

"I was the good guy with a gun that night in Saigon. I managed to shoot that Vietnamese assassin and kept him from killing Mai while you were writhing on the floor with two bullets in the shoulder."

Rebecca, he recalled, had never been one for false modesty or sulking. "Yeah, and you and Mai still would have been killed if it hadn't been for the Frenchman."

"Only because I ran out of bullets—and my aim was off because I was worried about you."

"You know what they say, sweetheart—close don't count but in horseshoes and hand grenades."

She wasn't impressed. "I'm the oldest of six kids. My father was killed by Vietcong guerrillas when I was eight. My grandfather's an outcast. I grew up in a part of Florida that isn't all beaches and air-conditioning and Disney World. We had poisonous snakes, mosquitoes, lizards, giant cock-roaches, spiders, the occasional alligator. I dealt with all of that, Jared." She crossed her arms under her breasts and gave him a scathing Boston Brahmin look that she could have patented. "You could have told me about Quentin."

"And how could I have justified it? 'Oh, R.J.'s had so much thrown at her in her life, what's a little more.'"

She scoffed. "Letting me believe you and Tam had had an affair wasn't exactly sparing me."

"What about the fortune in jewels you neglected to mention?"

"That's different."

"What's good for the goose is good for the gander." Sitting back, he searched her eyes, and the past fourteen years melted away. "The minute you hit Saigon you knew I was in love with you. If you'd really loved me, you could have forgiven me a fling with Tam."

He could see her swallow, but she wasn't one to back down. "And then what? Gerard would have shown up on *our* doorstep, and you'd have said, 'Oh, well, I neglected to tell you this back in 1975, but Tam and I never slept together.'"

"Think we'd have lasted fourteen years?"

Her jaw set hard. "You shouldn't have lied to me."

"I didn't. You asked me if my name as Mai's father was a mistake, and I said no."

"The intent," she pointed out, "was deception, and that's the same as a lie."

"The intent," he said, rolling onto his knees and moving in on her, "was to spare you from having to suffer for choices you didn't make. The intent, I'll have you know, was to keep the twenty-year-old woman I loved from getting killed because of something I'd seen and done." He put a hand on the headboard at either side of her, trapping her between his arms. "There's a nobility of purpose in what I did that you fail to see."

"You made a choice for me that wasn't yours to make."

His face was so close to hers he could feel her breath and the fire of her eyes. "Okay. What would you have done if I came to you in Florida after I got out of the hospital and laid everything on for you?"

She thought a moment. "You wouldn't have gotten the

chance. I'd told Papa O'Keefe and my five brothers what a heel you were, and we had the shotguns loaded, the driveway booby-trapped, the sheriff on alert—"

Jared was laughing, amazed at how good it felt. "I loved you, R.J." And he suddenly grew serious, taking in the sight, smell, closeness of her, and he whispered, "God help me, but I still do."

The memories that had been haunting Rebecca for hours receded, and there was only the present. For a change, it was all she wanted. Jared shut the door and she switched off the light. In the darkness, she listened to the wind and the sound of a siren in the distance, heard the bed creak when Jared sat back down, his bare feet on Eliza's old Persian carpet. She was stretched out on her side so that his hip pressed against her thighs.

"We'll figure out this business with Quentin and Gerard and the Jupiter Stones," he said softly. "We'll figure us out."

She put a cool hand on his arm. "I know we will."

Turning toward her, he rubbed the outer curve of her hip through the soft, silky fabric of her nightgown. She saw that his arms and chest were still well-muscled. There was a no-nonsense toughness to Jared Sloan often belied by his nonchalance and teasing nature. He was willing to make difficult choices; he had made them.

His hand slid over her hip to her waist, stopping just under her breast. "I don't want to rush you into anything."

She smiled and rolled onto her back, so that his hand fell onto the flat of her abdomen. "Rush me."

It was all he needed to hear.

He peeled off his jeans, and when he turned around, she was sitting up with her back to him, holding her hair up on top of her head. "I'll go nuts trying to get these buttons," she said. "Would you mind?"

There seemed to be fifty thousand of the tiny, pearl-like buttons.

"I'm liking this nightgown less and less," he muttered. "It looks like something Queen Victoria would wear."

"She might have, for all I know. I never really thought of buttons as a deterrent, but you only have to unfasten about ten of them. Then I can just pull it over my head."

"Can't I just tear it off?"

She glanced around at him with one of her scrimy Blackburn looks.

He undid the buttons. They were small and many and the job was pure torture, but the reward—

She gave him the honor of lifting the nightgown over her head and tossing it onto the floor. His breath caught at the creaminess of her skin, the softness of her breasts with their pink-pebble tips. How the hell had he gone on without her?

"R.J..."

"I know." Her voice was hoarse, and she brushed one finger along the edge of his sandpapery jaw. "It's been forever."

The curtains at her windows billowed in a breeze that cooled her overheated skin and made her shiver, until Jared came to her and they fell back together onto the narrow bed. She felt hot and light-headed and very aroused. She could sense his hunger in their kiss, in the searing wetness of his tongue. And with the taste of him, the heat of his body against hers, she knew she'd been wrong; it hadn't been forever.

It had, it seemed, just been yesterday.

He smoothed his hands down her sides, all the way to the middle of her thighs and back again, sliding them over her breasts, murmuring how beautiful she was, how much he wanted her. They kissed again, slowly, deliciously. He moved his hips against her. Rocked, swayed. Every movement was titillating and sexy.

She raked her fingers through his hair and pushed his head back so that she could see his eyes and he could see hers. "I can't stand it anymore."

"Good."

His voice was ragged, his eyes were dusky, and she knew he was perilously close to the edge himself. In the next instant, he thrust into her, and she pulled him in deep, crying out as they fell together.

It was a long, sweet, frantic fall.

Just before dawn, Jared eased out of bed and left Rebecca twisted in the covers, sleeping. And by the time he got downstairs, the cuckoo was counting out five o'clock.

He still didn't sleep, but it was just as well. By five-thirty Rebecca was sitting cross-legged on the rug in front of the couch, Sweatshirt curled up placidly in her lap. Jared watched jealously.

"I've got a new theory," Rebecca announced.

"Go ahead—shoot."

"Gerard never knew Tam had the Jupiter Stones the night she was killed. He wasn't there because of them, he was there because of *Quentin*. He knew what Quentin was up to, tried to stop it, and at the same time figured it was something he could use as leverage with Annette."

Jared frowned. "With Annette?"

"Right." Rebecca stroked her cat's soft ears. "She and Gerard must have known each other in 1959 when he was stalking the Riviera as *Le Chat*. Maybe he was in love with Annette, so he gave her the Jupiter Stones as a present."

"And then she fingered him as *Le Chat*."

"Nice of her, huh?"

"You want to explain how you know all this?"

She shrugged, then told him about the colored marbles she and Tam had found at the Winstons' *mas* on the Mediterranean Sea all those years ago.

"Mai's picture brought Gerard out of the woodwork," she went on thoughtfully, "because he was in Saigon the night Tam was killed and knew Quentin was responsible for her death—and nearly yours, mine, and Mai's, as well. His leverage with Annette—to get her to give him the stones—is what he knows about Quentin."

"Why does he want the stones so much?"

"They're incredibly valuable."

"Are we talking millions?"

"I should say. I'm sure he'd also like to nail Annette for turning him in thirty years ago."

The cat crawled out of Rebecca's lap, did one of his ugly cat stretches, and jumped onto the couch. He warily eyed Jared, then pounced, claws bared.

"You're in his spot," Rebecca informed him.

"Uh-oh."

Surrendering, Jared joined Rebecca on the floor. As it turned out, he liked it better that way. "So why does our Frenchman have a soft spot for you?"

She grinned. "You don't think it's just my big blue eyes?"

"Could be—"

"Oh, stop. I guess it's just because he and my father were friends and he doesn't want anything to happen to me. Who knows? He's an ex-jewel thief and a blackmailer, not a murderer."

"How much of this would you guess dear Aunt Annette knows?"

Rebecca sighed. "She's not a particularly sympathetic victim, is she? I would say, though, she must be aware of what Quentin did. That's why she hasn't asked anyone's help in dealing with Gerard. She's covering for Quentin."

"It makes sense," Jared said. "I wish I knew whether or not to talk to her about it—and your grandfather. There's no telling how much of this he's figured out."

On that, they both concurred. "We should get some sleep," Rebecca suggested, "and go at this again with clear heads. You okay?"

He laughed, kissing her lightly. "I'm fine."

"I'll take Sweatshirt back upstairs with me."

"No, let him have the couch. I'll just lie here on the floor and go to sleep knowing I'm going to dream about you."

"You're such a romantic," she said, but he could see he'd cut through her Yankee Blackburn reserve. *My God*, he thought, *is there hope for us, after all?*

Thirty

After hours of nightmares and tossing and turning—of obsessing about one thing and another—Annette gave up any hope of sleeping. She could feel Jean-Paul out in the street, watching her house, waiting for some sign that she was distressed—*reveling* in her discomfort. He wouldn't need anything so human as sleep. Climbing out of bed, she refused even to turn on the light and give him the satisfaction of knowing she couldn't sleep.

He was out there. She knew that much.

She pulled on her robe and ran her fingers through her hair, annoyed at how dry and stiff it felt—nothing but straw. She hadn't taken very good care of herself the past few days. There were still pins in her hair, and her digestion was miserable, and she hadn't done any proper exercise since seeing *The Score*. Ordinarily she took daily walks in the Public Garden or along the river to keep in shape. She went into her bathroom and shut the door, turning on the light and splashing her face with cold water. There were bags under her eyes and a grayish cast to her skin, a look of exhaustion and defeat about her that she abhorred.

When she'd dozed, she'd dreamed of Jean-Paul and herself during those passion-filled, erotic weeks on the Riviera. He'd been so incredibly sexy. She'd never wanted a man as much. Thomas Blackburn she'd wanted to *conquer;* Jean-Paul she simply had wanted to bed...over and over again.

She dried her face and went downstairs, careful in the semidarkness. Her knees were trembling. She heard one crack as she came to the first floor. *You're getting old, m'dear.* Nonsense. She was only sixty. Look at Thomas at seventy-nine—

I won't think about him or Jean-Paul!

Her mind was whirling with images and memories and possibilities...herself as the unfaithful wife, the manipulative mother, the corrupt businesswoman.

"Get hold of yourself, you fool," she snarled aloud. Even if Jean-Paul blabbed all over town, he couldn't prove any of what he'd have to say. Who'd believe that half-dead swine over her?

But what was Thomas up to?

Did he have the Jupiter Stones? How much did he know—how much had he guessed?

Dear God, I can't stand this!

In just her bathrobe, she walked out into the street, quiet just before dawn. She felt cornered and uneasy...and yet she had the glimmer of a plan. Perhaps she should make one last attempt to get Jean-Paul Gerard out of her life for good—and, while she was at it, Thomas Blackburn.

And all she'd be doing was following his advice.

She whirled around, looking up and down the street for the pathetic, distinctive figure of Jean-Paul Gerard, but she saw nothing. *Am I getting paranoid?*

"Can't sleep, *ma belle?*"

Startled, she flung around at him, and he was so close—
so very close. Why hadn't she heard him? His white hair
glistened in the murky light, and his scars made him look
frightening…monstrous.

The man was indestructible.

"It's a lovely night," she said, regaining her breath. "I
thought you might be out here."

He only smiled.

Their toes almost touched. She could feel his warm
eyes on her, and her dream came to her…the memory of
her arousal flooding over her. Even the current reality of
him—his ravaged face, his ugly teeth, his thinness, his
age—didn't stop her from wanting him. If he so much as
hinted he wouldn't laugh, she'd have dropped her robe
and made love to him there on the cold brick sidewalk.

"Jean-Paul." Her voice was sultry; she felt raw and vulnerable, her nipples straining against the filmy robe. Did
he still think her desirable? She swallowed, plunging
ahead. "Jean-Paul, I couldn't sleep because I've been wondering if I didn't make a terrible mistake thirty years ago."

He seemed amused. "It's taken you a long time to consider this possibility, *ma belle.*"

She ignored his heavy sarcasm. *I can't go on like this—
I have to do something.* "You see," she went on, "I lied to
you. My God—Jean-Paul, I never had the Jupiter Stones.
I just told you I did because I knew you wanted them and
I needed to hurt you because I thought you'd betrayed me
by stealing jewels from my friends, from people I knew—
because I thought you'd betrayed *me.*"

"Annette…"

She grabbed his hand; it was surprisingly warm, and so
callused—so hard. "No, hear me out. I've been upstairs
lying awake wondering if I made a terrible mistake when

I turned you in as *Le Chat*. I've been thinking…remembering… Jean-Paul, Thomas Blackburn needed money desperately then for his business venture—that absurd consulting company of his. He was in and out of France for several months." Removing her hand from his, she found her throat tight, her breath coming in gasps, but she made herself go on. "Jean-Paul, you were innocent, weren't you? You were never *Le Chat*."

Jean-Paul's expression didn't soften. "You know what I want."

"Yes, yes—the damn Jupiter Stones. Listen to me, will you?"

"Annette, do you think it makes any difference if I were *Le Chat* thirty years ago or not?"

"I'm telling you I made a *mistake*."

"Congratulations."

"Bastard—"

He shrugged, unaffected by anything she could say to him. "What do you want, Annette?"

"You think I have no feelings—you think I don't *care* about what I've done to you." She brushed tears from her eyes, but Jean-Paul was unmoved. "Thomas came to see me earlier. Were you out here then? Did you see him?"

"What if I did?"

"Then you know I'm telling you the truth."

"All right. I saw him."

She smiled. It wasn't much, but at least she had penetrated his skepticism. "Thomas told me he has the Jupiter Stones."

Nothing. Jean-Paul didn't even move.

"Did you hear me? *Thomas has the Jupiter Stones*."

"I heard you," he said, almost inaudibly.

"Gisela was his friend and he betrayed her. He stole the

stones that meant so much to her. And he's bred the hatred
between us all these years. He let me go ahead and turn you
in as *Le Chat.* Jean-Paul, he could have stopped me. He *let*
me ruin your life. Then when you turned up in Saigon in
1963, he arranged the ambush in order to kill you. Why do
you think he backed out at the last minute? Because he
knew what was going to happen."

"And what about 1975?" he asked.

She hesitated only for a moment…seeing Jean-Paul
coming out of Jared Sloan's Saigon apartment…feeling
that same terror she'd felt when she'd recognized him…
feeling herself jump and shudder when she'd fired her gun
into his face. And the relief. Feeling the washing, cleans-
ing, beautiful relief that at least she was free of him.

Only, of course, the invincible son of a bitch had lived.

"I was in Saigon to *stop* the assassination that night,"
she said quietly. "Tam had discovered Thomas was responsible for her father's death and tried to blackmail him
into helping her get out of the country. Thomas's answer
was to hire that assassin to kill her. I didn't know he was
responsible—I only just figured that out. But I knew she
was in danger. I wanted to help her, Jean-Paul. All right, I
didn't want her as a daughter-in-law, but we were close
when she was a little girl. I don't care if you don't believe
me, but I shot you because I thought you'd been a part of
the killing—"

Jean-Paul remained impassive. "I only want the Jupiter
Stones."

Annette clenched her fists. "And revenge against me for
things I'm telling you I was *duped* into doing to you!"

"Not anymore. Revenge would give me little satisfaction."

"I made a *mistake.* Thomas has the stones. He's had

them all these years and he's known you thought I had them. He's been using us both." She slumped, exhausted and defeated, and waved a hand in despair. "I don't know why I'm trying to explain myself to you. I know you hate me—you deserve to. But to make amends for my own idiocy, I'll get the stones from Thomas for you. Come to my house on the North Shore after lunch today. Let's end this, Jean-Paul, before someone else gets hurt."

Jean-Paul leaned forward, his face very close to hers. "I'll be there, Annette, but I warn you—if you do anything stupid, I'll kill you, as I should have thirty years ago."

"You don't believe me—"

"What I believe makes no difference. Give me back the Jupiter Stones, and we'll be finished." He brushed a curl off her forehead. "Sleep well, *ma belle*."

Thirty-One

—⚬⚬⚬—

Mai didn't relax until she was sitting on the subway into Boston, with Logan Airport and the long, long transcontinental flight behind her. She had hoped to be able to take a cab, but she had only twenty dollars left after buying her plane ticket—and she was lucky to have that much. Because she was over twelve she could buy a ticket without an adult. However, she had to pay full fare, and since she was flying on short notice, a one-way ticket was more expensive than she'd anticipated. But if she waited and took the 12:30 a.m. flight, she could get a cheaper fare. It meant hanging around the airport awhile, risking that her grandfather might figure out what she'd done and come after her, and staying up all night.

The other choices, however, were to go back to Tiberon and face the music or steal her way onto an earlier flight. What did airlines do to stowaways?

She'd bought the ticket for the red-eye.

She wasn't too worried about getting around Boston. Given her longtime desire to go there, she'd bought a dozen different guidebooks and had practically memorized them all. She knew that the subway would take her downtown and she could walk to Winston & Reed, the Winston house on Mt. Vernon Street, the Eliza Blackburn House, even Rebecca Blackburn's studio. Surely her father would be at one of those places. But where to begin?

It was just eight or so California time, after eleven in New England. Mai exulted in how much Boston met her expectations and in her adeptness at getting around in a new city. Her grandfather would just be getting up now and discovering her note. She hoped he'd understand. Her dad wouldn't—no question about that. He'd probably send her to reform school.

But she was worried about him, and if he couldn't understand that, then maybe she *belonged* in reform school. He'd always told her everything, always included her—but not this time. She didn't know who the white-haired man was or why her father had reacted to him like that, with a gun and that mean, mean-looking face. She didn't have any brothers or sisters, no cousins yet, and she'd never known her mother. She adored her grandparents but most of the time it was just her and her dad. She couldn't stand the idea that something would happen to him. What would she do without him?

She wiped tears off her cheeks with the backs of her hands and blamed them on the stiff wind as she walked across the wide plaza of Government Center, up toward Beacon Hill. She would try her great-aunt's house or the Eliza Blackburn House first. Her grandmother, who'd grown up on Mt. Vernon Street, had shown Mai pictures of the Winston house when she had visited Nova Scotia last summer. She thought she'd recognize it when she saw it. And the address of the Eliza Blackburn House was listed in one of her guidebooks, with an acidic comment about its current state of disrepair.

Her dad would be okay, she told herself.

And so would she.

Jared cursed and fumed and tried to hold back his terror as he drove Rebecca's car out to Logan Airport. She had offered a choice of the car or her truck. Thomas had muttered something about how many vehicles one person needed. A recording of a heart-stopping bestselling thriller had come on when he'd started the engine. Only R.J. The cornered innocent was about to bloodily uncorner himself when Jared popped the thing out. He settled for silence.

And speed.

And his relentless anxiety.

Mai.

"The little devil stole a few hundred dollars from me and made her escape like this was some kind of prison," Wesley Sloan, more worried than annoyed, had told him. "She must have slipped into the car with George when he went to the airport. She left a note saying we shouldn't worry, she was joining you in Boston and would be fine."

Mai the optimist.

"I'm sorry, Jared. She'd pleaded illness yesterday afternoon, and we just left her alone for the night. I didn't check on her until this morning."

"Dad, it's all right. I don't blame you."

"It's not as if she's been kidnapped. Jared, she's a resourceful girl. She'll manage. I'm on my way out to the airport now to find out what I can, but if I were you, I'd get out to Logan as soon as possible and check every incoming West Coast flight."

Jared hadn't wasted any time.

He got stuck in tunnel traffic and made a wrong turn in the airport and had to fight traffic to come back around and try again. Then he had to wander around forever to find a place to park. He cursed and fumed some more.

It was nearly noon and had been a bad morning from start to finish. Sleeping too late, getting up to the cold, raw reality of what had gone on between him and R.J. in the night. Loving her. Wanting her again. Not wanting to mess up her life again. Quentin was his cousin and that wasn't one of those things anyone could change.

Thomas and Rebecca had already been up grumbling at each other in the kitchen when Jared had stumbled in shortly after nine. They'd fixed coffee, juice, toast and wild blueberry jam, and ate breakfast in the garden, where the sun was shining between dark, threatening clouds. Jared had already decided to pay Quentin another visit. Perhaps he knew something about Gerard; perhaps Jared had misjudged him. In any case, they needed to talk. Thomas, however, suggested he exercise caution and not plunge ahead until he could assess the possible consequences of action versus inaction. Jared, however, had had fourteen years too many of inaction.

Munching on a piece of toast slathered with jam, Rebecca had explained to Thomas the theory that she, Jared and Sweatshirt had discussed just before dawn.

Thomas refused even to hear her out. "Rebecca, enough. The best thing you and Jared can do is go to San Francisco and let Jean-Paul, Annette and Quentin sort things out for themselves. Gerard has no bone to pick with you two or Mai. He came to San Francisco to see for himself whether or not Quentin's being Mai's biological father was common knowledge—something he could use. He doesn't need to touch her to get what he wants."

They'd just started to argue the point when Wesley Sloan had called.

Jared finally parked and raced into the airport. Every major airline flew into Boston. There were scores of connections Mai could have made to get herself to the east coast— scores of places she could have missed a flight, gotten on the wrong flight. Chicago, Denver, St. Louis, Dallas. Jared pushed back his panic. There were computers, checks and balances, security people. He'd find his daughter.

As he passed a bank of pay phones he decided to stop and call Tiberon for an update.

Maureen Sloan answered on the first ring. "Jared, I'm so glad it's you. Wesley just called. Mai was on a 12:30 a.m. flight out of San Francisco."

"Has it arrived?"

He heard his father's wife inhale sharply. "Over an hour ago."

Thirty-Two

The last person Annette needed drifting into her house was her son, Quentin, but there he was, looking even worse than she felt. A long, cold shower had revived her. She'd dressed in slacks, a simple cotton shirt and her tennis shoes, as if ready for an ordinary Saturday morning. Already she'd called Thomas and he'd agreed to bring the Jupiter Stones to Marblehead at one o'clock. *I can't believe he's had them all these years—or is he just bluffing?* It didn't matter. All she required was his solitary presence on the North Shore in a little more than an hour. The solitary part had been relatively easy; she'd exacted his promise he'd come alone. She knew he wouldn't go back on his word.

She'd already dispatched an eager Nguyen Kim to Marblehead. The years of idleness had been wearing on him, and he yearned for action. Well, now was his chance. She would leave Jean-Paul and Thomas to him.

In the meantime, she would tend to her son. She had made a late breakfast for herself and Quentin for the first time since he was a little boy and she had grudgingly slapped together peanut-butter and jelly sandwiches for him. They'd had servants, of course, but she'd considered waiting on her son part of a mother's responsibility. Quentin would hate her if she didn't make him the occasional sandwich. Thomas had been unimpressed with that kind of thinking. Motherhood, he'd told her, was a role, not a job. He'd sensed her deep dissatisfaction with traditional definitions of that role and had warned her to seek additional positive outlets for her energy and interests before she ruined herself *and* Quentin. Too late now, she supposed he'd say. What of it? She no longer cared what Thomas thought and hadn't asked his advice in the first place.

Quentin only picked at the miniature muffins she'd scrounged out of the refrigerator and reheated, adding a pot of coffee and a pitcher of orange juice and serving the whole mess in the sunroom that jutted out into the garden. Quentin had been complaining about Jared Sloan and Jean-Paul Gerard since he'd wandered in.

"I do wish you would relax," Annette told him impatiently.

"You should have seen Jared yesterday—"

"I did see him. Just ignore him. He's always enjoyed making you feel small and imbecilic." She rested back in her chair, her own breakfast barely touched, but she wouldn't eat until she'd accomplished everything she'd set out to accomplish for the day. It was a tall order, but she was up to it. Forcing herself to focus on her son's problems, she added, "Jared's hardly in any position to judge you."

Quentin sighed, shaking his head sadly. "But the way he talked about Tam. Mother, it was as if he blamed me for what happened to her."

"That's his own guilty conscience at work." Noticing the snappishness of her tone, Annette admonished herself to be more patient: her son deserved that much from her. "Quentin—listen to me, all right? Tam is dead...."

He shut his eyes, wincing as if it were news to him.

Annette could have throttled the weakling. Tam had been dead for fourteen years! Gritting her teeth, she continued. "What Jared has to say about her is, frankly, no concern of yours or mine. You've a perfectly fine wife in Jane. I suggest you remember that and stop fretting. I'm sorry to be so brutal, but it's obvious to me what Tam was."

Quentin lowered his eyes. "And what was she, Mother?"

"A Vietnamese tramp who *used* you." But Annette groaned, slumping down in her chair and feeling awful. "Quentin, Quentin. Why do all our conversations have to be this way? Every time we talk you maneuver me into berating you. Do you think I enjoy it?"

"No, Mother...."

"Then why do you do it? Why ask me about Tam when you *know* what I think? Here I am, trying to be understanding, and you won't let me."

He broke a muffin in half and proceeded to tear it apart, crumb by crumb. "I know—I'm sorry. Maybe I just don't feel I deserve your understanding."

"Oh, Quentin."

She sighed, feeling so damned sorry for him—and furious at the same time. He reminded her so much of Benjamin. *I'm not good enough for you,* he'd told her a thousand times. What the hell kind of man was that? How was she supposed to respect him—to *want* him?

Walking behind Quentin, she put her arm around his shoulder and hugged him fiercely. "You're my *son*. Quentin...don't you understand? You're all I've got. That's what makes me so hard on you, I suppose, but never, never think you don't deserve my sympathy. Now." She straightened up, patted him on the shoulder, and returned to her chair across from him. "What are your plans for the weekend?"

"I don't know—helping to sort out this business with Jared and Gerard, I guess."

"What's there to sort out?"

Quentin cleared his throat, looking at his mother as if she were the tough military-school teacher who always found fault with his answers. If only, Annette thought, he realized what an attractive, powerful, tough-minded man he could be. Even sitting there all worried and stricken, he was as handsome as any man she knew with his tawny hair, square chin, roguish smile and trim weekend clothes. She wished he wouldn't be so damned tentative all the time. *Stand up to me,* she wanted to say—but another time. Right now she just wanted him to get moving.

"Have you heard anything more from the Frenchman?" he asked.

"Jean-Paul Gerard knows I'll do whatever's necessary to protect you."

Quentin looked pained. "Mother, I'm so sorry…."

"Apologies don't help the situation, and feeling sorry for yourself or me will only incapacitate you. You should seize upon adversity as an opportunity to make yourself a better, stronger person."

"I suppose so," he replied, not knowing what else to say. He had risen before dawn and walked out on the rocks at the Winston house on the North Shore, unable to get Tam out of his mind. He couldn't think about her without the burning pain of regret in his stomach. Yet to attempt to explain his feelings to his mother would be futile. Not only would she not hear him out, even if she did, she'd never understand how, after all Tam had done to him, he still felt anguish over what he had done to her. Only after he had abandoned her had she turned to Jared Sloan. That Quentin had had little choice, that he had *intended* to go back for her, meant nothing. Only actions counted.

Her elbows on the table, Annette held her coffee mug in two hands and drank slowly, hoping the caffeine would revive her. She wished Quentin had the courage to meet her eye. What a hellish mess they were in. Thomas, Rebecca, Jared, Jean-Paul. Maybe she should have shot Jean-Paul while she'd had the chance—or let Kim have him. A dead man in her study wouldn't have been the worst thing she'd ever had to explain.

"I've decided to leave for France this afternoon," she said. "I hadn't planned to leave until next weekend at the earliest, but I was up most of the night thinking about this dilemma we're in. Frankly, I think the wisest course of action right now is for me to get out of the country. I usually don't like to confront problems by running, but I can't justify standing up to Jean-Paul when he might jeopardize the safety of others—you, Jared, even Rebecca. Whatever my personal opinion is of those two, I don't want to be responsible in any way for anything Jean-Paul might do to them to twist my arm. It's best I just leave. If Jean-Paul wants to deal with me, he'll have to come to the Riviera."

"Mother, are you sure? You could be leaving yourself open."

She smiled at his boyish concern for his old mother's safety; how sweet. What would he think of her if he knew how deliberate her actions were? "Quentin," she said philosophically, "it's my guess Jean-Paul Gerard won't dare step foot in France to follow me. I'm hoping—call it a calculated risk, if you will—that he'll just give up." She inhaled, then sipped her coffee, debating whether she should bother to go on. Finally, she said, "There's another side to this problem I haven't told you."

Quentin abandoned any pretense of eating breakfast. His mother's seriousness—her very blue eyes riveted on him, her lined face strangely pale—further upset his stomach and made him wonder if he should have come to her. He could have explained his fears to Jane, told her everything about Tam, Saigon, the Frenchman. He could have tracked down Jared and talked to him, tried to clear the air between them. Why had he come to his mother? Not for sympathy and understanding certainly; they were in short supply with Annette Reed. For advice? For hope? For strength and courage?

No, he thought, he'd come to her simply because that's what he'd always done.

"What's that?" he asked in a neutral tone.

"Thirty years ago," she said, "I brought it to the French police's attention that Jean-Paul Gerard was their much-sought jewel thief *Le Chat*."

Not wasting a word, she told Quentin about the Riviera in 1959, the jewel thief *Le Chat,* the popular race-car driver Jean-Paul Gerard, Gerard's flight from the country.

"I thought I'd never hear from him again," she explained, "but obviously I was wrong. He used you to get to me in 1974 with that blackmail scheme. Now he's trying again."

Quentin had listened quietly, horrified. "Mother, I had no idea. What you must be going through...to do the honorable thing and then suffer for it. And obviously I let you down. I gave him a way of getting to you—" Quentin paused and shook his head in sorrow. "I should have been more careful."

"All water over the dam now," Annette said briskly. "You committed a relatively minor transgression, Quentin.

You were twenty-two years old, and you allowed yourself to be duped. If you'd done something I considered really wrong—really inexcusable—I would have let you take your lumps."

"But I was just stupid."

She made no response.

"Why did Gerard wait all these years to come after you again? There must have been something in that article in *The Score*—"

"No, I doubt there was anything specific. *The Score* simply stirred up his old feelings of resentment, and he thought he might as well have another go at me." She pushed aside her virtually untouched plate of muffins. "The point is, Quentin, that he's after me, not you or Jared or Rebecca or anyone else. But if I were Jean-Paul Gerard, I'd think very seriously before I stepped foot into a country I'd left thirty years ago as a fugitive from justice."

Quentin nodded, admiring his mother's courage. He would have complimented her again and again, except she'd had enough of him.

"Go away for the weekend," she told him. "Let Gerard realize he's failed again and go sulk. Everything will be fine." And thinking of Thomas, Annette smiled and added, "I promise."

Jean-Paul relished the taste of the hot, bitter coffee from a twenty-four-hour store on Cambridge Street as he walked back up Joy to the intersection of Mt. Vernon. He'd been debating for hours whether or not to go ahead and meet Annette in Marblehead. What was she trying to accomplish with that nonsense about Thomas Blackburn being *Le Chat?* With Annette, he never knew. He had considered taking the next plane west and returning to the life he had in Honolulu. It wasn't much: odd jobs, a seedy room, too many trips to bars. He'd tried to make friends, but what was the point? He had a knack for getting good people killed.

He remembered Benjamin Reed's screams of agony as he'd slowly died.

Remembered Stephen Blackburn's courageous attempt to defend himself and his party.

And Quang Tai's absolute refusal to show fear or pain to the countrymen whose tactics he so despised.

I should have died that day, not them.

Jean-Paul had fought as long as he could before being wounded and relieved of his weapon. He had assumed the guerrillas would execute him, but instead they'd marched him off as their latest trophy, a French mercenary prisoner. They'd taken his gun and used it to kill others.

Five years of hell he'd endured.

Every day, every hour of his captivity, he had thought of Annette and what she'd done.

Stephen, Benjamin, Tai. All dead because she had lacked the fortitude to kill Jean-Paul and Thomas herself.

All dead because Jean-Paul had been stupid enough to go up against her again. Would Gisela have wanted him to reduce himself to blackmail—to endangering innocent people—to get to Annette Winston Reed?

He had survived his ordeal in the subhuman conditions of the jungle POW camp and emerged into a South Vietnam in the midst of all-out war. Sick and dispirited, Jean-Paul gave up on any idea of exposing Annette or getting back Gisela's Jupiter Stones—until Quentin Reed arrived in Saigon in the fall of 1973.

Quentin wasn't a bad sort, just naive and frightened, but he'd gotten himself into a jam. Jean-Paul had waited to see

if he'd extricate himself. He hadn't. At first he'd okayed
the drug smugglers' use of Winston & Reed planes, not
knowing exactly what they were up to. The next time, he'd
done it out of fear of reprisal. So Jean-Paul had stepped in
and threatened to tell the police what he'd done, using
Quentin's troubles as an opportunity to get to Annette. He
doubted he'd have gone so far as to turn Quentin in to the
authorities, but he was somewhat surprised when Annette's
bright, sensitive son had agreed to her demand he remain
in Boston and give up any hope of a life with Tam. Why
not just tell her to go to hell and return to Saigon and take
his chances?

It was probably just as well, on one level at least, that
he hadn't. In going after Annette through Quentin and his
misdeeds, Jean-Paul had ruined the smugglers' neat little
means of exporting their illicit product—but they didn't
blame him. They blamed Quentin. If he'd returned to
Vietnam, Jean-Paul would have been compelled, no doubt,
to save his life. He'd experienced a twinge of guilt at his
role in Quentin's abandonment of Tam, but Quentin could
have defied his mother and gotten Tam out of Saigon
without stepping into the country. Still, Annette would
have never tolerated a Vietnamese—and especially Tai's
daughter—in her family.

More to the point, Tam had known too much about
Annette. A survivor herself, smart, lively Tam had gotten
plugged into the same network as the woman she'd have
as her mother-in-law and, Jean-Paul believed, became suspicious that Annette had been responsible for her father's
death. Jean-Paul warned her not to seek vengeance.

"Vengeance?" Tam had laughed in disbelief. "I've seen
too much suffering in my country to bother with vengeance.
No, I'll use what I know about Annette to get what I want."

What she wanted was no less than a life with Quentin in the United States.

Jean-Paul had kept an eye on her and Jared, and had been appalled when Rebecca Blackburn turned up in Saigon. He waited for Tam to make her move, prayed she wouldn't...and hoped Stephen Blackburn's beautiful, crazy daughter would get out of Southeast Asia before anything happened to her.

Finally, in the predawn hours of April 29, 1975, Jean-Paul realized—too late—that Tam had gone to Annette Reed with what she knew about 1963. The Vietnamese assassin was Annette's answer to her demands.

Over and over he had pleaded with Tam to forget Quentin and just let Jared Sloan get her out of Vietnam, but Tam had wanted everything: her baby, Quentin, a life in the U.S. "Quentin loves me," she would say, so disarmingly.

As he started down pretty Mt. Vernon Street, Jean-Paul was reminded of the streets of Paris in his boyhood and was glad to shove aside the dark memories of Quang Tam. During his years of captivity, he had coped with his isolation and suffering by recalling every detail of his childhood with his eccentric, warm-hearted mother. Gisela had loved people and wanted them to love her, and she'd wanted to be somebody—not frantically, not jealously. Just for the fun of it.

"Why couldn't I have been born a baroness?" she would ask him, laughing.

So she became one. Then Jean-Paul became a successful race-car driver, and it was too late for Gisela to recant and claim her famous son without jeopardizing the life she'd come to love on the Riviera. Jean-Paul hadn't minded. He and his mother understood one another.

Had she died hating him?

He shook off the question, as he had for thirty years.

Automatically he glanced up at Annette's magnificent house. He spotted a dark-haired girl pausing at the wrought-iron gate and squinting up at the fanlight above the front entrance.

His stomach lurched as he recognized her.

Mai Sloan.

No!

Jean-Paul threw down his foam cup and felt his insides burn as he began to run.

The Jupiter Stones and justice—vengeance—weren't worth another life.

Not a child's life.

With his limp, he couldn't move fast enough. *And what are you going to do when you catch up with her? She'll only scream. Annette will come out and see she's Quentin's daughter—so obviously Quentin's daughter—and that'll be that. She'll whisk Mai inside….*

Jean-Paul slowed, wheezing.

He couldn't risk moving too soon.

Haven't you caused enough trouble? he asked himself. *You should have followed Gisela into the Mediterranean thirty years ago.*

Better than that, he should have killed Annette under the olive tree that miserable day when she'd handed him twenty thousand dollars in payment for the life she'd just destroyed.

There was no undoing the past; he could only make the present right.

Nothing would happen to Mai Sloan.

He settled into the shadows.

"Nothing," he said aloud, waiting.

* * *

Grateful that Quentin was about to leave, Annette went to answer the front door. She'd had all she could take of her son. But she was in a relatively good mood. There'd be an end to all this soon…finally. It wasn't the first time she'd had such a thought. When she'd gotten rid of Jean-Paul in 1959, she'd believed she was free. And then in 1963—for years she'd waited futilely for firm word that he was dead. And 1975. She'd shot Jean-Paul herself and would have made sure he was dead, but Nguyen Kim, her primary contact with the Saigon underworld, had insisted they leave at once for Tan Son Nhut. As it was, they'd only barely gotten out in the ARVN plane he'd commandeered. She shuddered at the memory of the artillery fire all around them, but they'd managed to arrive in Thailand safely. Annette had conducted some business there, quietly arranged for Kim's emigration to the United States, earning his undying gratitude, then taken a commercial flight back to Boston. For the next fourteen years she'd thought despite the uneasy status quo among herself, Quentin and Jared, at least Jean-Paul was dead.

She took a bite of scone and checked through the side window.

She gasped, recognizing the girl on her doorstep at once as Mai Sloan.

Her hands trembling, Annette opened the door. At first she thought the girl's Asian features were unexpected, then decided it was her Caucasian features—and then realized they blended together, inseparable, right.

Annette smiled her most gracious smile. "Hello, dear," she said, hearing the slight catch in her voice. "You must be Mai Sloan."

The girl smiled back, obviously relieved at her welcome,

but Annette had to call on all her powers of self-restraint
not to fall back into the entry and slam the door shut.

In particular when she smiled, Mai's resemblance to
Quentin—to *Benjamin*—was unmistakable.

Mai said, "And you're my great-aunt Annette, right?"

No, Annette thought, no longer any question—or
hope—left, *I'm your grandmother.*

Thirty-Three

Rebecca couldn't stop moving. Her grandfather had twice insisted she sit down because she was driving him crazy, but he himself had trouble standing still. They were in the parlor, trying to figure out where Mai Sloan could have gone. Jared had called from the airport with the news her plane had landed safely and she was on the loose somewhere in Boston. Was she headed to Winston & Reed? Quentin's condominium on Boylston Street? The Winston house on Mt. Vernon? West Cedar? Even Rebecca's studio was a possibility.

Rebecca notified security at the Winston & Reed building and called the watchman at her building on Congress Street, describing Mai as best she could. She left her grandfather's number with both.

Jared was on his way to Quentin's condominium on the Public Garden.

There was no answer at Annette Reed's house.

"I can't stand this," Rebecca said. "I'm going over to Mt. Vernon and have a look. Will you be okay here? You look exhausted."

Her grandfather gave her a pointed look. "I should say I got more sleep last night than you did."

She felt her face redden, but she really had no idea if he *knew* about her and Jared or was just making a good guess. "I'm not eighty," she told him.

"Neither am I."

"Grandfather—"

"Ah," he said, peeking through the front window, "my cab's here."

"Your cab? Where are you going?"

He ignored her question. "Find Mai and sit on her until Jared gets back. I've something I need to do."

"What?"

"I'm not used to having anyone worry about me anymore. Don't you start."

He headed into the entry, Rebecca on his heels. He paid no attention to her. Looking grimly determined, he got his old umbrella out of the coat closet.

"What aren't you telling me?" Rebecca asked him.

He sighed. "Isn't being cracked in the head by Jean-Paul Gerard enough to convince you there are dangers involved here?"

"You know Gerard isn't going to kill me. He just wants me out of the way—maybe for my own protection, who knows? The same with Mai. He's not going to hurt her. He had his chance in Saigon and saved her life instead."

Thomas added a rain hat that looked as if it had seen a few too many tropical storms. "I'll be back as soon as I can."

Acting on impulse, Rebecca grabbed his arm, even as she stifled a surge of panic. "Grandfather, please."

A kind of pain crossed his face. "Rebecca, please." He pried her fingers loose and held them tightly against his chest, reminding her of the powerful man he'd been in his younger years. "I know your brain is in overdrive as you try to put all these pieces together, but understand this—I will not have you hurt. This is *my* affair—*my* responsibility. It's something I should have dealt with thirty years ago."

"I was involved then. I was the one who found the Jupiter Stones in the first place."

"You were four years old."

"Mai wasn't a day old when that assassin tried to kill her, so age has damned little to do with it. If you're involved, you're involved. Let me help you—"

"Move aside, Rebecca," he said, not ungently, "before you discover how much strength your old grandfather has left."

She relented, and he let go of her hand. "Wherever you're going—do you need the Jupiter Stones?"

"At this point I doubt they'll make any difference."

Rebecca's eyes narrowed. "You know something, don't you?"

Out on West Cedar, the cab's horn honked impatiently.

"My dear, I have a doctorate in Asian history." He smiled mischievously, his eyes suddenly dancing. "I know a great deal."

His smile and teasing only accentuated how much Rebecca didn't want anything to happen to him—how much she couldn't bear to lose him. *Don't go away from me,* she thought. *Please, Grandfather, not yet.*

Biting her lip, she followed him out to the front steps. It was drizzling and chilly, and she thought of Mai wandering alone in the dank city.

"But do you know," Rebecca said to her grandfather, "that Annette Reed and not Jean-Paul Gerard was *Le Chat?*"

She'd intended her statement to rock her grandfather to

his very core—to make him stop and tell her what was going on, what the phone call earlier had been about, why he'd called a cab, where he was headed—but he merely frowned up at her from the bottom of the steps.

He said, "That kind of idle speculation will land you in court for slander."

She crossed her arms under her breasts and leaned against the doorjamb. "Not if it's true."

"Do you have any proof?"

"No—"

"Then it'd come to a choice between the word of a Blackburn and the word of a Winston. Two hundred years ago a Blackburn would have won. But today?" He tucked his old umbrella under one arm. "Ponder that while I'm off."

Rebecca had no intention of pondering anything. "It makes sense, you know. Annette had the Jupiter Stones in her possession in 1959. If Jean-Paul Gerard was going to spend the next three decades trying to get them back, why'd he give them to her in the first place?"

"I'm not listening—"

"Why do they mean so much to him? You were at Baroness Majlath's funeral. Any guesses?"

He refused to answer. His back to her, he walked out to the street.

Rebecca just talked louder. "Jean-Paul hasn't just been after the stones for the past thirty years. He wants revenge, too. If he was *Le Chat,* Annette only did what he might have expected her to do, so vengeance wouldn't really be a factor. But if she *framed* him and wrecked his life for something he didn't even do, he'd carry that grudge for a long time."

Thomas swung around abruptly, his face red, and

pointed the end of his closed umbrella at her. "That's enough, Rebecca. I suggest *you* learn to practice a little discretion."

The cab driver had rolled down his window. "Lady, buster—you want to talk or you want to get moving?"

"Do you mind if I go about my business?" Thomas asked his granddaughter quietly.

"You don't need my permission. So go ahead. Do what you have to do."

He gave her a mock bow. "Thank you."

"But Grandfather—am I right?"

If he heard her, he pretended not to, and Rebecca kicked the open door in frustration, adding another scuff and crack for the neighbors to complain about. But as she went back inside, she turned in time to see her grandfather blow her a kiss. She blew him one back, fighting sudden tears. He was an old snob and a man of secrets and riddles, and she loved him with all her heart.

"Where to?" the cab driver asked.

"Marblehead Neck. I'll give you more specific directions when we get there."

"You know it's going to cost you—"

"Yes," Thomas interrupted wearily, "I know."

He settled back against the ragged seat and prayed he was doing the right thing. Acceding to Annette's wishes, abandoning the search for Mai Sloan, not telling Rebecca where he was headed.

Aah, he thought, choices.

"You okay back there?" the driver asked.

Thomas nodded, exhausted. Rebecca had been right about that. He supposed he must look terrible. When a person reached the rather advanced age of seventy-nine, people tended to think he or she was going to expire any moment, without warning. Thomas wouldn't mind going that way—but not today, thank you. Not before he'd had a chance to finish things with Annette.

Until this week he hadn't really known she'd been behind Tam's death. He had always had that glimmer of doubt that Quentin, secure in his new high-level job at Winston & Reed and ever-afraid of his mother, might actually have put out the word that he didn't want his ex-lover coming into the country. But knowing Annette as he did, Thomas realized she was the more likely suspect.

Either way, Mai Sloan would have been in serious danger if Jared had stayed in Boston and pushed for answers. He had chosen to take her to San Francisco. Legally, she was his daughter. Thomas supported that decision. He continued to believe it had been the right one.

But Quentin...

Thomas, as much as anyone, knew how persuasive and charming and awe-inspiring Annette could be.

I should have whisked Quentin from her years ago and raised him myself—or tried to undermine her influence and get him to see his own strengths, get him to defy her.

He hadn't, of course. And Quentin had proved incapable of doing anything but worshiping his mother and believing every nasty thing she said about him, her own son.

"Oh, Annette," Thomas said to himself, so tired he could scarcely breathe, "whatever happened to you?"

The driver eyed him worriedly in the rearview mirror. Thomas smiled back, and they drove on.

Thirty-Four

━━━━━⟋⟋⟍⟍━━━━━

One of the great terrors of Annette's life was when her nephew had arrived in Boston after his close call in Saigon. She hadn't necessarily intended Jared or Rebecca to die that night. Her specific instructions to the man Kim had hired were to locate the Jupiter Stones and to make absolutely certain that Tam and her baby—Annette didn't even know if she'd had it yet—didn't leave the country. She had told him to use his discretion regarding anything unforeseen that came up. There were a variety of ways he could have dealt with two American witnesses, although, of course, shooting them was by far the surest.

Annette had no idea what Jean-Paul might have told Jared and Rebecca while they were in the Tu Do Street apartment together, or even before that terrible night. Jean-Paul could have told Jared everything during her nephew's eleven months in Saigon. Jean-Paul could have gone to Rebecca and boasted about being Stephen Blackburn's friend. Annette didn't know what the Frenchman had done, and that bothered her.

With Jared in Boston, Annette had dispatched Quentin

immediately to Europe, out of his cousin's path. As a further precautionary measure, she had had Kim follow Jared and thus knew he'd gone straight to Thomas.

That only augmented her fear.

As much as she could explain away the ambushes, affairs, robberies, Jupiter Stones and whatnot, Annette couldn't deny she had deliberately misled her son into believing Jared had fathered Tam's baby. She supposed she could admit she'd made a mistake—but then what? More questions? More accusations? A son who no longer believed in her?

And there was Mai, of course. Knowing Quentin as she did, Annette assumed he'd never forgive her for having ruined any hope of his and Tam having a life together in Boston. And he didn't even realize Annette had had the manipulative little bitch killed.

She still had the note Tam had written her:

Dear Mrs. Reed,
I know what you did to my father. I know about your illicit network here in Saigon. I know you were the jewel thief on the Riviera in 1959. I have the Jupiter Stones. I found them among your things before leaving France. You can have them back and I will forget everything I know about you, if only you'll let me have Quentin. I love him and he loves me. I know he'd never abandon me unless you made him, unless you lied to him. But help me, and I will keep my silence.

Tam had kept her silence anyway, hadn't she?
Annette had suffered the threat of Jean-Paul Gerard for

too many years not to know how to deal with another schemer swiftly and surely.

She wasn't sure what her nephew would prove to be.

He never did try to see Quentin or her. Instead he announced that Mai was his daughter by Tam, a tragic victim of those last violent, wrenching days of South Vietnam, and returned to San Francisco.

His mother mentioned that Jared had papers for the baby, and Annette entertained the possibility that Jared and Tam had slept together and he believed Mai was, in fact, their daughter. It would have had to be a casual fling. Jared was another honorable sort, and he and Rebecca had been so in love that a full-blown affair seemed unlikely.

But Rebecca apparently believed Mai was Tam and Jared's child, and no one was more surprised than Annette when Rebecca and Jared split up.

Taking the bull by the horns, Annette decided it would be prudent to do her part in keeping him out of Boston. She made it clear she objected to his fathering an illegitimate half-Vietnamese child and didn't want anything to do with her. He'd responded exactly as she'd hoped he would; she hadn't heard from him in fourteen years.

But if Annette had any lingering uncertainty over whether Jared or Quentin had fathered Tam's baby, seeing Mai at fourteen ended that.

She brought the girl into her home and silently prayed Quentin had taken the opportunity of his mother's absence to leave.

He hadn't.

He was in the kitchen when Mai smiled at him in the way that reminded Annette so much of Benjamin.

"Mai," Annette said, holding the girl by the shoulders, "this is your father's cousin, Quentin."

* * *

Mai...

Relieved and somewhat surprised by his mother's cheerful welcome of Jared's daughter, Quentin held his breath and stared at the girl, fighting to keep from crying. Everything about her reminded him of Tam—of how much he'd missed his cousin Jared being a part of his life. *This is their daughter, Jared and Tam's.* Quentin had long since forgiven them. He'd abandoned Tam, after all, at least in her eyes. He'd told her a thousand times he would love her forever, that no matter what happened when he went back to Boston to crawl on his belly for his mother's help, she should not give up on him. He'd be back or he'd get her to Boston. They must have been meaningless words to her. How many American men had made similar promises to her friends over the years? Perhaps she'd understood him at twenty-two better than he'd understood himself and had realized he'd never come back—not that he'd had the chance. How many *days* before she and Jared were at it?

When his mother told him Tam was pregnant and had moved in with Jared, his fantasies of swooping into Saigon and bringing Tam home abruptly ceased.

But he hadn't wanted anything to happen to her, and he hadn't wanted to lose Jared. He had been like a big brother to Quentin.

In a way, he supposed he'd abandoned Jared, as well as Tam. He could have gone to San Francisco anytime, defied his mother's wishes and risked Jared's throwing him out for what he'd done to Tam—risked his own discomfort at seeing Mai. Of course, Jared had shown no indication of wanting to see Quentin in the last fourteen years, either. Did Jared blame him for Tam's death? Did he think Tam would be alive if only Quentin had gone ahead and married her?

But Jean-Paul Gerard had tested Quentin's courage in 1974, and it had come up lacking.

"It's good to meet you," he said to his pretty cousin, his voice cracking as he vainly tried to sound cheerful, "finally."

Annette and Quentin were friendlier than Mai had expected from her father's rare descriptions of them and seemed genuinely glad to see her. Mai gratefully accepted a warm muffin and milk while her great-aunt busily rinsed the breakfast dishes and put them in the dishwasher. She was so different from Mai's grandmother, who'd once explained that her younger sister Annette had taken no interest in Mai for her own selfish reasons, not because of anything Mai was or had done. Annette, her sister had said, was essentially an insecure woman who desperately needed recognition and affirmation from everyone around her, but was also incapable of seeing her own weaknesses. Mai's grandmother talked a lot about the importance of self-understanding.

"Quentin, there's no need for you to waste your weekend hanging around here," Annette said. "I've got a lot to do."

"What about Mai?"

"Your father knows you're here?" Annette asked.

Mai made a guilty face. "Well…"

"He doesn't."

Mai nodded and admitted her father might not even know she was in Boston. She added, "Do you know where he's staying?"

"I'm afraid not, but we'll work something out. In fact—" Annette turned to her son. "Quentin, I know this will come as a shock, but Thomas Blackburn called earlier and said he'd like to meet me in Marblehead. Please don't interrupt and just listen. Thomas indicated Jared would be there, as well. I'm hoping this means we can work something out to make peace between our families. It's going to be a tight squeeze for me to get up there and back before I leave later this afternoon, but why don't I take Mai along? I can just turn her over to her father when he arrives."

"All right, but why don't I join you?"

"Perhaps you should keep an eye out for Jared and let him know I've got Mai and everything's okay. We'll see him in Marblehead." She turned to Mai and smiled reassuringly. "How does that sound to you?"

"Okay, but I guess I should let my dad know I'm all right…as soon as possible."

"I know several places he might be staying. We can try to call him on the car phone. How's that? And we know he'll be in Marblehead before too long—has he or your grandmother ever told you about the Winston house there? Your dad and cousin Quentin used to play there all the time when they were just boys."

"Grandmum showed me pictures of it." Mai beamed, remembering how much she'd wanted to visit the huge, rambling house. "I'd love to see it."

Annette dried her hands and then put one out for Mai to take. "Then let's go."

Thirty-Five

"Sofi—Sofi, it's Rebecca. I need your help."

She was pacing in her grandfather's kitchen. She still hadn't heard word from anyone—her building, Winston & Reed, Jared. She couldn't wait around for something to happen.

Sofi said, "Words I've despaired of hearing from R. J. Blackburn. What can I do?"

"I need you to come over here now."

"Done—"

"No, wait. I won't be here. Listen—I'm leaving the Jupiter Stones on my bed. Take them to a safe place. I imagine David Rubin can secure them. Nobody comes near them except Jean-Paul Gerard, Jared Sloan, my grandfather or me."

Sofi inhaled sharply. "Jean-Paul Gerard. R.J., isn't he a crook?"

Rebecca abruptly stopped pacing. "No. He's not a crook. If something happens and none of us is able to get the stones, tell the police the gems were found in Annette

Reed's possessions in 1959 in the south of France, but not recovered until now."

"Wait just a minute. What's this about 'if you're not able to'?"

Rebecca resumed pacing and answered as clearly and as concisely as she could. "I can't go into all the details right now. Tell the police Annette was *Le Chat,* and they've got to prove it and set the record straight. They have to admit they were wrong about Jean-Paul Gerard."

"R.J.—"

"Sofi, will you do it?"

"I'm on my way."

Rebecca hung up. The rain had picked up, the wind whipping it against the windows. As a little girl, she had loved to be in there while it rained. She'd color, read, play games with her brothers, just sit and watch the raindrops hit the puddles. Florida storms and the drafty O'Keefe house were different, but she'd brought her love of rainy days south with her.

It would be so easy, she thought, just to go upstairs and curl up on her bed and do nothing.

She dragged out her handbag, withdrew the red velvet bag of stones, and took the two flights of stairs two and three steps at a time and left the Jupiter Stones on her pillow.

Back downstairs, Athena was munching on an English muffin with pictures of dead bodies unfolded on her lap.

"I'm going out," Rebecca told her. "If an Amerasian girl—fourteen years old—comes by, sit on her until Jared Sloan gets back."

Athena glanced up with dark, intelligent eyes. "His daughter?"

"Yes."

"And if he asks where you are?"

"Mt. Vernon Street. He'll know—tell him it's all Annette."

Athena didn't need to repeat the instructions, just said, "Okay," and returned to her studying.

Rebecca headed out.

Jean-Paul hobbled down Mt. Vernon Street, knowing there was no longer any time…knowing he should have strangled Annette last night when he'd had the chance. He had jumped in front of the big Mercedes coming out of her driveway, trying to impede its progress out into the street. He'd pulled on the doors, but they were locked. He'd banged on the windows and screamed at Mai to run.

She'd looked nervous, but Jean-Paul had seen Annette's reassuring smile and heard her as she rolled her window down a few inches. "Don't worry—I won't let him hurt you." Then she'd turned to him. She knew she had him. "See you soon."

The powerful car lurched, throwing Jean-Paul off. He'd landed hard and cried out at the pain slicing up from his bad leg.

Now he needed a car, a way to get to Marblehead. There was no question in his mind that Annette was using Mai to lure him to her house there. It was a private setting. She could kill him—finally. And Mai? What would Annette do with the girl? Jean-Paul felt himself go numb with shock and pain. Annette would kill Mai. She'd tried once before, in Saigon.

What have I done?

Rebecca Blackburn swung around the corner. Her expression, her mouth set hard against the rain, reminded him of her father so long ago. She was already older than he had been when he'd died. "She's a relentless mix," Stephen had said affectionately of his young daughter, "of her mother and her grandfather."

No, my friend, nothing will happen to her.

But right now Jean-Paul needed her help.

Her gaze fell on him and she didn't flee, as perhaps would have been smart. She came to him, running hard and just daring him to try and get away. Instead he moved toward her.

Before she could speak, he said, "There's no time. Rebecca, I need a car. Annette—"

"I know about her."

Jean-Paul could see that she did, and a surprising sense of peace came over him as Rebecca looked at him without fear, without hatred, without confusion. For the first time in thirty years he had someone who believed in him. That it was Rebecca meant everything to him.

But he said, "It makes no difference."

"I have a truck. Come on—let's go. You can tell me everything on the way."

"No."

Already starting down West Cedar, she swung back around at him, her rain-soaked hair whipping into her face. Jean-Paul grabbed her by the shoulders and held her tight. If his action created any doubts about her conclusions about him and Annette, they didn't register in her pale, wet face.

"The keys," he said.

"If you want them you have to take me with you. My grandfather's in trouble, isn't he?"

"Give me the keys, Rebecca." He hesitated as his words had no discernible effect on her. Then, finally, he said, "Annette has Mai. She's going to finish what she started in 1975."

At Rebecca's stricken look, Jean-Paul acted, taking advantage. He grabbed her wrist and twisted it behind her back, sticking one hand into the pocket of her soaked jacket, then the other. He came up with a set of keys.

"Which truck?"

"You're hurting me—"

"You'll survive, but I'll break your arm if you don't tell me. Which truck?"

"You'll know."

Glancing down West Cedar, he saw what she meant. Amidst the upscale cars was one battered ten-year-old truck. He started to release Rebecca, but knew she would only chase after him. Even if she didn't have his soldier's experience, she was younger, faster and didn't have his bad leg. But he couldn't bring himself to break her arm. Adding pressure, he pushed her down to her knees. She cried out in pain, but he didn't release her.

"Let me do what I have to do," he said.

Then, swiftly and with calculated force, he kneed her in the side, catching her in the ribs. She doubled over in pain, momentarily breathless.

Moving as quickly as he could, Jean-Paul hurried toward her truck.

Rebecca caught her breath and forced herself back upright. Her arm ached; she could see the imprint of Jean-Paul's fingers on her wrist. The cold rain pelted down on her, but she ignored it. To get off West Cedar, Jean-Paul was going to have to drive past her.

In the next seconds, she heard the familiar rattle of her truck.

She was surprisingly steady on her feet, but to mislead Jean-Paul, she wobbled around as her truck came to the intersection of Mt. Vernon and West Cedar and slowed for a car speeding down Mt. Vernon.

Rebecca lunged and grabbed on to the back of the pickup, grabbing hold of the tailgate as Jean-Paul shifted gears and screeched sharply to the right, out onto Mt. Vernon. She could see Jean-Paul checking his rearview mirror. She hauled herself up and over the tailgate and went sprawling into the back of the truck, landing hard.

Jean-Paul slammed on the brakes at Charles Street, got out and walked around to her. "You don't give up, do you?"

"I'm going wherever you're going," she said, "even if I have to steal a car and follow you—"

"All right. We're wasting time." He put out a hand. "Come on."

Not trusting him, she ignored his offered hand and climbed down on the other side of the truck. Her arm ached, her side ached, she'd banged her knee leaping onto the tailgate—but Annette had Mai, and Rebecca didn't know where her grandfather was. She jumped into the passenger seat before Jean-Paul could get back behind the wheel and speed off without her.

"Why do you care so much about me?" she asked him as he thrust the old truck into gear and clattered onto Charles Street, heading toward Storrow Drive.

He looked at her and grunted. "Don't push your luck."

"No, I'm serious. You could have knocked me out or run me over. There's something going on between you and me that goes beyond a macho Frenchman's idea of protecting a helpless woman."

His white eyebrows arched, and for a moment she could see vestiges of the dashing race-car driver he'd been. "You're no one's idea of helpless."

"So why do you care about me?"

"Because," he said, "I'm too stupid to know any better."

* * *

Jared did everything short of taking on a half-dozen security guards and breaking in to Quentin's condominium in the elegantly subdued five-star hotel on the Public Garden. Chords of Mozart floated down the hall from the tearoom where a pianist in black tie was entertaining the sparse crowd gathered on love seats and wingbacked chairs, being civilized and very correct. The man at the front desk had suggested several times that Jared have a seat in there and await his cousin's return. A pot of tea and Mozart. Just what he needed.

Where's Mai?

"I don't have any change," he told the man at the front desk he'd been harassing. "I need to make a call—"

He pushed a telephone toward Jared. "Please," he said, "go right ahead."

His stomach burning, he dialed the Eliza Blackburn House.

"Put on a tape if you like," Annette told the nervous girl sitting beside her. They were already winding through the familiar streets of the picturesque seaside town of Marblehead. "It'll only be a few more minutes."

Mai hunched over toward the passenger door. "That's okay."

"You're still worried about that man, aren't you?"

Nodding slowly, Mai decided not to mention that she was also worried about her great-aunt. Going off with her to Marblehead had suddenly not seemed such a good idea when the Frenchman had pounced on the Reed car. Why had he told her to run? Why had he looked so scared?

"Do you know who he is?" Mai asked.

"I have no idea. Mai, I don't want to worry you needlessly, but…well, dear, I believe he's the man who killed your mother. Any proof we could get would be in Saigon—Ho Chi Minh City now. We'll talk to your father about him after we get to Marblehead, all right?"

Mai shut her eyes tight, trying to squeeze back the tears. She wanted to talk to her dad now. She didn't trust Annette Reed. No wonder her dad hadn't let her come visit Boston. His aunt was weird.

"Calm down," Annette said. "Everything will be fine."

The minute the car slowed down, Mai thought, she was going to jump out and run and call the police to bring her father to her.

Annette, however, gave no indication she'd be slowing down anytime soon.

Jean-Paul had Rebecca's truck cranked up to seventy as he negotiated the intricacies of 1A and corrected his passenger on the mistakes in detail she'd made in her rendition of the events of the past thirty years. The general scope of Annette's wrongdoing—and his own—she had exactly right.

"So in 1959," she said, "you and Annette had an affair and she framed you for a series of jewel robberies you didn't commit. Why didn't you stand up for yourself?"

"The evidence was against me—Annette had planted one of her own bracelets in my house and said I'd stolen it from her. And, Rebecca, who do you think would have believed me? I was a daring Grand Prix driver. She was a proper Boston housewife—"

"Who got her kicks stealing jewels from her wealthy friends and acquaintances." Rebecca winced. "I guess you were caught between a rock and a hard place."

"She warned me I was about to be arrested and paid me

to get out of the country—to avoid the embarrassment of our affair coming out."

"Did she realize you knew she was *Le Chat?*"

"No, she still doesn't." Jean-Paul gripped the steering wheel, remembering her attempt last night to get him to believe Thomas was *Le Chat*. A clever way, he now saw, to get them both out to the relative isolation and privacy of the Winston house on Marblehead Neck. He added, "She's convinced it's her secret."

"And that's what started everything else?"

"That and my own greed, my own inability to let the past be."

"You wanted the Jupiter Stones?"

"Yes."

Rebecca turned and stared out her window. "I have them, you know."

Jean-Paul stopped breathing. "What do you mean?"

And she told him…about Tam at six and herself at four in Annette's room…about infant Mai screaming on the helicopter and Rebecca scooping out the fortune in gems… about hanging on to them for the past fourteen years thinking Tam must have been planning to smuggle the jewels into the U.S., and that the Vietnamese who'd killed her had been after them.

When she finished, Jean-Paul was unable to speak.

Rebecca looked at him. "You've always thought Annette had the Jupiter Stones, haven't you?"

He nodded, the slow, dull, agonizing ache of regret working its way through him.

"That night in Saigon," Rebecca said. "You had no idea Tam had the stones?"

"No," he whispered. It was nearly impossible to utter a word. "She must have figured out everything and threatened Annette...." He broke off, choking back tears. "If only I'd left well enough alone."

"You risked your own life in an attempt to save Tam's—and you did save mine, Mai's, Jared's. You shot Jared to keep the Vietnamese from killing him outright, didn't you?"

"Yes..."

Tam, he thought. Beautiful, stubborn, determined Tam. All these years she'd had the Empress Elisabeth's gems. Had she realized their monetary value? With the Jupiter Stones, she could have bought herself a new life in any country in the world. But not Tam, Jean-Paul remembered. At twenty-two she had wanted love and happiness...a life with Quentin Reed. So she had used the valuable gems—the stones that could damn Annette as a liar, a jewel thief, and even a murderer—as a means to get what she wanted.

Help me, Madame Reed, Jean-Paul could hear her saying, *and I'll return the Jupiter Stones to you. Let me have Quentin...let me have a life.*

It was all so clear to him now.

Aah, Maman, I've failed you again.

Beside him, Rebecca asked, "What happened to you after that night?"

Annette, he explained, had slipped into Saigon to make certain Tam and her baby didn't get out. As South Vietnam had collapsed, her network had scattered, and, in any case, she was unwilling to delegate this particular nettling problem. Not until he had spotted her hired assassin going into Jared Sloan's apartment had Jean-Paul realized she was even in the city. Knowing he was probably too late, he had raced after the Vietnamese, but already Tam was dead. Jean-Paul told him Annette had sent him as backup.

Afterward, Jean-Paul had gone after her.

"I didn't know where she was," he said, in a neutral tone that surprised him. "That gave her an advantage."

She had shot him in the face and left him for dead in an alley.

Jean-Paul regained consciousness in a communist Saigon. All around him were *bo dois,* communist soldiers. His face was shattered, and his recovery, in hiding, was slow. It was eighteen months before he could escape with dozens of refugees in a fishing boat, a grueling experience for which even his years as a POW hadn't prepared him.

He got as far as Honolulu before his body gave out again, to malnutrition, dehydration, infection. The next months he spent on the streets just trying to stay alive. How could he possibly take on Annette Reed? He saw her picture in a magazine, read about her in cast-off copies of the *Wall Street Journal.* She was untouchable.

You've survived, he'd told himself. Be glad of that.

Not until he'd seen the copy of *The Score* had he known Rebecca, Jared Sloan and Mai had gotten out alive. He could have found out but hadn't. The picture was like a call to action. His final chance.

Stupidly, arrogantly, ridiculously, he had thought he could succeed this time in compelling Annette to give up the Jupiter Stones and to bring her to justice for the crimes she'd committed.

But Annette had never had the Jupiter Stones.

"I should have stayed in Honolulu," he told Rebecca.

She smiled with tragic understanding. "Isn't hindsight wonderful?"

As they drove on, she had her own gloomy thoughts to fight. She loved Jared. Nothing had changed after all. If anything happened to Mai…

"If you knew for certain you were doing the right thing,"

her grandfather had often said, "you wouldn't be making a difficult choice."

No crystal ball.

He had chosen silence in 1963. Twelve years later, Jean-Paul had chosen to risk his own life to keep Annette from adding to her body count. Jared had chosen to claim Mai as his own child and raise her.

Not easy choices, maybe not even the right choices— but they'd had to make a decision. And all choices, all decisions, had ramifications.

Was that something Annette understood? She had tried to kill Mai once already…*her own granddaughter.*

"We'll get Mai away from her," Jean-Paul said, reading Rebecca's thoughts. "Annette knows I was hesitating about going to Marblehead. She's using Mai to lure me."

"What do you think her strategy is?"

"To blame the last thirty years on your grandfather," he replied calmly, "and to kill him and me."

"But that's crazy!"

He fastened his warm, soft eyes on her. "Think about it, Rebecca. Is it?"

Thirty-Six

$\sim$ ⤜⤚⤛ $\sim$

The Winstons' house on Marblehead Neck was much as Thomas remembered from his first visit there with Emily, before World War II, but he wasn't the same man he'd been. As he stumbled on the slippery rocks and shivered in the biting ocean wind, he could see Annette as a little girl, climbing up to him, her hands filled with seaweed and periwinkles, her cheeks rosy and her eyes bright with triumph.

"Look, Uncle Thomas, look! Do you think I'll find a mermaid, too?" she'd asked.

"Keep looking," he'd said. "You never know."

"I'm going to show Father."

Minutes later, Thomas had seen John Winston angrily marching to the edge of the rocks with little Annette's treasures and flinging them as far as he could, and her mother taking her sobbing daughter inside to wash her hands and change her dress, telling her there were no such thing as mermaids.

All more than a half century ago and yet, Thomas thought, clearer in his mind than anything that had happened last year.

Behind him on the rocks, Nguyen Kim commanded him to stop. Thomas was perfectly glad to oblige. He'd read somewhere that balance and the legs were the first to go as one aged, and from this billy-goat climb down to the water's edge, he could attest to that theory's veracity.

They had come to a relatively level area of barnacle-covered boulders and tide pools below the tide line, well out of view of the house. With the gathering storm, the tide was coming in high, with huge, frothy swells. Already Thomas could feel the icy spray of the roiling waves on his face. Had Annette, he wondered, made her plan according to the weather, or were the turbulent seas just another of her happy coincidences?

He turned around, and Kim pointed to a rock and ordered him to sit.

"Barnacles are sharp," Thomas said.

Kim grinned. "Good."

Annette's Vietnamese bodyguard had met Thomas on the lawn and, without a great deal of fanfare, had revealed the gun tucked in his waistband and suggested Thomas lead the way down to the rocks.

Thomas had hoped the bastard would trip and accidentally shoot off his own balls.

He sat on the rock. The barnacles pricked his rear end, but it wasn't that uncomfortable—preferable, he supposed, to a bullet in the head, although that might be next.

"I gather Annette doesn't want me killed in her living room," Thomas commented.

Not answering, Kim removed a length of rope from his back pants pocket.

Thomas stiffened his jaw so that his teeth wouldn't chatter, but the cold had reached into his bones. "Afraid I'd come back and haunt the place, isn't she?"

"Your hands," Kim said.

With a resigned sigh, Thomas crossed his hands behind his back, and Kim immediately came round and whisked the rope around his wrists, Kim repeating the move with Thomas's ankles, the knots tight enough that what little circulation he had to his extremities was immediately cut off. He'd always had an irrational fear of having to have a hand or foot lopped off, but supposed that'd be a luxury now.

"You always were efficient," he said mildly.

Kim fastened his hard eyes on him. "I've only done what I had to do to survive."

"And what, might I ask," he said, unflinchingly meeting the Vietnamese's gaze, "is so bloody important about your surviving?"

"You're going to die today, old man."

Thomas gave him a cool, appraising look. "As I should have twenty-six years ago?"

Not responding, Kim gave the ropes at his captive's hands and feet a final tug and bounced back onto his feet.

"Nguyen Kim," Thomas said, rolling the name around in his mind, as if he hadn't made up his mind yet whether he recognized it or not. "Quang Tai's friend, weren't you?"

"I knew him."

"Did you know you were signing his death certificate when you tipped off your Vietcong friends on Annette's behalf?" Thomas's gaze didn't let up. "That was you, Kim. Tai trusted you. He told you my itinerary—and you, brave fellow, told the insurgents."

Kim remained impassive. "I was doing a job," he spat. "On your stomach!"

But Thomas wasn't fast enough for Kim, who grabbed him by the shoulder and thrust him onto a huge, flat boulder. Thomas felt the sharp barnacles bite into his cheeks.

"You're going to drown, old man," Kim said.

His feet crunching on the barnacles, he hurried off, leaving Thomas trapped at the water's edge, unable to do much beyond listening to the rhythmic sounds of the approaching tide.

Jared's call to Sofi Mencini shook him. She had gone over to Mt. Vernon Street herself, but saw no sign of Annette, Rebecca, Mai, Thomas or Jean-Paul. "I'm worried, Jared," Sofi had said.

"So am I."

"David's putting the stones in a safe at the store, but I'm calling the cops."

Jared agreed. "I'll join you as soon as I can."

Through the hotel's glass front doors, however, he saw Quentin climbing out of his white Porsche and smiling graciously at the uniformed attendants rushing to serve him.

Jared surged forward. An attendant moved to open the door, but not fast enough, and Jared banged through it, sensing the already suspicious eyes of the security guards on him. He didn't care. He jumped in front of Quentin, grabbed him by the front of his shirt, and smashed him up against his car.

"Where's my daughter?"

Quentin squirmed in terror. "Jared…what's wrong with you?"

"Answer me."

"She's with Mother. I thought—she said Thomas had called and you and he and Mother were all going to meet in Marblehead."

Jared froze. "Your mother has Mai?"

The attendant with the keys said tentatively, "Mr. Reed, you want me to get security out here?"

"No, it's all right," Quentin managed to say, Jared's grip on him already loosening. "What's going on, Jared? I saw Mai myself. She's fine. She looked a little tired, that's all."

"When did they leave?"

"A half hour ago, something like that. Jared, Mother's not a monster. I know she said some pretty cruel things about Mai at first, but that's over. They seemed to be getting along—" Quentin swallowed, white-faced. "Thomas didn't invite you to Marblehead? You don't know anything about it?"

"No."

"Jared, is he going to hurt Mother and Mai? He's an old man, and it just never occurred to me…"

Jared started for Rebecca's car, but stopped abruptly and turned to Quentin, still sprawled against his Porsche. "Answer me this, Quentin. Did Tam come to you for help getting out of Saigon in 1975?"

"What? No, I never heard from her after I left. I know that was wrong, and I don't blame you or her for what happened. I—I guess I was just stupid. I did really care about her, you know."

Jared felt as if his entire world was on fire. *Tam didn't go to Quentin for help, she went to Annette.* He stared at his cousin. "Then you don't know."

"What?"

Mai's your daughter….

"Get in," Jared said, pulling open the passenger door to Rebecca's car. "We'll talk on the way."

Thirty-Seven

❧◦⟞◦❧

All in all, Annette thought as she followed Mai onto the rocky coastline of her Marblehead Neck house, it was a solid plan.

It would be difficult to blame everything on Jean-Paul. He'd suffered too much. He'd had to flee his country; he'd endured five years as a prisoner of war; he'd been shot in the face. He was a decidedly seedy character, but still peculiarly sympathetic, unable to elicit the kind of hatred a highbrow like Thomas Blackburn could.

For all his talk of suffering, had *Thomas* ever really suffered? Ha! He'd lost his pusillanimous son—who would have died in Southeast Asia sooner or later. His daughter-in-law had fled back to the swamps of Florida with her passel of children, but there wasn't a Quentin among them. Had Thomas ever had to make the difficult choices to save a family member the way she had Quentin?

No, Thomas Blackburn wouldn't stir up much sympathy.

With him, Gerard and Mai dead, Annette could cover her tracks and she'd be believed. There'd be no ravaged, white-haired Frenchman to counter her, no scrawny old Boston

Brahmin who'd known her for her entire life, no fourteen-year-old Amerasian girl who looked too much like a Reed to pass for half-Winston, half-Sloan for much longer.

She would explain the tragedy in simple terms.

In 1959, Thomas Blackburn, in desperate need of funds for his new business venture, stole jewels from people his young friend Annette Reed had mentioned or introduced to him during his weeks in and out of France. When he was about to be caught, he'd framed the popular race-car driver Jean-Paul Gerard for his crimes.

In 1963, Thomas had caused the deaths of the three men, and the horrible five-year imprisonment of Jean-Paul Gerard out of his own arrogance. Jean-Paul had come to France looking for vengeance and a particularly valuable collection of gems Thomas had stolen from the Baroness Gisela Majlath, the Empress Elisabeth's Jupiter Stones. Thomas, however, had given the stones to Annette—presumably his way of paying favor to her for having accidentally led him to his rich victims. She'd thought the stones were just an amusing gift. It had never occurred to her that they might be the Jupiter Stones; indeed, aware of the dwindling Blackburn trust, Annette had assumed the stones had no real value beyond the sentimental.

In any case, Thomas had assumed he would no longer have to worry about the young Frenchman whose life he'd destroyed.

In 1975, he'd gotten the shock of his life. The daughter of his old friend Quang Tai had contacted him with an unpleasant ultimatum. She had discovered the Jupiter Stones among Annette's things when she was a little girl back in 1959, finally realized their significance and put together that Thomas Blackburn had been *Le Chat*. She'd already realized he was responsible for her father's death. Now she could use what she knew to get something she wanted: a life in the United States. If Thomas didn't cooperate and help her, she would expose him. She whipped herself up into a frenzy thinking she would succeed and, as a result, erroneously seduced herself into believing Quentin would look after her.

Thomas's answer to Tam's ultimatum came in the predawn hours of April 29, 1975.

Fourteen years later, Jean-Paul Gerard had tried once more to get hold of the Jupiter Stones, only Thomas put him onto Annette. An unsavory character to be sure, the Frenchman did, after all, have a bone to pick with her from his failed attempt to frame Quentin in 1974. So he'd come after her.

For reasons no one would ever know for certain—the main parties being dead—Thomas Blackburn had lured Jean-Paul Gerard and Annette Reed to Marblehead, each presumably, with a different story. Annette had gone so far as to take her nephew's daughter, thinking it was to be a peaceful gathering.

How wrong she'd been.

Annette realized events not yet carried out might require her to adjust the ending to the sorrowful day, but her present rendition involved a relatively straightforward scenario: Thomas kills Jean-Paul, but given his advanced age, he slips and falls into the ocean, drowning. Mai also drowns. Thomas dupes Annette into letting him take the girl out to the rocks, where he ties her up in an effort to use her predicament to lure a suspicious Jean-Paul out into the open.

"Definitely not a bad plan," Annette said to herself. If Rebecca or Jared tried to counter any of her facts, she'd just challenge their conclusions and demand to see their proof.

And there'd be no proof: Thomas, Jean-Paul and Mai would all be dead.

Of course, with them gone, Annette could always revise her story as necessary.

She would, of course, have made a valiant attempt at saving her grand-niece's life.

The girl was getting tired. "Aunt Annette," she said, "it's raining awfully hard. Don't you think we should just go back to the house?"

"No, no, it's just around that pile of rocks over there. Trust me, Mai, there's nothing quite like the Atlantic Ocean during a storm."

"It'll be safe?"

"Of course."

Jean-Paul, where the devil are you?

Annette spotted Kim on the rocks down near the water and waved, and when he raised one hand in answer, she knew he had Thomas Blackburn.

Finally.

Mai didn't see him. Annette directed her over the last pile of rocks, but the girl was obviously losing patience, and perhaps wondering what this stormy trip down to the ocean's edge was all about.

"Wow—look at the waves." Mai pointed, looking around at her father's aunt, but Annette could tell she was just being polite. The girl added, "They really are incredible."

They clambered over a large boulder, finally coming to the level, secluded area where Annette had suggested Kim take Thomas.

He was there, lying motionless on his stomach, his hands and feet tightly bound. His fingers were a ghastly white from the cold and lack of circulation. For a moment Annette thought he was dead, and she let out a sob, amazed at how awful she felt. Then he moved, raising his head and looking around at her, his face smeared with blood from the sharp barnacles. The tide was rushing in, coming closer and closer with each fierce wave, and the cold, clear seawater was lapping at Thomas, seeping underneath him. If the waves didn't take him, he'd die of exposure within hours.

Mai saw his bloody, skeletal face and screamed.

"It's all right," Annette said quietly. What an ending, she thought…but it wasn't her fault. When people had left her alone, she hadn't bothered a soul.

Kim jumped lightly from a rock, landing between her and Mai. He said something in Vietnamese to the girl, but she stared at him in mute terror.

"She doesn't speak Vietnamese," Annette said. "Let's not prolong this, Kim. Deal with her as you have Thomas, if you please." *I'll have to tinker with my story to include their hands being tied,* she thought. *Even if Kim has a chance to unbind them before the end, there will be signs they were tied.*

Mai's eyes widened at Kim's approach, and she edged back against the bank of rocks, away from the water.

"Mai," Thomas yelled, *"run!"*

She hesitated, not that it would have mattered if she'd bolted: Kim was extraordinarily fast. He seized the girl, and she began kicking and screaming, crying for her father to help her.

Annette couldn't bear it.

Thomas saw her look of discomfort and grunted. "You've never had to be a party to your own handiwork, have you? Stay, Annette. Watch."

"I don't have to defend my actions to the likes of you."

"You won't get away with this, you know."

She snorted and made herself laugh. "I already have.

You pride yourself on doing what you have to do to protect your family. Allow me that same pride."

"This isn't pride, Annette—this is desperation."

Mai was screaming now, a gutsy thing to do in Kim's heartless grip, and he smacked her hard across the side of the face and told her to shut up.

Annette had to look away.

"What kind of woman would murder her own grand-daughter?" Thomas asked in a low voice.

"I'm protecting my son."

"No, you're not. You're protecting yourself. You think Quentin's weak, but he's not. You're the one who's weak, Annette. Weak and insecure, frightened. I should have seen that thirty years ago, but my vision of you was always clouded by the misunderstood, unhappy child you'd been. I didn't want to see the selfish, evil woman you'd become. Annette, think of what you've done. And all because you couldn't admit to being a bored housewife who'd turned to stealing jewels from her friends."

Annette shuddered. So he knew. The chilly wind and the rain had soaked her to the skin, but she paid no attention, trying to shut out Mai's screams and Thomas's smug look.

"You were *Le Chat*," Thomas said. "Rebecca knows. I'm sure she's told Jared by now, Quentin, the police. Annette, don't compound what you've already done by adding more bodies to your conscience."

"You have no right to judge me. I made a few mistakes—"

Even in his agony, Thomas's eyes were clear and uncompromising, that riveting Blackburn blue that, Annette knew, would haunt her forever. "Mistakes, Annette? Benjamin, Stephen, Tai, Tam—mistakes? That was murder."

A monstrous wave crashed ashore, spraying all of them

with icy froth as it rushed between the rocks and crevices and almost inundated Thomas. The frigid water swirled four inches deep around him, under him, and he gritted his teeth against the cold, his entire body quaking, until the surf receded.

Kim had finished with Mai and dumped her onto the wet, barnacle-covered rocks beside Thomas.

Annette went over to the sobbing girl and squatted down, stroking her shining, wet hair with one hand. "I'm sad this is the way things have turned out, Mai, but I want you to know I had no choice."

"Don't believe her, Mai," Thomas said calmly. "She could have chosen the truth."

Mai shook off Annette's hand, called her a hateful bitch and flapped like a seal, managing to throw the older woman off balance. Annette went sprawling, landing on one knee. The barnacles cut right through her pants. Kim was beside her in an instant and offered to shoot Mai and Thomas both and be done with them.

"No, that's all right," Annette said, letting him help her back onto her feet. That was what she got for trying to be nice. "I don't want any bloodshed while I'm around. Just let the tide do its work. Jean-Paul should be here soon. Do not underestimate him, do you hear?"

"Don't worry," Kim said.

She gave him a withering look. "Don't patronize me. None of us would be here now if you hadn't underestimated him in the first place. Do your job, Kim. You've been paid well enough for it. Now, if you don't mind, I have to go."

And she about-faced, walking fast and never once looking back at the girl and the old man trussed up on the rocks, waiting for the tide.

* * *

"Get down."

Jean-Paul didn't wait for Rebecca to obey, but shoved her onto the floor of the truck as they came to a stop behind Annette's Mercedes. The rain was coming in blinding sheets now. Jean-Paul shut the truck off. As it rattled into silence, he warned Rebecca to stay down.

"I don't want to do anything that would jeopardize Mai's safety," he said. "Annette's bodyguard is out on the rocks. I'm going to find out what he's up to. You stay here until I get back, all right?"

"Jean-Paul—" She broke off, grabbing his hand, her eyes huge and strangely bright in the gloom of the early afternoon. "Be careful."

"I will, *ma petite*." He squeezed her hand gently. "And I'll look after your grandfather if I can. I've resented him for many years, but that's not important now. I can see I was wrong about him. I always thought he knew about me."

"That you weren't *Le Chat?*"

"That," he said, "and that I'm his son."

Rebecca stared at him, speechless.

Jean-Paul smiled. "You see why I care about you? Your father and I were brothers."

Annette reveled in the softness of the grass under her feet after her treacherous climb in the drenching rain back up to the house, and she ducked in through the side door. She grabbed a towel from the bath off the kitchen and went upstairs to peel off her wet clothes before she came down with pneumonia.

You can pull this off—just don't think about Thomas and Mai. You're doing what you have to do. Be strong!

As she wrapped the towel around her head, she stood

naked in front of her bedroom window and saw a decrepit truck in the driveway. Rebecca's, she thought with a fresh wave of panic. Before she could get hysterical at the prospect of having to include Rebecca Blackburn in her scheme, Annette saw Jean-Paul's figure limping across the lawn.

Good...

She tugged open the drawer to her mother's old tiger maple dresser and took out dry clothes, pulling the towel off her hair and wishing she could take time to blow-dry it. The warmth would feel wonderful after being out on the rocks. A long time ago—even before *Le Chat*—she had learned never to act out of desperation. That meant always having a contingency plan in case things began to unravel.

France was her contingency plan. Her personal jet was waiting at a private airport.

A feeling of calm came over her, and she began to hum as she got dressed.

The water never receded entirely now, and the cold had penetrated every fiber of Thomas's being, until he could no longer rely upon his own sense of coherency. It was pure agony. Worse was having Mai next to him, in the same unholy predicament, sobbing for her father.

"Mai," he said, coughing just to clear his head. "Mai, listen to me. We must use our ingenuity."

She sniffled and fastened her dark, lovely eyes on him, her terror slicing at his very soul. "The tide's coming in. We'll drown."

"Did you know when it's training its SEALs the navy does something called drown-proofing?"

Tears streamed down her face, but she managed to shake her head.

"They do," Thomas said. "They bind their hands and feet and toss the young men into the water and make them swim."

"And they survive?"

"Yes, they survive. Now, do you think you can roll over me and get to my other side? You'll be farther from the water."

"You've been out here longer...."

"Please, don't worry about me. You're smaller and younger—Mai, can you do it? It'll hurt. Barnacles are nasty beasts, but if you can stand it, perhaps you can shelter yourself from the tide and hang on until help gets here."

"My dad—"

"He'll come, Mai. I'm sure of it."

Another wave surged over the rocks and almost covered them this time, but Thomas was numb to the cold. He could see Mai's small body lift in the water, then smash down onto the barnacles. At this rate, she wouldn't even make it to high tide before being swept onto a wave and battered against the rocks, or even sucked out into the ocean.

"Mai..."

The pain had revived her. Biting down hard, she rolled onto her side, her back up against his side and groaned as the barnacles cut into her bound hands and wrists. The rain pelted onto her face as she used her momentum to carry her up onto Thomas's back.

He welcomed the warmth of her body on his.

"Hold on through the next wave," he told her, his voice hoarse.

The wave came, a huge swell that inundated him, but mercifully, only caught Mai underneath. Thomas could feel himself sinking into the barnacles. He couldn't keep up the effort. His body would simply give out.

"I think," Mai was saying, "if I get off you just right I

can sit up and maybe kind of crawl backward up onto the rocks. Should I try?"

Oh, Thomas thought, to be fourteen again. Her energy helped energize him. "Of course you should try."

"But if that woman—"

"We need to worry about the ocean right now."

"Why is she doing this to us?"

"Because she made a mistake a long time ago and couldn't face up to what she'd done. So she kept compounding that mistake until now, and she feels she has no other choice."

"I hate her."

"Yes, but she wasn't always like this, Mai. She's an insecure and frightened woman, and that makes her very selfish and mean. I'm not making excuses for her. Everyone's afraid sometimes. It's how we act when we're afraid that shows us what we are. Do you understand that, Mai?"

"I'm going to roll off you now and try to sit up. Okay?"

He smiled even as he heard yet another wave coming at them. "Okay."

"Your father and I were brothers."

Either Jean-Paul Gerard had gone nuts, Rebecca thought, or there was another fly squirming in the ointment. Right now it didn't matter which. Crouched down, she climbed back up onto the seat of her truck and peered over the dashboard.

Nothing but wind, rain, gray sky, gray ocean. Jean-Paul had already disappeared down onto the rocks.

Staying low, Rebecca cracked open the passenger door and slipped out, leaving the door slightly ajar, although with the crashing surf and howling wind, probably no one would have heard it even if she'd slammed it. *And who's around to hear it?* The place looked dead. She shuddered at her terminology. Grandfather, Mai—they had to be around here somewhere. Given what Jean-Paul had told her, she was positive this was where her grandfather had come.

Annette was going to make him her scapegoat...again.

Hunched over, Rebecca used the Mercedes as cover and crept onto the walk, the flagstones slippery in the pounding rain. She moved quickly, but no one came out and shot her or grabbed her and took her away. *Should I have trusted Jean-Paul? What if I've been gullible and he's no good after all?*

She shook off the doubt and kept moving. The walkway branched off, heading to the front of the house in one direction and around back in the other. She picked the one going around back and stood. If someone saw her, so be it. She tried to look innocently oblivious to what was going on and totally unafraid, but neither was easy.

She went all the way round to the side entrance, nearest the ocean. The door was unlocked. Inside the house was quiet and warm, as beautiful as Rebecca remembered from her few visits there as a child. As she recalled, she'd always gotten into trouble for one thing or another.

There were wet footprints in the kitchen. Fear rising in her throat, Rebecca followed them out into the hall and into the front entry.

Annette came down the stairs, buttoning the cuff of her shirt. "Why, Rebecca—hello." She sounded cheerful, and even smiled. "What are you doing here?"

"Where's Mai?"

"Out on the rocks with your grandfather. I was just looking outside. The weather's turned rather nasty—it's insane for Thomas to keep a child out there in these conditions. He wanted to show her the surf at high tide during a storm." Annette came to the bottom of the stairs, her cuff buttoned. "I hope nothing's happened to them."

Rebecca stiffened, restraining herself, and headed back to the kitchen.

"Where are you going?" Annette demanded, following.

"I'm calling the police."

"Why—Rebecca, obviously you're upset about something. What? What on earth's going on?"

Rebecca resisted the temptation to turn around and scream for her to just *stop,* but this was no time to lose control. She hunted around for a telephone.

A loud crack sounded outside.

Gunfire.

Annette shuddered visibly, and the color drained from her face. "What…"

"Save it," Rebecca said.

And she was out the door and running.

Thirty-Eight

The first shot struck Jean-Paul in his bad leg. It had missed his upper body only because he had dived off a boulder at the last split second. His landing in the tide pool below probably did him worse damage than the bullet that had seared his thigh. It wasn't that he felt any pain—that would come later—but that he couldn't move. He lay prone in the icy water, the tide washing over him.

"In the end," Nguyen Kim had said, "I win."

Jean-Paul searched with one arm for something with which he could pull himself out above the water line, but he cut his hand on barnacles and came up only with useless periwinkles, snails, mussels and slimy seaweed.

A wave surged over him. Cold, salty water filled his mouth and nostrils as his body was picked up by the powerful tide and thrown down again, along with the sea life clinging to the rocks. He didn't fight. The tide would ebb, leaving the tide pool quiet and still for a few hours, himself drowned…unless that wasn't good enough for Nguyen Kim.

The swirling water flipped Jean-Paul onto his side, and

as the wave pulled back, trying to take him with it, he could see Kim standing on the rock six feet above him.

Kim had been waiting for him. In the past, Jean-Paul might have taken him—in fact, had. But not today, with his body and spirit giving out. He had hoped, at least, his death would satisfy Annette and she would leave the others alone.

But of course, it was too late for that. Jean-Paul had seen the two figures huddled together against the battering tide.... Thomas and Mai...*no!*

He had jumped from certain death, and Kim had fired.

Now the Vietnamese was preparing to fire again and finish him off. Jean-Paul felt his leg burning. The rest of him was numb.

Then—for no apparent reason—Kim was catapulted through the air, yelling, his legs kicking. His gun went flying. He more or less rolled, slid and plunged onto a steep, rocky embankment a few yards from Jean-Paul, and his momentum carried him down into the ocean, where the tide smashed him back against the rocks.

Steeling herself against the pain in her ribs, Rebecca clambered down off the huge boulder, down to the tide pool where Jean-Paul was bracing himself for another round of pounding surf. He looked dead. Then he grinned weakly at her, and she cried out with relief, wading out to him. She grabbed him under the arms. Going with the oncoming wave, she used its momentum to drag him out of the tide pool. Then she scrambled, heaving and tugging, moving fast so they wouldn't get caught in the outward pull of the tide. Jean-Paul was scrawny and she was fit, but she still had to get him onto a rounded rock, above the water line.

She saw his blood-soaked thigh and understood why he wasn't doing more to help himself.

The rain beat down on her, and she half expected
Annette to appear on the rocks above them with another
gun, another attempt to kill them both.

With one last burst of energy, she hoisted Jean-Paul
onto the flat boulder where Kim had first landed. The rain
seemed to make getting a decent breath even more difficult than it already was with her bruised ribs and the
exertion, but she stayed on her hands and knees, gasping
for air, willing back the stabbing pain.

"Grandfather, Mai," she said, "where are they?"

Jean-Paul's eyes focused, and he tried to push up on his
hands. "On the rocks." He winced in pain, pointing. "They're
in the tide."

Rebecca could feel near-hysteria rising up in her. "And
Kim…"

"He's a killer. Save him for last."

"Will you be all right?"

"Go!"

Not needing to be told twice, Rebecca was off, clam-
bering over the steep rocks. Jean-Paul hated himself for not
being able to go with her. To lie here bloody and useless
was unacceptable.

He swore viciously in French.

Slowly, the pain beginning to register now, he pushed
himself onto his hands and one knee, and began to drag
himself over the rock toward the girl and the old man…
toward his father, damn both their souls.

The waves seemed to be coming in higher and faster and
more often, and Mai was terrified one would finally take her
and the old man. She still didn't know who he was. Barely
conscious, he was unable to speak. They had both managed
to sit up and worm their way to a more sheltered spot up

against a sleek, black boulder. There weren't as many barnacles there, but they weren't out of reach of the tide.

Mai was exhausted from fighting the waves. Even with the old man in front of her, trying to protect her, the force of the water was almost impossible to resist. She no longer even noticed the cold or the pain of her scrapes and cuts and bruises from being bashed round on the barnacles and rocks.

Dad...Dad, where are you?

Another wave was boiling in over her. She didn't even prepare for it, but simply let it come.

White-faced and staring blankly out the passenger window, Quentin hadn't spoken for the last five miles. Jared didn't try to get him to talk. Preoccupied with his own fears, he hadn't bothered to sugarcoat what he'd had to say: Annette—Quentin's *mother*—had deliberately misled him about Tam and had ordered Tam's killing and that of her own granddaughter.

"She's lied to you and used you," Jared had said brutally, "in the worst ways I can imagine."

"But why?"

"To save herself."

He'd explained what he could, not knowing if Quentin was able to digest anything beyond the fact that his mother had taken advantage of his guilt over his stupid involvement with the drug smugglers...that Tam hadn't fallen into bed with his cousin...that Mai was their child.

Jared took the turn into the Winston driveway in Marblehead too fast and ran up into the pristine lawn, but quickly righted the car and sped up toward the house.

Annette's Mercedes was coming at them.

It swerved onto the lawn to avoid a head-on collision.

Jared screeched on the brakes and jumped out. He didn't look back to see what Quentin was doing.

Annette had already rolled down her window. "Jared, I'm so glad you're here. I don't know what's going on—there were shots fired and Thomas has Mai down on the rocks. Kim's doing what he can to help. I'm heading for the police now. I've tried to call, but the line's dead. Someone must have cut it—"

"Give it up," Jared said stonily. "I know what you've done and there's no escape. If anything happens to Mai, I don't care where you go, there's no place you can hide from me. Got that, Auntie? Nowhere."

"You're dead wrong."

Behind him, Quentin said, "No, Mother, I don't think he is."

"Quentin…" Annette swallowed, no color at all in her face, and began to cry. "Quentin, don't let him poison your mind. I'm your mother. How could you believe I'd hurt anyone?"

"I'm going after Mai," Jared said, unmoved, and ran off into the rain.

Quentin fell in beside him. "You might need my help—I know every rock out there."

Jared clapped him on the shoulder. "Let's go."

They heard the Mercedes engine race, and Jared glanced back, seeing the big car bang into Rebecca's car, right itself, and go on. He had no idea where his aunt was going, but it didn't matter. He'd find her.

"Grandfather…*Mai!*"

Rebecca choked back her terror and slid down the black rock into the icy, thigh-deep water. The force of the swell pushed her up against the wall of the rock and she had to hang on to the edges of the rock to maintain her footing, hooking one arm around the slight figure of Mai Sloan. The girl was unconscious, and now, at high tide, every on-coming wave totally inundated her. Rebecca held on as the current tried to pull them back out with it.

Her grandfather's thin body floated up in the foaming water and went with the receding wave, pounding over the rocks. Rebecca could see his pale, bloody face, and she screamed for him. He didn't move.

Never loosening her hold on Mai, Rebecca shivered in the numbing surf and knew she didn't have the strength to hoist Mai up over her head onto the black rock. She would have to edge to her right where, about twenty feet away, the steep embankment of rocks gave way to a small cove. The tide wasn't as deep there. Rebecca would be able to leave Mai on the bank of sea-smoothed, softball-sized rocks and go back for her grandfather.

You can do this. Just stay steady and keep moving.

But as she peeled her fingers loose from their hold on the black rock, she could feel Mai being pulled from her. At first she thought it was the current, then she heard Jean-Paul's French-accented voice. "I've got her."

He was on his stomach on the rock above her, reaching one arm down and lifting Mai's tiny body by her soaked shirt. Rebecca helped shove her up to him.

And then Jared was there behind him, taking Mai, and Quentin leaped into the water with Rebecca and thrashed out into a roaring wave where her grandfather bobbed help-lessly. He got an arm around the old man, and they both disappeared in the gray swell. Rebecca dove in after them, losing her footing in the deepening water, the force of the tide trying to push her back. Barnacles cut at her hands and feet, and she banged against rocks as she fought to stay in control, not to let the tide seize her.

Leaving Mai with Jean-Paul, Jared came around to a rocky point off to Rebecca's left, where the water was just waist-deep. He jumped in, and Rebecca made her way toward him, guessing he'd spotted Quentin and her grandfather.

Within seconds, Jared pulled Thomas up and deposited him on the rocks.

Together, he and Rebecca dragged Quentin to safety. He'd bashed his head on a rock but was conscious.

Thomas and Mai, however, were another matter.

"Jared…" Rebecca bit her lip, unable to bring herself to ask.

But Jared understood. "They're both alive."

"We've got to get them warm," Rebecca said.

Jared nodded grimly. With a jackknife from his pocket, he deftly cut the wet, cold rope binding Thomas's hands and feet. He looked over at Quentin. "You're in no shape to carry him. Can you get Mai?"

Without a word, Quentin took Jared's jackknife and hurried back over the rocks to where Mai and Jean-Paul were. Jared lifted Thomas onto his shoulder and steadied himself before starting up to the house.

"R.J., I'll be back for you as soon as I can."

She climbed agonizingly to her feet and gave him a quick smile. "The day I let *anybody,* even you, Jared Sloan, carry me when I can walk…" She caught her breath and winced. "Just don't wait for me."

It was Quentin who called the police and the ambulance, who got out blankets while Jared and Rebecca peeled off Mai's and Thomas's soaked, tattered clothes. Ignoring their scrapes and cuts for the moment, they wrapped them in the blankets. Jared held his daughter and tried to will his own warmth into her.

"Nothing will change, Jared," Quentin said softly. "She doesn't have to know who I am."

"Yes, she does. I can't keep lying to her. Before it was to save her life. Now…there's no reason."

"I won't try and take her from you."

"Good, because I'd fight you every inch of the way."

"I just…I just want to be a part of her life, Jared. That's all. She's my cousin's kid, right?" He looked at the pale, pretty face. "She's going to be okay."

On her way up to the house, Rebecca had stopped to help Jean-Paul Gerard, but he'd shooed her off. "The rain's letting up—I'll be fine. Take care of your grandfather."

But now there was nothing more she could do for Thomas beyond what she and Jared and Quentin had already done, and so she grabbed a blanket and a first-aid kit and headed back out to the rocks. She'd taken a couple aspirin for her ribs. For now, it'd have to be enough.

The rain had stopped, and already the tide had begun to ebb. Rebecca went straight down to the black rock where she'd left Jean-Paul.

He wasn't there.

She scoured the immediate area and scanned the gray swells, but saw no sign of him. How far could he get in his condition? Frowning, she started back up to the house, hoping he hadn't just given up and lowered himself into the sea. But that wasn't Jean-Paul Gerard's style. He'd survived too much to give up now.

By the time she reached the grass, the police and ambulance had arrived. Jared pointed her out to a paramedic, and she tried to protest, but there was no arguing with medical types.

As they draped a blanket over her, she noticed that her truck was gone.

She grinned. Jean-Paul Gerard had stolen it.

Thirty-Nine

❧

The sky was an impeccable Mediterranean blue and the rose garden behind the stone *mas* in full bloom, a riot of pinks and yellows and reds. Annette enjoyed their scent as she came out onto the terrace. She would miss this beautiful old place, but sacrifices had to be made—and there was still the possibility everything would work out to her advantage. Already she'd cabled Quentin, letting him know that she'd left for France in a total state of shock, unable to fathom all the accusations being flung at her, and promising she'd fight to clear her name. No one had yet offered a shred of proof she'd done anything more than left for her annual trip to the Riviera a bit earlier than usual. Both suffering hypothermia and head injuries, Thomas and Mai hadn't yet been able to give their version of what had transpired at her oceanside house on the North Shore. Jean-Paul Gerard was missing and presumed drowned, and Kim's body had washed ashore.

Naturally Jared and Rebecca had come out unscathed. Didn't they always?

Annette had the glimmer of an idea in which she could

blame everything on her dead Vietnamese bodyguard, even ordering Mai's hands and feet bound. *I had to...he was going to kill me!*

Hmm, she thought. The story needed work, but it had possibilities.

But meanwhile, she had her contingency plan of last resort. Thirty years ago—after her brush with being "found out" as *Le Chat*—she had set up a Swiss bank account for herself and purchased a beautiful chalet in the Alps to which her ownership couldn't possibly be traced. Retreating there would mean giving up everything: Boston, Winston & Reed, Quentin. She would have to begin a completely new life—and at sixty years of age. It wouldn't be easy. At least she'd have the satisfaction of knowing Thomas Blackburn would finally have to acknowledge that she indeed knew what it was to suffer.

She planned to leave for Switzerland this afternoon.

However, she had one last loose end to snip off in her *mas* garden.

The sharp thorns of the rosebushes dug at her gloved hands and her sleeves as she reached among them, feeling around until she grasped the edges of a tall, heavy terracotta urn. She rocked it onto its edge and rolled it out onto the terrace.

The cremated remains of my pets are in there, she'd told various gardeners over the years. *Just leave it right where it is.* Of course, they had. They'd thought her quite the eccentric.

The plastic cover she'd taped carefully over the top was still in place. She grimaced at the layers of dead insects and grime, but just shut her eyes and peeled back the plastic. The top half of the urn was filled with hundreds of bits of cork, which she scooped out. In spite of the close call she'd just had on Marblehead Neck, she could feel the excitement building in her.

At last her fingers struck the familiar softness of the plastic-wrapped leather pouches she'd dropped into the urn in 1959. She hadn't touched them since.

One by one she brought them out: *Le Chat's* plunder. Diamonds, pearls, emeralds, gold, sterling silver—beautiful pieces of jewelry of every description. There was even one particular Art Deco piece, an interesting snake bracelet, that had caught her eye. It had belonged to a St. Louis socialite, one of Annette's Radcliffe classmates, who was still whining about its loss.

Nothing in these pouches, however, came close to equaling Empress Elisabeth's incredible Jupiter Stones.

If Annette had known Tam had swiped them all those years ago, she wouldn't have waited until 1975 to deal with the sneaky little brat.

Still, it wasn't the monetary value the jewels represented that made Annette's heart trot happily along as she indulged in the memory of those thrilling days. She hadn't become *Le Chat* for the potential profit, but for the excitement—the daring of it all. If she could go back to 1959, she wouldn't change a thing, except perhaps not shooting Jean-Paul when she'd had the chance.

"Was it worth it?" a female voice asked.

Annette jumped, startled out of her reverie.

Rebecca Blackburn looked stunning in a navy wrapdress and flats, her hair pulled back, no sign that her beloved grandfather was on the brink of death.

"Get off my property," Annette said, "before I call the police."

"Oh, don't worry. The police are already on their way."

Annette shot to her feet. "I want you out of here!"

Rebecca was unmoved. "Scream and throw a fit all you want. I'm not leaving. There are all kinds of warrants out for you in the United States, and the French police know you're here. They're going to detain you for questioning. I just thought I'd mosey on over and make sure you didn't try and make an exit before they could get here. Those *are* your suitcases on the walk out front?"

Annette didn't speak.

"Grandfather's going to recover. Mai's already talking like crazy. I know what you've heard, but it's not true. I thought you might like to know that."

Cursing herself for not having the foresight to bring a gun out to the garden with her, Annette bent down and gathered up her packages of stolen jewels. Her hair fell into her face, and she could feel perspiration springing out on her back and in her armpits. She hated this feeling of desperation.

"Don't try to leave," Rebecca said.

Annette glared at her, hugging the packages to her chest. "I'll do as I please."

"I didn't come alone."

"Oh—and I suppose you tucked Jean-Paul in your back pocket? Did he live, as well? Get out of my way, Rebecca. I may be sixty years old, but I can still knock you on your pretty behind."

But she could hear the back door creaking open, and her gut twisted as she saw the familiar tawny hair and the handsome, grim face of her son.

"Quentin..."

"Hello, Mother," he said.

Annette licked her parched lips and felt her spirit—her very soul—catching fire, blackening in the despair of seeing her son's expression. He knows, she thought. He knows everything.

Rebecca said softly. "How do you think I knew where to find you?"

"I did it all for you." Annette's voice was hoarse; she felt as if she were choking. "Quentin…don't look at me like that. Please! It was all for you. How could you have had a jewel thief for a mother? The police would have come after me if I hadn't given them Jean-Paul. Think of what that would have been like for you."

"If you'd considered me, you'd never have become a thief in the first place. And I'd rather—" He hesitated, his tone cold, but he was fighting back tears. Clenching his fists at his side, he went on, "I'd rather have had a mother who accepted the consequences of her actions. I'd rather have had a jewel thief for a mother than a liar and a murderer."

"Quentin, how dare you speak to me like that? I can explain…"

"No, Mother. You can't."

Annette snapped her mouth shut. She could see it was useless. He'd spent too much time already with his cousin and Rebecca. *They'd* never understand.

Suddenly she couldn't stand the way Quentin was looking at her—the way Rebecca, the little snot, was trying *not* to look at her. Hanging on to her pouches of jewels, she began to run.

She didn't stop until she came to the spectacular cliff above the Mediterranean where she used to take Quentin to watch the boats. The salty, fishy smells of the sea mixed oddly with the tangy scent of lemons, and she collapsed onto her knees in the tall grass, her packets spilling out of her arms. What was she going to do now? Where would she go? She couldn't imagine sticking it out with the French police. Calling in lawyers, making denials, thinking up new ways to explain the past thirty years.

"It's over," a voice said behind her, and she wondered if it were her own—her conscience. Then the voice went on, "You can't win this time, *ma belle.*"

Annette rolled back onto her heels and watched Jean-Paul limp to her. He was using a cane; she could see where his thigh was bandaged. She thought perhaps they'd both gone to hell, but far be it from Jean-Paul Gerard ever to die.

"Come on," he said, "I'll take you back to the *mas.*"

"I killed Gisela, you know," she said, feeling the warm breeze in her hair.

"Yes."

"She told me you knew I was *Le Chat* from the beginning—that you only took up with me to get her Jupiter Stones back." She blinked at him in the bright sun, remembering how they'd made love here on this spot. "Is that true?"

"Partly. I never expected to love you as much as I did."

"Were you Gisela's lover, as well?"

Jean-Paul shook his head sadly, moving closer. "No, Annette." His warm eyes locked with hers. "Gisela was my mother."

Annette fell back onto the grass and stared up at the sky, laughing. "Of course!" She giggled now as it all made sense. "Hungarian baroness—she was nothing but a French whore with a bastard child. To think of all the regrets I've wasted on her over the years—it's ridiculous."

"She tried to help you."

"She tried to blackmail me. She offered a 'deal' in which I'd return the Jupiter Stones, drop you, and promise not to steal anymore. In return, she wouldn't blab to the police about me. Can you imagine? Gisela 'Majlath' trying to wring me dry."

Jean-Paul's face reddened, the only indication that her words disturbed him. "She only wanted you to give back what was hers—"

"And what poor slob did she steal them from?" Annette sat up, feeling gloriously free. She picked bits of grass from her hair and looked out at the ocean. "You can imagine how furious I was, having someone like that interfering with my life, making threats. I gave her a good shove—just out of anger, really. Well, she slipped. She tried to hang on, but she knew better than to ask me to help her. I thought about it, though, but there was no way I was going to risk toppling over the edge myself. After all, I had a little boy at home." Annette brushed the flat of her hand over the very top of the grass, letting it tickle her palm. "Finally she just let go."

Jean-Paul shut his eyes and said quietly, to himself, "Aah, *Maman*...I should have been there to help you."

Annette climbed wearily to her feet. "You know, I've always thought that if it came to it, I'd be able to do the same—just drop silently into the sea."

Instantly alert, Jean-Paul put out a hand to stop her.

But she had already made up her mind, and he couldn't move fast enough on his injured leg. He threw down his cane and lunged for her, but she was running, laughing as she came to the edge of the cliff.

She didn't make a sound as she disappeared into the wind.

Forty

~~~

Mai was sitting up in her bed in a guest room at the Eliza Blackburn House. Despite her bruises and stitches, she looked mischievous and every bit the kid Jared couldn't live without. His mother, horrified by what had happened, had come down from Nova Scotia and insisted on spelling him, although he'd refused to leave Mai's bedside in those first crucial, terrifying hours after Rebecca had pulled her from the water. Now, ten days later, the doctors had told him Mai could travel soon, and he could take her home.

Home…was that still San Francisco for her?

"You've got to tell Granddad to cut it out," she said. "He's sent me flowers, balloons, a singing telegram—and now the nurses say he's sending *them* flowers and balloons to make sure they're taking good care of me. It's *so* embarrassing."

"Has he told you that you don't have to pay back the money you swiped?"

"No…"

"Then I wouldn't complain if I were you."

Mai decided a prudent change of subject was in order. "Have you heard from Rebecca Blackburn?"

Jared shook his head. He'd gotten used to single parent-hood and knew he couldn't leave Mai, but he'd have gone to France with Rebecca and Quentin if he could have. R.J.—he thought about her all the time. She hadn't come back to Boston after Annette's death. Shattered by the events of the past days, Quentin had brought his mother's body home and buried her in a quiet ceremony. His wife was sticking by him. Jared had offered to provide moral support for his cousin in any way he could, short of giving up Mai, but that, Jane assured him, wasn't on the docket.

With the guidance of a psychologist, as soon as she was well enough, Jared had told Mai everything. She took it all in stride. The therapist explained that given Mai's interest in Amerasians and the Vietnam War—the fall of Saigon, in particular—she knew more about what went on there than most. "It's been in the back of her mind for a long time that your name on her papers doesn't mean a lot," the therapist had said. "She's aware you're uncomfortable about talking about her mother or what really happened in Vietnam. Jared, she knows people got out with false papers. She knows what life was like for so many beautiful young Vietnamese women like Tam. She's not a baby you need to shelter. Give her some credit."

He was trying.

Mai took her box of Godiva chocolates—courtesy of Maureen Sloan—off her night table and picked out the fattest one she could find. "You're still in love with Rebecca, aren't you?"

Jared grabbed the box of chocolates from her. Naturally she'd taken all the semisweet ones. "Stay out of my love life, kid."

"Why? You meddle in mine."

"You're fourteen and I'm pushing forty."

She popped the chocolate in her mouth. "Time you got married, Dad."

It was the first time she'd called him Dad since he'd told her about Quentin and Tam.

She caught his expression. Chocolaty saliva dribbled out of the corners of her mouth, and she suddenly looked very frightened. "You're still my dad, right? No matter what?"

"Mai…yes. I'm your dad. Forever."

He swept her into his arms and held her.

For the first time since her husband's death twenty-six years earlier, Jenny O'Keefe Blackburn came to Boston. First she visited her husband's grave at Mt. Auburn Cemetery. Then she visited her father-in-law in his "hidden" Beacon Hill garden. His head was still bandaged, but he was doing just fine, sitting at a small wrought-iron table.

"Someone should have knocked you on the head a long time ago," Jenny said, smiling as she set a pot of pink geraniums on the brick courtyard. "I remember you consider cut flowers a waste. You can plant these in your garden and see what becomes of them. Thomas—" She began to cry; she'd promised herself she wouldn't. "Can you forgive me?"

He waved a bony hand in dismissal. "There's nothing to forgive."

"I wanted someone to blame—"

"You didn't do or say anything I wouldn't have. Jenny, there hasn't been a day I haven't wished I'd gone on that trip instead of Stephen."

"I know." She pulled up a chair and sat beside him, taking his hand. "It's been so long, Thomas, and I don't mind saying I've missed you, in my own way."

He squeezed her hand. "How are the children?"

"They're fine. I brought pictures. And my father sends his best. He says you're invited to come down and sit on the front porch with him and drink iced tea anytime you want."

"Is it warm this time of year?"

"Quite."

"Good. Never mind my concussion, we'll leave this afternoon—"

Jenny laughed. "You're as impossible as ever. As it so happens, Father and I are planning a family reunion for Memorial Day weekend. With all the daughters-in-law and grandchildren, we've gotten to be quite a horde."

"I considered you a horde in 1961."

"You can't get to me anymore, you know. I've come too far. I've raised six children on my own, I own a damned citrus grove, and I've lived within spitting distance of my father for twenty-six years. I've toughened up."

"You've never remarried," Thomas said.

She shrugged without apology or regret, then smiled. "I'm only fifty-four. You never know." Her pale blue eyes never leaving him, she said, "What about Memorial Day? I'm not going to beg, but you've got great-grandchildren you've never seen...and grandchildren who need to get to know you."

His eyes misted. "Jenny..."

"And if you're worried about paying for your ticket, please don't."

That brought him up straight. "I have no intention of accepting charity—"

"What about a share in Junk Mind?"

Thomas sat back and gave her an appraising look. "Go on."

"When Sofi and Rebecca were starting out, they got

anyone and everyone they could to invest in their crazy scheme. I did, the kids did—and so did you."

"I didn't give a penny toward that game."

Jenny cleared her throat. "Um, do you remember that Chinese porcelain vase?"

"The one that came over on one of Eliza's ships in 1797?"

"The *ugly* one with the screaming eagles painted all over it."

"Eagles were a tremendously popular motif in the new republic—"

"Thomas, the vase was ugly."

His incisive gaze fastened on her. "Was?"

"Well, I'm sure it still *is,* it's just not mine any longer. And I did say mine, Thomas, because as I recall you did give it to me—probably because you knew I thought it was ugly. Anyway, I sold it to a very rich old woman in Palm Beach and invested the proceeds to Junk Mind in your name. The money's in some kind of trust. I worked it all out. I know you'd probably rather have the vase back. If you'd like, I'll give you the woman's number and you can badger her until she relents. You'll have enough money to buy ten more like it if you want."

"There's only *one* like it."

"Thank God for small favors."

"How much am I worth?"

She grinned at him. "That's a loaded question, but if you want a dollar amount, you'll have to talk to Sofi."

"Why not Rebecca?"

"This one was between just Sofi and me. Being a Blackburn, Rebecca would have insisted on telling you, and I didn't want to deal with you. I wanted the girls to have the money, but I didn't want to profit myself from selling anything that had meant something to you—so I just did what I did."

Thomas smiled and leaned forward, kissing her on the cheek. "I don't know who to call first, Sofi or a travel agent."

"Then you'll make it?"

"I think I can live another week or two."

"The kids'll be thrilled. Oh, Thomas." Her voice cracked, and she couldn't believe she was crying again. "I'm not sure Rebecca will make it, but you've probably seen enough of her to last you a while. If she has any sense, she'll be in San Francisco. Jared's taking Mai home tomorrow, and I picked him out as my one-and-only son-in-law thirty years ago."

"Where is Rebecca now?"

Jenny sighed. "France."

To the disgust of the purists at the next table over in the sidewalk cafe, Rebecca sipped on a tall glass of iced café au lait and tried to decipher an article in the morning edition of the Paris *Le Monde*. Finally she pushed the paper across to Jean-Paul Gerard. "My French rots. Does this say what I think it says?"

He glanced at the headline and smiled. "Probably."

The last ten days had transformed him. Springtime in Paris was just as gorgeous as everyone said, and he'd hobbled on his cane, dragging Rebecca from one sight to another. He'd told her about Gisela and how he was her "whim," the child she'd wanted. She hadn't wanted any of her regular lovers for the father: she'd wanted an honorable, intelligent, good man…a friend. In late 1934, Gisela found herself in French colonial Saigon on a lark, and she discovered that Emily Blackburn had died the previous year and Thomas was totally bereft. Emily had been her friend, as well, and Gisela and Thomas fell into each other's arms for comfort. And she'd decided…*him*. He'd be the father of her baby.

And so it was.

An honest and open person, she'd told her son everything, but explained that Thomas had never had an inkling he'd gotten her pregnant. And she'd made Jean-Paul promise he would leave it that way.

"Then he never knew?" Rebecca had asked.

"No—but I resented him for it. I thought he should have recognized me…seen himself in me. But I favor Gisela, and what can I say? It just never happened."

Now he folded up the newspaper and drank some of his espresso. "It seems," he said, looking at her over the rim of his cup, "the Louvre has received an anonymous donation of the Empress Elisabeth's Jupiter Stones."

"That's what I thought it said."

"They came with a typed note explaining that the empress—an eccentric woman given to whims—had, at one time, taken to wandering through the gardens of Riviera cottages. One night in the early 1890s, she came upon a girl who wasn't frightened of this strange, wealthy, powerful woman, and they talked until dawn, at which point the empress gave the girl a bag of 'pretty colored stones' in gratitude for those moments of peace and friendship."

"Gisela's mother?"

"Yes."

Rebecca drank some of her café au lait and let an ice cube melt on her tongue. "You got the stones from David Rubin?"

Jean-Paul grinned. "You'd graciously put me on the list of people to whom Sofi could relinquish them."

"And you smuggled them into France."

"The least of my difficulties getting here."

"You know, I'd have given you the stones. You could have sold them if you'd wanted. They're worth an incredible fortune."

He shook his head sadly, his eyes distant. "That's never been why I wanted them. They were Gisela's, her prize possession—not even a possession. A gift. Her mother had never sold them, and neither had she."

"So neither would you. The Louvre's probably got a staff of hounds on your trail by now. They'll get the whole story."

"Good," he said with satisfaction.

"You know," Rebecca said, sitting back. "You could do *me* a favor."

"Anything."

She laughed. "I should hold you to that, but you'd better hear me out first. Grandfather's been threatening to leave the Eliza Blackburn house to me—just what I need. I already own enough decrepit buildings. It needs new wiring, new plumbing, painting, fixtures…. You could take me off the hook."

"You're not going to stay in Boston?"

"Nope. I haven't paid my rent in two months—Grandfather's probably drawing up papers to evict me now. I'm wrecking his cash flow."

"Rebecca…"

"Don't say no yet. Think about it."

"You don't understand. I've never had a father. And I promised Gisela—"

"There's one thing you're forgetting, and that's Thomas. My grandfather. Your father. Think about him, Jean-Paul. Then make up your mind." And she smiled suddenly, and jumped up, hugging him and ignoring all the peculiar looks they got, her the rich chestnut-haired young woman, him the battered, white-haired man who looked twenty years older than he was. "I'm glad you're my uncle."

Jared turned off his computer and gave up on trying to get any work done. He couldn't concentrate. Back two days from Boston and all he'd managed to do was make a mess of every project he started. Mai was catching up on her homework and doing famously; she'd even started delivering papers and washing windows to earn the money to pay back her grandfather. Rebecca had sent them a postcard of the Eiffel Tower and scrawled on the back some nonsense about tumbleweeds coming to rest. Jared couldn't see the correlation between Paris and tumbleweeds.

All he knew was that he missed her.

Feeling restless and out of sorts, he walked across his small yard and started fiddling with the pots of geraniums on the rail of his deck. He and Thomas Blackburn made a pair when it came to gardening. He pinched off a few yellowed leaves before he gave himself up to the spectacular view. San Francisco wasn't Boston, but it was where he belonged. He couldn't take Mai away from her friends, the only life she'd known—not now. If that meant losing R.J....

He couldn't. He had to think of a way not to lose her.

Behind him, the wooden gate creaked open, but it was too early for Mai to be getting home from school.

"Don't you ever worry about earthquakes?" Rebecca asked as she walked up onto the deck. "I've been in San Francisco two hours and keep waiting for the ground to start moving under me. Of course, Grandfather says he wouldn't live in Florida because of the poisonous snakes and the alligators, but Papa O'Keefe says he wouldn't live in Boston because of the blizzards. I guess it depends on your perspective."

"R.J...."

She went on breathlessly, "You just have to decide what you can live with and what you can't. I got used to snakes, alligators and blizzards. I can get used to earthquakes."

She was putting on a grand show, but he'd known her

since she was born and could see she was nervous. Having her there, close to him again, made his head spin. This was the woman he loved…would always love.

Without looking at him, she went over and sat in the rope hammock, giving it a little push with her feet. It was all Jared could do to keep from touching her. She was the one who had to make the trip west, who had to make the decision whether or not she wanted to be a part of his and Mai's life…whether or not she was ready to settle down and understand that a kid had to be in school and he had professional commitments.

But he wasn't altogether certain that if she asked him to fly off to the South Pacific, he wouldn't pack himself and Mai up and go.

It was her show, and he let her talk.

"I figure," she went on, "you live in San Francisco, you learn to nail down the furniture and not display the glassware."

Jared leaned against the rail. "You planning to live in San Francisco?"

Her eyes—so blue, so gorgeous, so scared—avoided his. "Thinking about it. The Boston branch of my studio went out of business."

"The Boston branch?"

"I've decided to open up a West Coast branch. I've got the design for my stationery and business cards finished." She pushed off again, swinging gently in the hammock. "I'll get them printed up as soon as I have an address. Not a temporary address, either. A real address."

Jared was gripping the rail; he noticed his knuckles had turned white, and tried to relax. "You could afford to buy half of San Francisco—"

She looked at him—finally. "I don't want half of San Francisco."

"R.J.," he said in a low voice, "you're making me crazy."

She pretended not to hear him. "All I want is a place to work—which is easy enough to come by—and a room with a view. You wouldn't by any chance know of one of those, would you?"

"Rooms with views can be hard to come by in this city."

"What do I have to do?"

"Have lots of money you don't mind spending or know someone. Since you're a Blackburn," he said, straightening up to stand beside her feet, "and there hasn't been a Blackburn born who likes spending money, I guess you'd better know someone—preferably," he added, "someone who likes you a lot."

"Aha. Guess who's the only person I know in San Francisco?"

With one foot, he lifted up her toes and gave her a push. "Who?"

She grinned at him, keeping her feet up so she could swing freely. "You're not going to make this any easier on me, are you?"

Jared shrugged. "I haven't dumped you out of that hammock and carried you upstairs yet, have I?"

She looked at him in mock innocence. "Does your room have a view?"

That did it. He grabbed her on the upswing and pulled her into his arms, feeling the warmth and weight of her and loving her. She clasped her hands at the back of his neck and laughed. "Jared—I love you."

"Good thing, because you know what?" When she shook her head, he held her close and said, "I love you. R.J., I've always loved you—I'll never stop loving you. But, darling, my room doesn't have a spectacular view."

As it turned out, it just didn't matter.

Forty-One

❧❧❧❧

Thomas had enjoyed his trip to central Florida, particularly the groves and the ample screened front porch and the children—the *masses* of children. Jenny had reminded him there were only five great-grandchildren circulating about, but he counted his six grandchildren and their assorted spouses and sweethearts as part of the throng. Rebecca did turn up, with Jared and Mai—more heads to count. Thomas had surprised Rebecca by forgiving the two months back rent she owed him. He'd been in touch with Sofi, and Eliza's vase had indeed brought him financial peace of mind. He was already in touch with the woman in Palm Beach.

Rebecca, in turn, hadn't surprised him or anyone else when she announced a fall wedding at Wesley Sloan's house in Tiberon. That meant another trip. At least, Thomas thought, amused, he could afford it.

He felt better than he had in years. The carpenters would start in the morning. They declined to call themselves carpenters—they were restoration specialists or something, but in Thomas's mind, a man with a hammer was a carpenter.

It was a warm June evening, and Athena, who'd been

in her glory during his recovery, was beating the tar out of him at the new edition of Junk Mind. The doorbell rang, and he used the interlude to consider a ridiculous question about a cartoon character. He peeked through the window onto the doorstep.

Jean-Paul Gerard was leaning against the wrought-iron rail and trying desperately, Thomas thought, to look as if he didn't give a damn whether or not he was sent on his way.

Gisela's son...*my son.*

Rebecca had told him about Jean-Paul after her return from Paris, saying the secret had been his promise to keep to Gisela, not hers.

Thomas opened the door. "Come in, son," he said. "Welcome home."

Turn the page for an exciting sneak peek at
THE ANGEL
by Carla Neggers.
Available in paperback
June 2009
from MIRA Books.

Beacon Hill, Boston, Massachusetts Evening,
June 17

Not for the first time in his life, Simon Cahill found himself in an argument with a snob, this time in Boston, but he could as easily have been in New York, San Francisco, London or Paris. He'd been to all of them. He enjoyed a good argument—especially with someone as obnoxious and pretentious as Lloyd Adler.

Adler looked to be in his early forties and wore jeans and a rumpled black linen sport coat with a white T-shirt, his graying hair pulled back in a short ponytail. He gestured toward a watercolor painting of an Irish stone cottage across the crowded, elegant Beacon Hill drawing room. "Keira Sullivan is more Tasha Tudor and Beatrix Potter than Picasso, wouldn't you agree, Simon?"

Probably, but Simon didn't care. Keira Sullivan was supposed to have made her appearance by now. Adler had griped about that, too, but her tardiness hadn't seemed to stop people from bidding on the two paintings she'd donated to tonight's charity auction. The second was of fairies or elves or some damn things in a magical glen. Proceeds would go to support a scholarly conference on Irish-American folklore to be held next spring in Boston and Cork, Ireland.

In addition to being a popular illustrator, Keira Sullivan was also a folklorist.

Simon hadn't taken a close look at either of her paintings. A week ago he'd been in Armenia searching for survivors of a moderate but damaging earthquake. Over a hundred people had died. Men, women, children.

Mostly children.

But now he was in a suit—an expensive one—and drinking champagne in a chandeliered drawing room on the first floor of an elegant early nineteenth-century brick house overlooking Boston Common. He figured he deserved to be mistaken for an art snob.

"Beatrix Potter's the artist who drew Peter Rabbit, right?" Simon swallowed more of his champagne. It wasn't bad, but he wasn't a snob about champagne, either. He liked what he liked and didn't worry about the rest. He didn't mind if other people fussed—he just minded if they were pains in the ass about it. "When I was a kid, my mother decorated my room with cross-stitched scenes of Peter and his buddies."

"I beg your pardon?"

"Cross-stitch. You know—you count these threads and—" Simon stopped, deliberately, and shrugged. He knew he didn't look like the kind of guy who'd had Beatrix Potter rabbits on his wall as a kid, but he was telling the truth. "Now that I'm thinking about it, I wonder what happened to my little rabbits."

Adler frowned, then chuckled. "That's very funny," he said, as if he couldn't believe Simon was serious. "Keira Sullivan is good at what she does, obviously, but I hate to see her work overshadow several quite interesting pieces here tonight. A shame, really."

Simon looked at Adler, who suddenly went red and

bolted into the crowd, mumbling that he needed to say hello to someone.

A lot of his arguments ended that way, Simon thought as he finished off the last of his champagne, got rid of his empty glass and grabbed a full one from another tray. The event was catered, and guests included a wide range of people—academics, graduate students, artists, musicians, folklorists, benefactors, a couple of priests and a handful of politicians. And at least two cops, but Simon steered clear of them. Most people were dressed up and having a good time.

"Lloyd Adler's not that easy to scare off," Owen Garrison said, shaking his head as he joined Simon. He was lean and good-looking, as all the Garrisons were. Simon was built like a bull. No other way to say it.

"I'm on good behavior tonight." He grinned, cheekily putting out his pinky finger as he sipped his fresh champagne. Owen just rolled his eyes. Simon decided he'd probably had enough to drink and set the glass on a side table. Too much bubbly and he'd start a fight. "I didn't say a word."

"You didn't have to. One look and he scurried."

"No way. I'm charming. Everyone says so."

"Not everyone."

Probably true, but Simon did tend to get along with people. He was at the reception as a favor to Owen, whose family, not coincidentally, owned the house where it was taking place. The Garrisons were an old-money family who'd left Boston for Texas after the death of Owen's sister, Dorothy, at fourteen. It was a hellish story. Just eleven himself, he had watched her fall off a cliff in Maine and drown. There had been nothing he could do.

Simon suspected that childhood trauma was the central

reason that Owen had founded Fast Rescue, an Austin-based international rapid-response search-and-rescue organization. They could put volunteer teams in place within twenty-four hours of a disaster—man-made or natural—anywhere in the world.

Fast Rescue had arranged the Armenian mission. Simon had become one of its volunteer search-and-rescue specialists eighteen months ago, a decision that was complicating his life more than it should have.

Owen, a top SAR specialist himself, was wearing an expensive suit, too, but he still looked somewhat out of place in the house his great-grandfather had bought a century ago. The decor was in shades of cream and sage-green, apparently Dorothy Garrison's favorite colors. The first floor, where the drawing room was located, was reserved for meetings and functions, such as tonight's reception. The second and third floors comprised the offices for the Dorothy Garrison Foundation.

Owen glanced toward the door to the main entry. "Still no sign of Keira Sullivan. Her uncle's getting impatient." Her uncle was Bob O'Reilly, one of the cops there tonight. Owen's fiancée, Abigail Browning, was the other one. They were both homicide detectives with the Boston Police Department. O'Reilly was a beefy, freckle-faced redhead with a couple decades on the job. Abigail was twenty years younger, slim and dark haired, a rising star in the homicide unit.

She was also the daughter of John March, the director of the Federal Bureau of Investigation and the reason Simon's association with Fast Rescue had become complicated. He used to work for March. Sort of still did.

He'd decided to avoid Abigail and O'Reilly, because they both had a nose for liars.

"Any reason to worry about your missing artist?" he asked Owen.

"Not at this point. It's pouring rain, and the Red Sox are in town—rained out by now, I'm sure. I imagine traffic's a nightmare."

"Can you call her?"

"She doesn't own a cell phone. No phone upstairs in her apartment, either."

"Why not?"

"Just the way she is."

A flake, Simon thought. He'd learned, not that he was interested, that Keira was renting a one-bedroom apartment on the top floor of the Garrison house until she figured out whether she wanted to stay in Boston. He understood wanting to keep moving—he didn't live on a boat by accident.

"Abigail's bidding on one of Keira's pieces," Owen said.

"The fairies or the Irish cottage?"

"The cottage, I think."

They were imaginative, cheerful pieces. Keira had a flair for capturing and creating a mood—a part-real, part-imagined space where people wanted to be. Her work wasn't sentimental, but it wasn't edgy and self-involved, either. Simon didn't have much use for a painting of fairies or an Irish cottage in his life. No house to hang it in, for one thing.

Irish music kicked up, and he noticed five young musicians in the far corner, obviously enjoying themselves on their mix of traditional instruments—an Irish harp, bodhran, tin whistle, mandolin, fiddle and guitar. They'd use what a song required.

"The girl on the Irish harp is Fiona O'Reilly," Owen said. "Bob's oldest daughter."

Simon wasn't sure he wanted to know any more about Owen's friends in Boston, especially ones in, or related to people in, law enforcement. It was all too tricky. Too damn dangerous. But here he was, playing with fire.

Owen's gaze drifted back to his fiancée, who wore a simple black dress and was laughing and half dancing to the spirited music. Abigail caught his eye and waved, her smile broadening. They were working on setting a date for their wedding. Whenever it was, Simon planned to be out of the country.

"You can't tell her about me, Owen."

"I know." He broke his eye contact with Abigail and sighed at Simon. "She'll find out you're not just another Fast Rescue volunteer on her own. One way or the other, she'll figure out your relationship with her father and that I knew and didn't tell her. Then she'll hang us both by our thumbs."

"We'll deserve it, but you still can't tell her. It's classified. We shouldn't even be talking about it now."

Owen gave a curt nod.

Simon felt a measure of sympathy for his friend. "I'm sorry I put you in this position."

"You didn't. It just happened."

"I should have lied."

"You did lie. You just didn't get away with it."

The song ended, and the band transitioned right into the next one, "The Rising of the Moon," which Simon knew well enough from his days in Dublin pubs to hum. But he didn't hum, because if he'd been mistaken for an art critic—or at least an art snob—already tonight, next he'd be mistaken for a music critic. Then he'd have to rethink his entire approach to his life, or at least start a brawl.

"In some ways," he said, "my lie was more true than the truth."

Owen stared at him. "Only you could come up with a statement like that, Simon."

"There are facts, and there's truth. They're not always the same thing."

A whirl of movement by the entry drew Simon's attention, and he gave up on his explanation as he noted a woman standing in the doorway, soaking wet, water dripping off the ends of her long blond hair.

"The missing artist, I presume."

But even as he spoke, Simon saw that something was wrong. He heard Owen's breath catch and knew he saw it, too. The woman—Keira—was unnaturally pale and seemed to struggle to keep herself upright, her eyes wide as she appeared to search the crowd for someone.

Simon surged forward, Owen right behind him, and they reached her just as she rallied, straightening her spine and pushing a wet lock of hair out of her face. She was dressed for the woods, soaked and obviously shaken, but even so, she had a pretty, fairy-princess look about her with her black-lashed blue eyes and flaxen hair that hung almost to her elbows. She was slim and fine boned, and whatever had just happened, it hadn't been good.

"There's a body," she said tightly. "A man. Dead."

That Simon hadn't expected. Owen touched her wrist. "Where, Keira?"

"The Public Garden—he drowned, I think."

The Public Garden was just down Beacon Street. "Are the police there?" Simon asked.

She nodded. "I called 911. Two Boston University students found him. We all got caught in the rain, but they were ahead of me and saw him first. He was in the pond. They pulled him out—they're just kids. They were so upset. But there was nothing anyone could do at that point." Despite her obvious distress, she was composed, focused. Her eyes narrowed, searching the crowd. "My uncle's here, isn't he?"

Simon glanced back into the room. The well-dressed crowd and the sparkling room—the lively Irish music and tinkle of champagne glasses—were a contrast to the stoic, drenched woman behind him and her stark report of a dead man down the street.

Detectives Browning and O'Reilly were working their way over to Keira from different parts of the room, their intense expressions indicating they'd already found out about the body through other means. They'd have pagers, cell phones.

Abigail got there first. "Keira," she said crisply but not without sympathy. "I just heard about what happened. Let's go into the foyer where it's quiet, okay?"

Keira didn't budge. "I didn't see anything, or the patrol officers on the scene wouldn't have let me go." She wasn't combative, just firm, stubborn. "I'm not a witness, Abigail."

Abigail didn't argue, but she didn't have to because Keira suddenly whipped around and shot back into the foyer, water flying out of her hair. Simon knew better than to butt in, but he figured she'd decided she'd rather discuss the dead man with Abigail than with her uncle, who was about two seconds from getting through the last knot of people.

Simon wished he still had his champagne. "I wonder who the dead guy is."

Owen stiffened. "Simon—"

"I'm just saying."

But Owen didn't have a chance to respond before Detective O'Reilly arrived, his jaw set hard, clearly not pleased with the turn the evening had taken. "Where's Keira?"

"Talking to Abigail," Owen said quickly, as if he didn't want to give Simon a chance to open his mouth.

O'Reilly gave the unoccupied doorway a searing look. "She's okay?"

Owen nodded without hesitation. "Remarkably so. She's not the one who actually found the body."

"She called it in." Clearly, that was plenty for O'Reilly not to like. He sucked in a breath. "How the hell does someone drown in the pond in the Public Garden? It's not even a real pond. It's about two feet deep."

Good question, but Simon clearly wasn't on O'Reilly's radar and he preferred to keep it that way.

The senior detective glanced back toward his daughter. She and her ensemble had just finished a song and were taking a break. "I need to go with Abigail," he said, addressing Owen. "You'll make sure Fiona stays here until I know what's going on?"

"Sure."

"And Keira. Keep her here, too."

"She got caught in the rain. She'll want to change—"

"Yeah, good. That's fine. Just don't let her go traipsing off somewhere. She's like that. Always has been."

"There's no reason to think the drowning was anything but an accident, is there?"

"Not yet," O'Reilly said without elaboration, and stalked into the foyer.

Simon didn't mind being a fly on the wall for a change. "The uncle doesn't get along with his daughter and niece?"

"They all get along fine," Owen said, "but they're a complicated family."

"All families are complicated, even the good ones." Simon moved closer to the foyer doorway, just as Keira started up the stairs barefoot, wet socks and shoes in one hand. She was prettier than he'd expected. More or less drop-you-in-your-tracks pretty. He noticed her uncle scowling at her from the bottom of the stairs and grinned, turning back to Owen. "Maybe especially the good ones."

Ten seconds later the two BPD detectives left through the front door.

The Irish ensemble started up again, playing a quieter tune.

Owen headed for Fiona O'Reilly, who cast a worried look in his direction even as she and her ensemble launched into a new song. She had freckles, but otherwise didn't resemble her father as far as Simon could see. Her hair had reddish tints, but really was blond and long like her cousin's, and she was a lot better-looking than her father. Simon thought Owen had said Fiona was nineteen. She looked younger.

People in the crowd seemed unaware of the drama over by the door. Caterers brought out trays of hot hors d'oeuvres. Mini quiches, little flaky buttery things oozing cheese, stuffed mushrooms, skewered strips of marinated chicken. Simon noticed Lloyd Adler pontificating to an older couple who looked as if they thought he was a pretentious ass, too.

Simon went in the opposite direction, making his way to the back wall where Keira's two donated watercolors were on display.

He'd bid on the one with the cottage, just to give himself something to do.

It was a white stone cottage set against a background of wildflowers, green pastures and ocean that wasn't in any part of Ireland that he had ever visited. He supposed that was part of the point—to create a place of imagination and dreams. A beautiful, bucolic place. A place not of this world.

At least not the world in which he lived and worked.

Simon settled on a number and put in his bid, one that virtually assured him of ending up with the painting. He could give it to Abigail and Owen as a wedding present. If he was invited to the wedding, he'd make sure he was in another country that day. But he could give them a present.

He acknowledged an itch to head down to the Public Garden with the detectives, but he let it go. He'd seen enough dead bodies, enough to last him a long time. A lifetime, even. Except he knew there would be more. There always were.

Instead, he'd find another glass of champagne, maybe grab a couple of the chicken skewers and wait for a dry, calmer Keira Sullivan to make her appearance.

MIRA®

From the author of *Trapped*

Chris Jordan

In a small New York town, a deranged young man holds more than one hundred schoolchildren hostage...

After a tense standoff, the gymnasium suddenly explodes. Fortunately, all the students escape. All, that is, save ten-year-old Noah Corbin. Noah's mother, Haley, is frantic. Was her boy killed? Or did someone take him?

Haley hires former FBI agent Randall Shane. However, as Randall investigates, Haley is forced to admit a dark family secret...one that leads to the Rocky Mountains—where an entire county is owned by a cult. A cult with secrets they are all sworn to protect. No matter what.

torn

"Jordan's full-throttle style makes this an emotionally rewarding thriller that moves like lightning."—*Publishers Weekly* on *Taken*

www.MIRABooks.com   MCJ2575

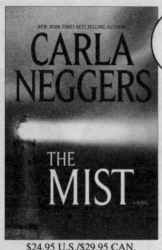

NEW YORK TIMES BEST SELLING AUTHOR

CARLA NEGGERS

THE MIST

$24.95 U.S./$29.95 CAN.

REQUEST YOUR FREE BOOKS!

2 FREE NOVELS FROM THE ROMANCE/SUSPENSE COLLECTION PLUS 2 FREE GIFTS!

YES! Please send me 2 FREE novels from the Romance/Suspense Collection and my 2 FREE gifts (gifts are worth about $10). After receiving them, if I don't wish to receive any more books, I can return the shipping statement marked "cancel." If I don't cancel, I will receive 4 brand-new novels every month and be billed just $5.49 per book in the U.S. or $5.99 per book in Canada, plus 25¢ shipping and handling per book plus applicable taxes, if any*. That's a savings of at least 20% off the cover price! I understand that accepting the 2 free books and gifts places me under no obligation to buy anything. I can always return a shipment and cancel at any time. Even if I never buy another book from the Reader Service, the two free books and gifts are mine to keep forever.

185 MDN EF5Y 385 MDN EF6C

Name _____ (PLEASE PRINT) _____

Address _____ Apt. # _____

City _____ State/Prov. _____ Zip/Postal Code _____

Signature (if under 18, a parent or guardian must sign)

Mail to **The Reader Service:**
IN U.S.A.: P.O. Box 1867, Buffalo, NY 14240-1867
IN CANADA: P.O. Box 609, Fort Erie, Ontario L2A 5X3

Not valid to current subscribers to the Romance Collection,
the Suspense Collection or the Romance/Suspense Collection.

Want to try two free books from another line?
Call 1-800-873-8635 or visit www.morefreebooks.com.

* Terms and prices subject to change without notice. N.Y. residents add applicable sales tax. Canadian residents will be charged applicable provincial taxes and GST. Offer not valid in Quebec. This offer is limited to one order per household. All orders subject to approval. Credit or debit balances in a customer's account(s) may be offset by any other outstanding balance owed by or to the customer. Please allow 4 to 6 weeks for delivery. Offer available while quantities last.

Your Privacy: Harlequin is committed to protecting your privacy. Our Privacy Policy is available online at www.eHarlequin.com or upon request from the Reader Service. From time to time we make our lists of customers available to reputable third parties who may have a product or service of interest to you. If you would prefer we not share your name and address, please check here. ☐

BOB08R

CELEBRATE
60 YEARS
OF PURE READING PLEASURE
WITH **HARLEQUIN**®!

Look for Silhouette®
Romantic Suspense in April!

Love In 60 Seconds

Bright lights. Big city. Hearts in overdrive.

Silhouette® Romantic Suspense is celebrating
Harlequin's 60th Anniversary with six stories that
promise to bring readers the glitz of Las Vegas,
the danger of revenge, the mystery of a missing
diamond, and family scandals.

**Look for the first title, *The Heiress's 2-Week Affair*
by *USA TODAY* bestselling author
Marie Ferrarella, on sale in April!**

His 7-Day Fiancée by **Gail Barrett**	May
The 9-Month Bodyguard by **Cindy Dees**	June
Prince Charming for 1 Night by **Nina Bruhns**	July
Her 24-Hour Protector by **Loreth Anne White**	August
5 minutes to Marriage by **Carla Cassidy**	September

CARLA NEGGERS

32586	TEMPTING FATE	___ $7.99 U.S.	___ $7.99 CAN.
32038	NIGHT'S LANDING	___ $6.99 U.S.	___ $8.50 CAN.
32516	THE WIDOW	___ $7.99 U.S.	___ $9.50 CAN.
32455	ABANDON	___ $7.99 U.S.	___ $9.50 CAN.
32419	CUT AND RUN	___ $7.99 U.S.	___ $9.50 CAN.
32237	BREAKWATER	___ $7.99 U.S.	___ $9.50 CAN.
32205	DARK SKY	___ $7.50 U.S.	___ $8.99 CAN.
32104	THE RAPIDS	___ $6.99 U.S.	___ $8.50 CAN.
66972	THE CARRIAGE HOUSE	___ $6.50 U.S.	___ $7.99 CAN.
66970	ON FIRE	___ $6.50 U.S.	___ $7.99 CAN.
66845	THE CABIN	___ $6.50 U.S.	___ $7.99 CAN.

(limited quantities available)

TOTAL AMOUNT	$ _____
POSTAGE & HANDLING	$ _____
($1.00 FOR 1 BOOK, 50¢ for each additional)	
APPLICABLE TAXES*	$ _____
TOTAL PAYABLE	$ _____

(check or money order—please do not send cash)

To order, complete this form and send it, along with a check or money order for the total above, payable to MIRA Books, to: **In the U.S.:** 3010 Walden Avenue, P.O. Box 9077, Buffalo, NY 14269-9077; **In Canada:** P.O. Box 636, Fort Erie, Ontario, L2A 5X3.

Name: _____

Address: _____ City: _____

State/Prov.: _____ Zip/Postal Code: _____

Account Number (if applicable): _____

075 CSAS

*New York residents remit applicable sales taxes.
*Canadian residents remit applicable GST and provincial taxes.

MIRA®

www.MIRABooks.com

MCN0309BL